# Hadassah
## One Night With the King

TOMMY TENNEY

# Hadassah

# One Night With the King

## TOMMY TENNEY

### with Mark Andrew Olsen

BETHANYHOUSE

MINNEAPOLIS, MINNESOTA

Published by Bethany House Publishers
11400 Hampshire Avenue South
Bloomington, Minnesota 55438
www.bethanyhouse.com

Bethany House Publishers is a Division of
Baker Book House Company, Grand Rapids, Michigan.

Printed in the United States of America

ISBN 0-7642-2737-8 (Hardcover)
ISBN 0-7642-2892-7 (Large Print)
ISBN 0-7642-2893-5 (Audio)
ISBN 0-7642-2909-5 (International Trade Paper)

**Library of Congress Cataloging-in-Publication Data**

Tenney, Tommy, 1956-
    Hadassah: one night with the King / by Tommy Tenney with Mark Andrew Olsen.
        p.   cm.
    ISBN 0-7642-2737-8 (alk. paper) — ISBN 0-7642-2892-7 (large-print pbk.)
    1. Esther, Queen of Persia—Fiction.  2. Xerxes I, King of Persia, 519-465 or 4 B.C.—Fiction.  3. Bible. O.T.—History of Biblical events—Fiction.  4. Iran—History—To 640—Fiction.  5. Women in the Bible—Fiction.  6. Queens—Iran—Fiction.
I. Olsen, Mark, 1954-  II. Title.

    PS3620.E56H33      2004
    813'.54—dc22                                                    2003021804

# Dedication

*To every little girl who would be queen . . .*
*But especially to the Queen of my life.*
*And to our three girls, every one a princess.*

*Acknowledgments*

Mark Andrew Olsen is a talented and creative writer, and he provided a wealth of experience for our collaboration on *Hadassah*. Being a novice fiction writer, I questioned my ability to write effective dialogue. Mark helped educate me on this and other pieces that contribute to writing a novel. Downloading my research on Esther, he took my "architect's drawing" for the plot and themes and began to build the story on the foundation I had laid. Many hours of phone conversations and multiple drafts passed back and forth between us until my original vision for the story of Esther was completed. Thank you, Mark, for your significant contribution to this effort.

Larry Walker has assisted me editorially on many writing projects. Rarely can the phrase "my friend" be added to the phrase "my editor." Larry can wear both badges equally well. His research assistance on this project was invaluable.

Much thanks also to Carol Johnson, an incredible editor with a fine eye, a soft voice and a red pen.

# Cast of Characters

**Hadassah Kesselman:** A modern-day Jewish bride-to-be.

**Hadassah (Star, Esther):** A beautiful young Jewish girl raised by her cousin, Mordecai.

**Mordecai:** A Jewish man who works as a palace scribe at the King's Gate in the Persian capital of Susa. "Mordecai" is a derivative of the Persian name "Marduch."

**Rachel:** Mordecai's Jewish housekeeper and Hadassah's confidant.

**Jesse (Hathach):** Rachel's grandson and Hadassah's friend.

**Xerxes:** King of Persia from 486 to 465 B.C., also known as Ahasuerus.

**Memucan:** King Xerxes' chief advisor, the Master of the Audiences.

**Hegai:** Royal eunuch in charge of preparing the Queen candidates for their night with the King.

**Haman:** An Amalekite warrior, also known as the Agagite, who fiercely despises all persons of Jewish descent.

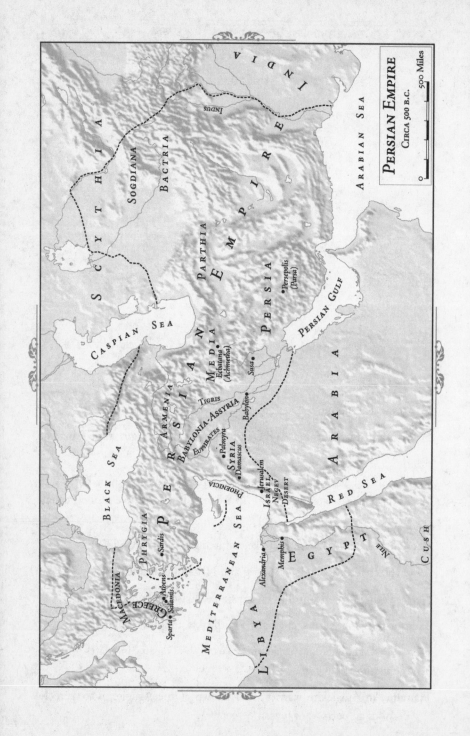

PERSIAN EMPIRE
CIRCA 500 B.C.

500 Miles

INDIA

Indus

ARABIAN SEA

SCYTHIA

SOGDIANA

BACTRIA

EMPIRE

PARTHIA

PERSIA

Persepolis
(Parsa)

PERSIAN GULF

CASPIAN SEA

MEDIA
Ecbatana
(Achmetha)

Susa

ARABIA

ARMENIA

PERSIAN

Tigris

BABYLONIA-ASSYRIA          Babylon

Euphrates    Palmyra

BLACK SEA

SYRIA  Damascus

PHOENICIA

RED SEA

PHRYGIA

Sardis

Israel  Jerusalem
NEGEV
DESERT

MACEDONIA

Athens

GREECE

Sparta  Salamis

Alexandria

Memphis

EGYPT

Nile

CUSH

MEDITERRANEAN SEA

LIBYA

# Contents

## Hadassah Kesselman

### THE JERUSALEM STAR SOCIETY PAGE

*". . . the Kesselman/ben Yuda wedding promises to be
the social event of the summer. . . ."*

*Chapter One*

ISRAEL MUSEUM—JERUSALEM—PRESENT DAY

"Father, where are you taking me?"

The old man turned shakily upon his cane, paused at the top step and looked toward his daughter while still panting to catch his breath. Despite the wrinkles that had lately etched their way across his face, she could still recognize the sly smile that always signaled his toying with her.

"Why, Hadassah, this is the Shrine of the Book. You've been here a dozen times."

"Of course, Poppa. I know that."

As if to punctuate her statement, she glanced about the monument. Her gaze rose into the cobalt blue Judean sky where the Shrine's celebrated dome thrust its odd, milky white swirl. She noted again its fluid shape, meant to evoke the ancient jar lids that once sealed the beloved scrolls now housed inside. Just beyond, her gaze settled briefly on a jutting slab of ink black basalt—the famous architectural apposition of Darkness against Light. "Ideological structure," her ninth grade teacher had called it years ago, just before using the term in a test question.

*Ideological structure: designing a building for a symbolic as well as a functional purpose. . . .*

"But why today?" Hadassah continued the conversation in the modern Hebrew with which she had grown up, though she also spoke fluent English. "With the wedding just a few days away? This is no time for sightseeing, Poppa."

He smiled again, indulgently this time, and waved her on up. "My child, have you ever known me to waste your time?"

It was an odd question to pose so flippantly, but she pondered it nevertheless while she scrambled up the steps after him. In fact, he had always been a quiet, mild-mannered father, and she had to admit after consideration that he had never been one to yank her about on useless errands.

She reached him, and he laid his arm upon her shoulders. "Just follow me," he said with a smile that grew wider and more inscrutable by the second.

Still locked in their amiable stalemate, they entered the lobby where tourists waited in line to see the world-famous Dead Sea Scrolls. For the first time her father did not approach the counter for a ticket but merely waved at the cashier and received a solemn nod in return. They walked through the entrance passage with its smooth, rounded walls intended to emulate the cave at Qumran, site of the scrolls' discovery. And then, presumably like the young shepherd who had found them half a century earlier, they emerged into a cool, vaulted space: the main hall.

Despite both her bewilderment and her familiarity with the room, Hadassah could not help but glance around. One of the wonders of modern architecture, the luminous inner hall of the Shrine of the Book never failed to seize her imagination. Overhead, the curved underside of the dome shone with countless horizontal grooves, each one capturing a different hue in the sunlight that filtered from a window at its apex. Rising from the floor, just beneath this aperture, stood a huge scroll handle—as though someone had half-buried a giant Torah upright in the floor.

A hush overtook the pair as they entered the chamber, as both its acoustics and the solemnity of its contents discouraged noise. But her father was not here today to peruse the softly lit parchment tables. He crossed the room and immediately started down a nearly hidden stairway that led into shadow below.

"Poppa?" she asked.

She saw only the back of his hand motioning her to follow, then disappearing into the gloom. Hadassah shook her head and frowned, then followed him. A door opened into soft half-light. She followed him through it into a carpeted hallway that branched off into three additional corridors.

And there, smiling in anticipation, stood—

*Aunt Rose?* "What are you doing here?" Hadassah asked, incredulous. Aunt Rose lived in America. The two had not seen each other for four years. Rose was indeed flying over for the wedding, but Hadassah was sure she was not due for another few days.

Rose leaned toward her with a knowing smile and simply engulfed her in a hug. And that was when, over her aunt's ample shoulder, she saw the rest of the women. Standing in a corner, strangely quiet and still, were Grandma Grossman, Great-Aunt Pauline, Aunt Connie and two more elderly matrons she only faintly recognized, yet all were facing her with intent and shining eyes.

As soon as she disengaged from Aunt Rose, the women converged on their youngest descendant *en masse*, crying softly and creating a tumult of greetings and congratulations. Although she responded in pleasure and surprise, this gathering, on this day and in this place, filled her with an intense curiosity and even a sharp sense of foreboding.

*What in the world is going on here?* She pulled away and shot her father a questioning glance.

"My dear, I brought you here to maintain an ancient tradition," he said as though he'd read her mind. He turned to the group while jerking his thumb dismissively in her direction. "Ladies, Missy here did not even want to come today. I practically had to drag her over—I thought she'd call a nursing home to haul me away before I could get her in here."

The women all laughed knowingly, which did not help the bride-to-be's disposition. Her father faced her again, and this time his expression had changed completely; she could even see a surprising gleam of tears in his eyes.

"Your mother would have brought you here herself, were she still with us," he said huskily, then paused a moment. "And, of course, I wondered if I would last long enough to see you actually find your beloved."

It was true. She *had* been picky, taking her time to find the one she would want to wake up with every morning for the rest of her life.

Now her father was off again, hobbling down the center hallway with his cane, the line of old women in tow. She shrugged and followed. He paused before a large metal door recessed into the wall. Then he stopped and took a maddeningly long time to extract first a folded piece of paper from his pocket, then his glasses with which to read it. He looked up, punched one of the buttons in a wall-mounted keypad, then glanced down for the next. The whole process took several minutes. Finally the door clicked open with a *whoosh* of compressed air. The group filed in without a pause, as though they had gone through many times before.

A vast underground room sprawled before them. Subdued lighting emanated from somewhere under glass-covered table rows. A stout woman of about fifty wearing a museum uniform and a world-weary smile stood in front of them with her hands clasped before her.

Hadassah had always known that most of the Shrine's workings were underground. She also knew that the Dead Sea Scrolls were periodically rotated from public areas to subterranean chambers in order to reduce their exposure to light. But she had never known of this chamber or any reason her relatives might have for congregating here.

"You are members of the family?" the uniformed hostess asked in a smooth voice.

"Yes, we are," her father said loudly.

"And who is today's bride?"

Her father turned back to her and motioned. "Hadassah."

The woman smiled knowingly. "A most apt name." Then she stepped forward, gave another reassuring grin and shook Hadassah's hand before leading her toward one of the waist-high tables.

"Please, Hadassah. Step forward and sign."

"What am I signing?" she asked.

The museum staffer looked sharply at her father. "So she has been told nothing." It sounded like a statement but was actually a stern question.

Rather than answering the woman, her father turned to Hadassah. "My dear, I apologize for all the secrecy and uncertainty. But you must understand. For nearly three thousand years the mothers of our family have been keeping these pages a secret until a bride's wedding week."

"*What* pages?"

He sighed heavily, as he always did when she showed impatience, and swept his arm toward the display.

"These tables hold the remains of a private family parchment. In more recent times, the government has been kind enough to safeguard it for us because of its enormous historical value, but it belongs to the family and is completely private, for our individual use. It is our single copy of a letter written, in a way, just for you—given by someone very special to your grandmother nearly one hundred times removed."

"Okay. Who gave it to her?"

"Queen Esther."

"Queen Esther—of the *Tanakh*?"

"No. Queen Esther from the corner bakery." He reached out

and touched her hand to show he had meant no offense. "Yes. The Esther of old. It is a memoir she wrote in her later years to a younger Jewish girl also chosen as a candidate for Queen of Persia, just as she had once been. Tradition has it she never wanted these words to end up in public, framed in some Palace museum, but she wanted its message reserved privately for every bride of royal standing descended from its recipient for time everlasting." He bit his lower lip, and a thick tear rolled down his cheek, which he quickly swiped away. "Now you know why your mother insisted so strongly that you learn to read Hebrew fluently."

"So, would you care to sign here at the end?" repeated the museum attendant, with the faintest hint of insistence. She pointed to the left, as Hadassah would have expected since the document was written in Hebrew—from right to left.

Then she realized what she was being asked to do and recoiled. "You mean—actually sign the end of the document *itself?*"

The woman nodded and almost smiled. "This is a piece of living history. And you are its latest addition."

Hadassah exhaled forcefully. She could feel her mind reel under an unfurling stretch of antiquity suddenly far more colorful and vibrant than any she had contemplated before. To think that she— modern, busy, disorganized Hadassah—led a life linked to a saga stretching back nearly three thousand years . . . that her everyday existence was now connected to a story she had known only upon the printed page or in tales of rabbinical legend on synagogue scrolls . . . It made her heart pound. She was truly becoming a part of its history.

Feeling almost dizzy, she followed the staffer to where the long table ended, where a length of the ancient parchment now lay shockingly exposed to the elements. A gold fountain pen rested beside the manuscript, waiting. She stopped for a moment.

Just above a blank space near the end of the scroll stretched a long array of signatures in an endless variety of feminine handwriting. Some of the scripts flowed, some were meticulously squared, some thick and strong, others wispy and ethereal with their inks fading under the onslaught of time.

She bent down and peered at the names. The first almost assaulted her with its immediacy, for it was the signature of her own mother. Strangely, the sight of such familiar handwriting in this place startled her, caused her heart to skip a beat and her eyes to moisten. It seemed for a moment that Momma was not dead and buried in some faraway grave but standing beside her, steadying herself with that fragile hand she had laid upon Hadassah's shoulder so many times in her later years.

The museum attendant cleared her throat and shifted her feet from side to side.

Hadassah ignored her, wiped her eyes and started to read the names above her mother's. Ruth Sarason, her grandmother's maiden name. Elizabeth Prensky, her great-grandmother's. On and on: aunts, cousins. Names she did not know but which sounded distantly, vaguely familiar. She blinked away more tears and looked even farther—the parchment was now growing crowded with increasingly faded and ancient names. She became overpowered by the feeling that she was some impudent interloper getting ready to deface an item of infinite value and age.

She looked even farther and saw where the signatures began and the actual text ended—faded and barely discernible, archaic Hebrew script traced in a sure and graceful hand.

"We bring you here to honor the tradition," her grandmother said, breaking the spell with her trembling voice. "But we also have a modern Hebrew translation of this letter printed in book form for you to take home."

Her father had bent over and now struggled to hold up a richly embossed, thick leather tome.

"Do I have to read it *now*?"

The women laughed. "No, dear," her father answered, cradling the volume in his arms. "Just take it home and read it over a few days like you would any good book. Like the others did whose signatures you see."

She thought for a long moment and then turned to the whole group, her voice sounding weak and small to her own ears. "Am I a royal bride?"

Aunt Rose answered. "You are, sweetie. We took a vote," she said kindly. "You are a bride fit for a king."

Hadassah turned away, as much to hide her tears as anything else, and started to cross the room back toward where the document, under its glass protection, ended.

"Men of our family have died to preserve this," her father said beside her in a voice still thick with emotion. "My father missed his boat to America so he could take the time to store it in a basement in Amsterdam."

She kissed him on the cheek, remembering her grandfather's death at the Nazi camp Treblinka, then looked down at the first line.

"Just sign," he said softly, his face now quivering freely. He struck the book's cover with a dull tap. "Then you can read it all."

She nodded, handed the box with it precious medallion to her father and sat down before the faded document. She lifted the pen with trembling fingers, bent toward the glass, took a deep breath and signed.

*Hadassah Kesselman.*

---

Dear Candidate for Bride of the King,

I am sure this letter will come as a great surprise, as I have never actually spoken to you, let alone given any indication that I wished private communication between us. However, the truth is that I have much information of the highest importance to share with you.

Please do not tell anyone of this letter. Certainly tell none of the other girls. The only one you can trust in your harem is the one who gave you this: the King's chief eunuch. You know him as the Chamberlain. If you cannot read, he will read it for you, and he is trustworthy beyond life itself. I should know.

But I write you, my dear girl, on the eve of your own time in history, with vital information to impart.

I saw something in you when you first appeared at the harem, something that others must have seen in me almost thirty years ago.

Even among the crowd of young women I noticed a peculiar gleam in the eye, a regal hold of the head, an uprightness of posture, an unusual poise and self-possession.

Now, I know that such qualities are mere features of one's outward appearance. And even less significant perhaps—they can be mere habits of disposition. But what they appear to say about you, about your character, is far more profound. I believe I discerned an integrity, a depth, in you that set you apart from the other young, beautiful maidens brought in from the provinces for the King.

More important still, I spotted you praying in the Palace orchard yesterday morning, and besides reminding me indelibly of myself, it sealed one thing for me. From the manner of your prayer I'm convinced you must be a follower of YHWH, like me. That you are a Jewess and follow the living G-d is the supreme factor in my decision to contact you in this manner. (You will notice throughout this memoir I use the traditional Hebrew abbreviated forms in referring to Deity out of reverence for the Almighty One.)

What I have to tell you can be introduced this way. Some years ago I was exactly where you are now. I, too, was a royal concubine in training. I, too, possessed certain qualities that gained me favor with those in authority. But you do not seem to have what I had and sorely relied on: a godly mentor.

I would be that for you: if you will heed my words.

I will start by saying this. Shortly you will be ushered into the King's bedroom, and potentially into his life. In all likelihood, you will never come this close again to such an opportunity for this kind of power and influence. You must treat this time with him as the most precious and pivotal hours you will ever spend. You have no idea what all could result from that one night. I myself, despite spending a year in its preparation, tended to undervalue that time as mere competition, never fully understanding at that time how my success or failure could change the course of history.

Danger often lurks where destiny beckons. That is why the right approach demands even more than just prudence or solemnity. It calls for G-d's anointing and a healthy dose of wisdom gleaned from the Sacred Texts. There is, in fact, a specific protocol to approaching the King's presence. Most who come to him never know this, and this ignorance dooms their most valuable time in his company to insignificance. I would teach you this protocol, for it is both simple and a great source of inspiration and blessing. And besides, I want you to be the Queen. I want my former place of influence occupied by another child of YHWH, someone who will stand for righteousness and mercy in the Empire when times call for it. I want your night with the King to prove as successful and providential as my own.

I have no idea how much you know of my story or the events that surrounded it. I can only hope that you know me as more than the slightly stooped figure who waved at your group the morning of your arrival at the harem. If you've been blessed with some schooling or you come from an observant Jewish family, as I believe you do, then you may know me as the legendary past-Queen. I was once a most powerful figure at court.

But do you know my story? My whole story? The whole breathtaking account of what the G-d of my fathers wrought through the events of my life?

I do not ask this because of some old woman's penchant

for storytelling or recognition. I ask you this because telling my story may be the only way of impressing upon you the utter importance of what lies ahead for you.

There are parts of my story that I did not know at the time they were occurring. The historical background with which I begin my tale is found in the Sacred Texts. I have only been able to reconstruct the whole over much time and many conversations with those who were there—or those who knew someone who was there.

Horrible deaths occurred while my story unfolded. Our whole people could have been wiped out forever had I not listened to the voice of G-d and those He sent to counsel me in preparation for my night with the King. In fact, you yourself would not be alive if I had not heeded the sage advice of my own mentor, along with the inner voice of G-d's Spirit.

I have no idea whether your evening with the King will involve as much intrigue, as incredibly high stakes, as mine did. I hope for your sake it is more peaceful.

But I do know one truth for certain.

*One night with the King changes everything.*

### Haman, son of Hammedatha

KETHUVIM ESTHER 3:10

*". . . the king removed his signet ring from his hand and
gave it to Haman, son of Hammedatha
the Agagite, the foe of the Jews."*

*Chapter Two*

BABYLON—CIRCA 492 B.C.

One early, horrific event punctuates my memory of childhood. Most likely it is my earliest because it is the worst—because its horror drowned out every childish whimsy that came before it.

My family was on an extended trip to Babylon, a visit with my aunt and uncle's family to celebrate my seventh birthday. In fact, it was the last conversation I ever had with my father and mother. It concerned my receiving the gift, a gleaming golden medallion engraved with the pattern of a six-pointed star. I remember crying out in delight and holding the luminous gift up to the light.

"Oh, Poppa, did you make this for me?" I asked.

"No, my dear. This has been precious to our family for many years. In fact, your great-grandmother brought it with her from the Promised Land."

"You mean *Israel*?"

"Yes, Hadassah. That is what I mean."

At those words, I clasped the pendant even tighter to my breast and gazed at my father in wonder. I remember that my mother laughed her warmest, kindest laugh and reached out to ruffle my hair. "It is a star, Hadassah, and we gave it to you because you are our bright star and because we want you to carry on this family legacy and all it stands for. You can put it on, dearest, but you'll have to wait awhile before keeping it on for good. This is a woman's neckpiece."

"Oh, I know—but can I wear it tonight? Just for tonight?"

I remember that my parents exchanged a glance to consider my request and that in my mind's eye I thought I spied a gleam in both their eyes, a twinkle of love for me and of affection they held for each other. My mother looked back at me and smiled again. "Yes, my dear. You may wear it tonight."

So I slipped the medallion around my neck and immediately snuggled down to sleep on my blanket, anxious to begin my night with my newly beloved treasure, this family heritage of which I had only the barest understanding.

I was startled awake in the night to screaming and a thrashing frenzy of movement in my family's room. And a flash of light: the glimmer of moonlight from the open door upon the curved blade of a raised scimitar.

The sword did not stay raised for long. It swept down with a swift confidence, an utter ferocity of purpose whose motion alone has haunted me for years. Thank G-d the darkness hid what came next, for now that I recall it from an adult's perspective, the sound was fully sufficient to tell me what was taking place. A long, glistening arc of light, a whistle of sound, and the strangle of a breath escaping my mother's lungs. The impact close by told me she had fallen hard, right next to where I lay on my pallet on the floor.

I rolled out of my blanket to her side, and I suppose the reflex saved my life, for in the dark and confusion, I blended into my mother's silhouette. I remember feeling a jarringly opposite pair of sensations: at once the known—the usual outlines of her torso, the curve of her shoulder, the smell of her person—and secondly, the sheer lifeless weight of these once-familiar limbs. By now I was in shock and, thank G-d, completely incapable of uttering a sound. There was something else—a viscous liquid coating her clothes and mine that had not been there just seconds ago.

Knowing what I know now about children, I cannot believe I did not cry out. What seven-year-old lives through such terror and does not scream? The Lord must have stilled my tongue. Especially given what came next. In trying to make my mother speak and comfort me, I traced up her shoulder, but I could not find her face.

My exploring fingers located a warm ring of flesh and sinew.

I recoiled—not necessarily from a full mental understanding of what had happened to her, but from the sheer strangeness of it, the sudden change in a body that at that age I knew better than my own. An icy flood of combined dread and bewilderment cascaded down my senses. I knew, somehow, that something profoundly mine, the anchor of my being, was forever changed.

As I write this years later from a thorough understanding of the tragic horror of it all, I grieve once more for that long-ago lost child, almost as if she is someone other than myself. On the other hand, I also can relive the personal anguish even though my awareness at that time, thankfully, was limited.

Next to me, the shouting and slashing and falling continued. A pair of men was slaughtering my family. My nose was filled with overpowering and terrifying scents—an earthy aroma that I would later learn was blood, the sweaty odor of the attackers, even the goatish, salty smell of my own all-encompassing fear.

Over the screams of my brother and father I distinctly remember hearing the throaty male laughter of the intruders. It was low in timbre, more bass than I'd ever heard in my father's voice, even in the morning at his gruffest. And it had a quality I had never heard before and have never heard since. All I can say is that it reminded me of animals: a combination of baying dogs and the howling of hyenas.

I must have stayed too traumatized to even draw in a breath, let alone exhale to utter a cry, because they never heard me or saw my prone form in the blood beside my mother's body. Or perhaps they thought me dead, which, considering the state of my mind, probably was not too far from the truth.

I will say more later on about the massacre of my family and that of Mordecai, for it is certainly the dominating event of my childhood—perhaps even of my life, although clearly that is debatable considering what came next. But the reason I subjected you to this account is to show you that I of all people have cause to lament the violent taking of life.

Which is why I find such irony in subsequent events. I have discovered that the hatred at the heart of this story originated in a beheading that *should* have taken place almost five hundred years previous to this time. That botched execution led, through the years, to the butchery I've just described and, even later, to the entire story at hand. I know this sounds mysterious, so let me explain and trace for you the terrible influence of this long-ago event into the present day.

*Chapter Three*

THE NEGEV DESERT—1039 B.C.

t first sight, King Saul thought the warrior might be injured by the way he stumbled and swayed toward him. Granted, the barren desert plain between them lay knee-deep in corpses and the jumbled detritus of battle. And yes, the sun shone high overhead in a summer's cloudless sky. Yet it seemed clear that the figure approaching him labored with some unusual burden. Saul stood, raised his hand to his forehead to shade the sun and saw.

The soldier was dragging a man by the hair. Toward him.

Saul sighed, turned away and spit into the merciless Negev dust. The liquid actually caused a faint sizzle and the daintiest release of steam from the hot sand under his sandals.

True, he welcomed his subjects' enthusiasm for warfare. But it also wearied him that their battle lust caused them to forget an order so straightforward and simple. He had made it clear to his unit commanders that they were to kill every Amalekite, man, woman and child. These weren't even his orders, to be frank. In fact, Samuel had told him that G-d wanted the enemy's livestock killed, as well. But now it looked like the old custom of taking spoils and capturing enemy leaders seemed to have supplanted his direct orders.

So be it. Ever since Samuel had appointed him king, Saul had become convinced that the old prophet was burning with an inner fire born of jealousy and hate. It seemed obvious that Samuel had relished a little too strongly his previous years as ruling judge of Israel, for he had certainly approached the choosing of a king with mouthful after mouthful of grumbling and dire warnings.

*G-d did not want this,* Samuel had muttered. *You'll regret this. You'll pay. G-d wants the direct link between himself and the people left intact.* He had gone on and on and on. Even the people had become convinced of Samuel's self-interest, which was one reason they had so lightly regarded his warnings when Saul became king.

*On account of my height,* Saul reminded himself as he stooped down to reenter his tent for a moment of respite from sun and heat—and responsibility. *My accursed oversized height,* he thought again for the thousandth time.

Saul had never wanted to be king. He had always felt self-conscious about his size, and now the mere length of his limbs made him a perennial object of withering and burdensome attention. No one would understand what an ordeal that was, despite the obvious appeals of being monarch.

And then there were the military campaigns. Saul definitely harbored mixed feelings about the incessant circuit of death Samuel had made him embark on since coronation. Granted, the aversion had dimmed after his armies' recent unbroken string of victories. He had to admit that the people's sudden adulation had soothed his discomfort, even warmed his relationship with Samuel. But often the sheer horror and drudgery of war, not to mention the lingering possibility of defeat, made it almost unbearable. He would rather have stayed home planning the construction of a proper royal abode or summoning the kingdom's fairest maidens for consideration as possible Queen.

*But now comes this prisoner.* Saul sighed wearily. He would surely be forced to rebuke a soldier whose actions he inwardly did not oppose, all for the sake of appeasing that cantankerous old priest. He left his tent and steeled himself for the task.

The soldier had drawn close now. He bowed low, then released his prisoner's hair, causing the head to hit the dirt with an audible thud. "Your majesty," he said, "I give you Agag, king of the Amalekites."

A collective gasp went up from the scattering of soldiers around the area. Saul peered at the prone captive and a chill of recognition cascaded down his spine. He had fully expected the prisoner to be a leader of some sort, perhaps a general, but not the king. Yet the tattooed blood markings on the man's back and shoulders were indeed those of the crazed figure that had waved his countrymen on to death and jabbed obscene gestures in Saul's direction just a few hours before. It was he, all right. *Agag.* The filthy, murdering demon worshipper was now his prisoner, the most notorious rapist and mass murderer in the known world and king of the clan that had mercilessly ravaged the children of Israel years before on their journey north from Egypt.

In short, his nemesis. Not only that, but in many ways the human nemesis of G-d himself.

The thrill of superiority made Saul stand straighter and taller, suddenly unashamed of his stature. All the demeaning concessions and negotiations with old Samuel now faded into oblivion. He was king of a conquering army, and the knowledge made his head swim.

His soldier gave Agag a kick across the shoulders, sending him face first back into the dirt. "Your Majesty, there's more. My men and I have kept back this pig's household riches. You should see his livestock alone, your Majesty. We're bringing it all to you now, even one of his wives who was traveling with him for you to—ah—do your bidding before she's also exterminated."

A quiet voice warned Saul that Samuel would fly into an absolute rage at this disobedience. G-d's mandate had been clear and specific. *Kill them all. Kill them instantly. Livestock included.* In fact, Saul thought with a suppressed chuckle, Samuel probably would have hewn this soldier's head from his shoulders for insubordination if he were on hand. Or tried, for there was no telling what this seasoned Hebrew fighter would have done in his own defense.

But thank goodness Samuel was back in Gilgal, attending to his endless sacrifices. And Saul had to admit that it felt good to contemplate taking the fallen king's possessions. Who knows, he might even sacrifice a portion to G-d to appease any displeasure—in case Samuel's rantings actually represented the Lord's wishes. Yes. He would make a great pious show of burning these riches back to the elements. Maybe even fashion the gold into some sort of candlestick or icon for the tabernacle. Maybe the Levites would begin to appreciate him a little bit, and the gift could spark a thaw in the fierce opposition born of their loyalty to Samuel.

Saul walked forward to the prisoner, grasped his long hair and pulled hard, forcing his face upward.

"Look at me, you swine," he growled.

Agag whispered something in his native tongue.

"What?" Saul whirled around and waved over his interpreter.

"Spare me" came the translation.

Agag spoke again, louder now, and the translator leaned into Saul's ear. "Please spare my life, your Majesty." Agag shuffled his knees under him and managed a kneeling position. He even pulled his hands together as though in supplication. "It is well known that you Hebrews serve a merciful god. That you are people of justice. Please show me mercy, as a tribute to the mighty one who gave you this victory."

Saul could not help looking up and around him at the gathered crowd. Had even his own subjects shown him such verbal deference lately? It felt good, this stream of abject tribute from another sovereign, especially one who had shown him and his people such complete loathing in the past.

Saul looked away at another disturbance approaching on the

desert floor. Farmers? Through the quivering desert haze he could make out oxen, sheep, donkeys laden with goods—no, there were Israelite soldiers driving the herd.

*Ah, yes.* The spoils of Agag's household.

He turned to the captured king. The time had come for a royal pronouncement. He pursed lips and drew his eyebrows together, scrambling to muster the proper eloquence.

"Agag, your people are Israel's oldest foe. And a needless one, I might add. We asked for nothing but safe passage when we approached your lands so many years ago. Yet your people murdered our aged, our women and children. Since then you've pillaged and plundered our ranks without quarter. Well, I hope you saw the carpet of bodies on your way here today, Agag. It is all that remains—or should I say *you* are all that remains—of the Amalekite race. My G-d has decreed that your people be wiped forever from the face of the earth."

Impulsively he added, "As for *your* fate, I shall hold you prisoner until such time as I decide whether to slay you personally in obedience to YHWH's command or merely let the widows of your victims stone you to death. Meanwhile, tonight you can listen to the sound of me ravishing your wife. Begone."

He ordered Agag dragged away and chained in a nearby guardhouse, then retired to his tents. It had been a long and weary day. Hard work, all this killing. Such hard labor that he reclined on his pillows and promptly fell into a deep afternoon sleep. When he awoke, the tent stood dark but for a few candles his servants had lit in the corners. He rolled upright and fought to regain his clarity. And then he was reminded of his impulsive threat to Agag.

*I have some raping to do.*

In the intoxicating moments following Agag's capture, the prospect had stirred him with lewd anticipation. But now, his head swimming with sleep, his senses tinged with nausea, the prospect did not seem as enticing. Maybe he would let the night pass along with the idea. Only the guards would know he had not made good on his statement.

He heard a shout. *"Stop! Stop!"* His eyes flew wide open. His heart thundered in his chest.

He jumped to his feet and raced outside. He saw the retreating forms of soldiers running away into the darkness of a ravine behind the camp.

"What happened?" he shouted.

"The Amalekite woman!" a voice cried back from the blackness. Saul thought simply that the women had escaped, which to him was no great disaster. Then the voice finished, "She laid with him!"

The full import of this revelation grew slowly within Saul like a gradual rising of floodwater. First, that his finest men had been eluded, which was only a slight embarrassment. So the doomed king had enjoyed a final night of pleasure. A trifling jibe for a condemned man, nothing more.

Then it came to him. This could become a major embarrassment.

And his heart sank. "She laid with him!"

*What if? What if she's—? No, no, she cannot be with child. . . .*

# Chapter Four

*A*ll the troubling *what if*s in the world did in fact align themselves against the hapless Saul. His soldiers searched all night, but the fleeing woman eluded capture. The next morning Saul gave up on the hunt and moved his camp to Carmel, where he built a cairn in his honor at the occasion of defeating the Amalekites. Then he ordered them on to the tabernacle at Gilgal.

There he rushed to Samuel's tent, eager to tell him the news of their ancient foes' extermination. He found the old man prone on the tent floor in an attitude of supplication. The aging prophet rose slowly and fixed a baleful, tear-stained face upon Saul.

"Blessed are you of the Lord!" Saul exclaimed. "I carried out G-d's command concerning the Amalekites."

Samuel stood in silence, obviously wincing while his joints straightened. He pointed a bony finger in the direction from which Saul had entered.

"Why, then, are my ears suddenly full of the bleating of sheep and the lowing of oxen?"

38

Saul could feel the blood drain from his face. He had hoped to placate the old man with news of their overwhelming victory. After all, what was a slight deviation—a surviving king, a few expendable wives and some spoils for sacrifice—next to the extermination of an entire nation from the face of the earth? *I should have known better,* he told himself in a flood of exasperation. *That old pain in my side always finds one tiny matter and turns it into some enormous issue.*

"It is no great thing," he attempted. "The people brought them from the Amalekites. Along with their captured king and a wife. I spared the best of the sheep and oxen for a sacrifice before G-d. But all the rest we've destroyed."

The knowledge of that escaped woman, full of Agag's seed, burned inside him, and he looked away from Samuel's intense gaze.

In the seconds that followed, Samuel's features were consumed by the most profound expression of sadness Saul had ever witnessed in another human being. And during that moment Saul realized something he could hardly bear to consider. His stomach began to churn with the knowledge that Samuel had never been the enemy of his reign, for it was now equally obvious that the old man's heart was in the process of breaking.

Saul realized something else, as well, from the old man's shattered look. *He, Saul, had just lost his throne.* Perhaps not immediately, but for all intents and purposes he had just ceased to be king. And all of a sudden, despite his constant misgivings and self doubt, he now wanted nothing more than to save his crown.

At that moment Samuel straightened the stoop in his neck and drew to his full height. The grief that had overwhelmed his features suddenly coiled into rage. His nostrils flared and his arm reached far above him, index finger jabbing at the tent roof. Even the towering Saul recoiled a bit before the old judge's newly imposing figure. "Saul, let me tell you what the Lord said to me last night!" he shouted.

"Tell me," replied Saul, trying a placating tone.

"Although you were once small in your own eyes, did you not

become the head of the tribes of Israel? The Lord anointed you king over Israel. And he sent you on a mission, saying, 'Go and completely destroy those wicked people, the Amalekites; make war on them until you have wiped them out.' The Almighty required a complete purge of this evil, disease-ridden nation. Why did you not obey G-d? Why did you pounce on the plunder and do evil in the eyes of the Lord?"

"But I did obey Him," Saul insisted. "I went on the mission the Lord assigned me. I completely destroyed the Amalekites and brought back Agag, their king. The soldiers took sheep and cattle from the plunder, the best of what was available, in order to sacrifice them to the Lord your G-d at Gilgal."

Samuel shook his head and the skin of his face began to take on the color of a calf's liver. As he opened his mouth to respond, his jowls quivered with a rage that seemed to instantly engulf his body. "Does the Lord delight in burnt offerings and sacrifices as much as in obedience to His commands? To obey is better than sacrifice! To heed Him is better than the fat of rams!"

As Samuel's voice rose in pitch and ferocity, King Saul felt life and strength draining from his entire body. His long limbs, which had once carried him with strength and energy, now sagged into lifeless rags, and he nearly staggered as he stepped backward. Finally he hung his head and replied, "I have indeed sinned. I violated the Lord's command and your instructions. I was afraid of the people and so I gave in to them. Now I beg you—please forgive my sin and come back with me so that I may worship the Lord."

But Samuel shook his head, his rage clearly growing by the moment. "You have rejected the word of the Lord, and the Lord has rejected you as king over Israel!"

Saul felt himself blanch further and slowly shook his head. He could not believe something as minor as a single prisoner, a matter he had thought Samuel might even overlook, had somehow exploded into the end of his kingship.

When Samuel was through proclaiming the end of Saul's reign

in a voice full of both anger and grief, he stopped, huffed loudly a few times and turned to a nearby guard. He said, "Soldier, bring me Agag, king of the Amalekites. Drag him into my presence *now!*"

Samuel at this moment seemed as alive and possessed with as much vitality as a man half his age. With an impulsive sweep of his arm, he pushed aside a tent flap and marched out into the sunlight to await the prisoner. Saul reluctantly followed.

A short while later, a cordon of soldiers walked up with the pagan king striding proudly in their midst. As he approached the prophet, it was clear from his confident gait and expression that Agag believed he was about to be released.

Samuel stepped within a single cubit of the Amalekite's face and shouted in his best proclamation voice, "*As your sword has made women childless, so will your mother be childless among women!*"

Agag had barely enough time to register his miscalculation and utter the words, "No—please . . . Have mercy . . . please!" He sank to his knees with a terror upon his face more abject than he had worn all day—for he no doubt knew from reputation that the old prophet would not entertain further delay or change his mind.

In a single motion the patriarch wheeled around, unsheathed the sword from a nearby soldier's scabbard, and without pausing heaved the blade with a mighty two-handed grip. A combined gasp ripped from the crowd of assembled watchers, for the old man's torso twisted and turned, and with a flash of reflected sunlight the blade whistled down across Agag's shoulders. Its edge swept through bone with a metallic ring and hissed through his neck's remaining flesh—the king's once expressive head toppled almost comically from its perch and fell with a thud in the dust. Without pause the rest of his body crumpled from its knees and sprawled at Saul's feet.

Still spewing its crimson stream, the severed head seemed to stare up at Samuel with an almost aggrieved expression of combined sadness and reproach—but the old man neither uttered a word of pity nor halted his grisly work. Bending over at the waist, he swung downward and sloppily cleaved the torso in half, and then, with loud grunts that the bystanders could not distinguish between exertion or rage, he chopped off Agag's arms and legs.

Finally, his momentum spent, Samuel straightened and tossed the sword with a gesture of disgust down into the jumble of gore and limbs at his feet. He fixed Saul with eyes as cold as the now-vacant gaze of the dead king. Then, just as quickly as it had overtaken him, the renewed vigor left Samuel's body, the stoop returned to his shoulders and a moment later he was again a wizened old man.

The old prophet of Israel shuffled off without a word and departed within the hour for Ramah.

In light of Samuel's execution of her husband, those who knew of the escape of the Amalekite queen, fleeing somewhere through the desert canyons of the Negev with the seed of her race alive within her, now felt its portent for evil.

The truth was, Saul and his men had carelessly allowed scores of Amalekites to live, bands that subsequent kings would be forced to deal with in years to come. But the woman did not know that. She was only aware that she carried the survival of Agag's royal bloodline within her. And of that she was correct.

As it came to pass, this woman possessed the hardiness for which her people were legendary, and she survived. With the determination that came from believing she was the last of her kind, she passed herself off as a widowed countrywoman to a band of Kenites whom the Hebrews had ejected from her capital just before their attack. The shepherds eagerly wed her off to one of their unmarried sons, and her survival appeared won. Life became hard but assured. She helped her new extended family tend their sheep until her pregnancy became too ungainly.

Then, in the spring of the following year, she gave birth to a sickly baby boy. The family accepted this child as the offspring of her dead husband and welcomed him as their own, nursing him carefully to health.

At night, though, while her new husband was away tending flocks, the young woman would whisper to her son in a language the Kenites would not have understood. She would whisper to him that he was the son of Agag, last king of the Amalekites. He carried not only the royal line within himself but the very survival of their people.

She whispered something else, too. It was about the Hebrews, the children of Israel. *They are responsible for your miserable fate*, she would wrathfully breathe into his ear. *Kill any one you find, even if it costs you your life. Their death is your blood, your reason for living. Someday one of your offspring will find a way to kill them all.*

That boy would leave the Kenites at age fifteen with a bride from the nearby village. He would sire nine sons, who would themselves father thirty-five. The Amalekite race had regained its Jew-hating foothold upon the lands of the Hebrews. And from that day forward generation upon generation passed upon the earth, each one gathering unto itself increasing levels of hatred and the means to wipe G-d's people out of existence. Each mother cooing to her baby tales of Hebrew treachery. Each father fanning the flames of his children's resentment and rage.

Five centuries later, the right descendant was born not far from where his ancestral mother had given birth to Agag's son.

His generation would be the one to stage the ultimate revenge.

That man was named Haman.

And I know now that he was leader of the horde that slaughtered my family. I know this because that night I saw one more feature of these murderers, a distinguishing mark that is indelibly etched on my memory. When their "work" was done and they swaggered out the door, I saw the moonlight upon their blood-spattered backs. And beneath the flecks of blood I saw their insignia traced in white—a strange cross shape with each arm broken and twisted in the same direction. For some reason, the sight of that insignia frightened me as much as my own brush with death, as much as the horrible death of my mother, whose lifeless body now protected me. I had never had such an all-consuming reaction to a mere symbol before. Maybe it was the association with evil, cruel and cowardly men. But somehow it seemed deeper than that. I felt as though my spirit had recoiled into a place I had never been before.

For years I did not see the sign again. That is, until, as a new arrival, I began to catch brief, terrifying glimpses of it around Susa's Royal Palace, where the sight of it upon some soldiers' backs made me inexplicably shudder and begin to weep like a baby. Some time later I would learn of these men's origins.

And that is how I know.

# Chapter Five

WILDERNESS OF ZIN—497 B.C.

*T*he poor traders never saw it coming.

Granted, they were heavily armed with the latest Egyptian bows and leather shields. And they were certainly on guard, for the region they were crossing was a notorious haven for marauders. They were even being escorted by a contingent of local guides, who in addition to steering them through the impossible maze of gullies and ravines known as the Wilderness of Zin, pledged for their fee to offer protection from attack.

The guides' leader halted the camel caravan as the path ahead traced a fork-shaped split. His dark eyes darted above the folds of his scarf as though he was probing the craggy rock face for their proper route. But then a pair of vultures noisily took flight from a perch just ahead, and he abruptly lifted his arm.

Suddenly all six of his men gave a shrill shout and violently kicked their camels into a trot. Before the traders could respond and follow, the guides had disappeared around the first rightward bend. The travelers had no time to dwell on the abandonment, for as soon as their betrayers were gone from sight, a rain of flaming arrows began to pour down upon them.

Although one of them fell shrieking from his saddle with an arrow piercing his neck, the rest were well shielded. But the arrows' true purpose soon revealed itself. One of them landed to the side of the one hapless trader's body, and with a soft thump its flame shot forth in a thin sheet of fire a cubit or so above the ground.

*The vapors*, thought Majiir Sunwadi, the group's leader. He had smelled vague odors and seen a faint reflection of sunlight wafting above the path, sure signs of a nearly invisible cloud of fumes, another of Zin's notorious features. He had heard of these strange mists igniting the night fires of the careless, but he had never heard of their strange properties being used in attack.

Sunwadi cursed loudly as his camel groaned in terror and reared backward in an attempt to escape the flaming veil. He fell, reached forward and pulled his sword from its sheath. He hit the ground and his ankles roared in pain, first from the impact of the high fall, then from the singe of the flame upon his skin. But the fire only lasted an instant, its fuel just as quickly consumed.

He rolled over and came up on his knees, holding the sword with two hands beside his face. The trained stance.

He needn't have bothered. He looked up into a wall of lances. His band was surrounded by a veritable rampart of hard leather, razor-sharp blades and eyes even harder and colder than the weapons themselves.

*Amalekites*, he told himself with a flood of fear and resignation. The remnant spawn of King Agag's once mighty people.

He dropped his sword. He motioned for his men to do the same, and the clatter of falling swords echoed across the rocks. One thing he knew: the first rule of survival in these situations was complete and abject surrender. The Amalekites were superb warriors, so fluent in killing that Sunwadi had often inwardly confessed a perverse admiration for their skill. They were swift and expert in their craft, and no one in the Fertile Crescent dared deny it.

The line of pirates shifted forward, and Sunwadi found himself standing, back amidst his dismounted men and their animals.

They were marched in a tied-up huddle for several hours. Eventually the ravines played out and they climbed atop Zin's treacherous terrain, tracing a narrow summit with the desert splayed out for miles beneath them. Sunwadi had just allowed himself his first furtive glance at the land's beauty below, when they abruptly turned down into a ravine sheltered by a surprising grove of palm and olive trees. Its soothing shade canopy soon blocked out the oppression of the sun, and he could sense his men's mood lifting. Even their captors began a lively jabber in their strange language, and their gestures grew more animated.

He briefly allowed himself to think of his wife and son, back in Palmyra. Now, walking into the cluster of tents that marked the raiders' hideout, he wondered if he would ever pick up the boy again. The Amalekites were known for being maddeningly fickle captors. They might torture and kill you or just as easily treat you as an honored guest and merely ask for tribute upon your return.

*I'll be glad to offer tribute on my next time through*, thought Sunwadi. *Especially since there won't* be *a return trip*. This disaster had sealed his resolve to stay off the road. His dead companion was the young nephew of a close friend back home. He'd have a hard time explaining that the hard-headed young man had refused to don the proper armor, complaining of the heat, and that his stubbornness had cost him his life.

A short, fat man with a glistening black beard sauntered forth from the main tent, energetically probing his teeth with the tip of a thick tongue.

"Who is the leader of this band?" he shouted in accented Sumerian, their native dialect.

"I am," Sunwadi replied in a voice made gravelly by the dust.

The man said nothing but motioned inside with a jerk of his head and led the way into the tent. Sunwadi followed him onto a shadowed carpet of rugs and matched his cross-legged pose. As his eyes adjusted he spied a staggering array of gold and silver adornments, as though the tent were some sultan's gilded palace. Chains hung from the tent's seams and support ropes. A small ebony pony stood behind him, inlaid with lapis and jade and filaments of gold. In the far background shone the sulking eyes of a beautiful woman dressed in the provocative clothes of a concubine. He looked away, not daring to indulge his eyes. There was no surer way to be killed than to be caught ogling the head man's woman. Of that he was certain. He turned at the sound of the man's voice.

"My name is Haman. Haman the Agagite. Have you heard of me?"

He nodded. "Your legend stretches across the land, sire."

"And what is your name?"

"Majiir Sunwadi, sir."

"And where are you from?" asked the fat man.

"Palmyra," Sunwadi answered.

"What are you carrying?"

"The usual. Spices, medicinal herbs, silk swaths, jewelry, foreign trinkets."

"Hmmm. Why have I never seen you before? You avoiding me?"

"Oh no, I am not. In the past I have hired guides who must have regrettably avoided your acquaintance. For whatever selfish reason, I do not know."

The man narrowed his eyelids and grinned in response. He obviously liked Sunwadi's answers. Then, just as quickly, his countenance changed: his eyes grew into bright and beady sapphires, and his teeth clenched reflexively.

"Tell me, do you conduct business with the Hebrews? You passed through their country. I won't stand for that."

"Oh no. As you said, their land is a passage through which I must cross. But my men and I do nothing more than buy the occasional bit of provision or the right to water our animals. No, we're headed to Egypt, where the premium prices are."

"We'll see." The man leaned over, hate and some other un-identifiable emotion undulating in waves across his features. "My men are taking a sample of your wares. If I see anything Jewish-made, I'll kill you where you sit."

The man shouted in another tongue to someone outside. A flap opened and one of the bandits brought in an armful of Sunwadi's merchandise. He leaned forward and let the baubles fall onto the carpet with a long tinkling sound. Haman began to poke through the pile with a coquettishly wandering index finger, as though only mildly interested in the haul.

"Nice quality," he said, although his gaze was only half fixed on the items. "Hah. What is this?"

He had held up a piece of rosewood inscribed with a curious symbol, a square cross with its ends twisted at right angles to each other.

"What do you call this insignia?"

"It has many names, sir, for it is revered by many nations, including Greece, Troy, Egypt. It's said to have orginated in India. The Greeks call it the gammadion. It is the most ancient and powerful emblem known to mankind."

"Really. Powerful, you say." The bandit's eyes seemed to glitter the more he stared at the sign. "You know, my friend, I have been looking for a suitable icon to adopt as the insignia of our . . . tribe here. This one—well, it intrigues me."

"It is yours," Sunwadi said abjectly.

"Of course it is. Hey, Oman, what do you think? The Riders of the Twisted Cross!"

"I like it," said deep-voiced Oman, a massively shielded warrior standing near the tent entrance. Haman stood and turned to him.

"Kill the peddler," he said, without even a look back at Sunwadi. "I don't want anyone else but us to know where we obtained this."

A hand pulled Sunwadi painfully from his seated position by the knot of rope on his wrists. He was yanked to his feet and shoved outside.

As the blade whistled downward, Sunwadi thought of his wife and son and silently bade them good-bye. The last thing he heard in this world was Haman's laughter filtering out from the tent's interior. Then the ground rose up and struck him beside the face, and his world went black.

# Chapter Six

PERSIAN PROVINCES—CIRCA 490 B.C.

*H*aman did in fact utilize the strange Indian symbol that had so captivated his imagination. Indeed, his men embraced it with a swiftness and a possessiveness that surprised even him. They began to etch the eerie twisted cross onto their battle gear, paint it onto their garb and even tattoo it onto their skin. And they found, over time, that the unity created by their common image bore out the effect Haman had sought. Their ferocity began to escalate. They fought more savagely. They found, in fact, that they started to seek out battle, to fight more than was needed just to keep themselves alive through piracy.

At one time they had merely been good enough fighters to scare their prey and protect their loot. No more. Now they began to roam in search of people to attack, whether loaded with bounty or not. Hebrews who fell into their clutches came in for especially bloody treatment. To those they showed no mercy. Whole families were put to the sword without exception, and Haman insisted, with particular emphasis, that even their livestock be destroyed.

Throughout the region, the name of Haman was spoken with whispers and shivers. Traveling through the area became a nightmare for all but the most well connected and well protected. The sight of a twisted cross scratched or splattered in scarlet paint—*or was it blood?*—upon a trailside boulder became the emblem of imminent peril.

One day Haman and his scouts came upon a column of well-armed and disciplined soldiers of an army they did not recognize. From his typical perch atop a limestone cliff, Haman himself watched them make their way. What he saw made his blood run cold. They clearly were not Egyptian. Their ranks were straight, even into the dozens of rows. Their capes and boots were completely clean and utterly alike—woven of what appeared to be gold. The raiment of an empire. He breathed in raggedly. He'd never heard of this powerful force.

Then he made another jarring observation: the sun was shining off their breastplates.

These soldiers were armored in metal. He had *never* seen that before. He turned to his chief warlord and whispered, "We will not attack these men. They are a breed these parts have never seen. I will try to befriend them."

He jumped on his horse and sped away down the slope. Moments later, the column's scout raised his fist and the riders behind him ground to a halt. Ahead of the soldiers waited a man on a beautiful horse, holding out a hand.

The sizable rider, whose helmet plumage and carriage bespoke high rank, cantered his splendid mount over to the newcomer. After looking him over for a cool minute, the soldier spoke.

"Would you be Haman, by any chance?"

Haman could not prevent himself from grinning like a boy at the question. "Yes, I am. And who would you be, revered soldier?"

"I am Satrap Xeril Artemis, of the Royal Empire of Persia."

"Persia," Haman repeated, more out of surprise than an attempt to clarify the word. His shoulders immediately stiffened at the knowledge. Did these men mean him harm? He had certainly plundered his share of Persian convoys, stolen his share of Persian goods.

The captain laughed. "Do not fret, my good man. We do not come to seek retribution for your crimes against the Persian state, although I hear they are many."

"My heart rejoices, most kind satrap."

"And I hope to bring it even more joy when you hear the errand upon which I have sought you. I wonder if you have any place to which we might retire and discuss matters privately?"

Haman's eyebrows rose in droll agreement at the satrap's suggestion. He smiled broadly and waved a quick gesture to his men. "I would be honored to host you and your men at our humble desert camp."

The two parties rode side by side through the desert—polished Persian legions and ragtag Negev marauders eyeing one another warily for any sign of ambush or treachery. The sun was past its highest point when they reached Haman's oasis camp.

Haman's men dismounted and hurriedly exhumed several amphoras of prized Greek wine seized from a long-ago caravan. The two leaders retired to Haman's tent as the libations began to flow and spirits to rise.

Sitting in the relative cool of the bandit's tent, Satrap Artemis watched his host closely and began to silently reappraise the man. He had not missed a detail upon entering the robbers' lair—its bristling weapons caches, opulent furnishings, the variety and volume of its plundered spoils. *These men may have a ragtag appearance*, he concluded, *but they are skilled fighters*. Despite his familiar and bustling manner, Haman's narrow eyes bore a cold ruthlessness that also glittered on the faces of all his men. Remembering the impaled skeleton that had greeted their arrival, the satrap smiled inwardly and told himself, *The reports on these Agagites are true—they're tough* as sun-dried leather! I would hate to be their enemy, but they may make perfect allies.

"So, satrap," said Haman eventually, pouring a second goblet. "What brings you to our desolate straits?"

"We come to claim this land for the Empire of Persia and its almighty king, Darius. We have heard of how sorely your predations in these parts have disrupted the Egyptian economy. And since King Darius intends to subdue this entire region, we have actually come to ask for your help."

"I will give you whatever aid my men and I can muster."

"Good. My lord and I ask only for you to do what you do best. To rape and pillage. Since you have already done such a worthy task of causing the Pharaoh grief, we would like for you to turn your attentions to Egypt itself on the Emperor's behalf."

"Attack Egypt?"

"Well, maybe not attack the entire nation. Our armies will do plenty of that in time. But harass, maybe. Pester their northernmost outposts. Weaken their defenses. Distract their scouts. If you can burn a city or two, all the better."

"Can I kill any Jews I find?"

The satrap shrugged. "I know of no prohibitions against harming Jews. But I suppose they would be treated like any other local civilians."

Haman rubbed his hands together, his eyes gleaming. "Sir, consider me the newest and most willing raider in your Persian army. Call me your advance force, if you will."

The Persian slapped a hand across Haman's shoulder. "Excellent. And there will be more opportunities for raiding if all goes well. This could be a good chance for you to catch the eye of our leadership and advance in position and rank in the Empire."

"Where could I raid after that, may I ask?"

"Well, I'm not promising anything. But if this goes well, I could give you permission to attack Babylon. The old capital has been a bit arrogant of late and stands in need of a good trouncing. Of course, it could not be traced back to the Empire. It would have to be blamed on ethnic tension or some other source."

Haman's greed swept through him like a tidal wave. He had never even considered ransacking Babylon, once the world's strongest city.

In only a moment, a snap of the fingers, his prospects had broadened far beyond his wildest dreams.

And Haman did indeed attack Egyptian positions on his side of the Red Sea. His attacks were successful. As a result, six months later his Persian liaison gave him the go-ahead to attack Babylon. His men still would not be wearing the insignia of Persia, and they would have no official sanction from the Empire. They were undercover murderers, little more. Yet behind the scenes, the Empire would help Haman do his dirty work. A city gate left open. A sentry called in for the night. A defense force mysteriously away on maneuvers.

A subdued city of Babylon, a too-arrogant child whose hand had been slapped, now leaned increasingly on the stablizing strength of the Persian Empire.

And that, my young friend, is how a band of Hebrew-hating Amalekites came to be in Babylon, far from their native territory, massacring not only my father Abihail's family but many Jewish homes in the city and some of Babylon's leading citizens.

The blood of my family won Haman great favor within the Empire. In fact, within days after the Babylon bloodbath, he was summoned to Persepolis, where the king appointed him satrap over his native Negev deserts.

And the stage was set for Haman's ultimate assault on those he hated so much.

## Hadassah, daughter of Abihail

### KETHUVIM ESTHER 2:7

"... had neither father nor mother. The maiden
was shapely and beautiful. ..."

# Chapter Seven

BABYLON—CIRCA 492 B.C.

$\mathcal{M}$y second memory took a long time to form. It is a composite, really, a sadly familiar slice of the years following the murders. The memory is one of awakening ever so gradually from a cold, thick fog, a choking mist that dissolves from around my vision as slowly as eternity itself.

Oh yes, and the fog is pain. I know that. Even as a child, I realized it. I look back and I am walking, one slow step at a time, out of an endless cloud of anguish.

Did I tell you? Of course I didn't. I hardly ever tell myself.

I was the only member of my immediate family left alive.

As it was, the murderers were not content to slaughter my mother, father, brother, uncle, aunt and three cousins. Or, as I would later discover, leading citizens of Babylon and all but a few dozen of its Jewish citizens. The Empire had stayed true to its plan—arranging for the conquered city's homeguard to be deployed on "maneuvers," all Imperial sentries mysteriously called away from their posts. Then it had ensured that the Ishtar Gate stood open and unwatched for the first time in centuries. The way for their cowardly massacre had been smooth indeed. The tweaking of mighty Babylon's nose was complete.

And as they swaggered out, one of the murderers found the time to throw a torch into the middle of the room. It is a wonder it was not extinguished by the deep puddle of blood that had collected there. But instead, it sprouted vigorously into flame and began to consume the remains of my family with an almost willful aggression.

I remember the first sound of the fire's eruption as a respite from the awful silence that had immediately settled as the last attacker departed. I had lain there, wishing time to stop, desperate to postpone the moment when I would have to open my eyes and deal with the cause of the awful stillness in the room, absorb the grisly verdict of my fingertips. But then I heard a great soft thump followed by the crackling of fire and realized that the last man had made one last act of violence. I was lying in the farthest corner from the door and truly at great risk of burning alive. Outside, the whinnying and galloping of horses had subsided. The murderers were gone.

So I shakily stood in the sudden glare, not looking around me but keeping my eyes fixed on the door and the freedom framed there. I wanted to run, but here's something I remember vividly: standing suddenly after so many minutes with every muscle clenched had caused my legs to go numb. I can clearly recall trying to coax my feet forward, even pawing at the floor with my tingling yet utterly unresponsive instep. Panic began to chase my heartbeat and inflame my gestures. It struck me as almost ironic—though I would not have known the word—for my entire lower extremities to be frozen at a moment like this, but the fire was roaring toward me, and I could honestly picture myself becoming a human torch, unable to move in time. I began to gasp. Slowly, through a million pinpricks, my feet started to respond. I took a step with the slowness and exaggerated effort of a ninety-year-old.

And then, possibly prompted by the recalcitrance of my limbs, I became instantly paralyzed with a limb-numbing kind of fear, the likes of which I had never felt before and seldom since.

I simply could not move an inch, even to save my own life. I could not have been more immobilized had someone tied me with a rope. I watched the flames approach, felt the heat grow unbearable, but found myself as fixed as a statue.

In the next moment, the image of myself as the last victim of this attack burst whole into my mind, vivid and realistic. Somehow it seemed, for the briefest of seconds, utterly reasonable and proper that I should soon die. It was in the order of things. It made sense.

And then, just as quickly, it did not. Now it made no sense whatsoever; in fact, in the blink of an eye its reasoning became offensive to me. I felt pain and looked back. The fire had raced around the ceiling's corner and had now swallowed a linen curtain tucked above a windowsill, only five cubits away. I sensed an actual rage in the flames, a vast and powerful hatred of my body in its intact state. Suddenly the thought of myself as its victim struck me as repugnant. The very notion of remaining frozen and accepting of this fate now made me feel like a cowardly accomplice to my own horror.

So I began to fight again. Not willing to accept the excruciating slowness of my steps, I actually hopped, as though jumping would liberate me from the rebellion of my legs. I hopped again, farther this time.

I could feel the heat across my back and the hem of my nightrobe beginning to sear my skin. The flames were now a storm in my ears. I dared not look back, for I had seen them speeding across the fabric for me. Like prey, I was like a small, innocent animal being stalked for death by an uncaring and implacable foe.

Now, at long last, I screamed. Not in grief, as I could have, but in frustration and terror.

Twisting my torso with the strain, I willed my legs to move. And they did. Still not nearly as fast as I wanted them to, but they shuffled forward. Cubit by cubit, the door grew closer—but by now it, too, was sheathed in a glowing inferno.

I heard a loud crack that was not fire and glanced up to see from the corner of my eye a ceiling beam crash down behind me and land heavily on the floor. Agony lanced through my brain, my shoulders, and as the pain began to scream down my back, I realized the timber itself had been aflame.

I looked again at the burning doorway, and in a judgment not borne of experience or sophistication—merely a raw, innate knowledge that however dangerous the door was, it stood only a handsbreadth away from the outside, from open, free, cooler air—I started to run. I do not remember realizing that my legs were now capable of flight. I only recall that they did run, and while I tripped over burning wreckage I knew with a wild exhilaration that nothing would knock me off my feet now. I passed through a brief assault of heat, then fell into the flickering night and rolled upon the ground.

All I remember next is the sound of shouts. Less than a second later I felt hands upon me, wrapping clothing around my body, pulling me, rolling me farther into the dirt.

Through the tumult I heard one voice that I recognized. It was the deep yell of my cousin Mordecai, my uncle's eldest son. He had not been in the home because, as we all knew, Mordecai was a highly spirited young bachelor who often stayed out late with his friends. A knot of onlookers had been holding him back from the fire, into which he might well have plunged himself in suicidal grief. It was clear from the sight of the inferno that no one would survive that blaze.

Mordecai was screaming to be released when I stumbled from the doorway, still covered in my mother's blood, flames rising from my garments. He gave a great cry and launched himself on me, the first to reach my side. Still crying out at the top of his lungs, Mordecai threw off his robe and proceeded to quench the fire.

I do not remember much after that.

In fact, I have only a few specific memories of the next few years. Only numbed impressions. I do know, because he told me, that Mordecai immediately carried me to the home of a physician, who bathed me in aloe and a poultice of other Oriental herbs. I believe that is why, to this day, I bear no scars or marks from the ordeal. It can only be miraculous that my body escaped unscathed. The scars from that night I carried in my soul.

And that is how the next chapter of my life was born.

*Chapter Eight*

SUSA—CIRCA 493 B.C.

*I*t has taken me a lifetime to remember the events I just related to you. I spent nearly as long trying to forget them. In fact, even writing them here has taken a surprisingly exhausting amount of effort, calling up grief I did not know I still harbored this many years later.

I know from his stories that Mordecai took me in as the sole survivor of his family and adopted me as his own. Almost as if he, too, had jumped through a doorway of no return, there was no hint of the careless, reckless youth he had been. We left Babylon shortly after the massacre, after the feeble attempts and ultimate failure of the Persian authorities to hunt down and punish those responsible.

He tells me the story of purchasing our passage on a Bedouin convoy along the royal road to my hometown of Susa. I was still so deep in shock that he reports having been forced many days to hold me in the saddle, slumped against him. The effort must have been extremely tiring, but he never made any inference of having resented it, not ever.

The only tokens I had of my family were the birthday pendant I had been wearing on that fateful night and the warmth of my parents' words as they gave it to me.

This memory of my family would indeed become one of the last to fade, thanks to Mordecai's admonition and my gradual attachment to the necklace. He kept it hidden away, but he would bring it out on occasions such as my birthday, then carefully return it to its hiding place. It came to mean more and more to me as I grew older, and I yearned for the day it would be mine to keep. That had been my parents' final admonition to me—that I should wait until I was a woman to wear it. It was my one tangible link to my past, and it retained that significance long after my parents' faces had disappeared from my memory.

We could live in my family's old house, Mordecai says he told me. He had remarked that it was the only place left for us, but I think he also knew how much I would appreciate sleeping in my own bed, with familiar sights on every side. But I don't think dear Mordecai considered how painful it would be to see these places without the beloved family who had once inhabited them with me.

No, instead Mordecai, ever trying to cheer me up, reminded me that we were in the capital of the Persian Empire and therefore relatively safe. Not *actually* safe, that is, but less imperiled.

How wrong he was. But I will tell you *that* story in its proper order.

According to our family lore, upon our arrival in Susa we contacted a childhood friend of Mordecai's father, a fellow Jew named Elias. Soon this friend helped Mordecai secure an apprenticeship at the Palace scriptorium. And so it is here, in the home of my birth, surrounded by the ghosts of my dead family, that I passed the long, sequestered years of my childhood.

Several images shimmer into focus from that time of slow awakening. The towering green canopy of the palm tree in the center of our garden. An impossibly high span of outer wall, smelling of old plaster, which blocked out the winter sun. The frozen eyes of my cherished clay doll, Tirzuh. The broad, wizened smile of Rachel, our housekeeper and my closest childhood confidant. Mordecai's face gazing down at me, his eyes brimming with tears of affection, his smile tremulous but full of caring and love for me. I do not myself clearly remember Mordecai's demeanor before the killings, only what I had heard adults saying about him. But somehow, as I grew to know him, I became convinced that he was now far more serious and burdened than he had once been. A freer, more whimsical version of him surely lay hidden behind the solemn and caring man I now saw every day. In my childish self-absorption, I forgot that Mordecai, too, had his enormous griefs and losses. As well, he had inherited the traditional Jewish burden of carrying on our family name, of passing on its heritage.

In those days, my adopted father—and eventually I began to think of Mordecai and address him as *Poppa*—was a thick, soft man whom no one would mistake for a common laborer. Rachel always said that in Israel his build would have revealed him as a priest, especially had he belonged to the tribe of Levi. He wore an admirably full beard that turned gray with surprising quickness during those first few years. He kept it trimmed square and long, though in the curled Persian style rather than the Jewish. Most remarkable about him were his eyes, which were brown and large and always darting alertly about to assess his current surroundings or the character of someone nearby. He radiated an air of warmth, competence and intelligence, yet also a wariness that never rested.

Mordecai did not marry. At the time he was content for me to believe it was out of devotion for me, and I'm sure that played a part. But now I also think he remained a bachelor because he was so concerned about betraying his Jewishness. He could not bear the thought of either marrying a known Jewess as the Torah mandated or, worse yet, marrying a Gentile woman and having his secret revealed upon their wedding night. Either scenario would have filled him with dread, for if I remember anything about my beloved guardian, it is the incredible care he took to disguise his Jewish origins. Besides his Persian name, he dressed as a Persian, talked like one, and only a handful knew he was not.

This care even reached deep into our home, where he required Rachel and me to converse in Persian—although when he was telling stories from our Hebrew history, he slipped into the familiar language of my early years with my parents.

I especially loved the stories of Sarah and Abraham, Rebekah and Isaac, and the bittersweet love story of Jacob's Rachel and her sister Leah.

So I grew up knowing both languages well. Now, you may hear me speak of Mordecai's pains to appear Gentile and conclude that he was less than a brave or dedicated Jew. And that would be completely false, as you will soon learn, although I see the paradox. No, Mordecai was a secret and yet a dedicated, observant Jew—with but one notable exception: neither of us attended services at the local synagogue.

The Jews of Susa, as I would soon find out from Rachel, were actually a sizable and privileged minority. They were the merchants and money-changers, and, based on the Code of Hamarabi our Persian rulers had concluded that at least tolerance toward their strange ways and strange god was the wisest political course. They administered their own house of worship and lived under the civil authority of their prophet, though owing ultimate fealty to the King. But to identify publicly with this community would have posed too great a risk for Mordecai. The memories of our family's holocaust were too vivid to feel at ease, even among our own people. We considered ourselves fugitives of a sort, survivors of a massacre whose perpetrators remained at large. Toward that end, he maintained a respectable standoff with the high priest, who came over several times to plead the case of ending our seclusion.

The prophet-priest, a thin, swaying man with the burning eyes of someone who had once survived near starvation, stood in our home and argued convincingly that our ultimate safety lay in identifying with his numerous and influential flock. And Mordecai, without once losing an attitude of profound deference, repeated the facts of our narrow escape and the sense of danger that still haunted us both. Finally the man would toss up his arms in mild resignation and leave, both appeased and exasperated at Mordecai's respectful manner and his assurances that we kept all the observances. Indeed, Mordecai was rearing me in the knowledge of G-d's ways.

Actually, Mordecai kept his heritage hidden only out of concern for me. Had he been alone in the world, I believe he would have cast all cares to the wind. For that matter, I am sure he would have cast himself into the flames of his family's home that fateful night and willingly perished. Only the strong arms of his neighbors kept him from it. And then the sight of me stumbling through the doorway, wreathed in flame and coated in my mother's blood.

In fact, I have never known nor imagined a man more committed to his religion. Within the confines of our home he faithfully observed, and taught me, every Hebrew ceremony and tradition imaginable. During the early years he did so without great enthusiasm, for his faith was battered and wounded in those days. (When I think about it, his disillusionment with G-d may have played a bigger role in his arm's-length stance with the temple than he would care to admit.) Nevertheless, he maintained his outward faithfulness through it all.

Eventually the faces of my parents and brother receded from my memory and blurred into a melancholy haze. They were rarely spoken of directly, except when the occasional Jewish ritual required us to refer to our fathers and mothers. As a result, I actually grew to picture my home with Mordecai as overhung by a dark cloud. It hovered just below the ceiling, its shadow gray with all the memories and losses we dared not discuss. I actually had frightening dreams about it. The cloud would hang over my every waking hour, always present, ever looming at the back of my vision, and fill me with a dread and foreboding far more terrible than its mere appearance would suggest.

I did not blame Mordecai for this oppressive silence, at least not until many years later. But my lack of guile did not keep me from recognizing an underlying unhealthiness in our lives.

If anything, though, the unspoken grief we shared translated itself into an intense kindness between us. I suppose that is partly because Mordecai and I were all the relations left to each other in the world. Another reason may be the secretiveness of our Judaism, which bound us together in another layer of silence. But I have to say it is also because Mordecai was basically a kind and highly principled human being, qualities that soon began to distinguish him in the capital and earned him a respected place as court scribe.

How much more would I have worried had I known that the band of murderers still roamed my native Persia, still seeking my blood and that of all my people? That even as I walked through the years of my childhood, an ancient conspiracy to wipe the children of Israel and their memory from the earth was even now gathering strength—coming together like an evil growth joining its errant shoots? That rather than a safe place, the capital of Susa would soon become the most dangerous place imaginable?

I am not sure I would have survived even the thought of it. Had I even contemplated such a possibility, I'm certain I would have scurried under my bed, curled up like a small cat and melted into the comforting darkness, never to emerge again. Had you found me there and pulled me from my hiding place, my mind would have been gone, departed forever to a place of safety and peace.

But somehow, in my naïve state I did not consider such a possibility. My immediate surroundings felt safe, so I did not think about an attack ever happening again. Nor about the men who would not rest until I was dead if they even suspected that I could identify them and their horrendous deed.

That is not to say that the secretiveness did not affect me deeply. From the youngest age I recall thinking that I was different, yet forbidden to speak of why. In fact, since I saw virtually no one beyond Mordecai and Rachel, I wonder how I came to even have a basis for comparison.

The greatest reason for feeling different lay in the fact that I was a virtual prisoner in my home. I grew up to be a shy and socially maladjusted girl, of that I am sure. Strangers—the few who came by the house for this or that purpose, or the Jewish children Rachel would sometimes bring into the home to play—frightened me. Many days I would back into my favorite corner of the wall and cower, my head lowered. Strangers had killed my family. I had not seen the murderers' faces. How was I to know this wasn't the stranger who had done it? Or at least someone who would betray me to them?

Mordecai tried hard, when I was young, to put a good face on it. Being Jewish was a gift, he would tell me, and then he'd recount tales of this faraway place called the Land of Promise that was supposed to be our homeland.

And it worked, for a while. Even though it rarely became more than a background story, in those days it gave me comfort. Actually, I never witnessed hostility toward Jews until years later, when I left the four walls of my home and encountered humanity at large. Essentially I grew up as the sheltered only daughter of a Palace functionary in the capital of the world. At least, that is how I saw it. In those early years, I was content—for a while.

The truth is, I grew up sequestered both by physical isolation and by emotional devastation—I realize that now. But not knowing anything different, I did not consider it an aberration. I was only grateful for the embrace of a comfortable and expansive home. I played alone under Rachel's watchcare and listened to her stories of Israel and its kings. And I grew.

I only suppose that if I possess any depth of person at all—and I use this term only because others have used it on my behalf—it must be due to the equal depths of grief and inwardness that my childhood traumas had carved out in my soul. I grew up a quiet child, I've already pointed out. In fact, Mordecai informs me that I hardly spoke for nearly a year after the murders. I must believe him, for of that period I remember absolutely nothing. The fog obscures everything. And I must admit that although I would not wish my losses on anyone, I do believe that long periods of silence and introspection do a great deal to enrich a person's spiritual and emotional dimensions.

I still would trade these qualities in a heartbeat to have spared my father, mother and brother their horrible encounters with death.

THE ROYAL ROAD, NEAR SUSA—LATER THAT YEAR

Haman the Agagite stopped his horse at the top of the very last bend in the great Persian highway, raised his hand to shade his eyes and peered longingly ahead. Below him, shimmering from heat waves and distance, lay the capital of Susa, its broad scattering of white rooftops nestled against the hilltop jumble of the Palace itself.

He grinned fiercely, exposing his teeth to the hot desert wind in the process. He reined back his shying, impatient mount. Finally here he was. Ever since he'd heard of the Persian Empire for the first time, he had coveted this arrival, this city. Not only was it the seat of staggering power, the repository of untold riches, but he'd been told that the place was stinking with Jews. He had heard a drunken soldier mutter once that there were more Jews in Susa than in Jerusalem itself.

*Just think of the fun to be had,* he told himself. *Wealth to plunder. A king to overthrow. And Jews to kill by the score.*

*Paradise on earth.*

And he, already a satrap, was one of the King's key governors, the Princes of the Faces. He was already positioned. The generals knew him from the raids they had conducted together, along with several reprisal attacks against Egypt and Babylon. A lifetime of pillage had turned him into their anointed expert on low-level raiding—a painless alternative to costly, full-scale war. Soon he would call for his family and the rest of his private army, summon the men back from their current raids against the Greeks and show this city who was boss.

Haman laughed out loud, kicked his horse in the side and galloped off toward his blissful future.

# Chapter Nine

Sometime after I came to live with Mordecai and he adopted me as his daughter, he sat me down on our home's rooftop and made several revelations to me. I remember that it was a spring day, a rare cool day in Susa, and a recent rainstorm had given the air a briskness and pleasant fragrance. Yet despite the milder temperature, Mordecai's face was stiff and his voice was rough with the strain of his disclosures. He looked me in the eye only when he was through speaking.

"Hadassah," he said, "there is a great deal I have not told you. You see, I did not seek employment at the Palace and residence in Susa merely for the pay or the prestige of the position. I also went there with the intention of discovering more about who killed our families. I believed that if I could find that out anywhere, it would be here."

"And did you find anything?" I asked, my eagerness giving my voice a high, girlish lilt.

He nodded yes. But his eyes did not express joy.

"I found out some. I gained access to the royal archives and found, for one, that they were not Persian soldiers. There has never been an order for any unit of the Imperial army to kill Jews. However, permission had been given for a punitive raid mentioned in records against Babylon. But it was to be a politically motivated and politically targeted attack. It had no mention of focusing on civilians, let alone Jews. No, the murders were carried out by an outside mercenary force. A private squad under the protection of the Empire. I have a suspicion they may be Amalekites, for the records I saw keep mentioning a man called The Agagite, a name that refers to an ancestor of the Amalekites. This worries me greatly."

"Who are the Amalekites?"

"Well, Hadassah," he replied, his voice growing soft and contemplative, "you know that our people once had a homeland in a faraway place called the Promised Land, also called Israel. As a matter of fact, many of our distant relatives left here to return some years ago, when Emperor Cyrus gave his cupbearer, Nehemiah, leave to return there and rebuild our temple."

"Yes, of course, Poppa," I answered with a slight chuckle. "I know of this land, Israel. You speak of it all the time."

He ignored my jibe with no more than a patient dip of his eyelids, his usual reaction, and continued. "Well, many, many years ago, when our people were still a band of wandering former slaves, we passed through the land of the Amalekites right before settling in Israel. And they were very cruel to us. In fact, without our having done anything to them, they set out to kill and torture as many of our ancestors as they possibly could."

"Why?"

"Because they were servants of the Evil One, the spirit who hates G-d. And not only does that spirit hate *G-d*, but because we are His chosen people, he hates *us* very fiercely, too. And the Amalekites worship either him or one of his foulest spirits."

"But, Poppa, what can you possibly do to them once you do find them, these Agagites—or Amalekites, whatever they're called?"

He laughed. "Hadassah, you are so perceptive. The answer is, I don't know. I only know that I have this overwhelming feeling that G-d wants me to find them."

And in Mordecai's recent state of mind, that settled it. Any edict attributed to G-d in our household was not to be questioned, not for a moment. I myself did not possess the maturity to distinguish His voice from the multitude of childish choruses going off in my head, but I grudgingly admired Mordecai's unwavering certainty that he could hear it clearly. And I must admit: at this point in our lives he could lay as strong a claim to hearing G-d's voice as anyone I could think of.

You see, Mordecai had begun to take in traveling or itinerant Jewish brothers and sisters. He still had not relented to the local high priest's insistence that we join the temple, but their impasse had calcified into a sort of grudging respect. The cause of harmony had been helped when Mordecai had put out the word that any Jewish person seeking shelter, for reasons clandestine or otherwise, could knock seven times on our door and receive a hot dinner and a place to sleep as long as he or she needed it.

The procession of takers for our offer started slowly at first. I remember our inaugural visitor, a teacher. He immediately began a tradition of our guests sitting with Mordecai around the dinner table for hours, even on into the small hours of the morning. I think my cousin began to think of it as a nominal price of lodging for our guests to sit and pass along every piece of gossip or legitimate intelligence they could possibly remember. We learned a great deal that way. And Mordecai would never forget to eventually throw in the perennial question: *Do you know anything of a band of Empire-sanctioned mercenaries riding around with this emblem and killing Jews?*—and at that he would carefully unfold a cloth upon which he had traced their vile insignia, then fold it hastily before the person even had the chance to respond. I had learned only many years after my own first traumatic glimpse that Mordecai, too, had seen the broken cross on a fleeing back that horrendous night.

Mostly he heard rumors, for the legend of these killers had apparently spread far and wide, especially among Jews. Perhaps Mordecai's own constant badgering was responsible for some of that. But these entreaties never produced much information of value.

Yet Mordecai did learn a great deal about the realm at large during his frequent visits to the Palace. After all, as the capital of a huge empire, Susa was visited by merchants, travelers and dignitaries from all over the known world. From Mordecai's careful ears as well as the accounts of our visitors, I learned of a huge athletic contest known as the Olympian games, for instance. Local boys were gathering in the land of my empire's enemies, Greece, to revel in the excellence of sport. I learned that Greece was ablaze with all sorts of ideas about people being equal to one another and that they explored these freedoms through elaborate stagings of these readings called *theater*. Of course I learned endless tidbits about the labyrinthine machinations of Persian Palace life—the jealous Princes of the King's Face, the scheming generals, the wrathful Mothers of the King. I also learned who was impaled that week and who beheaded.

And then from our exhausted traveling visitors would come news from that place Mordecai usually called the Promised Land. A strange expression would overcome him when such things were spoken of. It was a wistful look, almost as though he were on the verge of tears. And his voice would rise and adopt a breathy, almost feminine tone.

"Tell me, have they finished rebuilding the temple?" he would ask. "Have they resumed the sacrifices? Has the *Shekinah*, the presence of G-d, returned to the Holy of Holies?"

# Chapter Ten

There was one visitor in particular who, my young Queen candidate, became the prime reason for my relating this whole part of our lives. He was a wiry old man, slow of foot and even slower of speech. His coming to us had been wreathed in an unusual frenzy of preparations and high security. He was a very important man, we were told in cryptic terms, but nothing more. He had been brought to our door by a small group of muscled young Jewish men who declined Mordecai's invitation to enter and promptly disappeared into the night.

I remember my first sight of him. He wore a torn and heavily stained canvas robe tied at the waist by a length of twine. He had a nose longer than any I had ever witnessed on a person and a straggly beard that must have seen fuller, thicker days. He fixed a rheumy yet sincere gaze upon Mordecai and extended his hand, which was bony and nearly the size of a small dog.

"Mordecai. May our Lord YHWH bless you for your hospitality."

"Thank you, Revered Priest," he replied. "Please consider this your home in Susa. We are honored by your presence, Jacob."

The old visitor shakily sought out the nearest chair and sank into it with a loud exhaling of breath that I fleetingly mistook for the creaking of bones. In the process, I must admit that he also expelled a burst of flatulence, which caused both Mordecai and me to examine our sandals with wry, wavering smiles. And he did not smell like spring flowers anyway, our visitor. Evidently he had traveled a great distance with only camels and Bedouins for companionship. In fact, the sight and smell of him made me wonder if our open-door invitation had not led us a little too far afield.

But while devouring a pot of my lamb stew and gulping draught after draught of our best Persian wine, he also began to speak, and I soon learned that Jacob had just come from Jerusalem, where he had been one of the first priests to offer sacrifices in the newly rebuilt temple. He had traveled to Persia to receive an offering from Susa's Jewish congregation and return with it to Jerusalem. He told us, excitement coloring his voice, that King Xerxes also was making a contribution. Mordecai had told me this newly ascended Persian ruler had received the throne from his father, Darius, and had previously been the Crown Prince of Babylon. In Hebrew his name was "Ahasuerus." I thought of all this as our ancient guest was talking about the Persian king's gift.

In a moment all Jacob's elderly idiosyncrasies were forgotten. He began to speak of temple life and of Jerusalem as the undisputed seat of G-d's presence, in a voice that grew stronger and more emphatic by the second.

And then Mordecai asked the fateful question. "What was it really like to enter the Holy Place, the dwelling of the Almighty?"

The old man turned to his host and raised his eyebrows high. I could not tell whether he was giving Mordecai a quick reappraisal or glaring at him for his impudence. Then I saw that his eyes were watering. As he was completely motionless at that instant, I wondered if he was suffering some sort of internal breakdown.

But then he looked away, and two large tears rolled over the creases below his eyelids only to disappear in the sparse hairs of his beard. No, I could tell he was not angry at Mordecai for asking the question. He was merely preparing his reply with all the strength he could muster.

"Ah yes, the perennial question. Or at least it once was. Ah, my son . . ." and he trailed off. Then he turned around quickly, with a surprising ferocity in his eyes. "It's not just what you think, you know. Everyone thinks it is all fear and trembling. And some days it was. Especially in my early years. But I will tell you the truth. The memory that keeps my heart strong and my head clear is the thought of days when my heart was pure before Him. When I had spent time reading the Sacred Texts, preparing myself beforehand, had sung His praises, asked for forgiveness of my sins, I would enter the temple and suddenly be engulfed in His presence. . . ."

At that moment he jerked his head back and stared into the ceiling as if he were seeing some opening into heaven itself. He made a small keening cry, like that of a newborn child. Then he looked down and his gaze was turned so inward he seemed to have forgotten we were even present. Several more tears fell from his cheeks onto the table. Finally he looked up again, not quite back to the ceiling but just over our heads, as if meeting our gaze would have simply been too much at that moment.

"G-d really does have a presence, do you know?" He asked it almost petulantly, as though his proximity to tears was due to some skepticism on our part. "My whole being would throb with this awareness of His person. I thought I could feel His heart. And at such times I was glad everyone else kept their distance, because often I would dance and laugh and weep and sing and shout all at the same time because my chest felt like it would truly, truly burst if I did not. I felt—I felt . . . well, have you ever seen a young child greet a beloved father after a long absence? The little arms pumping, the little legs churning, the leap into his arms, the tears in the father's eyes? I felt like that. A child so overcome with joy at His return that all I wanted to do in this world was to leap as high into His bosom as I could. And I could feel His tears, too. That's the wonder of it, don't you see? I could feel His Spirit being fed, His heart gladdened, His pain—yes, His pain—being healed somehow." He halted his speech and looked down into his lap somberly. Then he said very quietly, almost a whisper, "I could feel G-d's pain. In fact, I thought of it on my journey here whenever I looked out at the eternity of the desert. G-d's pain because of sin and evil and heartbreak was vast and endless and searing. I can still feel its weight upon my soul."

He looked at me with a glance that had suddenly grown edgy and piercing. Then he shook his head, obviously disappointed. "That's only a tiny part of it, don't you know?"

He threw up his hands in a gesture that spoke of futility and allowed them to fall back limply onto his lap. "I also felt struck by lightning. I tingled with a knowledge that I stood in the presence of the Being who created the universe, who created me. And that anything could happen. I could be ushered into glories unspeakable. I could be granted the kingship of Israel. I could be struck dead. Who knows? When you are in the presence of the King of Kings, destiny—not just your own, but the world's—can change in the twinkling of an eye."

And I began to stare, even at my young age, for I was almost certain that I could feel it myself at that moment. A sensation like when someone stands behind you and you feel their eyes upon you, and the hair begins to tingle across the back of your neck. You feel their presence. My heart began to race, my cheeks to flush. Something wonderful was happening.

Now, maybe you are a more holy person than I. I make no pretensions of great righteousness. But for me, this was the first time. In fact, I had spent the previous years angrily denying to myself that G-d could actually exist. After all, I had reasoned, if we were His chosen people, why did my whole family die? Why did my tender mother, my quiet, freckle-faced brother, my brave and handsome father have to lose their lives to the blades of men for whom the taking meant less than to kick a dog? Why did He not protect them—after all, they were chosen people, too! Why did so many others have to die horrific and tortured deaths? The whole attack had felt like the acting out of an evil intelligence, a foul intention. Not the will of a good and loving G-d.

You can imagine how jarring it was to feel G-d's Spirit fill our dining room and our hearts to bursting that night. The sensation seemed to increase even as the old man continued to speak.

"I always believed," Jacob continued, "that the catalyst for these times of blissful closeness to Him was that I had focused my attention on Him, not on myself. Not on the fact that the Master of the Universe, may His name be blessed, stood in *my* presence, and I in His at that moment. I could not even think of such a thing, although I suppose it was true. No, like that little child, I was completely enraptured by His arrival and His presence, and my own part in the matter was completely forgotten. Then, of course, as He surrounded me and wrapped me like an infant in those Abba arms, it became even more impossible to turn a thought unto myself. What caused His joy was not my puny righteousness—*my* holiness, which would have been like filthy rags to Him had He chosen to examine it. In that moment His charity—His favor—was far too great to scrutinize my fault. Again, it was not about *me*. Not about me at all. What caused His joy was seeing my rapture at His presence and the communion that it sparked. That is what gladdens His heart. Often I have to remind myself that the example of parenthood is not accidental. He *is* our Father. He is many other things, too, of course. But He is every bit as much a Father, and more, than any man whose heart has ever ached at being separated from his little ones."

Jacob took one last gulp of stew and leaned back on the bench, wiping his pathetic beard with an edge of his filthy tunic. "I never forget those moments with the King of Kings, not ever. Today, I suppose I am the most expendable person you could imagine. An old, infirm man. One good whack of a bandit's sword would do me in. Yet I remember, without vanity I hope, that I have stood in His presence and found favor with Him. And no one can ever take the joy, the knowledge, the certainty of that away."

# Chapter Eleven

*M*y dear young maiden, you might still be wondering what could be the significance of this latest anecdote. And so I will tell you this. In ways that I can only attempt to explain to you, Jacob's words were the reason, at least the *earthly* reason, for everything that came next. Although I didn't truly realize it at the time, it laid the foundation for decisions that wound up saving my life, and yours, as well, if you're a Jewess as I suspect. Please be patient with me and I will show you why.

You see, Mordecai's life was not the same after that night, and neither was my own. Without speaking of it to the other until much later, we both began to feel in the days that followed an unmistakable inner urge to regain the sense of His presence we had felt during the old man's visit.

We responded to that urge in vastly different ways.

Jacob left our home two days later, and we never saw him again. Word came some time later that his caravan had been beset by bandits while returning to Jerusalem with his offerings, and he had died of his injuries in the desert. Mordecai bowed his head and whispered a prayer upon hearing the news. I simply turned away and walked out into the courtyard.

Once again, I told myself, G-d had failed to protect His own. But I couldn't help but ask myself what Jacob would say about it. Somehow the memory of his description of the Presence, at least for the moment, won out over my accusations against God.

The visit had caused Mordecai to renew his fervor toward G-d. He began to pray alone, for no official reason, and take his religious life far beyond the mere dictates of tradition—even though tradition had once been of supreme importance to him. He began to study his scraps of Torah in the morning before leaving for work and before retiring to bed in the evening. He began to pepper his speech with mentions of the Lord and His will. He grew more purposeful and enthusiastic in his observances of Jewish holy days. Needless to say, each of these newfound habits annoyed me more intensely with every passing year.

I, on the other hand, turned the other direction. Realizing that G-d was real, palpably so, actually filled me with a fresh resentment that I could barely contain within my reserved demeanor. Somehow, dealing with my anger toward Him was easier when He had been simply a relic of tradition, a remote institution of my ethnic heritage. Knowing that He was real and approachable, and that I could personally experience those realities, made Him the perfect arm's-length target for my rage.

And yet, fearful of angering this newly real G-d, I also kept these emotions to myself and made a pretense of following Mordecai's inner renewal. I prayed with him, sat obediently during the chants and rituals. We kept the weekly Shabbot, well—religiously.

Slowly, even more gradually than my grief had dissipated, my anger began to grow. And soon I began to feel my first stirrings of rebellion against the solitude, a longing for escape. Rachel's presence helped, of course, or I would have gone mad within weeks. Her constant humming and puttering about the house provided their own never-ending source of companionship. And the various grandchildren she brought by at least relieved the tedium somewhat.

From her earliest days with us, Rachel had constantly told me of my physical attributes. "What an exquisite face you have, Hadassah," she would coo over me, always grasping my head in some painful vice-like grip or other. Soon she became so enamored with my girlhood appearance that she began to bring over her favorite grandson, Jesse, a rather sallow-faced, sad-eyed boy.

"From a good family he comes," she was given to announcing anytime I expressed the typical disdain toward the presence of a boy. "You could do worse than marry him someday. That is, if your father lets you admit you're a Jew."

She did not speak those last words as much as spit them out, for she was a faithful member of the local flock and opposed Mordecai's reticence, often with tirades, which had grown louder and more frequent over the years. Rachel emphatically believed that visibility, not assimilation, was the key to Jewish survival in this new land. Of course, so was eventual immigration back to Israel—a goal that she spoke of in husky, sentimental tones but never seemed to pursue with much seriousness.

I disrespected Jesse not out of elitism but good old-fashioned disgust toward any young males. Eventually Jesse and I became friends, but not until several years of taunting and pestering had passed.

Despite the company, some days the sheer repetition of sights, sounds and smells in the house would oppress me so deeply that I felt I might suffocate. I would have to wait impatiently until late at night, after Mordecai's raspy snore began to drift from the room next to mine, to slip out into the cool night air and climb onto the roof.

Once there I would crawl as quietly as I could over the moldy remains of palm leaves, trying hard not to think about how peculiar I would seem getting caught in such a strange perch. I would stay low and move as stealthily as possible to the lip of the outer wall, then peer out as carefully as a spy.

People were still about at that hour, enjoying the evening breezes. I would lie there by the hour, soaking in the sheer variety of it all and the imprint of something new upon my eyes. I could glance across a hundred rooftops and see a dozen family excursions, domestic quarrels, moonlight sales transactions. I could even see the towering pillars of the Royal Palace upon their height, their bases flickering in the torchlight, the tiny silhouettes of royal guards highlighted in the glow.

The Palace seemed so far away then. Its very heft, its exalted site high atop the north of the city, decreed matters of great consequence. Decisions of life and death. Important people living out lives of gravity and privilege.

I glanced away most of the time. Such an intimidating sight was not necessary to clear my head. I required only the sight of passersby: a camel train, a sneaking youth or even a soldier or two. The sight of a stranger—that mysterious looming bane of my childhood nightmares—had grown from an object of terror to one of curious longing.

Soon thereafter forces of nature joined the fray.

# Chapter Twelve

*I* awoke in panic from a nightmare of a masked man kicking me in the stomach. I could hardly breathe. My midsection kept pulling me downward, trying to double me over, refusing to relax. Instead it heaved in wave after wave of agonizing constrictions.

Because the last time I could remember waking in the night with a crisis was the night of my parents' death, all the old terrors washed over me once more. I could actually hear the men grunting again as their swords plunged into my beloved family. Scorching their way through my very bones, I could feel the screams of my mother and brother. I could see the flames rising up to hide the carnage. Worst of all, I could feel every ounce of terror, fear, rage and grief I had felt so long before.

"What is happening? What is happening?" called Mordecai, rushing over with features slack from a deep sleep. I had never seen his eyes so glazed over and inert.

"I don't know!" I answered, holding my midsection and rocking back and forth with the pain. "It hurts so bad!"

I cried out. Mordecai remained motionless, his eyes as wide as two gold pieces.

"What is it?" I screamed. "I swear, Poppa, I did nothing! I touched nothing! I was fast asleep!"

Mordecai did not even seem to hear me, so great was his paralysis. Yet even through my panic and pain, I could tell from his eyes that he was coming to a realization. One he had not expected. One that remained a complete mystery to me. Finally Mordecai saw the evidence upon the fabric of my night clothing and knew for certain. "I am so sorry," he said, almost moaning in his remorse. "I didn't think. I didn't prepare. . . ."

And then he turned swiftly and hurried for the door.

"I have to go," he said, his face pale. "I know—it's terrible to leave now, but Rachel will know what to do. I must go and fetch her."

He was almost out the door when he stopped abruptly, turned around and said with as much tenderness as he could remember to summon, "By the way, my dearest, there's nothing wrong with you. Nothing at all. I—I can't explain now, but Rachel soon will. Just please wait there and do not move, will you?"

Now, I do not relay this episode to convey yet another milestone in my growing-up years or to illustrate Mordecai's ineptitude or any such thing. I tell you this because "becoming a woman," as Rachel called it when she eventually arrived, had a profound effect upon me.

To put it simply, puberty caused my stored-up rage to surge and break out of its restraints. And the target this time, I am ashamed to say, was my poor dear lifesaver, Poppa Mordecai.

To his credit, Mordecai tried to atone for his omission in preparing me for that day. He took the necklace given to me by my parents and draped it around my neck.

"You are a woman now," he said in a low voice. "I remember how your parents wanted you to wear this when you had finally left childhood behind. It is a special symbol of our people, and you should always wear it proudly."

"I thought it was just a family heirloom," I countered.

"No. It is far more than that. It is the very symbol once painted on the shields of David's army. For many of our people, it has become an emblem of sorts, since God's law forbids us to have graven images."

"It's not just a star?"

"It *is* a star. Some even call it David's Star. But this sign is much more. Whenever you see it, wherever you see it, you can know that a child of Israel, one of your people, has left his mark."

A few days after that first menses, after spending a dreadful day curled up in my bed, I took a shaky walk around the yard. It was frightfully hot, yet I was too grateful to be outdoors to even notice. Rachel's grandson Jesse walked haltingly beside me—actually a few steps behind me, afraid to come too close in case I would snap at him once more.

I was hardly aware of his presence. From the first moment I had stepped out into the daylight, I had become seized by the most ferocious sense of confinement and alienation I had ever felt. Suddenly the expanse of our courtyard became a prison, its walls the ramparts of a dungeon wall inching inward with every passing hour. Mordecai was my jailer, a sadistic depriver of adolescent joys.

So the first thing I did was dispatch Jesse with a mean-spirited diatribe about the peskiness of young men. I am ashamed to say this, especially in light of the near future, but such is the wont of so many adolescent girls.

On his way out, Jesse reentered the house to bid his grandmother good-bye and left from the front door without another word. Several minutes later, Rachel emerged, wiping her hands against her lap. I bristled and turned away, for I was certain she was about to upbraid me for my treatment of her favorite grandson. But instead, she took my arm and awkwardly sat down with me in the shade of the center palm tree. And that is where I finally learned the truth of what had just happened to me.

Somehow Rachel felt the need to veer her object lesson into the provinces of male anatomy and sexuality, a subject that rendered her nearly incoherent. The words stammered out of her in staccato bursts. I had never heard her speak so nervously, her eyes turned away from me and her face grim with determination. When her descriptions brought her to the need to specifically describe parts of the male body, she nearly halted, paralyzed by her struggle to capture the safest nickname or euphemism.

I nearly seized her by the shoulders to shout at her, "Rachel, for heaven's sake, I've caught glimpses of Mordecai and even Jesse; it's fairly obvious they are different from us. That makes it undeniable! And it's something they hold in the hand—I have it pretty well figured out!"

But instead I kept my lips tight and still and listened to her elliptical trip through the wonders of all the subjects the adults in my life had never seen fit to teach me.

When Rachel finished, she simply stopped, as though her lurching flow of words had finally exhausted her capacity for speech. A long pause fell between us. I have wondered since if she was waiting for me to ask questions or say something, or whether she truly was finished and simply refused to utter a word more than the occasion required. But before I could find out, without the least warning I felt my lungs start to heave, my shoulders shake and my eyes begin to stream with tears. I had never wept like that in my life. I felt possessed by some foreign being whose only form of communication was deep, even violent sobs.

Rachel reached her arm around my shoulders with a dutiful expression and began to explain that my predicament was nothing to be frightened or sad about. It was a natural thing that happened to every girl. Everyone understood that.

But if anybody did *not* understand that day, it was Rachel. For you see, I was not weeping about the frightening facts of menstruation or sexuality. For the first time, I was weeping for my dear dead mother. The sensation of being in her arms, hearing her warm voice whisper to me about what a beautiful little girl I was—that feeling had washed over me as fresh and powerful as though she had died only yesterday. And my emotion was not merely grief; it was a profound sadness—that my mother's "beautiful little girl" had now become a woman, had progressed into her childbearing years without her momma being able to share a moment of it.

I explained none of this to Rachel. In my weeping state, I felt it beneath me to explain the truth to her. I simply went on sobbing loudly with my face in my hands. Finally Rachel shook her head in dismay, no doubt convinced that such a reaction should take only a minute to run its course, then stood and returned to the house. I sat and tried to force my tears to stop. I failed. My body was on a ride of its own making, and it certainly had no plans to consult me about the best time to end.

It has taken me many years to fully understand the layers of emotion I experienced that day.

The first layer was, as I've just described, an unexpected wave of delayed grief over the death of my mother. But below that, just below it in fact, was my first taste of adulthood, with all its undertones of yearning and independence. In short, it had finally occurred to me that I was growing up. Time was not standing still anymore. I had now entered my childbearing years, yet I remained a virtual inmate at the hands of my benevolent despot of a father-who-was-not-my-father. I was a woman now, for G-d's sake. Yes, my little friend, I was in the frame of mind to use His name for my own ends, I'm sorry to say. The fact that I wasn't even allowed to leave the house filled me with resolve. Something had to change!

## Chapter Thirteen

*I*t was only a matter of weeks before these emotions escalated into an unquenchable thirst to physically leave the home. One day as I stood behind Rachel stirring the soup pot, I asked her a question.

"Momma Rachel," I began, using her favorite appellation, "I remember you have said that Jewish folks like to dress up and fool people into thinking the girls are boys and boys are girls."

"That is true," she answered. "There is a long tradition among our people of using clever disguises, in play and in times of danger, as well."

I thought for a moment, absorbing the news and planning how to use it.

"Rachel, you know how badly I wish to see the city. Would you dress me up to look like a boy? Maybe even a non-Jewish one?"

I remember that she turned to me and shot me the sharpest glance I had ever witnessed from a woman. And yet I could not tell if she was actually displeased with me or merely seized with a sudden and very acute curiosity regarding my question.

"Why *not* Jewish?"

"Oh, you know. Mordecai is so careful, after—well, you know."

"Yes, but he would never let you leave the house in the first place. You know that."

"Yes. I was hoping you would keep it between us. And I would feel that I had not disobeyed him so badly by dressing as a Persian."

She laughed and tapped me on the head with a wet hand.

"That is you, Hadassah. Trying to disobey without breaking any rules." She shook her head sideways for a long moment, her expression rueful and amused. "Yes, I will help you, my dear. I think he is wrong to keep you cooped in here like this. You must know, Hadassah, that I will bring up the matter of letting you leave these walls to Mordecai."

"That's fine," I said. "That's wonderful, in fact."

And Rachel did not let me down. She arrived the following day carrying a bundle filled with not only the clothing we'd discussed but a wealth of cosmetics and accessories.

First she wet my hair from a pitcher of well water, then rolled it tightly around my head. Next she tied a scarf snugly around it and placed a large shepherd's hat atop the whole mass. I changed into loose-fitting desert clothes, slipped on some worn sandals and presented myself for inspection with arms held wide.

Rachel frowned. "I don't know, Hadassah. You still look awfully delicate." She stood, walked outside and returned with a handful of dirt, which she proceeded to rub onto my cheeks. "Just for a little character. A little roughing up."

She examined her work and shook her head appraisingly. "My love, will you let me send a friend along with you? Someone to watch over you, make certain nothing bad happens?"

I scowled. "You mean Jesse, don't you?"

She shrugged disarmingly. "Maybe—have you got someone else in mind?"

"Yes," I huffed. "No one."

"Hadassah—"

"I'm serious. It won't mean a thing with one of *you* tagging along beside me." I regretted the rudeness of my words as soon as they left my mouth yet felt too engrossed in the emotion to apologize. Instead, I laid a hand on Rachel's shoulder and smiled grudgingly.

"I'll be all right," I said.

"Just don't say a word. Promise me? If anyone hears your voice they'll make you out for sure, and someone will assume you're a runaway slave. You'll get frog-marched into the garrison, and it'll take days to sort out. . . . You just don't want that sort of thing. Promise?"

"I promise." And I meant it. Someone could have dropped a boulder on my toes and I would not have uttered a sound.

And so I walked out of Mordecai's door for the first time in years. Alone.

My young friend, I cannot describe to you the exhilaration I felt walking down that street. I felt like the wind was new, more brisk, cooler upon my face. It seemed like my legs were full of energy, my feet as light as air. I fought the urge to throw out my arms and burst into song. What a feeling! By the time I'd reached the corner and turned back—and caught Rachel peering at me through a barely opened crack in the door—it seemed like I had become a new person.

I waved cautiously at Rachel, barely suppressing a giggle of excitement, then turned toward the open road. It was midmorning, and the lane adjoining our home featured its usual moderate foot traffic. I passed a donkey cart loaded high with bags of rice. Wonderful—the driver did not even catch my eye, so weary and fixed was he upon the road ahead. How silly of me, I admonished myself, to think I would attract every gaze simply because I was excited to be here. I realized in an instant, as I passed a group of young men holding skewers of lamb meat, the elementary lesson that everyone has his own worries and concerns for the day. It wasn't about me. All I had to do was blend in, stay quiet and unobtrusive, and I might as well have never been there. Strange. New concept for a girl accustomed to being the center of her household's attention.

I kept walking until I stood surrounded by views I had never seen from my rooftop perch. Entirely new sights and smells assaulted my senses from doorways and outflung awnings—a rack festooned with small cups of foreign spices, the unprecedented sight of a fire spit from which a roasted pig sent its aroma drifting in clouds of woodsmoke, around the corner an ornate stand hung with jewelry and items of clothing from faraway lands.

Then I realized, and I turned—I was completely out of sight from my home. I had truly ventured forth at last. I made a mental note of how to return and continued uphill, keeping the Palace rooftop straight ahead as my guide. I crossed the dried-mud bridge over the equally muddy Kerkha River and walked on. It seemed the farther I went, the more exotic and crowded the streets became. Soon the sound of barkers, haggling shoppers, workers and soldiers shouting became louder than any sound I had heard since that of thunder in a summer storm the year before.

Finally, my long climb ended at some sort of open plaza, I turned a corner and there it was. The majestic portico, the mighty arch of Xerxes, with the King's Gate soaring dizzily behind it, a wonder of height and expansiveness beyond any image I had ever conjured. I tried to picture what it would be like to live in the Palace, surrounded by vast gardens and servants and unspeakable opulence. Rachel had told me that much of the gold in the world was now hoarded within that building.

My mind could not contain it. So I simply gazed for a long moment, trying to catch my breath.

*Chapter Fourteen*

nd so many people! I had forgotten that the King's Gate was
the center of commerce not only for Susa itself but the
entire Persian Empire. My eager eyes traveled across the intricate
spectacle, the swirling patchwork of color and detail and motion.
There were columns of soldiers marching through the crowd in a
line so precise you would have thought someone had drawn it with
a pen. The sun shone majestically off their breastplates and lance
tips. There were camel necks craning above the crowd, their humps
trailing through the throng like islands in a sea. Canopies of bright
red, purple, gold and rich yellows protected piles of glinting foreign
goods—pitchers and vases and bolts of silk and beaded curtains and
kettles and even curved, threatening knives and sabers—from the
elements.

And the sound of it—the harsh exclamations of a thousand hag-
glers, barkers shouting out the wonders of their goods, laughter of
passersby. The noise reached a volume I had never considered possible.

Trying to absorb it all, I realized that I was standing against the tide like a stone in a river's current. A sharp nudge in the shoulder made me look up into the cross glance of a thin, very brown, turbaned man. The wheel of his cart crunched slowly by me, just inches away from my big toe. Then a middle-aged woman loaded with heavy slings across her shoulders grazed my arm and shouted at me in a language I could not understand.

I began to fear for the survival of my disguise, so I turned to reorient myself for home. This had certainly been enough excitement for one day, at least for this first time.

And then it hit me. *Mordecai might be here—somewhere*. He had told me he often spent hours just outside the portico, dealing with royal vendors. As soon as the thought exploded in my mind, I realized this was what I had wanted all along: to see Mordecai on my own, from the covert vantage point of my disguise. A way to silently mock him, perhaps—to flaunt the boldness of my transgression—even though I would never reveal myself.

But could I find him in all this crush of humanity? I turned back toward the Palace itself and willed myself to navigate the thickest part of the multitude.

*Act like you know where you're headed,* I spoke to my hesitation. *You belong here. You have a destination in mind. You just don't know where it is.* . . . I teased myself with the barest hints of a smile as I moved forward.

Then the Palace walls grew closer, and I caught more glimpses of the guards, their faces tense with concentration and purpose. Their fists clutched thick, tall lances. At their waists shone jewel-encrusted handles of scimitars. The sight made me blanch and suddenly feel quite tiny, quite frivolous in my adolescent adventure. *What am I thinking?* Who was I to believe I could walk into such an official, solemn place simply in pursuit of a lark?

I turned away from the soldiers and allowed my curiosity to overcome my intimidation. Maybe I would just walk over *this* way, along the high wall lined with tent stalls—and then I saw him. He was sitting on the thick cushion he brought home every day, a small sunshade over his head, holding his stylus against an easel erected in front of him.

I had never seen him in an environment like this, so confident, his face devoid of the worry and doting affection that often constricted his features when he was around me. He squinted with the effort of forming a precise letter stroke upon the sheet, then looked out over its edge—and looked right at me.

I averted my gaze in a panic and turned away. My heart galloped suddenly in my chest. *Has he seen me?* Surely he had felt the intensity of my gaze, the lingering pause of my scrutiny. I did not even turn back to satisfy my curiosity. I began to run as fast I could through the crowd.

And when I started forward once more, I ran straight into the lanky form of a young boy. I looked up warily only to meet the familiar smile of Jesse, Rachel's grandson. I could feel my face instantly tense into a scowl. Upon my own soul—so much for my sense of utter freedom and abandon! And then I realized that Rachel had surely ordered him on his little surveillance mission, and my anger redoubled. My ally, my helper had betrayed me.

"What do you want?" I grumped crossly.

"Nothing. Just to make sure you're safe," he said with a slight grin.

"Well, you can go back to your precious grandmother and tell her I'm fine. I don't need anybody like you spying on me."

"Oh," he said knowingly. "I'm sure you're fine. Only tell me, Hadassah, or whoever you are, what is the way back to your house?"

Why, that was easy. I turned and craned my head only to realize that half a dozen streets fanned out from the square, each identical to the one that had brought me here. I sighed heavily and planted my hands on my hips. The sun was scorching my face. My elaborate clothing began to feel heavy and hot. My head became confused with weariness and fatigue.

I turned back to him and put on a world-weary expression.

"Well, don't sit there gloating, you big goat. Why don't you help me?"

"I'm sorry," he persisted, his expression lit with a perverse joy. "Did I hear you say the word *help*?"

"Yes. Friends are supposed to help each other."

"Friends. Fine. Follow me."

At that he turned and began to run, long, loping strides through and around the milling people. I followed, only too happy to have someone who knew the way. An odd version of my previous exhilaration returned as I wove my way daringly around a never-ending assortment of people, desperate not to lose sight of Jesse's back. Soon a clearing emerged in the crowd and I actually caught up with him, glancing over at his flushed features as I matched his strides. He just smiled, for Jesse was a good-natured and kind soul; then he jerked his chin back toward the Palace portico. I shrugged and followed him through the dregs of the marketplace to where the people stopped and the abruptness of Palace wall began.

"Where are we going?" I asked.

He turned around and smiled for an answer.

"Aren't we going home?"

"No. Since we're here already, I'm going to show you a special place."

I started to object, but he turned again and began to run. I could only shrug once more and follow. After we ducked behind a stand selling roasted figs and nuts, I followed him up a steep rise behind the canopy and the merchants' tethered donkeys. We climbed to a clearing above the crowd, and I stopped to catch my breath. He seemed about to pause and consider the awesome view, but instead Jesse threw his elbows back and started to run forward. I feared he was about to fall off the incline back into the market below, but he launched himself into the air and vaulted with his feet carving the air beneath him. I rushed forward to see him land flat on the back of a gryphon, one of the giant half-eagle, half-lion statues that flanked the portico itself.

Laughing in the breeze, he turned back and waved to me. "Come on!"

I shook my head. The view was quite sufficient from here.

"Are you a coward? Shall I call you Hadassah the Mouse?"

I cringed at his words, for no one had ever called me a coward before. Besides, I knew enough of Jesse's little jibes to realize that if I failed this test, I might very well hear about it for years. Hadassah the Mouse might well follow me to my grave.

Without consciously making the decision, I felt my legs flex, my fists clench and my arms start to pump up and down. I propelled myself forward, planted my foot and jumped.

And for a glorious moment I felt all the freedom and lightness of a bird.

A second later the unyielding statue's flank struck me hard upon the shins. I splayed gracelessly against the stone but held on. A hand reached down into my field of view and I grasped it, held it firmly and pulled.

The next second I was astride the gryphon's back, sitting behind Jesse as if we were actually riding the beast. I looked down and felt my mouth fall open. Below us stretched a dizzying sea of turbaned heads, bright canopies and milling livestock. Not only the market-place but all of Susa stretched on in a vast patchwork of rooftops and jagged streets to the edge of desert and the snow-capped mountains beyond.

I felt exposed up there, prominent beyond all hope of concealment, yet as I looked down I noticed something remarkable: no one was looking at us. At least nobody I could spot. The market had a life of its own, and that milling existence did not cease, nor did it care, for the existence of two exhilarated youth.

I felt like someone spying in plain sight, snooping on someone too stupid to turn around and even sense my presence. Could Mordecai see me? I craned my neck back in the direction of his spot and saw nothing. My hands—where were my hands?—oh my, I suddenly realized I had encircled Jesse's waist in a manner that felt, well, somehow it did not feel as innocent as child's play anymore.

Jesse hiked up one leg and swung around to face me, his own features clouded by an expression of curiosity and anticipation. With a quickness that made me jump, he reached out and pulled off my shepherd's hat, brushed the dust from my cheeks, ruffled out my hair. I no doubt looked like a girl again. The air suddenly grew thick—and not from heat. I felt my head lighten, my cheeks flush. But I did not pull back. Suddenly Jesse was the center of the universe, the epicenter of my fracturing field of view.

And then he did it. He leaned forward and brushed his lips against mine. I pursed my mouth against the pressure and felt the most delightful sensation. *More* than that, of course. I felt a shock of intimacy, of a closeness beyond embarrassment. And then confusion. What in the world had just happened? I had never entertained, for even one moment, my thawing feelings toward him. I would later learn that there are women—a large portion of women—who spend hours, days even, basking in their contemplations of men. Believe it or not, I was not one of them. The flush of my affection for Jesse felt like the breath was being squeezed from me.

Then the moment passed, and shyness overtook me. I was now ready for flight and a return home. I swung one leg back to the other and jumped to the ground, a leap that left the soles of my feet tingling.

With a crunching sound behind me, Jesse joined my descent. He quickly returned the hat and scarf to me, which I jammed onto my head as best I could. Wearing a smug grin that did not dim in the ensuing minutes, he ran to the nearest street opening. I recognized it as the one leading home.

On the less-traveled avenue we increased our pace and actually began to sprint downhill. The nearly *parasang* of distance I had traveled that morning in about an hour took far less time on our downward run. Small bits of laughter escaped through the panting of our lungs. I loved it. Confined for years in a courtyard home, I had never experienced the sensation of crossing a large distance with such speed before, especially using my own feet.

An old woman beating a rug on the sidewalk looked up at me strangely, then stared at me, and I realized then that I was not running like a boy. I looked back at Jesse. How did he do it? What were his strides like, and how were they different from my own? I began to swing my arms emphatically and plant my feet on the ground before taking the next step.

And I almost ran into his back. He was standing, and stopping alongside him I realized why. We were home. The unfamiliar exterior of my childhood abode stood before me, as unchanged as if I had never left.

I was panting with the unusual physical activity as well as the excitement of my adventure. Then it hit me: the thought of coming back to spend my typical confined afternoon filled me with a sense of dread I could feel in my temples.

I turned to Jesse. He flashed a smile that made him look manlike for the first time in all the years I had known him and grasped me by both arms. He leaned toward me and I thought he was going to kiss me again, but instead he turned slightly and grazed my cheek with his lips. Shivers wracked my spine.

I quickly pecked his cheek in rather perfunctory reply, then turned, took a deep breath and reentered our abode. Rachel, of course, breathlessly awaited my report, and I tried my best to fill the hours with every minute observation that had come my way in such a short time. Every observation, that is, except for the tantalizing events with her grandson.

Three hours later Mordecai returned, seemingly his usual self. Yet my guilty mind thought it caught him eyeing me closely several times from his corner stool.

Did he know? Was he unsure of what he'd seen and trying to gauge the possibility?

I never found out.

## Xerxes, son of Darius

KETHUVIM ESTHER 1:1

*". . . who reigned over a hundred and twenty-seven
provinces from India to Nubia."*

## Chapter Fifteen

SUSA—CIRCA 480 B.C.

*T*he heart of my story, the part that you perhaps have heard of, begins one stifling hot summer day in my nineteenth year. I was used to the heat having known nothing else. I had heard that the King and his court would occasionally escape to Ecbatana for a reprieve from summer temperatures. I was sitting at the table pounding out Rachel's unleavened bread when Mordecai came through the door, breathing heavily. He usually didn't return before sundown.

He fumbled with his outer tunic, the purple velvet piece he'd saved up months to buy and usually folded carefully. Today he briskly tossed it over the sill of an open window, his cheeks flushed the color of a ripe apple.

"I've been invited to a banquet with the King!"

I stopped as though struck by a witch's spell, my fingers frozen white with flour. I had been daydreaming about life in the Palace all afternoon. My face must have asked the question.

"The King's chancellor has just given a general invitation for everyone in Susa to attend a royal banquet lasting for seven whole days. It's the tail end of a military convocation that has been going on for six months. King Xerxes has been whipping his generals into a frenzy over going back to war against Greece. Now he wants to demonstrate the people's affection for him. There'll be food and wine from all over the Empire, and dancers. None of which I have any use for, of course." He chuckled and looked over at Rachel, whose expression had already grown disdainful.

I felt my lips form the words, then heard them as though they'd floated out of another person's mouth. My head became light and dizzy, filled with a sort of filmy gauze, when my ears actually heard the statement meet the open air.

*"I want to go."*

A year before he would have dismissed the words without even glancing at me. After all, I did not leave the grounds. But something about my new stature and the tone of my voice made him stop quite abruptly and meet my eyes with a dark, appraising look.

"What did you say?" he asked, no doubt for time to collect his thoughts.

"You said 'everyone in Susa.' Well, I am someone in Susa, and I want to go. I want to see the Palace."

"It'll be a drunken brawl. It's the last place I would take you outside of this house."

"Then why," asked Rachel, already cocked sideways in her defiant posture, "is a good, observant Jew like yourself going?"

"Because I have to. I'm a Palace scribe. I have to be there. Be seen in attendance by the court. It's—oh, you wouldn't understand."

Rachel threw down the small rag from her shoulder with an exasperated sound.

"Mordecai, you need to go almost as little as Hadassah does."

"Besides," he argued, "the whole celebration will last seven days. I won't be able to come home for a whole week."

"Then let me meet you for the final night," I said.

"The final night is the worst," he answered with a shrug.

"Everyone has been drinking for a solid week. It's not safe for a woman of purity."

"Wait a minute!" I cried out. "I have hardly ever been outside these walls in my life! I hardly know what other people look like—in my imaginary world everybody is middle-aged and Jewish, because I don't know any better! And to make things worse, I'm getting older—"

"You're older," he repeated with a dubious look.

"Yes. *Older*," I spat out, still riding the steam of my agitation.

But Mordecai began to shake his head like the sage of the centuries. "No. No, my dear. You have no idea what questions I would raise coming in with a beauty like you. 'Oh, the bachelor Mordecai has found himself a winsome young concubine. Look at that luscious maiden!' And then if I explained that you were my daughter, I would have to answer even more questions, as I've told everyone I was never married. Even if I were to lie and say that we were neither lovers nor relatives, I would then open the door to countless questionable, even obscene, proposals and physical danger. The King himself might take a fancy to you and keep you as his concubine. And then I would never see you again. It is just too complicated and dangerous."

"All right, then. I'll go as a boy."

His eyes grew wide.

"I've done it before, Poppa."

His eyes doubled in size.

He sat heavily on his stool, his eyes glazed over with the look of a man in furious thought. A man whose view of things has just been twisted upside down.

"You've left here without my permission?"

"Yes." The word gave me a perverse thrill even as I said it.

"You've gone to the Palace?"

"The portico plaza—once."

"In a disguise."

"Yes, Poppa."

"Well!" He looked up at Rachel, questioning with his eyes whether she'd been an accomplice to this calamity. He turned away with the weariness of an old man. Of course, she would have to be an accomplice to some degree, no matter what. She was charged with always knowing my whereabouts. He sighed as though the fate of the world rested in his hands.

"I'll follow along behind you and not say a word," I continued. Then, as I saw he was beginning to actually contemplate my idea, I turned conciliatory. "Please? You know it will be the most exciting day of my life. To go from being a shut-in to a guest in the Royal Palace?"

When he began to chuckle grudgingly, I knew my case was won.

## Chapter Sixteen

*I* began working on my disguise with Rachel hours before sunset on the banquet's last evening. Mordecai returned home for a quick bath, then waited for me and watched incredulously while my transformation took place. Shaking his head, he playfully threatened to change his mind if I came out looking too much like a boy. Then, as Rachel's work progressed, he lamented my emerging as too *pretty* a boy. He threw up his hands in mock outrage at the thought of being considered a lover in the Greek fashion of which he had heard whispered.

Finally, sent on our way with several grudging Jewish blessings from Rachel, we left our gate and were immediately swept into the stream of revelers making their way toward the Palace.

I felt like I had been transported to heaven. The setting sun cast colors of fire against the horizon, and a pleasant hum rose from the crowd. Yet it seemed the volume and thickness of its composition rose with every passing step. By the time we reached the gryphon statues at the portico, the slow current had become a flood.

Mordecai reached out and grasped my hand in a grip so tight I almost felt my knuckles were breaking. Unlike on my previous trip, there was no need to fight the tide to reach my destination. Today we were carried along whether we liked it or not. The massive arch I had admired on my previous adventure now swept past me like an afterthought. The swiftness of its passage did not keep me from looking up, admiring its soaring grandeur and imagining that I was all alone—some favored guest of Persia entering on a royal summons, clad in exotic robes and jewels.

My fixation did not last long. The Palace's entrance was truly only the beginning of its wonders. I heard a curious sound beneath me and looked down to see that my feet were treading on marble of the most intricate gold-veined pattern. Looking beyond my own moving legs and feet, I saw a ground covered with this gorgeous stone. All about us lay thick, green foliage and parks ringed by flowers of violet, fuchsia, crimson and pink. *The royal gardens*, I remembered with a dizzy sensation. In a culture obsessed with cultivating the perfect household garden, those of the Royal Palace were legendary as the finest in all the land.

The crowd suddenly parted around a pool bluer and longer than any body of water I had ever beheld. Its surface seemed to reflect the azure blue of the desert sky as flawlessly as glass. At broad intervals along its sides stood marble benches lined with perfectly colored statues of beautiful young women. Real guards stood at attention between the benches, nearly as still as their stone counterparts.

"Royal concubines," Mordecai whispered.

I frowned, startled, and realized what he'd meant—one second after, one of the female statues actually moved. The figures were real women, dressed in silk robes that shimmered in the sun. I blanched, feeling suddenly quite plain, awkward and poorly dressed even for a boy.

Then the whole scene lurched and stumbled, almost pitching me onto my face. I fought to regain my footing and looked up again, for the source of my predicament was Mordecai himself, yanking me forward with the impatience of someone dragging a toddler to his bath.

One moment later a mountainous stone arch crowded out the sun. We were inside the King's Gate—if such an enormity could even be called "inside." I was used to low ceilings and a sense of warm confinement. Here was a cool space as tall as a dozen rooms. Susa's own Jewish synagogue now seemed a dim hulk compared to this immensity. I blinked and squinted, craned my neck and walked on. I wondered if I should even try to make a visual inventory of what I was seeing—the richness of detail was too much to absorb, at least at this brisk pace. My senses felt filled to overflowing.

I heard Mordecai's voice whisper to me, low and conspiratorial. "Try not to seem too awestruck," he said. "It makes you stand out."

I winced at my own childishness and tried to relax my face into a mixture of nonchalance and faint amusement. I'm sure now, reflecting back, that my new expression was only slightly less ridiculous than the former; such is a youth's sense of nuance. But I should be more charitable to my former self. After the years of confinement, this was an almost shocking immersion in the outside world, and I was trying my best.

Suddenly we were outside again, and the mass of walking humanity parted around a huge marble building. "The inner court," Mordecai said, pointing. "That's where the King's throne is located. Where he transacts his business and meets with his advisers. Our destination"—and at that he pointed upward, for the third edifice stood as tall as a mountain—"is there. The Central Hall."

# Chapter Seventeen

I glanced up, for we were passing between a row of columns so tall and massive I could have sworn their summits were piercing the sky. At the foot of each one a soldier stood as motionless as if he were part of the carving. At once I winced and recoiled, for a river of western sunlight was gleaming through the columns and glinting off the blade in one sentry's grip. I fought back a rush of memories from that long-ago night, squared my shoulders and looked onward with a sense of defiance.

Had only one of these Palace columns stood before me, I could have spent an hour arching my neck backward to marvel at its height, its intricate carvings and the gracefully curved bulge midway up. But dozens of these monoliths now towered against my horizon in row after orderly row. I tried to count and stopped at the number forty, my mind drenched in awe, with several more rows to go. The hall's breathtaking expanse and majesty made human scale seem antlike. I saw figures walking around the outermost columns and realized I could not throw a stone even half the distance.

Between the nearest of these stone giants hung vast tapestries the size of houses along purple cords, woven in hues of white and violet and fastened between silver rings on which glinted the setting sun. Their rich hues seemed to shimmer like liquid in the torchlight. Something sparkled at me from below, causing me to look down and gasp: the floor now consisted of a fine mosaic inlaid with precious stones and gems!

I looked at Mordecai, who met my gaping expression with a smile and a little shake of his head. I immediately tried to adapt a more natural face. We moved forward slowly. The crowds ahead were beginning to disperse, for on every side stood tables piled high with food in more varieties than I even knew existed. I saw a row of braised geese, baked ducks of every size and form and whole-baked chickens whose shapes were eroding beneath the guests' unceasing fingers. I fought back my retching reflex at the sight of an entire pig, its body baked brown and half eaten, upon another table. Several other fowl and beasts of unknown species lay in various stages of being devoured by the masses.

On another table, through a throng, I could make out row after row of golden goblets, every row a different height and shape, filled with what I could only presume was wine. A phalanx of stabbing hands was rapidly emptying the table.

I looked away for a moment and tried to find a normal sight upon which to rest my gaze. My ears chose this as their own occasion to assault me with not one but countless sources of tumult. This definitely had the look and sound of a celebration that had been going for a while. Streams of human chatter and shouting seemed to roll their way toward me from wholly separate parts of the building.

Then, suddenly, Mordecai and I stopped, and through the shoulders ahead of me I could glimpse the reason why. We had reached the end. The floor ahead suddenly vaulted upward and culminated in a platform crowning steps lined with more purple tapestries anchored by golden rods. Smaller columns, themselves tall enough to support the highest building I had ever seen until that day, held more hangings upon the landing. Large palm fronds waved slowly up and down over a gathering of gold-rimmed couches. And atop the platform stood the greatest sight of all: the King and his entourage, in clothes gleaming so brightly I wanted to shade my eyes.

*Which one is the King?* As I could not make out a throne, discerning him from the array of revelers proved difficult. Then I saw a formation of soldiers, scimitars drawn in their fists, and traced their glances to an apex. And there, more golden than any of the sights I had seen thus far, lounged a man around whom the light seemed to glow with an unearthly radiance. I made out broad shoulders, dark hair and a beard that had clearly been dipped in some sort of crystalline glitter. He wore a golden robe that draped not only beside him but for yards on either side. It seemed to have been carved of solid gold, until he moved and the whole wonder folded and moved with him.

A commotion broke out among the guests, and a large drunken man broke away from the assembly and stumbled onto the bottom step. He jerked his goblet high into the air, spilling its contents over himself, and yelled, "To His Majesty's health!"

The King glanced over and smiled, and the celebrants around me began to raise their own rejoinder to the toast. But then the man, seeing the favorable reaction from Xerxes, let out a guttural shout and began to scramble drunkenly up the steps.

I heard Mordecai gasp loudly at my side.

And then I saw why. Two royal guards stepped deftly over. The soldier nearest the drunken sop swung his axe blade far behind him and then forward again in a savage slicing motion. It was unclear which happened first: the head falling from the intruder's shoulders and the torrent of blood that erupted from the falling torso or the great communal moan that rose from the guests. The head bounced down the steps with discernible sound in the sudden stillness, spewing bright blood all over the purple rugs, then clearing a swath into the crowd when the gruesome object struck the floor and rolled a few cubits farther.

From his perch, the King shook his head with a rueful smile of mock disappointment at the man's folly. Then he held up his goblet as if to say, *Too bad—it seems we ruined a nice toast.* A eunuch rushed over to him with a *riatin* from which to refill the goblet.

At once a sea of goblets rose around me, along with the deep clamor of a thousand male voices in unison, shouting out a single word: "Xerxes!" And a thousand goblets tilted to pour wine into a thousand throats—all except mine. I was trying not to vomit from combined disgust and sheer panic. Once again, my own private nightmare came rushing back to me.

Mordecai leaned sideways toward me, more unobtrusive than ever. "It is an offense punished by death to approach the King without his bidding," he said, his voice a hoarse whisper. "Unless he lowers his scepter or gives some sign of his interest in the person, the sentence is immediate."

His private commentary was interrupted by the hasty arrival of two Palace aides who dragged the dead body away and ran back for the severed head and a quick swab of the floor with sea sponges. Then Mordecai glanced up, and I followed his gaze. The King had summoned a group of men from the platform with an imperious wave of his arm. The men had arisen and gathered around the royal person. Noise in the room seemed to diminish somewhat as the revelers sensed that a subject of some importance was being broached.

"These are the royal eunuchs," Mordecai whispered to me. "Hadassah, do you know what a eunuch is?"

I nodded his way in the affirmative, only slightly lying. I had a vague notion of men against whom the ultimate affront had been committed.

"These are the special ones," he continued. "The only ones allowed to move freely between the worlds of male and female. Some say they're the most influential persons in the kingdom—

even though they're little more than slaves."

Several moments of intense discussion followed upon the dais, its topic known only to this intimate circle—at least for the moment. Whatever the eunuchs' suggestion, it found favor, for the King finally raised his goblet again and shouted something that I could not discern until it was repeated by the crowd.

*"Vashti!"* went the echo.

The King threw back his head, appearing to laugh, and the cry rose again, louder this time.

"Vashti!"

Vashti was the name of Xerxes' queen. Legend had it she was the most beautiful woman in the world—and Mordecai had never said anything to dispel the notion. She also was of royal lineage, giving her the additional rank of Royal Consort.

A cluster of men scurried down the steps and made a human wave part before them. The dispersal came within a few guests of where I stood, and I saw them closely. They were middle-aged men, arrayed in so much gleaming filigree that I did not know if they were staggering from the drunkenness that clearly flushed their faces, the weight of their clothing or both. One of them raised another goblet from his side and shouted her name again, as though trying to incite the crowd. They seemed to need little inducement, for soon the chant rose, "Vashti! Vashti! Vashti!" It showed no signs of diminishing.

Mordecai shot a glance of disgust my way and shook his head. He moved closer and whispered, "I told you this was no place for a beautiful young woman."

"Why are they so anxious to see her?"

"It's not just to see her, young one. It's to *see* her. Understand?"

I shook my head.

He sighed deeply and shook his head. Apparently he had not wanted to elaborate. "They'll want Vashti to disrobe and parade her nakedness for the crowd. She has been hosting her own banquet for the wives and concubines of the King's officials."

I suddenly realized that my mouth had gone completely dry, a sign of the nervousness and shock I was laboring against. I tipped my face upward toward Mordecai and asked him where I could find some water. He shook his head and motioned toward the wine table. I had never tasted the fermented fruit of the vine. He had expressly forbidden it. "It's all there is," he said, shrugging apologetically. He stepped forward with me as I struggled to lift the heavy goblet to my lips. What flowed down my throat was at once entrancing and painful. Even as it burned, I felt my head swim in a delightful way, and a rich, musky aroma overwhelmed my senses.

I lowered the goblet and shook my head with my eyes suddenly as wide as they had been all evening. Then I looked around me in alarm, realizing that I had exhibited a most unmasculine reaction. Sure enough, three large-bellied, tall, middle-aged men began to laugh heartily at my bewilderment.

"How old are you, son?" the closest one bellowed to me.

I started to answer, but a quick movement from Mordecai reminded me of my constant need for silence. As poor as my disguise was, my fledgling attempts at vocally imitating a boy were far worse. So I feigned a knowing chuckle and pointed at my throat, as if some oral malady were responsible for my reaction to the wine.

I turned from the men and stepped away, only to be knocked back by a violent shove—I barely found my footing in time to look up at the one who had struck me. The man was walking as fast as one can without actually running. I immediately recognized him as one of the seven who had gone out to fetch Vashti only moments before. He no longer seemed drunk; in fact, it seemed like every nerve in his body was quivering from some sort of savage inward fright.

"Vashti! Vashti!" several of the men began again upon the sight of him. But the man paid no heed to anyone around him. He bounded up the steps toward the King. The royal guards stepped forward for a cursory reexamination of his face, then parted their axes and let him enter.

Now, dear reader, it is obvious to you that I was not upon the platform at this moment, so I was not privy to the strained conversation that took place. However, having served as Queen of Persia for a number of years, I know my history, and I can tell you with utter confidence what was said next and the subsequent events. Of course, it is also a matter of well-recounted public record, so my telling will be of little surprise to you, I am sure.

# Chapter Eighteen

*H*arbona of Lydia, the unfortunate eunuch selected to return with the obviously bad news, had already voided his bladder into his clothes by the time he reached the top of those velvet stairs, for he knew that his King was at once an expansive and a capricious host who did not suffer negative tidings gladly. He no doubt silently thanked his Persian god Ahura for the layers of robes he had worn in addition to his gold filigree, then proceeded to choose his words with the supreme effort of not bursting into tears, relieving himself further or both.

Watching him, I noticed at once the strangely feminine tilt of his head, the lilt in his high voice, his soft skin. This conversation was recounted to me thus:

"My King, there has been a most disconcerting turn of events, one which my fellow servants and I have labored mightily to reverse."

"Speak plainly, my friend. How dire can it be?" Xerxes was standing on the dais at this time, towering over Harbona.

"Well, your Majesty, Queen Vashti refuses to come."

There was a pause. The King's jaw muscles churned, and his facial complexion turned the color of a ripening apple. "You jest." But a glance at the face before him confirmed the truth.

"She also refuses to give a reason, your Majesty. But even after lengthy pleas and and warnings from myself and my two fellow emissaries, she maintained her refusal."

The King grew very still, and apart from the hue of his face, he gave no further clue as to his emotions. Then he turned away and stumbled toward the center group of couches.

"The witch turned me down," he muttered. Only a few heard this, but I learned of it later.

The communal gasp that came from among the King's closest advisers no longer reclining upon their respective pillows held a portent of death. These courtiers were deeply schooled in all matters of law and protocol, and their main function was to keep His Majesty constantly informed on these matters. "According to law," the King asked in a halting yet deep voice, "what is to be done with Queen Vashti for not obeying the command of King Xerxes delivered by the eunuchs?"

Memucan, the King's Master of the Audiences, rose shakily to deliver his opinion. "Queen Vashti has wronged not only your Majesty but also all the princes and all the citizens of your Majesty's provinces," he began slowly, but his words and tone gained strength as he continued. "For Queen Vashti's conduct will become known to all women and cause them to look with contempt upon their husbands and say, 'King Xerxes commanded Queen Vashti to come into his presence, but she did not come!' And today, all the women of Persia and Media who hear of the Queen's conduct will speak in the same manner to all the King's princes, even to every husband in the land, which will result in great contempt and anger."

I was standing more than forty cubits from the base of the royal stairs as these words were spoken, so I could not hear all that was being said until the end, when his voice became a shout. Yet I was deeply cowed by the great silence that had once more fallen over the crowd. Instinctively I knew that something solemn and earth-shaking was taking place. Mordecai stood unusually still and sober, his eyes radiating a fearful alertness. He leaned toward me and whispered, "The man speaking is Memucan, the second most powerful man in the Empire. He is Master of the Audiences. He controls the King's thousand bodyguards, called The Immortals, and decides who can enter into the King's presence. Some say he is the ultimate power in the realm."

Above us, Memucan finished his oration. "If it pleases the King, let a royal edict be issued by His Majesty and let it be written in the laws of Persia and Media so that it cannot be rescinded, that Vashti should come no more into the presence of King Xerxes, and let the King give her royal position to another more worthy than herself."

The gasp that then rose from the royal platform was so loud and exaggerated that I thought some royal pantomime was being performed.

Indeed, the assembled entourage was aghast then awed at the boldness and severity of Memucan's pronouncement. For indeed, Vashti was Queen of Persia at that moment. Had she appeared, even this learned consort of the King would have been compelled to bow low and kiss her outreached hand.

And in fact, I can tell you that Memucan had taken what to any other man was an intolerable risk, especially with a king as given to whims as Xerxes. But perhaps he had accurately read the King's rage and merely given voice to what His Majesty felt unable to express. In either case, Xerxes swerved drunkenly around and bellowed, "Make it so!" Then he pointed to one of the satraps in the corner and spoke in a lower voice. "You. Haman! You're a backstabbing murderer, forgive the slur, but come here!"

And Haman the Amalekite, summoned months before with all the other satraps for the military portion of this banquet, rose warily. His girth unmistakable, he approached Xerxes, and the King draped one arm unceremoniously around the old raider's shoulders.

Xerxes leaned salaciously into Haman's ear, as though he were about to anoint him with a kiss. Instead, he whispered, and while no one else but Haman heard the words, nearly everyone on the platform blanched at the hardened sneer that twisted the King's features as he spoke them.

Haman nodded, smiled slyly, bowed once before the King and bounded down the steps into the crowd.

And, dear Candidate, what I will tell you next elicits nearly the same overwhelming fear and revulsion as happened the first time. As Haman rushed past where I was standing, his cloak flew up and revealed just a glimpse of something I thought I had wiped from my memory. My knees nearly gave way as I recognized that cruel emblem I had seen long ago after the murder of my family. *The twisted cross!* I clung to Mordecai's arm, arguing silently but fervently that I *must* have been mistaken—it simply couldn't be.

I later learned that Vashti was dragged screaming from the Palace even as I stood there watching her husband squeeze the last dregs from his glorious party. She and her belongings were deposited outside the King's Gate in the swiftest and most sudden reversal of fortune Persia ever had the occasion to witness. And as word of this spread through the Persian provinces, the message to women was indeed clear.

What Haman would do next would result in my life being changed forever—again.

Not long after, on a cold and moonless desert night, a group of eight horsemen rode quietly into the darkness of a wealthy Susa neighborhood not far from the King's citadel. The men, all of whom wore identical twisted crosses permanently tattooed on their backs and on their tunics, tied their horses to a young tree and ran without a sound to a nearby home. The large, white dwelling was flanked like all the rest by a high mud wall. The men vaulted it without a moment's hesitation.

As though they were following some internal map, they ran

without pause into the dwelling, padded quietly up the stairs and entered a large bedroom there. In the low bed slept the publicly banished and now privately undefended Vashti, former Queen of Persia.

At once she sprang forward in her bed, her legendary raven hair tousling around her. A dark hand clamped over her mouth. Two more hands grabbed the sides of her heaving shoulders. And then a long blade began to stab—up, down, up, down, up, down. . . .

The King's whispered order had been carried out.

All I could think, when I finally heard the rumor whispered to me by Rachel, was how silent killers in the night had slaughtered my own mother in a similar fashion.

# Chapter Nineteen

THE ROYAL PALACE, SUSA—THREE DAYS LATER

A mere dozen cubits away from the royal bedchamber, the Great Hall stood abandoned, its floors finally swept clean and scrubbed free of the stains and spills that the prolonged revelry had left behind. Even the Inner Court behind it stood empty, save for one lone sentry.

In the King's private chambers languished the reason why. The sovereign of all Persia lay prone upon his giant bed, where he had remained for three days without going any farther than his nearby bathroom. Just outside the room's walls stood a phalanx of servants, courtiers and advisers at vigil, wringing their hands and whispering anxious phrases of bewilderment and frustration, some even daring to advise.

At the end of the third afternoon, Master of the Audiences Memucan slowly pushed open the door and entered. The floor between him and the sleeping platform was strewn with golden food trays, broken dishes and scattered food. Memucan stepped gingerly around them and approached the bed.

"Your Majesty—"

"You, of all people, have some nerve coming in here," interrupted Xerxes. "You're the one responsible for all this."

"Responsible for what, your Majesty?"

"For my banishing the Queen, what do you think? And, of course, for what came next."

"Your Majesty, may I remind you that I did not recommend for anyone to harm the Queen," he said quickly, "merely banish her from her position."

Xerxes rose in his bed now, his hair tousled and his beard twisted in three directions. "And what does one do with a banished queen, you idiot? Let her go out and become a symbol of martyrdom? An icon for the very rebellious female spirit that earned her dismissal in the first place? No! I had no choice but to order her dispatched! It's what any king would do in the circumstance!"

"Yet now your Majesty seems quite dismayed at having done just that," he dared say.

"Being a king is hard, dirty business. You of all people should know that. Sometimes it calls for actions that turn the stomach. I did not invent the rules, you know."

"No, sir. You did not. But may I point out that the rules also require your Majesty to appear at court, fit and powerful, for all to gaze upon and blanch in fear and respect. Your dismay over Vashti seems to have impaired that capacity."

Xerxes now stepped from the bed, jumped down the small step to the bedroom's enormous floor and fairly leaped upon Memucan.

"You watch your tongue, do you hear? I'm still King, and with a snap of my fingers I can still have you 'harmed,' as you so delicately put it!"

Memucan gently pried the King's fingers loose from around his neck and shrank back toward the entrance.

"What can I do to enhance the King's state of happiness?" he finally asked.

The answer came low, almost guttural in its tone. "Nothing!"

"I could find His Majesty a new queen," Memucan finally offered. "A new Vashti, only more beautiful and far wiser. First we would assemble a new batch of eunuchs, then the finest young virgins from across the land. When Hegai is through cleaning them up and making them presentable, I could bring them one by one to your bedchamber."

It took some time for the smile to become visible upon Xerxes' face, but soon he was beaming. And nodding his agreement to the idea most forcefully. This would take the attention away from the whole sorry incident and get his people speculating on who the next Queen of Persia would be.

### STREETS OF SUSA—TWO DAYS LATER

The army patrol was upon the boys before they even had a chance to bolt. Even had they been given the opportunity, the knot of Jewish youth would have probably stood their ground, for quite often soldiers turned out to be their childhood friends and the patrols rarely more than a passing spectacle.

But this time, the orderly stomp of formation gave way to the wild clatter of booted steps upon the cobblestones. The soldiers sprinted up to Rachel's grandson Jesse and his three companions and quickly encircled them with a bristling ring of spearpoints. The blunt end of an unseen spear beside Jesse swiftly knocked him behind the neck, hard, and sent him to the ground like a heavy sack of grain. Five pairs of rough hands reached down and seized him. Jesse shouted loudly and waved his arms like someone possessed of a wild spirit.

He saw only whirling sky and thickly muscled arms and then the sides of an army chariot. The point of a spear, quivering in his face, made the outcome quite clear should he attempt an escape.

His ensuing minutes were a jumble of terror and pain, along

with a host of wild, tumbling questions: *What have I done wrong?*
*Were we breaking some law? Where are they taking me?* Followed by
the most mind-numbing, blood-curdling question of all: *Are these*
*my last moments on earth?*

After an eternity of this torment, he opened his eyes to the towering sight of stone walls on his right. Then came a sharp turn and
a high wooden door tilting outward. A gate. He took in a breath,
and the realization washed over his senses like a bath of icewater
across his limbs.

*The Royal Palace.*

He was pulled from the chariot floor, and thick hands took his
hands and feet. He was indoors now, being pulled through one long
hallway, then down stairs. Then darkness. He fell hard.

# *Chapter Twenty*

*I* awoke at the same instant Mordecai did that morning, for it was still dark and our door sounded like it was being pounded off its hinges. A high, shrill voice wailed from the other side. It sounded vaguely familiar, but it was forming a sound somewhere between a hyena's laughter and a widow's funeral cry.

Mordecai bounded from his room. By the time he reached the front door I was peering around my bedroom door, my heart pounding in alarm and fear.

"Rachel?" he cried.

"Yes!" came the hysterical voice from the other side.

I gasped when Mordecai threw open the door and we were greeted by the sight of Rachel as neither of us had ever seen her. Her hair was tangled and askew, her eyes wild and red with tears, her back bent over as though she were misshapen. She appeared to have aged a decade in just a few hours. She shuffled in and resumed her weeping the instant she was inside.

"It's Jesse! It's Jesse!"

My blood ran cold as I heard this. Mordecai had come home late, bearing news from the royal barracks, news of a new kind of conscript that had made my heart sink even before this dire lament.

"What happened?" he asked, almost shouting at her for coherence.

"I don't know! He's gone! He's been missing since the afternoon. His father and mother searched the streets. We only heard rumor of an army patrol taking away groups of boys—"

Mordecai reared back with a deep, loud breath. I recognized the gesture; it was his reaction to very bad news—such as when I had told him about my excursion into town dressed as a boy.

He sat down slowly, his face growing paler by the second, his breathing like that of a man trying to make himself remain alive. At the sight of his reaction, Rachel fell to her knees and began to shake. "What is it? What is it, Master Mordecai?"

He only shook his head, his gaze an eternity away. Finally it came to rest on poor Rachel. He lowered his hands slowly onto her shoulders and took another deep breath.

"Rachel. I don't know. I'm so sorry—I can't guarantee this is what happened, but someone has to tell you—"

"Oh, my G-d! Oh, YHWH!" she began to pray and wail in anticipation, her eyes still fixed on Mordecai.

"I heard a strong rumor today at the Palace that five hundred handsome young boys had been captured and taken to the citadel to be turned into eunuchs."

At that, Rachel's eyes fluttered to the top of her eyelids, her head threw back and she fell heavily onto the floor.

When Jesse came to his senses it was still dark. The room was lit only by a pair of candles somewhere above him. It was cold, and he was naked. He was lying on a flat, hard surface. Wood. A table. His head felt numb; his senses swam wildly. Dimly, as though through a layer of mud, he started to realize something. *I feel drunk.* Several years before he had sneaked several long pulls of the Shabbot wine and faintly remembered the sensation of it. He was sure someone had slipped him a foreign substance.

And then, the most startling sensation of this whole event—large male fingers grasping his private parts. He heard the clicking of metal and the sound of a blade being sharpened.

Then came a male voice from somewhere in the gloom, low and menacing, speaking to no one in particular.

"Look at this: another Jew. They think they're so different, even down there they have to do things their own way."

And another voice, from the opposite side. "They think it makes them special. Just get it over with."

Then Jesse felt a sensation between his legs which, had he been conscious in the moment that followed, would have made him pray for death.

I was on the street before I knew it, before I even realized what I was doing. My legs were doing their own thinking, churning beneath me as fast as they could, my arms clawing the air, my bare feet flying above the ground without a care for whatever roughness lay beneath them. My lungs heaved, but not from the exertion; they were trying to stay inflated through sobs that threatened to tear every breath from my body. I felt like my mind was a passenger barely hanging on to some overheated stampede, for my limbs now had a will of their own.

And I knew where my headlong run was taking me: northward, uphill, toward the Palace portico. He would be there, as young and innocent as he had been just a short while before, riding the gryphon. He just had to be.

As the distance fell away before me, I inwardly began to shout at G-d, the vague Hebrew entity whom I had never fully trusted.

*So, is this your idea of caring for your own? Is this your gift for me upon reaching womanhood? For the supposed Creator of the Universe, you certainly have a strange way of showing your power. In fact, if this is your idea of sovereign watchcare, then opt me out! I'd rather be a Persian and worship their god!*

I was just beginning to feel the burning in my joints and legs when abruptly, sooner than I had expected, the portico square lurched into my sight.

The plaza I had seen crowded so thick that its ground was invisible now stood empty. A patch of dirt, surprisingly small. A great silence now reigned where the clamor of people had once roared almost unbearably. The sun was just beginning to rise, and a wedge of yellow sunlight was starting to chase purple shadows down the Palace wall. The square's only occupants were the Palace guards at the far end. I could feel them following me closely with their eyes.

I raced up to the gryphon statue and circled it with desperate speed. Beneath it was a pile of donkey droppings. I started to run up the incline we'd taken for our jump. But clearly the space above was empty.

Taking advantage of my pause from the exertion, fear and rage now began to well up inside of me to the point that I felt I would burst. My chest still heaved, not from a lack of air but from the effort of holding in my emotions. And then I held them in no longer: I threw back my head, took a deep breath and screamed at the top of my lungs.

"Nooooooooooo!"

How could they take a flawless young man, as new and perfect as nature could make him, and maim him like that? I'd barely had time to form a coherent picture of what made him distinctly male, and now *that* had been cut away and thrown aside like a bit of trash. His manhood, part of his deepest core, now shorn and discarded— the sheer callousness of it was beyond belief. Beyond my ability to fathom. The uncaring power of the Empire now seemed to loom over me with an almost physical sense of ruthlessness.

I fell to my knees and bowed my head. Out of the corner of my eye I could see that the guards had lowered their lances a notch and now stared at me openly. It had been a stupid, indulgent thing to do; I realized that at once. Yet even today, looking back from the calmer viewpoint of an older woman, I cannot say those feelings could have been restrained. My childhood cloud of foreboding had returned. Doom and tragedy seemed to have reasserted their control over my destiny. For someone that age, it was almost too much to bear.

With as much slowness and reluctance as I could possibly convey, I stood. I turned toward the road home and let the downhill pull of gravity, more than my own effort, move me forward. I walked into full sunlight and felt warmed a bit, inwardly and outwardly. Doors were now starting to open and sleep-swollen faces beginning to peep outside. I passed an old woman tossing out her evening's slop bucket from the safety of her doorway and swerved to avoid the splash. Another matron pulled out a canvas awning to shield her home's window from the early sun. A man whose unclad belly hung down over his waist gazed up into the sky, assessing the weather.

*How can they act normally on a morning like this?* I thought despairingly as I passed. *Don't they know? Do they not have a son, a nephew, a cousin taken in yesterday's roundup?* Mordecai had told me that five hundred young men had been herded through the Palace gates. Surely the city should be filled with wailing and every person's countenance downcast and grieving at the dawn of a day like this.

I was beginning to approach the turn onto our street when I saw Mordecai in his night-robe, running up the empty lane waving his arms wildly, shouting. I could barely tell who it was. I could not make out his words, but I stopped in my tracks. Then, struck by his hysterical appearance, I started toward him and home.

"What is the matter?" I shouted back.

He waved even more wildly and shouted more forcefully, but the louder his voice became, the less I could understand him. So I crossed a few long steps into our street to hear better.

And that is when I heard what Mordecai was shouting about.

From behind me, uphill from him, came the sound of marching feet. I turned, and only then did I hear Mordecai's shout clearly for the first time. It sounded eerily like the cry that had just ripped from my chest a few moments before.

"*Noooooooooo!*"

I backed away from the center of the street, away from the oncoming column, still not understanding the cause of Mordecai's extreme reaction. After all, army patrols happened all the time—it was certainly an occasion for prudence in choosing one's path but hardly cause for that sort of anguished cry.

I flattened my back against the wall, wanting to make sure I obstructed nothing of the soldiers' progress.

But the column veered and came straight toward me.

Before I could take another breath I was surrounded by soldiers. I could feel a dozen pairs of eyes travel up and down my body and even though I was clad in nightclothes, I wished immediately that I could have yanked on a heavy cloak.

One of the men, not a soldier, stepped forward from the rest and eyed me slowly from head to foot. I began to feel embarrassed at the disheveled state of my appearance, as I had bolted straight from my bed when this adventure had started. The man turned to a soldier behind him.

"A little unkempt, but still, she is beautiful, no?"

The other nodded, his eyes glued to the upper part of my body. "You're right, sir. She is stunning. A great face, a most appealing figure. She must be the beauty they told us about."

The civilian nodded his agreement with a smirk that sent a cold chill through my veins.

Just then the sound of tumult came up the street; Mordecai had finally reached the scene and was shouting, out of breath, nearly incoherent with panic.

"Please! Do not take her! She is exempt! She is exempt!"

The man frowned and turned Mordecai's way. The soldiers parted quickly to clear the path between the two men.

"Why is she exempt?" the soldier barked.

"Well, for one thing," Mordecai answered, pausing to try and recover his wind, "she is a member of a foreign people. . . ."

"Which one?"

"Well . . ." Mordecai gritted his teeth in his effort to decide whether to answer.

*"Which one?"* came the question again, this time more impatient.

Mordecai shook his head no. "Forget it. It was a lie—I take it back." Then he fixed me with a tear-stained look. "My dear, don't mention anything on that subject. Don't say anything, no matter what you do, about, you know . . ."

I numbly nodded my assent. Only Mordecai would have thought about the stigma of my Jewishness at a time like this.

"Look, it doesn't matter. This is a royal edict," the man interrupted, his voice growing more clipped with every passing second, "and to royal edicts there are no exemptions. The only question for you is, is she a virgin?"

Mordecai stopped still, his eyes darting from side to side in search of an answer. Finally he began to shake his head.

"She is not. She was—she was raped by bandits a few years ago."

Unfortunately, the man turned to me with a reappraising glance just as I grimaced at Mordecai's lie.

"What?" I began to protest. "But I *am* . . ." Again, the imprudence of youth and inexperience.

The soldier turned back to my uncle. "You're lying. I have a mind to have you run in."

"I am a royal scribe," Mordecai babbled, pleading now. "I'll give you anything. I'll pay you any price."

"Yes, I recognize you. From the King's Gate. And I am the King's agent in Susa, charged with finding virgins for his bed. We heard a rumor that one of the most beautiful young women in the kingdom lived in hiding somewhere around this neighborhood. How long has she resided here?"

Mordecai's jaw flexed grimly. It was then that I remembered the times Mordecai had escorted me beyond our home with his hand gripping my elbow to steer me forward—my eyes downcast as he'd instructed, our gait swift and hurried. He had been trying to protect me from prying and lascivious eyes. I glanced his way with the briefest look of gratitude, then back at the agent whose swaggering figure filled my sight.

"Sir, if you were not a Palace aide," the man sneered, "I would have you run through with a sword already. Now answer me. How long has she lived here?"

"Her whole life," Mordecai replied after a long pause.

And that is when I truly began to understand the soldiers' intent. They were going to take me into the Palace, just like Jesse. I would not be mutilated, but probably—my mind spun with the conclusions—I would become one of those girls on the benches, one of the gilded statues, one of the disposable women, a mere Palace decoration. . . .

Worse still, Mordecai had often described these women's solitude to me. They lived as virtual prisoners—something I had once considered myself—yet without friends or family to comfort them.

As the realization began to sear its way through my body, an attitude that had begun as mere bemusement swiftly turned to terror. I shrank back into the wall, wishing with all my heart that I could melt into the bricks and disappear.

The agent stepped toward me and brought his face within inches of mine. I could feel his gaze upon me like a physical blow. Then his fingers found their way into my hair; I recoiled only to have my shoulders pinned against the wall. Rough hands groped at places no one had ever touched before.

"Careful," said a voice behind us. "If she's that beautiful, she may end up as your queen before it's all over."

The man in my face snickered and backed away a little. Suddenly I was looking at his back.

"All right, men," he said loudly, "return two days from now and take her. We'll give the man some time to clean her up and dress her decently."

The King's agent leaned into Mordecai's face. His eyes went cold. "A favor," he said, almost in a low growl. "From one royal staffer to another. If she's not out on this street two days from this minute, ready to go, it'll be your neck and hers. You understand?"

Mordecai nodded numbly.

And prepare we did. Mordecai stayed home from work the next two days, claiming sickness—and "sick" was actually close to the truth in describing his overall state during that period. In fact, many moments during that span found me afraid that he might succumb in some manner to the extreme distress my predicament had plunged him into. Perhaps concern for him proved a welcome distraction for me, for I often thought he was taking the news worse than I was. After a determined consideration of the options, we came to the dismal conclusion it was death or cooperation. There was nothing else.

When he was able to keep his emotions in check, Mordecai maintained a running commentary on the protocols of Palace life and the best strategies for maintaining my purity and faith as a follower of YHWH. He refused to sleep or allow me slumber; instead my poppa rocked from side to side like some mystic reciting an endless creed, his eyes focused on nothing in particular, intoning his ceaseless instructions without pause. On and on it went—admonitions on keeping a godly diet, on following the commandments, on dealing with the eunuchs and other officials, on conducting myself with the other candidates. The longer he continued, the more I realized that he was not just trying to prepare me for a rushed departure but actually seeking to compensate for a whole lifetime of social deprivation.

"Tell no one of your Jewishness," he muttered over and over again. "It will become an issue. It could actually mean your life."

By the time he began to speak of how to approach my time with the King, Mordecai's themes had begun to flow together in a seamless verbal torrent. "I know you are frightened by what your capture implies, but my dear, you must realize that there are greater things to fear than the unknown regions of sexual intimacy. Much more than the King's bed partner is at stake. Hidden powers are jockeying for position here. Just stay as observant a Jew as you can. Privately, G-d will understand the things you are compelled to do upon pain of death. And you *will* be forced to break some commandments. But try your very best not to. Remember who you are, even if you keep it silent. Keep up your prayers to the Lord. Do not follow the others—the common sentiment—but remember what I taught you about the Word of G-d."

I suppose Mordecai's alarming behavior helped shield me from the full shock of my impending fate. I spent the two days in a sort of daze, trying my best to absorb the best of what he was attempting to impart and at the same time distinguish his true nuggets of wisdom from product of mere panic. In the end I slipped into a sort of numb state of my own, a mindset that I can barely remember to this day. Thank G-d, the time passed all too swiftly.

The fateful dawn arrived. I stood just inside our door arrayed in a fine tunic that Rachel had purchased for me at the King's Gate bazaar. Rachel had come early, and I was bathed, perfumed and beautified to the best of her experience. I now recall with some amusement that I actually believed myself to be as clean and fragrant as a girl could possibly be, that any further beauty treatments before it came to be my night with Xerxes would just be futile excess. How little I knew! And how naïve! I was able to form the phrase "my night with Xerxes" not understanding even a small portion of what that meant.

Finally, just as we stood to face the door and all the fearfulness awaiting outside, he turned to me with tears in his eyes.

"Hadassah, my dear," he said in a broken voice, "I think it is best if you leave your star necklace with me."

I gasped in shock and dismay. For some reason, surrendering the one relic from my dead family seemed like the cruelest loss of all—more grievous somehow than losing my freedom, my innocence or even my future.

Yet I knew from the crushed look upon Mordecai's face that he had my highest good at heart; it was no easier for him to ask it than for me to relinquish it. So I numbly felt my fingers reach to my neck, unclasp the medallion and hand it to him. Then I turned back for the door, opened it and stepped outside into a chill morning and the sun's bright rays emerging over the tops of nearby buildings.

Right on schedule, the synchronized slapping of boots on cobblestone was heard approaching our place. Rachel began to sob; Mordecai merely draped an arm over my shoulder, squeezed hard and stared at the opposite side of the street. The only motion in his face was that of his lower lip, which now quivered, I must admit, like that of a baby.

And then they were beside us. Today's column was far more military and precise than the one that had found me two days before. After their captain had barked out his order to stop, the men stared straight ahead. The only sign of their humanity was the faint wisps of air pluming from their mouths in the night-cooled air.

I almost fainted, for my breath was now rasping in my chest, shallow and halting. I tried to speak but my spastic throat would not form a word. My knees gave way, and I would have fallen but for the three pairs of male hands that immediately grasped my arms and held me up.

Through my tears and the lurching sway of my sight I could see Mordecai back away, his hands held pleadingly in front of his face. He was no longer in control of his faculties.

"No! No!" came all the pathetic plea he could muster.

The men pulled me farther into their midst, their grip so strong that keeping my feet was no longer necessary. They started to carry me uphill.

"The East Gate!" Mordecai began to shout, tearing at his hair, his eyes wild with grief. "Meet me at the East Gate when you can—I'll be there!"

I wanted to acknowledge his instruction, but all I could manage was a single word.

*"Mordecai!"* I screamed.

"Keep the commandments!" he shouted after me, his voice beginning to dim. "Remember! Keep the commandments!"

The same houses I had passed on my quiet return home now flowed past like mournful reminders. The early risers I had seen a few days before were now staring wide-eyed at the commotion.

"Come on, girl, it's not so bad," the King's agent said from my left. "You're not going to be executed. You're going to spend the best twelve months of your life, get bedded by the King and even stand a decent chance of becoming Queen of Persia. There are girls lining up all over the kingdom to be considered for this."

And that, believe it or not, is the first time I heard a clear statement of my future.

## Chapter Twenty-one

*T*he soldiers led me up the hill and through the Palace's front portico. I thought of the euphoria with which I had entered only days before, seemingly safe in my pathetic disguise with my protector Mordecai by my side. The Palace had then seemed the most awesome and wondrous place I had ever imagined. Now, knowing what had happened to Jesse, the place loomed as a fate worse than death. A chamber of horrors and of unknown, unspeakable outcomes.

The soldiers turned left just inside the portico and walked me beside the lovely reflecting pools I had once admired. We turned away from the great buildings I had visited for the banquet, that cataclysmic event that seemed to be changing everything, and walked for some distance toward a tree-shrouded enclosure of graceful, low-slung structures.

Upon reaching the compound's front doorstep, the soldiers paused. A heavy wooden door swung open and a well-clad, richly muscled man appeared.

"Already?" he said. "The voluntary ones have not even started to come in."

The King's agent laughed derisively. "We've heard rumors for years that the most beautiful girl in the Empire lived right under our noses, in the Hebrew quarter," he replied. "And look at her. How could you see that and not see a Candidate for Queen?"

"I understand," said the man in the door in a low voice. "All right, you can go now. I'll take her from here."

The hands that had gripped my arms for what seemed like forever now released me in less than a heartbeat. I almost fell to the ground, so accustomed I already had become to their painful grasp.

But now I felt other hands bear me up—softer, gentler. I looked up into the eyes of the man from the door. He was older, probably in his fifth decade, and though his face bore the distant expression of a world-weary citizen, I saw also a warmth, almost indiscernible in its source, radiating from him. His skin and expression seemed oddly feminine. And then it struck me. *Is he a. . . ?* And then thoughts of Jesse and fears for him flooded my mind. I let out a small whimper and swayed a bit.

"Here, little one," the man said, steadying me with a firm grip. "It's all right. I know the whole thing is very frightening. But I promise you'll be fine."

He guided me inside to a dark and cool interior room, an antechamber of sorts, lined with thick velvet pillows. "Believe me," he continued, "the method was not of my choosing. But this kind of edict puts everyone on edge, especially soldiers. Everyone is so anxious to advance. Here, you're so shaken up, let's take you straight to your room. What is your name, my dear?"

"Ha—" I started, intending to give my full name, but I then realized that its Jewishness might give me away. So instead I stammered, grasping for a name. The first thought that occupied the vacuum in my mind came with overwhelming emotions. "Star," I said weakly, recalling the beloved necklace given to me as a child. "My name is Star."

"That is a lovely name," he said in a soothing tone. "Star, my name is Hegai. I am His Majesty's royal eunuch. The King's Chamberlain, I am also called. And don't you worry, little one. I will make sure you are pampered beyond your imagination."

Through a thick gauze of shock, I remember thinking that what he described sounded inviting. But I was incapable of response. All I knew was that I was being led down a marble hallway, then turned into a high-ceilinged bedroom floored with real stone and lit by a large window open to the courtyard.

"Here. Now you rest," the man invited.

I lay down on a bed, a low platform softened with layers of sheep's wool, pulled a thin blanket of surprisingly soft material over myself and quietly cried myself to sleep. I dozed fitfully as bizarre scenarios careened over each other in my mind. The fact that I was sleeping on the Palace grounds seemed like but one of my delirium's fantastic inventions. I awoke a few times to the sound of movement in the hallway outside; twice I heard girls whimpering followed by the voice of our host, comforting them as he had me.

I awoke, opened my eyes and almost rolled from my bed in combined shock and confusion. For nearly all of my life, I had slept and awakened in the very same bed in the very same room. Now, blinking open to the sight of a strange wall, a strange ceiling, a strange light, I bolted upward while my breath shuddered in gasps.

Slowly, my panic subsided and the realization of where I was began to seep into my consciousness. I recalled traumatic snatches of my capture: the world reeling around me, the soldiers' hands reaching for me, Mordecai's pleading voice, the looming shape of the Palace gates as they swayed into sight.

The room was filled with that half-light that is difficult to distinguish between evening and morning. I stood on the tips of my toes and craned my neck to see over the edge of the high window. The landscape before me shone in the sunlight. I had slept a few hours. The back of a flowering cherry tree partly obscured my view of the marble terrace, the pool at its far edge, and the hulking shapes of the Palace's great halls crowding the horizon. *I could sneak out* came my first thought, until I pondered further and realized that every gate in the forbidding outer wall was under heavy guard. I ruefully considered how I had always thought of the Palace guard as keeping intruders out—not keeping terrified occupants in.

*Am I a prisoner?* came the lingering question. I didn't exactly feel like one; the room certainly did not seem like a cell. And yet I definitely was here against my will. Maybe the next hour or two would tell.

I turned back to the room, aware that sleep was over for now. Walking to the entrance, I tried the handle of the door and pushed it open silently. The hallway was spacious and cool with that airiness unique to stone spaces. I tiptoed out to an open-air courtyard filled with small trees and an enclosed smaller pool. The place's stillness and elegant beauty at this hour took my breath away. The golden light was kissing the walls' pale olive and the water's cool blue depths with all the richness of a painting. I had never seen such a serene and beautiful sight. Circling the pool, I came to a large open room filled with couches and tables. Empty, overturned wine goblets and rhytons were strewn across the furniture and floor. I turned away and returned to my room.

And then I remembered Mordecai's final words. *Meet me at the East Gate!* And I knew what I had to do next.

## Chapter Twenty-two

It was no great feat to escape the house itself. I had only to grasp the lip of the bedroom window, pull myself up, scoot over the sill, then jump down to the other side. Once there I stood perfectly still for a long moment, trying to acclimate myself to the new acoustics and listen for any disturbance I might have aroused. I heard only soft breeze through the leaves before me and a slight lapping from the nearby pool. I peered out through the foliage, trying to gauge where my greatest risk of detection would be. Would this compound have its own guards? Or were they all at the outer gates?

I saw nothing, so I tiptoed ahead, keeping to the shade nearest the wall. My next task was to determine in fact where east was. I noted the location of the sun, then glanced outward to the mountainous Palace halls I had visited so recently and tried to make out the King's Gate, which I knew to be the southernmost part of the Palace. Of the three highest rooftops, I chose the closest, as it was from the King's Gate that I had first glimpsed the harem compound.

Since that shape was southernmost, and the other rooftops lay on a north-south axis, and the sun was in front of me, I realized that east lay behind me, beyond the harem buildings. I continued to follow the wall until I knew I had come to the back side, then plunged forward into the garden foliage. After fighting my way through a thicket of lush bougainvillea, I reached an old gate that opened onto yet another structure. Its low roofline blended almost completely into the rich garden canopy. I avoided coming too close by staying on my side of the gate and darting from one palm trunk to another. I could not keep from peeking around, though, and what I saw brought me to a sudden and complete halt. A dozen young men stood under a loud stream of running water that cascaded from a corner of the roof. They were naked and tied together at the ankles by a thick wet rope. I thought I saw red rivulets in the stream trickling away from their crude bath.

I looked away, my virginal curiosity overcome by the gruesomeness of what my mind was telling me. These were the new eunuchs, I realized. Jesse would probably be one of them—if not one of the bathers, then one of their companions inside. I shuddered and, feeling faint, slowly moved away on my quest to reach Mordecai.

I slipped as silently as I could toward my calculations of east. A row of bright golden flowers flanked me for a while, nearly as tall as my waist. I passed through the shelter of a small apple orchard, then squeezed through a hedge on its far side. I finally shook my head, amazed. How large *was* this Palace? Besides the largest buildings in the world, how many forests, how many gardens and enclosed buildings could it possibly encompass?

Suddenly I found myself standing face first against the Palace wall itself. Finally, the end of it. I turned left, then right. Which way was the East Gate? I gambled on right and began to hurry. The sun was now setting, and the protecting shadow a small comfort. But I could picture an alarm being given for the escaped Jewish girl, packs of heavily armed soldiers stalking the gardens for my tracks. I had to get to the gate.

Up ahead, the wall was broken by a thick column and a wide gap. I sighed in relief. The East Gate. I tiptoed up to the column and peered around. From my narrow view through the iron bars I saw a flash of white tunic and burlap bag. Merchants and shoppers going about their final business of the day. No soldiers; but I could see only the farthest end of the gate's aperture.

I decided to take the chance. I slipped around, looked through the bars and, instead of a soldier's, the face that greeted me was Mordecai's, looking worn and tired. It was clear that he had been standing there since I had been taken, on the chance that I would come. He cried out at the sight of me and rushed to the gate.

"Hadassah! Are you all right?" He was weeping.

I could not form a response; indeed, from my very sight of him I was undone. A loud sob ripped forth from the bottom of my lungs as I leaned forward to take hold of his outstretched hands through the bars. It was more than crying—what overwhelmed me was a mixture of weeping and shouting for joy. I grasped his fingers and covered them with kisses and tears. I felt as though I had not seen him in years. Just being close to him, drinking in his person, his nearness, seemed like the most refreshing spring water to a desert wanderer. I had a flash backward in time to that conversation with old Jacob, when he described the young child so overjoyed at the sight of his father.

"I'm fine, Poppa," I finally managed. "Hegai the chamberlain is a very nice man and the quarters are quite comfortable. I have no complaints."

A semblance of reassurance seemed to come over him when he heard those words. Then he thought of another concern. "Have you met any of the other girls, Hadassah? What are they like?"

"None of them yet, Poppa. I have been here only a short time." And hearing myself say those words brought rushing back the fact that I was to stay here for the rest of my life. My composure collapsed in an instant. "Can you get me out?" I pleaded. "What can you do, Poppa Mordecai? You're a Palace worker."

He shook his head and tears began again to stain his cheeks. "This is a royal edict, Hadassah. I have made inquiries. I think I can walk past the front of the harem every morning and we can talk, but that is all. Other than that, nothing is to be done. Nothing, that is, except to bear this fate like a worthy child of Israel."

"You mean I'll never go home? I'll never sit down to dinner with you again?" My weeping seemed to twist the sound of my speech into the parody of a whining toddler, but I did not care. I reached forward to touch Mordecai's hair as I said it; he did nothing to resist, for he was in tears as thoroughly as I was.

"I'm afraid so, my love," he said, the last words nearly unintelligible over his sobs. At length he gained control of himself and cuffed me lightly behind the neck.

"Do you remember the things I told you?" he asked, looking directly into my eyes.

"Of course. Of course I do."

"Please. Swear to me you'll follow them as though your life depended on it. Because you know it does."

"All right. Yes, I will," I said with penitence in my voice. Suddenly the things I had once rebelled against at home had become precious icons of all I stood to lose. "I swear, Mordecai. I swear it to you. In fact, I have already done one thing." I lowered my voice and looked quickly around. "When they asked for my name, I realized that Hadassah is Jewish, and so I gave another one. For some reason all I could think of was my medallion necklace. I told them my name is Star. If you need to find me for some reason, that is how I am known. Star of Susa."

He nodded wistfully. "A wise decision, my dear. I should have thought of that myself." Then he, too, looked about him anxiously. "Go, my precious one. And when you can, meet me in the court-yard across from your building. Early morning is the best, and I can go from there to my work. If I am kept from the actual Palace grounds for some reason, look for me here in the evening."

I nodded through a fresh flow of tears and leaned through the bars to kiss him on the cheek. As he walked out of sight, weeping, I pushed my arm through the bars and called after him like the wife of a condemned man. I shouted his name through sobs until finally, just at the edge of my vision, he turned around, his face as shiny as a rain-slick stone, and lifted his hand in blessing.

My return trip, undertaken through a cascade of tears, seemed to take but a fraction as long as the earlier trek. This time I circled as far as possible around the male compound and kept to the thickest bushes. In but a few minutes I was walking back to the courtyard pool as though I had just stepped away for a moment of solitude. A familiar male voice sounded behind me.

"Star, right? From what I hear, an ill-timed walk is what landed you here in the first place."

I turned to the sight of Hegai, resplendent in a white silk tunic that seemed to magnify the setting sun. "I am told I ought to be grateful to have landed here, as you say," I answered.

"And well you should. This is the beginning of a wonderful life for you, or it can be if you let it. Women all over Persia dream of living in the royal harem. No annoying husbands, no burdensome children or families to feed and clothe and clean up after every hour of the day. Instead, a life of leisure and luxury unimagined. Every once in a while, a night of passion with the most powerful man in the world. Who would not be grateful?"

I looked at him and tried to give him the best answer I could without surrendering my dignity. "You are indeed persuasive, noble Hegai. I shudder to think what this harem would consist of without your convincing oratory."

He smiled knowingly. "You have a point, young Star. I do my best to lighten morale. As I always say—puffy eyes and tear tracks never did anything to enhance a woman's beauty. But somehow—" and at that he paused and gave me a deeply piercing look—"I don't think that will be a problem for you. You are a very beautiful and poised young woman, my dear—oh, and now, what is your *real* name?"

His question seemed to quiver between us in the morning air like some sort of raindrop suspended in mid-flight. I made a decision—probably not the wisest of my life, but in the long run, one of the most fortuitous.

"I would rather not say, sir."

"It will remain a secret between us. I promise. And my dear, if you have not guessed yet, no one in the world knows more about keeping secrets than a royal eunuch."

"All right. It is Hadassah. It means 'myrtle.'"

"Hadassah." He said the word and looked up into the sky, searching his memory. Then he nodded and fixed me with a satisfied grin. "Jewish. You are a child of Israel."

"Please tell no one, sir. I simply cannot allow my origins to become a matter of common knowledge."

"Why? Jews are well respected, even revered, throughout the kingdom."

"By His Majesty's government, yes. But we have enemies everywhere, sir. My own family was murdered by a group of marauders. I have lived in fear and seclusion most of my life. Please, sir. I would like to present myself as a modern Persian woman. Nothing more."

He pursed his lips in thought and nodded toward the ground. "All right, Star. Your real name and race are forgotten."

"Oh, except for one thing, I'm sorry to ask."

"What is that?"

"My diet. My adoptive father has begged me to remain true to our dietary laws. I wonder if you might speak to the kitchen staff about making one or two small additions to your menu that I may obey his wishes. Nothing radical, sir. Just a few dishes that will actually improve the health of anyone who shares them."

"Your request is granted, my dear. My dear young 'Persian' woman," he agreed with a slight emphasis on my assumed nationality.

# Chapter Twenty-three

And this, my dear Queen candidate, brings me to one of my strongest instructions for you. If my story has struck the least chord of sympathy within you, then I urge you to heed this advice.

*If you want to gain the King's favor, listen to the Chamberlain.*

You will be given a gatekeeper, a person who knows intimately the King and whose favor will do much toward gaining that of His Majesty. Listen to this person, for he speaks in the King's stead. He knows every one of the King's preferences and tastes. Heed his admonitions as well as you heed mine—or better. Seek his counsel, then follow it as if your life depended on it—for it may indeed be so.

It was in my case.

You may say that's fairly elementary advice. But of hundreds of girls who came to Xerxes' harem when I did, I was the only one who lived by this axiom. Nearly every other candidate allowed the luxury and stature of living at the King's Palace to go to her head.

For many of them, the intoxication of incredible luxury eventually overcame the fear and anger at being taken. For others, having defeated high odds and already been recognized as the most beautiful in their districts made them think of themselves as having arrived exalted and exempt from the normal rules and dynamics of human courtesy. Among other things, many began to treat Hegai as some sort of personal footservant. Some of them were daughters of nobility, whose sense of superiority and privilege now raged unchecked. Their families' hopes of royal accession rested on their shoulders, so these girls knew no bounds of ambition and treachery in the pursuit of their goals. What all these young women from various backgrounds and levels of social standing had in common was inexperience—we all were virgins.

And Hegai, ever the wise one, did not bridle or openly protest this uncalled-for treatment—although in the Palace hierarchy he was far more influential than any of us. He merely dropped the girl who acted this way from his list of favorites. And just as quickly, her chance of becoming queen effectively ended. The girls had no idea, of course. They were too wrapped up in their own elation to even notice they had fallen from any sort of standing. They simply went about their indulgences and chased after the esteem of the other girls—the last group from whom a prudent person would ever seek approval.

Even though Hegai was not a follower of YHWH, I found him over the months to be a wise and principled man. Every morning for weeks, a group of girls newly arrived from some far-flung province would meet their first dawn as Queen candidates in the harem. He would gather them by the pool and give them the same speech I had heard on my first morning.

He would stand by the water, adopt a nurturing, grandfatherly expression and say, "Young women, if I do not stray badly from the truth, I would say that each of you is experiencing a wide, even conflicting set of feelings right now. Exhilaration. Fear. Alienation. Homesickness. Anticipation. Loneliness. Joy. And probably a dozen other possibilities I have not named. If I can, let me heighten the joyful emotions among those. You have just become part of a highly select group, the most beautiful virginal young women in the entire Persian Empire. And if the Greek women I have seen are any indication, you are the most beautiful young women in the entire world."

Invariably, a modest patriotic cheer would go up at those words. Nothing, in those days of war, could stoke the fires of a dutiful young Persian like some slighting reference to the Greeks.

Soon, his comforting, reasonable tone and his words would quietly begin to dry teary eyes and settle anxious hearts. "And because of your youth and beauty, and maybe some other qualities that we will discover in the weeks and months ahead, you have a chance to be selected as the new queen of this whole empire." He would smile and say, "You may think I've been nice to you because it's my duty—actually, I'm being nice because one of you will be my queen someday, and I'd like to keep my head right here on my shoulders."

This time laughter, albeit somewhat nervous.

"Remember that you are not concubines, at least yet, and no one is allowed to treat you as such. You are Queen candidates, every one of you. Now, here is what your next twelve months will consist of. You will be immersed in the most complete regimen of luxury and indulgence any woman has enjoyed in the history of the human race. You will be fed the finest, richest foods Persia can offer. In a few moments you will be given a large supply of rare cosmetics from India, Lebanon and Egypt. For six moon cycles, you will be pampered with treatments of myrrh, the King's favorite essence. When you have been so thoroughly soaked in myrrh that you secrete its fragrance through your very pores, then will come six additional months of treatment with a wide assortment of spices from around the world. How does that sound?"

And then, invariably, would come the loudest, most sincere cheer of the day.

"At the end of that year, we will begin the process of selecting each of you for a night spent in the King's bed. That night, you can choose any garment, any amount of jewelry you wish to wear in with you. The decisions will be entirely your own. At the end of the night, whatever the King's ultimate choice may be, the jewelry and the clothes you wear are yours to keep. And should you not be chosen, you will take them with you to the concubines' harem, across the Palace courtyards. There I will help you adapt to the life of a Palace concubine—one of the most envied and luxurious lifestyles in Persia today. Should you be chosen as Queen, the royal bride—and I presume one of you will—then, well . . . there is no limit to the power you will wield—except the King's."

More clapping and cheering, after which the group would break up for a breakfast of rich baked goods and roasted sweetbreads. I routinely stayed away from such breakfasts, opting instead for a small pitcher of water and a few oranges from the orchards.

It turned out to be no difficult task keeping the dietary laws; I simply followed the habits Rachel had instilled in me most of my life. With the noon meal and dinner, the girls were served a sweet wine made from honey. The concoction obviously earned their rapid allegiance, but since I knew such a drink would never find its place in Mordecai's household, I avoided it. At first I had anticipated facing some scorn from my fellow candidates, but as it turned out no one ever noticed what color liquid was in my goblet or the fact that I had not approached the wine table.

And besides the satisfaction of obeying my race's religious laws, I enjoyed another unexpected benefit: While every other girl swiftly gained a visible fat layer around her hips and thighs, I remained slender. None of the other girls could explain how I did it—I of course said nothing about the dietary laws or their source, although I gave plenty of general advice about staying away from the rich and fatty foods.

I hope it does not sound like I held these young women in contempt. Far from it. In fact, though I was not the oldest of the girls, many of them began to seek my company for counsel. Perhaps they sensed the regard Hegai already had expressed for me. Or maybe they discerned that something in my upbringing had imbued me with a certain reserve upon gaining the Palace, rather than the hedonistic abandon that the others had embraced.

Eventually, I did make some friends among the other girls. But the emotional rigors of the competition ahead seemed to limit our closeness. The sense of loneliness never really went away, a feeling I had been familiar with my whole life.

And Jesse—I simply would not let my mind stray his direction too long. My thoughts and images of him had acquired the same sense of palpable horror as those of my family's murder. Something else I struggled to forget.

In fact, during those early days the only thing that would occasionally jolt me from my isolation would be the fleeting sight of that twisted cross trotting by on the side of a warhorse in the distance or briefly seen on the tunic of some figure in a crowd. I never failed to shudder and weaken at the briefest glimpse. For a time I harbored the mistaken conclusion that those two lines, crossed like the first letter of Xerxes' name and then twisted to the right at the ends, was the King's royal emblem. Thank G-d I soon learned better and the origin of the symbol soon faded into mystery—for I never could have given myself, no matter the consequences, to a man who bore that hateful sign as his own.

*Chapter Twenty-four*

Upon returning to my room that very first night after the emotional reunion with Mordecai, I began to feel an actual physical ache in my chest, the pain of a heart breaking. One fact made itself immediately clear to me—that the heart in question was not my own. I searched my feelings to try and place the strange emotion. No, the heart I could feel breaking was not Mordecai's, either.

Then I heard the voice of old Jacob again as he spoke in our home, as clearly as if he had stood there with me in the room.

*"I felt like a child so overcome with joy at His return that all I could do was leap as high into His presence as I could."*

And then I realized what I was feeling. It was the same presence Mordecai and I had both experienced so vividly upon Jacob's departure.

The presence of G-d himself.

The grief of a great Father's heart, as deep and warm as that of ten thousand earthly fathers and more, all at once poured itself into

mine. And a question poured in along with it. It came not as a voice
but an unspoken lament. . . .

*Why could you not weep for my presence, and rejoice at finding it, the
way you weep for Mordecai's? Like a child rejoining its parent?*

The power of this question struck me so forcefully that I felt my
knees buckle under me. My eyes, which had dried only a few
minutes before since my parting with Mordecai, started to pour
tears uncontrollably. Long buried, like my own tears for my parents,
my tears for G-d shredded from me like old skin. I could hardly
catch my breath; the grief was so fresh that it actually ripped the air
from my lungs. I bent over my bed and tried to mask the sobs, not
wishing to be mistaken for some homesick girl.

What was this sudden strange attraction for G-d, the same G-d
I had avoided, even rejected? Why did I *now* feel a pull that had
eluded me for so long?

*Stop. Stop*, I pleaded. The broken heart felt as if it was beating
wildly inside my own chest. I could feel its power, its agelessness.
Yet because it was divine, its sorrow was so much deeper—it
coursed through my body like the throb of a bowstring across a
violin.

But it was more than emotion—it was a person. The sensation
of His nearness and His love for me brought back, for the first time
in years, the tangible feel of my mother's love. Sensations returned
full force. The proximity of her cheek. The warmth and softness of
her breast against my face. The distinctive smell of her. The velvet
cooing of her voice.

I wept for them both, my mother and my Creator. So intense
was the grief that it left my chest feeling hollowed into some inner
crater—sapping my last ounce of strength yet leaving me to weep
on.

*But if you're real*, I found myself crying silently to Him, *then
why? Why did you let these bad things happen to me? Why all the death
and loss?*

This time the answer came to me.

*When those horrible things took place, my heart broke with you. I wept for you as strongly as you weep now.*

In the depths of my being, I gradually came to the realization that I had forgiven Him. I understood. The breach of those last few years was gone. But not my tears—I now wept because I knew for certain I had caused the sadness I had felt. My rejection and resentment had broken G-d's heart as badly as all the tragedies that had ever scarred my life. I resolved there and then to try and atone for the pain I had caused Him with every minute left to me on earth. I was a Jew in spirit now, not just by lineage.

And from that fateful morning on, I found that I could feel His presence more in that pagan, foreign environment than I ever had in the familiar confines of Mordecai's home. It truly seemed He was flanking my steps, a silent yet wise companion, His Spirit whispering into my innermost being words of instruction and exhortation.

G-d spoke to me about my challenges ahead. The first words of wisdom that came to me had to do with my upcoming night with the King.

*It is not about you. It is about the King. Focus on him.*

And I resolved, in the months ahead, to do just that.

It must have been a jarring sight for those accustomed to crossing the Palace grounds every day: a crowd of nearly one hundred beautiful young women moving across the terrace, chattering and calling to one another like an oversize flock of geese.

Hegai wore a grim expression and seemed not to notice the clamor behind him as he led us toward a cluster of Palace outbuildings. The loud procession traced its path beneath the shadows of the Inner Court, circled its massive bulk, then left it behind and after nearly half a mile of seemingly aimless wandering, came to a broad, low-slung building ringed by soldiers. We stopped before a pair of solid-brass doors crossed by half a dozen bars and locks. Two soldiers at sentry stepped forward and demanded Hegai's orders, which he promptly held out for their perusal. One of them read the tablet carefully, then nodded approval to his companion. The men turned back and spent several minutes sliding aside the bars and twisting the locks. Then they leaned into the doors and slowly pushed them open.

At once, the group fell silent.

The open doorway revealed a vast hall shrouded in near dark-ness—its shadow seeming to yawn heavenward and engulf us with the suddenness of a storm cloud passing over the sun. One guard lit a torch and gave it to Hegai, who carried it into the gloom. And then, like a spark thrown into a gas pit, the room filled with light.

It took us only a second to see the reason. As far as the torch's glow could reach blazed a glory of reflected gold. I almost put my hands over my eyes—so brightly gleamed the room before me. I squinted, allowed my eyes to focus and still could not find a single object on which to comfortably settle my gaze. The radiance was too stunning to absorb.

The nearest objects to present themselves clearly were glittering tiaras in a row. Behind them stretched a near-forest of hanging strands of necklaces, jewels and trinkets. A commotion immediately began when three girls converged upon the display, clawing at the baubles and one another in a cacophony of shrieks and insults.

"Stop!" Hegai yelled at the top of his lungs—the first time I had ever heard him raise his voice. "This is one of the kingdom's most important rooms, and you will treat it as such!"

Chastened, the three girls turned around with their arms slack at their sides.

"This is the bounty room," Hegai continued, his tone stern, "where the Crown stores the plunder of three dozen countries until it is needed for royal use. What you see before you includes the fortune of Babylon, gold from the pharaohs, the wealth of Phoeni-cia and countries you've never even heard of. Today, they all lay at your disposal. What you choose to wear, subject only to the dictates of good taste and beauty, will be yours for the keeping. All you can wear out of this chamber is yours."

Then the previous roar of female delight erupted again, and I watched the group break up into countless shrieking, grabbing figures. Several more torches were brought in to illuminate the room's endless reaches as the girls burrowed their way through the rows of piled-up gold jewelry, their voices echoing shrilly across the metal stacks.

I was the last girl to reach the rows. Not only did the girls' behavior disgust me, but I felt at a loss the moment my gaze fell upon the stolen riches of so many conquered nations—no doubt including my own. I walked through the aisles and let my eyes drift across the staggering array of wealth; unlike the others, I felt empty and aimless. From the sounds of gaiety around me, the candidates were finding plenty of trinkets and jewelry, but I saw only gaudy relics. How in the world did they know what to choose? How did they have the least idea what would appeal to Xerxes?

I heard steps behind me and turned to Hegai, who was standing close with a concerned look. "Is everything all right, Star?" he asked.

"Oh certainly, Hegai. I'm just a little overwhelmed, is all."

"I'm watching you, and awe is not what I see in your eyes. Please. Tell me. You haven't selected a single thing. If you do not hurry, all the best pieces will be gone. Despite the amount of spoils here, only a finite number are actually wearable by a young woman."

I took a deep breath and decided to tell him the truth. "Hegai, my problem is this—I can pick out a hundred objects that might have some appeal to me, but what does the *King* like? What does *he* prefer? I won't feel capable of truly pleasing him on that night until I know more about him."

Hegai did not answer. He simply stood there unmoving, the faintest hint of a smile upon his lips, his head shaking slightly. I was becoming concerned, thinking I had violated some unknown protocol. *Why does he not reply*, I asked myself frantically. Finally I spoke up.

"Master Hegai, did I offend you in some way?"

At my words he shook his head more vigorously and began to laugh. "No, no, Star. Far from it. You see, this is the first time a girl, or anyone in the harem for that matter, has ever asked me that simple question. Can you believe it?"

"No. It seems like the first question one would ask."

"Indeed it does, my dear. However, this place does not lend itself to focusing on others, as I'm sure you have noticed by now."

"Well, will you teach me? Or at least give me some idea? I really want to know."

"Yes, Star. I will teach you. And I'll do more than that. You've just solidified your position as my favored candidate. Prepare to move out of your present quarters. I am giving you the double suite and seven handmaidens to serve you, as befits the leading candidate. Your conduct will serve as an example for the other girls, and I will repeatedly exhort them to follow your lead. I'm sure you are equal to the task, are you not, Star?"

Now came my turn to stand and dumbly nod my head yes. I had anticipated being answered with a few sentences of instruction, nothing more. A rumor had circulated at lunch that one of the girls could be chosen as a favorite over time. I had not given it further thought.

But Hegai was not finished. He abruptly grasped my hand and pulled me back into the stacks of jewelry. "I know just the piece for you, dear Star." For a moment, hearing his voice like that, I flashed back to Rachel sifting through her bag of disguises for my first stolen trip out of the house. My eyes misted over at the thought—until Hegai's own rummaging brought me back to the present. He stood up with a triumphant look. "Aha!" He reached over and placed a small metal object on my palm.

"Don't look at it until we leave," he said with a conspirator's smile.

And I did not. I kept my fingers tightly wrapped around the piece until the treasure hunt had ended and I had filed out of the building with the other girls. Nearly a dozen of my peers, seemingly every inch of their bare skin encircled by bracelets and hung with jewels, turned to me with perplexed looks. "Why, Star, you didn't get *anything*!" one of them nearly yelled at me. "Are you stupid?"

I only smiled, and then, when we had left the building's shadow, I allowed my clenched hand to open.

I gasped.

My hand had seemed to report a familiar shape, but I had not dared to believe it. Yet there it was—a Shield of David, six-pointed star, with a precious stone shining from its center.

It was a near replica of the one given me by my father—my one link to the past—which I had been compelled to tearfully leave behind on the morning of my departure for the Palace.

I could almost feel G-d standing just behind me, a smile playing upon His face as He rejoiced at the chance to allow me this un-expected gift. As I had so often recently, I wept silently, grateful for the rich sensation of His presence. Quietly, I averted my face from the others and whispered a humble prayer of thanks.

## Chapter Twenty-five

*A*nd so after just a few dozen nights in my original simple but elegant room, I moved into a luxury suite featuring its own sitting area with a goose-down divan and three deep chairs, a separate bedroom and its own expansive bathroom. Now I truly felt like I was living in a palace. The beauty treatments would now come to me. Instead of waiting in line by the pool, I would lie on my bed and wait for the masseuses to tiptoe in and begun their work.

No, I cannot claim to have been mistreated, that is the honest truth.

My life in the harem house rapidly settled into a very predictable although incredibly pampered routine. I would wake before dawn, change into loose clothing and walk out into the courtyard for some early morning stretching exercises. The excursions also served, of course, as my occasion to meet Mordecai on his way to work at the King's Gate. I would hug him tightly through the gate, my affection for him having only grown deeper with time away from his home, and bring him up-to-date on harem gossip. This, of course, had far less value for him than his Palace gossip held for me. Mordecai seemed to know everything about the endless hierarchies and political game playing behind these marble walls.

In those days Xerxes, who had barely escaped with his life during earlier Grecian Wars with his father, was obsessed with his long-planned counterattack against Athens. More than anything, he wanted to go down in history as the man who conquered Greece. As a result, the Palace was filled with talk of war—was the King's authority stable enough to risk years away in battle? Who would emerge as his key general? And who would serve as High Regent during his absence?

Echoes of these great rivalries reverberated only dimly at the harem; we heard of them and realized their importance yet heard very little of their latest developments. Because much of the time the information Mordecai possessed was even more current than Hegai's, I gained an extra edge—yet another reason why other girls came to speak with me.

I gradually allowed myself to linger longer at the gate with Mordecai. I had little cause to spend much time at the breakfast table. Long after he had left for work I would remain outside and stretch, then find a secluded spot in which to pray. What had once been a ceremonial function—a series of loudly spoken pronouncements, a ritual Mordecai performed in private, one that I had once assumed to be a mumbled series of incantations—had now become an intimate means of communication with a divine presence who now felt closer to me than my own self. I found that I could not pray loudly or formally; I simply conversed with G-d.

Even as my time of private prayer ended each day and I took the morning's myrrh bath, I asked G-d to show me ways of following Him. After drying off, while the masseuse's hands kneaded the fragrant myrrh oil into my back for an hour, I continued silently speaking to Him.

The first time I rose from my hour's massage, my body redolent with myrrh—and realized I would be receiving a similar treatment that afternoon and every afternoon after that for the next six months—I felt like the historic Queen of Sheba Mordecai had taught me about. I could not help but take pleasure in the experience, but ever before me was the destination—one night with the King.

And Hegai, for his part, stayed true to his pledge—he began to periodically, tidbit by tidbit, educate me regarding the King's preferences. Sometimes it would be a hurriedly whispered phrase as he rushed past me at poolside: "He likes women lean; stay true to your diet!" or "When it comes to clothing, simplicity is better; that is for certain." Then, twice in the first six weeks, he appeared at my door and spent several hours discussing the King's personality. It seemed like almost a welcome outlet for him—a place to express his opinions on countless royal subjects with little fear of reprisal.

Xerxes, by Hegai's account, was surprisingly insecure for being the ruler of all the civilized world. As a result, he could be given to wild whims and erratic behavior depending on who was influencing him at the moment. Paranoid about being assassinated, he was constantly on the watch for signs of loyalty or treachery. Either one could bring wildly varying reactions.

As for matters of the bedroom, Hegai knew far less, yet more than anyone else. Xerxes was an adventurous lover, I was told—assuming he truly fancied the girl. He had spent his youth with captured beauties from Alexandria, Damascus and Cush and had found that a woman in fear for her life made for a vivacious and compliant partner. This knowledge tended to make him act gruff and intimidating.

"The governing paradox of sexual love," Hegai told me, "is that the quickest way to ruin your own pleasure is making it your first priority. Center your attentions on your partner's bliss, and your own will find expression along with it."

I smiled warmly at advice like this, for it conformed so well with my overall philosophy toward the King. *Focus on him. Focus on him.*

It had been our elderly friend Jacob's refrain, and now it would be mine.

"Be willing to try anything, but remember that your artless virginity is also part of capturing His Majesty's interest. You must be both maiden and harlot as the moment calls for," Hegai told me on another occasion.

I agonized before G-d about the morality of the whole encounter. Could I be considered married to Xerxes at the occasion of my deflowering? Regarding this dilemma I received no clear word, no definitive response from on high. But over time, I became convinced in my spirit that I was doing my very best, that I was here for a good reason. A reason that would reveal itself over time.

And Mordecai confirmed this in his hurried and whispered conferences with me each morning. He quoted passages from the Song of Solomon to guide my thinking and preparation.

As for my seven maids, I resolved to treat them like younger sisters, like the female companions I had never had. I shared bits of news and Palace conjecture with them and elicited their stories one by one during late-night discussions in my suite. I assured them that if they had not already been in royal service, all of them would have made superb Queen candidates—I am not certain they all believed me, but I think they appreciated the sentiment.

Afternoons were long, languid stretches at the harem. Many girls spent time in the sun by the pool, adding a deep suntan to their diminishing list of physical attributes, since Hegai had explained that the King preferred fair-skinned women. Others caught up on any beauty treatments that they had happened to miss during the morning hours.

I spent much of my afternoon time engaging in a clandestine activity: reading books from the royal library. Since, as you know, Persian women are not supposed to know how to read, I had my handmaidens discreetly bring various scrolls and parchments on the pretext of a mission for Hegai. Then they would deliver them to me out in the thickest part of the garden, across from the eunuchs' house. There I would curl up on a thick mat of fallen banana leaves and devour works of history and philosophy.

Or at least pretend to.

What I was really doing there, besides doing a bit of perfunctory brush-up work on my reading skills, was watching for an opportunity to make contact with Jesse.

I had first inquired about him on my third day there and learned that all eunuchs would convalesce for a week before beginning their training and would not join us for another few months.

That was far too long. I cared about Jesse, although the chaos of my capture and subsequent adapting to my new environment had largely crowded him from my mind. Our kiss on the gryphon statue had taken place a relatively brief time before, yet it now seemed like it had happened in another lifetime, to another person. Now that I had given myself time to reflect, I remembered how things had changed so dramatically between us in those days just before his capture. For years he had merely been the annoying young boy who tagged along with his grandmother. While entertaining to a lonely, isolated girl, he had been little more than a pest with dubious hygiene. Then he had become a friend. And puberty had added yet a new dimension.

I had noticed even before the kiss how Jesse was growing into a lanky, handsome young man. But the kiss seemed to have released something within me. I felt like I had been suddenly introduced to a whole new crop of emotions. My future as a woman, once a barren and worrisome set of images in my mind, now began to include brief, tentative scenes of being Jesse's wife. I had discovered, much to my surprise, that the scenarios did not displease me.

Thinking of it there in the orchard, I shook my head in disbelief. How drastically things had changed! Now I was promised—if not in marriage then at least in body—to the King of Persia, a flamboyantly jealous ruler. And Jesse was now sadly shorn of much that had once made him a man and a husband-to-be. Yet I cared for him deeply nevertheless, and I determined that I could not allow us to exist so close to each other without making at least an attempt to see him.

## Chapter Twenty-six

One afternoon in the orchard I rolled up my parchment, set it down on the leaves and began to weave my way through tree trunks to the edge of the old unused gate I had discovered during my first day's explorations. I had heard voices earlier, and sure enough, some of the young men were playing a game of catch with some sort of inflated animal bladder. They wore only swatches of linen tied around their waists; their bodies resembled those of every other lean, muscular young boy I had ever spied from my old rooftop. I stopped and stared for a moment and found myself surprisingly taken with what I saw. For the moment, their grim fates were forgotten—they leaped, ran and wrestled one another with all the fervor and impetuousness of typical male youth. They were beautiful; I had to admit it. The loss of their manhood had not yet made its effect known upon their bodies.

Jesse, once again, was not among them.

Finally the game broke up and most of the young men dispersed, leaving only an exhausted pair languishing upon the marble terrace. I stepped out just enough for them to see part of me, then lifted my fingers to my lips indicating quiet.

One of the boys cocked his head and frowned earnestly in my direction. I stepped out just a bit farther and waved, adding a small smile. He elbowed his companion. The two scrambled to their feet and began to carefully make their way forward into the trees. Finally they came within a few cubits of me. Their eyes were wide as saucers. Either their training had led them to fear the females of the species or they were aware of the possible consequences of this little meeting. Maybe both. Strangely, I felt no fear—tension, but no fear.

"Who are you?" one of them asked, his voice sounding strangely high pitched.

"I am Star, a Queen candidate from next door."

"Do you know what kind of trouble you could drag us all into with this kind of contact?"

I shook my head. "No, although I know it wouldn't exactly be permitted. But I have a question for you, and then I'll never bother you again. Where is Jesse? Is he here? Is he all right?"

The tallest one, closest to me, winced at the mention of Jesse's name and looked down to the ground.

"Are you a friend of his?"

"Yes, I am."

"Jesse is not doing well. He is inside, in bed, and has been there since the day of his arrival. He—well, he is deeply despondent and will not move. He has been beaten several times to get him going, but that has only made matters worse."

"What will happen to him?" I asked, feeling the pull of dread within me.

"I'm not sure. If he does not get better, it could range from simply releasing him to his family to executing him. It depends on how exasperated the head eunuchs become."

I took a deep breath and made a rash decision. "Please get me in to him."

"Are you crazy? The whole place is filled with eunuchs in training. We couldn't sneak in a horsefly."

"Fine. Then take me in through the front door. I am the lead Queen candidate and have the favor of Hegai, head harem eunuch. I will take my chances."

The two boys glanced at each other grimly. The taller one sighed heavily. "The others are in a protocol training session that just started. We're missing it ourselves. You just might make it in undetected."

"Yes. Let's go."

They both shrugged at the same moment and turned back for their building. I followed closely, trying to hide behind their broad backs. We crossed the marble, entered through a side door and found ourselves in a stone hallway much like the one in my harem abode. I could hear a man's voice loudly haranguing from a nearby room, and I steered away. The lead boy motioned to a closed door with a jerk of his chin. I raised my hand in thanks and waved them off, then entered the room. Curtains were drawn; the space stood in a deep gloom. I paused for a moment to let my eyes adjust, then moved forward.

"Jesse?" My voice felt small and weak against the despair that seemed to pervade the room. Finally the shape of a bed resolved in my vision, then the form of a body in the blankets, sitting upright.

"Hadassah?" The voice was only vaguely familiar, a breathier, weaker version of Jesse's once vibrant baritone.

"Yes, it's me," I answered and suddenly found myself lunging to his side, my throat constricting in the effort not to cry. I felt my way around his shoulders and wrapped him in a spontaneous hug, nudging my face into his neck to hide my grief.

"What in the world are you doing here?" he asked. I realized only then that he had no idea I had been taken. How could he? My capture had occurred after his own.

"I'm staying right next door," I replied. "I was taken as a Queen candidate just two days after you were captured. In fact, I'm here in a way because of what happened to you." I tried hard to control the emotions I was feeling.

He pushed my shoulders back and took a close look at me, his gaze piercing and deeply troubled. "What do you mean?"

"When your grandmother came over and told us you were missing, Mordecai realized right away what had happened. He told her, very carefully, very reluctantly. But I became so upset that I ran out. I lost my mind; I ran all the way to the portico. The gryphon statue."

Jesse's expression softened. "I'll always remember that, Hadassah."

"Me too. But on my way home, I was cornered by an army patrol. They were with the King's agent in Susa, and they decided I would make a good candidate, so they gave me two days' notice, after which they hauled me up to the citadel. I've been nearby ever since."

He shook his head, wide-eyed, as though I had told him something impossible. I could tell he considered his ordeal so terrible that he could not imagine my being anywhere close to him.

"They've given me a new name," he said mournfully.

"Yes, they also have done so for me. Mine is Star."

"I am now Hathach. I hate it. My real name came from the line of David. I don't even know where Hathach came from. For all I know, it is some pagan god."

I placed my hand on his arm. "Please, Jesse, it will be all right. You're in good company. Remember our Jewish brothers Daniel, Hananiah, Mishael and Azariah? They were all given pagan names when they entered royal service. And look how G-d remained with them and used them to accomplish His purposes. Besides—you will always be Jesse to me."

He smiled at me then, and I felt a flood of gratitude for him and his presence with me there in that intimidating place.

"Oh, Jesse," I wept in spite of myself, "I can't believe what has happened to us! One minute we're young people with all of life before us, and the next we're committed to—you know . . ."

My words seemed too much for him to absorb. He looked away from me, down at the floor. How much life had been drained from him in those few short weeks! He had been a mischievous boy with a gentle soul. He had been growing into the kind of man who would walk through town with his head held high and a marked twinkle in his eye. The kind of man everybody liked.

Now I could not distinguish his expression from that of the blind beggar Mordecai had once invited home for dinner. Empty, hopeless and despondent.

I grasped him by the shoulders and shook him gently, lowering my head to try and capture his vacant gaze. "Listen, Jesse. You have to stay strong, for me—for both of us! I need you, do you hear me? I need your support if I'm going to make it through this!"

He rested his stare on me, only slightly roused from his stupor. He finally spoke in a voice barely above a whisper. "Hadassah, you've never needed me a day in your life. You are so strong; you just never knew it. I imagine you'll find out now. If anything, I've needed *you.*"

"But that's not true! Especially now. Please, Jesse. Please get better. Listen, I've already become the favored candidate—I have privileges, I have Hegai's ear. I can help, I can get away to meet you, I can do a lot of things if you'll just get up out of this bed."

He laughed softly. "My shy little Hadassah—Queen of Persia. Wouldn't that be ironic?" Then he smiled weakly, laid his head back on the pillow and gave my hand a long squeeze. I took that as hope for tomorrow and crept away. Thank G-d, no one saw me leave.

## Chapter Twenty-seven

And so my peculiar afternoon ritual took shape.

I returned to my room that day feeling like someone had reached into my heart, grabbed it tightly and squeezed it without mercy. Jesse's demeanor had the specter of death to it. I did not even try to imagine how he had suffered. The mere thought of a boyishly innocent personality like his being thrown into that kind of cruelty filled my veins with ice water. I knew the feeling, of course. I knew how it felt to have a child's trusting heart shattered by the hatred and violence of men. But I had thought I was the only one in the world to live through such a thing.

In the week that followed, I slipped away to Jesse's area with gifts of foods the eunuchs could not receive—luscious fruits, meats, exotic candies and pastries. Eventually I was hearing encouraging reports of Jesse's recovery. And then came the wonderful day when he met me himself, looking more like the Jesse I knew and loved. So another tradition was established. Jesse would meet me and we would visit briefly, tentatively. Sometimes our meeting place would be empty, so I would leave behind presents along with encouraging notes.

And I noticed gradual improvement in Jesse's alertness. He began to smile more often. His sentences grew longer.

Of course, I had told Mordecai the very next morning about my visit. He uttered a deep sigh of relief upon hearing my report; not because he considered my words good news, but because it was enough just knowing Jesse was alive. Rachel would be so relieved, he told me. And I knew from the words he chose that Mordecai would not reveal to her the full extent of her grandson's state. Then his old fear returned just as quickly. "Don't get caught crossing boundaries," he warned. "And remember. Do not let them know you are a Jew." I simply nodded my agreement once again and kissed him on the cheek.

Despite his fears, the next morning Mordecai met me with a package from Rachel: a small satchel filled with dates and several sentimental knickknacks. Jesse's eyes filled with life upon receiving it, giving me my very first glimpse at the Jesse of old.

After the five hundred new eunuchs had been introduced to the candidates they had been castrated to serve, as I already told you, Jesse had begun to join me in the orchard for our afternoon talks. Very soon, these times started to rival my morning meetings with Mordecai as my most anticipated and encouraging encounter of the day. I would often bring treats from Rachel smuggled in via Mordecai, and he would tease me with memories of our childhood. It was not long before Jesse had completed his training as a eunuch, and the time had come for him and his colleagues to begin their duties.

Jesse and I resolved never to reveal our acquaintance, for the fact seemed fraught with potential consequences. But it was difficult not to cheer or applaud when the crowd of young men was presented to the candidates at poolside! I avoided even the slightest eye contact with him from across the terrace, afraid that even that small connection would somehow give away our friendship.

A collective groan came from the young women when Hegai explained that because of the closeness in ages, the eunuchs would all serve the young candidates at large instead of being assigned to one girl. I had hoped, of course, to somehow have Jesse assigned to my detail. But perhaps it was for the best.

The weeks and months passed, each day essentially the same as the one before. Besides being a Queen candidate and enjoying the luxurious lifestyle it entailed, I now had a secret bodyguard—Jesse, who would gladly fight to the death anyone who so much as looked askance at me—and I had the ear of Hegai, the royal eunuch. The days of long massages and myrrh treatments flowed into one another. Then, suddenly, they were over.

Then the second regimen began—perfumes and spices.

Only the discipline of my daily prayer time kept me from self-centered hedonism.

Somewhere around the seventh month, I felt myself beginning to lose sight of what life had been like before I was waited on hand and foot, before my sole responsibility was to submit myself to hours of baths, massages and cosmetic treatments. I could understand how the other girls, without the support and the spiritual foundation I enjoyed, could lose their emotional bearings entirely.

And lose them they did. I saw girls berate Hegai because a rain-shower had interrupted their sunbathing. I saw them tease a girl nearly into killing herself because she had darker skin than the others—ignoring the fact that their own poolside hours had rendered their skin several shades darker than before. I saw them divide into cliques that exhibited as much sullen hostility toward one another as rival armies. Had our compound been consumed by fire, I doubted some days who would have deigned to rescue whom.

I must admit that I denied myself very few of the pleasures of being the favored candidate. The higher standing afforded me extra beauty treatments—milk baths, extra massages and hours of facial cosmetic experiments. I do not think a single caravan passed through Susa from the exotic lands of East and West without one of my handmaidens scouring them for something I might employ. In the course of that year my face and body underwent the ministrations of sea sponges from Tyre, scrubbing salts from the Dead Sea, olive skins from Judea, coral sand from Egypt, ground fish scales from the Red Sea and more liniments and potions from Indus and the Orient than I could count. I learned how to outline and shadow my eyes with Egyptian kohl and galena, blush my cheeks with mulberry juice, redden my lips with flecks of iron oxide and stain my fingernails and toenails with crushed henna. I learned how to crouch for hours, a thick blanket around my body, over a small urn spewing out the sweet smoke of myrrh and incense. Before long, even my hair smelled of incense.

And throughout, Hegai continued to instruct me in the King's desires. One of his chief pieces of advice I will pass on to you. You most likely are a virgin, and I hope you are, but since the King is far from virginal, the biggest factor you must overcome is his jadedness. He has seen and enjoyed every sort of female body. He is experienced in every lovemaking technique ever developed—from India to Greece. He has heard every come-on phrase, endured every coy approach the mind of a young woman can invent.

So what do you do?

Well, it's simple, actually. If the King suffers from an excess of invention and artifice, then go the other direction. Be as simple, as straightforward, as you possibly can. Rely on what G-d gave you, not the treasury or the royal wardrobe. That is the strategy that— well, I know you know the outcome of this story, but I will hold its details in reserve nevertheless.

As time grew short, Hegai even began to instruct me in the sexual practices the King preferred. Since I was the most ignorant of possible virgins, the mere fact of intercourse took days for me to absorb. I seemed to live in a state of perpetual embarrassment. But how much more there was! Every new revelation, every new technique revealed took days of shock in order to accept.

After one particular session with Hegai, I found myself deeply despondent. I had no idea my body was supposed to be used in this manner—the thoroughness of my preparation was exposing me to facts from which the other girls had been spared, and no doubt for good reason.

While Jesse and I strolled beside the East Wall that afternoon, I asked him: was I right to submit to this kind of exploitation from a pagan? Or was I supposed to refuse him and accept my death? Did the Jewish code by which I vowed to live mention a penalty for an act some might label fornication—even though it was coerced?

Jesse said nothing for a long while. But even as we made our way beneath the trees and beside more gardens, I could tell his mind was furiously at work. At last he turned to me.

"Hadassah," he said, using the Jewish name he employed only when we were alone, "the Torah tells us to do, and not do, many things. One of the things it tells us to do is be fruitful and multiply. Well, what the King's men did left me incapable of obeying that commandment. Does that make me a nonperson? A non-Jew?"

"Of course not."

"Well, thank you. But why not? After all, I am violating a commandment."

"Because you have no choice in the matter. You did not surrender your manhood willingly. It was taken from you by force, under pain of death."

"Exactly. And so it is with your virginity."

A weight seemed to lift itself from my shoulders and waft away in the breeze. I reached over and gave him a quick squeeze about the neck. "You're right, of course. Oh, Jesse, I am so glad you're here."

He looked down with a scowl. "Yes, but after you go in to the King . . . Suppose you're chosen."

"Let us *hope* I am chosen. It is the only way any of this will have meaning. Jesse, somehow I believe all of this is part of my destiny—even though I don't understand it all yet."

"Yes, but you'll be taken away forever," Jesse interrupted. "These walks of ours will end. I won't see you anymore."

"Are you out of your mind?" I asked. "Being Queen only gives me more power to do as I wish, to do good. The Queen of Persia can visit an old friend anytime she wishes. I could name you to my personal detail. I could even have you released to your family."

He smiled wistfully at the last suggestion. "Yes, but as what? A man who cannot marry, who cannot start a family? No, I fear I am condemned to being a royal eunuch for the rest of my life. And still, I have hope. I have this stubborn sense that my life has meaning, that I am doing an important work in helping you remain safe and your identity protected."

"You know something, Jesse," I said as tenderly as I could, "I asked Hegai the meaning of your Persian name—I did it casually enough," I said at his look of consternation. "He told me 'Hathach' means 'The Good One,' and this you truly are." I clasped his hand, and he smiled.

"Well, anyway—as Queen, I can do many things to make your life, and ours, far easier."

He turned to face me and flashed a grin. "You just win, all right?"

I knew then that being chosen Queen was the only way my life—or his—would ever be made right. Beyond that, it was in YHWH's hands.

## *Chapter Twenty-eight*

*I* put the same question to Mordecai on the following morning. Was I defiling myself by allowing that first night to go forward?

Mordecai's response was immediate and profound. He obviously had been thinking—and praying—much about this. He shook his head and replied, "No, Hadassah. A thousand times no. G-d gave us the law to guide our choices, not guarantee our outcomes. You never chose this fate for yourself. You will not approach the King's bed voluntarily but as someone whose life might be required of her if she refuses. And even then, I do not want you to act reluctantly or sullenly for him. Act as though he will certainly be your husband, my dear. Remember how many arranged marriages happen these days. Well, perhaps your heavenly Father has also 'arranged' this one—who knows? Think of that other bride who did not know her husband—Rebekah. Do you remember her story?"

"Yes, Mordecai," I nodded.

"Well, Rebekah did not know Isaac, and yet she trusted in the fact that God had ordained their union. And it turned out to be one of the most important and successful marriages of all time. Besides, you might even find something about the King appealing."

"But what about the law? What about the proscriptions against fornication?"

"My dear, fornication is the willful flaunting of G-d's commands concerning the confining of sexual intimacy to marriage. I do not think that is what you will be doing. Like I said, you focus on making godly choices within the course available to you, and He will guide you. I do not know why G-d allowed you to be taken in such a manner. I do not know His mind or His intricate reasons. But I know He has a purpose for you. I am convinced He has placed you here deliberately. And the only way you can aid that purpose is to do your best in everything you attempt. That includes competing to be Queen with all the skill and planning you can bring to this endeavor. As Queen you will be his wife, a most honorable and worthy position under Jewish law."

I almost laughed in amazement. "I never thought you and I would ever have such a conversation."

"I know, dear Hadassah. It is so far from what I hoped for you, or anticipated." Grief colored his voice and brought tears to my eyes.

I sighed with the heaviness of a woman carrying burdens beyond belief. "I pictured myself marrying a good Jewish young man—Jesse, since he was practically the only one I knew—then settling down to have children and raise a family."

"I hoped as much for you, dear. But, you know, I learned long ago, after the deaths of our families, that sometimes we have to live with far less than our highest wish. Yet even then, G-d walks through the disappointment with us. We are not second-class persons to Him just because our lives have taken us to some low places—some of them of our own making, some of them not. I believe even then He can do mighty things through us. He can reveal a purpose for our suffering. Your story is not over, Hadassah. In fact, I'm convinced it has hardly even begun."

I threw myself into Mordecai's arms and held him as tightly as I could. How grateful I was for him at that moment! I think G-d knew I would never have survived without my beloved poppa's daily encouragement.

But the sadness . . . I thought back, still grasping him tightly, to the days when I was just a girl languishing inside his warm, comfortable home. Days when my biggest concern was the weather permitting me to spend time in the garden or having to eat Rachel's horrible lentil soup for lunch. Those days now lurked around the edges of my mind like some imagined folk tale, the invented story of some other girl in some other time.

But I could not afford to spend my time pining for that past time in my life. The present demanded all I could give. And more.

And that is why I vowed to master even the subject of the intimacy of the marriage bed to the best of my ability. I resolved that I simply had to win this competition and become Queen. Winning would be my vindication and would restore my honor. Beyond that, I did not know. I would emerge as possibly the most influential woman in the world—nearly unthinkable—or a discarded woman living in the high-class equivalent of a brothel.

Now, please understand—my determination to win did not mean my efforts would resort to mean-spirited and underhanded tactics like some of the other girls. But I certainly planned to avail myself of every advantage offered me. That included winning a place of affection in the other girls' hearts, rather than alienating or subduing them. I routinely made my seven handmaidens—whom I never could have kept busy anyway—available to serve the other candidates, provided they treated them with respect. I hosted in my suite overnight some of the candidates who had not won the greatest popularity and suffered under the shadow of obscurity within the harem. I made my cosmetics and beauty aids available to all. I passed on advice to those who asked me for it. ·

And in so doing—you must understand this—I did not dilute or weaken my position but rather underscored my standing as the most deserving candidate in the minds of most of the girls in the harem. That perception, I was to discover, would be invaluable to me.

I hope, of course, that as a follower of YHWH you recognize how this plan was scriptural, as well. The Sacred Texts teach us to love God supremely, to honor our parents, to not lie or cheat or steal. When we follow these commandments, I believe He ordains our path so that what might seem like weakness turns to our advantage. Obeying His laws, I was beginning to learn, put me within a heartbeat of being transformed from a peasant into a princess—from a commoner into a queen.

Although not dressed for stealth, and in spite of his girth, the man moved swiftly and silently through the darkened orchards and gardens that lined the outer walls of the Royal Palace. The fringe of vegetation had given him a perfect cover all the way from the King's Gate to the proximity of the candidates' house. Now, within sight of the moon-shrouded dormitories, he began to slow his progress and watch.

He did not have to wait long. The figure of a girl tiptoed past the pool and moved carefully away from the marble's edge into the gloom of the nearby orchard. She walked up to him with her arms folded before her—whether for warmth or as a buffer against her unease was impossible for the hidden watcher to tell.

They spoke in the softest of whispers.

"What can I do for you, sir?" Her voice held just the faintest tremor, though the words were cold enough.

"First of all, you need to realize that I know who your father, Carshena, is. I know his aspirations—though he is a prince, he wants more."

"What aspirations? He wants me to be the Queen—that's only natural for someone of royal lineage."

"Do not patronize me, you little fool. Everyone in the kingdom knows what the Princes of the Face scheme every hour of the day.

That's why your father forged your family papers and has kept your family connections a secret."

"Are—are you going to tell Hegai about me?" This time the tremor was unmistakable.

"No. That is, not if you do exactly as I say. We can create our own special arrangement, one that is mutually beneficial. The fact is, I will soon be king."

"You are teasing me, sir," she replied in a shocked voice. "Royal subjects should not speak this way, especially within Palace walls."

"Listen, girl, I have royal guards on my side and an army of men set to enter Susa. I *will* be king. So working with me will not exactly be the worst thing that could happen to you."

"What do you want from *me*?"

"Just two things. First, I want you to keep your eyes and ears open. I want to know if any of the candidates are Jewish."

"What is that?"

"You know. Hebrew. One of the Israelites."

"Oh, yes."

"If you find one, I want you to tell me. The Jews are a filthy and rebellious people, an internal threat to Persia and to my plans for the Empire. And then I want you to use this"—and he held up a small flask that reflected the light shining off the pool water—"to assure their failure and that of any other rival you consider especially formidable. It is not life threatening; it will simply make them very sick for a day or two. Enough to wipe out a competitor's night with the King. Can you do that?"

The girl nodded quickly. "Anything that keeps another candidate from winning, I am more than ready for. I want to be Queen more than I want to breathe."

"Good. And who knows: maybe if you don't become Xerxes' queen, you can be mine. You are quite delectable. You'll last a lot longer on the throne that way, anyhow. As I said, I'll be King of Persia before the year is out. In any case, your family will fare much better if I have your cooperation." As her eyes widened in fear, he finished with, "Now go, my lovely. Be on your way and be on the lookout for the signal of our next meeting."

She nodded in semi-shock and walked away. The man stood still for a long moment, either relishing the outcome of the conversation or watching for signs of detection or both. Finally he sighed and hurried off.

The man had not looked up, however. Even had he done so, he might have missed the intent eyes and hidden form of a eunuch who was resting in the crook of a tree, sheltered from sight by the massive trunk of a gnarled ornamental pine. The young man had seen the clandestine encounter and, concerned for the candidates' security, had sat watching mere yards from where the two plotters had stood.

Eyes staring wide in shock and amazement, the eunuch slid down the trunk and soundlessly ran back toward his own quarters.

The very next day I met Jesse for another of our afternoon talks. He seemed morose, even despairing. While I came up expecting my usual hug, he sat cross-legged, staring at the ground. I was not even sure he had noticed my arrival. I immediately sat next to him and leaned close.

"What is the matter, O Longface?" I began, trying to humor him.

Then he looked up and into my eyes and I saw that jest was out of the question today.

"You have to win," he said in a lifeless voice.

"Well, yes. We've already established that, haven't we? Even my father, Mordecai, has told me that."

"No. You *have* to win. It is a matter of life and death."

"Why are you being so melodramatic?" I leaned back to better view his expression. "What in the world are you talking about?"

"Two reasons. First of all, over in the concubines' quarters, another one of them killed herself yesterday." Jesse stopped and looked away from me. "She hung herself from the ceiling by a knot in the very same dress she wore on her last night with the King."

His voice had dropped almost to a whisper.

I remember the feeling of horror and pity that nearly overwhelmed me.

"The concubines' house is a sad place, Hadassah," Jesse finally continued when I could not bring myself to respond. "Far different from the candidates' harem. I mean, to those on the outside it seems luxurious and secure. But these women sit around all day watching their lives go by, waiting in vain for the King to summon them. Did you know he has to invite them *by name* back to the Palace, or they will never go there again? That means if he does not remember you from your very first night with him, you are doomed. And Xerxes has his favorites. Two-thirds of the women are never called on unless he gets restless and bored. They sit around gossiping and complaining and tormenting their servants in order to pass the time. It's a place of bitterness and rejection. And worse. Another concubine was executed last week for slander against the King. She was passing on bedroom secrets, actually. But word of it slipped to the wrong people. I'm telling you—under the pampered-looking surface, life is not worth dung in these places. I would die for you rather than see you end up there."

"Oh, Jesse," I mourned, "don't talk that way." Remembering there were two reasons, I reached to touch his arm. "Is the other as bad as this one?"

"No. It's worse. You have to win because there is a plot underway in the Palace, and one of your competitors is part of it. If she and the people behind her have their way, any strong candidate will be poisoned, and every Jewish candidate could be killed. And after that, King Xerxes will be assassinated."

This time I shuddered. "Are you just trying to frighten me, Jesse?"

He shook his head with an expression that made the truth of it very clear. "I wish I were, Hadassah. But I have a friend who overheard it with his very own ears. A large, powerfully dressed man came and gave this girl a flask of poison to make every leading candidate sick before her first night. He was plotting for her to become Queen and join some imminent treasonous scheme. He told her to report back to him with the name of any candidate who is Jewish. And he told her he'd become King very, very soon. The implication was he would do away with all Jews as soon as he assumed power."

"This is terrible," I whispered. "What can we do? Maybe I can tell Hegai. He respects me. Maybe we can find out who she is and have her expelled, or—"

"You cannot expel her. You cannot because her name is Misgath and her true father is one of the Princes of the Face."

I sat very still and thought for a long time. I knew Misgath, and as I pictured her, her involvement surprised me but little. Misgath seemed to be a dour, spiteful girl with a perpetual scowl and a superior attitude. She mostly kept to herself, which no doubt was a relief to the rest of the young women.

"What about the man? Can we tell—"

"The other eunuch did not recognize him. The only thing about him that he could see in the darkness was some kind of strange insignia tattooed on his arm. Some kind of *X*—he wasn't sure if it was a royal sign for Xerxes, except that the arms were twisted and broken off at the ends."

I gasped and felt my body go cold. *"A twisted cross?"* I asked, hardly able to draw enough air into my lungs to form the words.

"I suppose you could call it that."

I suddenly found myself actually struggling to breathe. The twisted cross was no longer a distant memory, a fleeting symbol.

*It is growing closer.* The panic felt like a rope about my neck.

"So what do you want me to do?" I finally asked, my voice now leveled by a grim sense of resolve.

"Win. That's the best thing you can do. Win the King's favor and become his queen. That is our only hope—for you, for your family and mine, for the Jews of Persia."

The stakes had now risen, I realized as I made my way back to my suite.

# Chapter Twenty-nine

*F*inally the year-long preparation was coming to a close. I suppose it would sound jaded and ungrateful to say that I had grown weary of hour-long baths, massages, herbal treatments and cosmetics sessions. But I can say that if she must experience it every day, day in and day out for a year, a girl can grow weary of almost anything.

By the end of that first year I was a different girl than the simple, wide-eyed commoner who had been brought into the Palace twelve months before. I walked differently. Talked differently. I looked different. I knew the special diet had given my body a leanness and maturity that radiated forth with every movement. I certainly smelled different. I had even begun to notice that Mordecai, who doused himself daily and whom I had always considered the height of refinement, now smelled earthy to my transformed nostrils. The truth is, it had taken me a whole year to reach Palace standards of readiness for the King. And the efforts had borne fruit.

The candidates' harem nearly throbbed with nervousness and

anticipation of what came next. No one knew who would be called first; no one wanted to be that first girl, either. Rumors abounded, most of which only added to the fears and uncertainties.

Those last months were filled with frantic scrambling for goals yet unmet—losing extra weight, choosing proper facial paint and hairstyle—and also selecting the wardrobe and accessories. Since every girl would be allowed to keep the accessories she wore that night, and since we had free rein of the royal treasury from which to make this selection, this last item ranked among the most hotly contested of the year.

I did not attend the girls' next field trip to the bounty room, but Jesse described for me the mad dash into the piles and racks of hanging necklaces, diamond earrings and rings captured from nations across the world. He chuckled as he told me of the clawing, the screaming, even a near stampede for one particularly long and thick strand of pure gold that hung from the neck of a marble mannequin.

I stayed away because, as I've already indicated, I had a different plan. It consisted of wearing a simple gown and only one adornment. Having heard Hegai's repeated descriptions of the King's interests, I came up with the idea myself, then shared it with Hegai. His eyes lit up, and he laughed out loud. "His Majesty will be most pleased, I'm thinking."

Then he patted me on the back and strode off. I took his response as his vote of approval.

I planned to enter wearing a simple silk gown of pale blue and a single piece of jewelry. And that I intended to leave behind as a gift—the means by which to remember my name.

ROYAL BEDROOM—INNER COURT—SUSA

King Xerxes of Persia threw back his third wine goblet, gulped down the remaining liquid and swore loudly. He had forsworn carnal relations for longer than he ever had since puberty, all in the hopes of being ready for tonight and the nights to follow with this new crop of candidates. Now he'd been forced to wait so long on the girl that in the meantime he'd surely drunk away his potency. *She'd better be wonderful*, he thought.

"Is she coming?" His slurred shout echoed across the vast marble floor and seemed to rise into the towering ceiling.

The twenty-cubit-tall door to his room opened and threw torch-light into the draped silk curtains of his bed's canopy. Memucan entered. Neither the aide's stride nor the rest of his body betrayed anything of his news. He reached the bed and glanced down at his hands, which clutched together seemingly of their own accord.

"Your Majesty, the girl has become . . . ill."

*"What?"*

Memucan suddenly adopted a paternal, indulgent expression. "She is very beautiful, I will attest, but she is sixteen and, I fear . . . a bit . . . delicate."

"So what is it—is she expelling her dinner at this very moment?"

"No, your Majesty. That occurred a short while ago. It could just be her nerves getting the better of her."

"Well, unless she is in the middle of a seizure, I want her brought in here." He hurled the goblet down to the floor, where it rattled loudly in the empty chamber. "Have guards carry her in if need be. My word, all she has to do—"

"It shall be," answered Memucan quickly; he then turned on his heel and left the room.

Xerxes threw back his head onto the pillow and sent another long groan up into the heights of the room. He lay there until the light emerged again and two silhouetted figures tiptoed his way. His curiosity forced him to grudgingly raise his torso and swing his legs over the bed for a better view.

The first thing he saw was reflections of light bouncing off gold. Was it some sort of golden scabbard advancing toward him? Xerxes furrowed his brow for a better look. Yes, a head did emerge from the cuirass of precious metal—a petite set of features framed by a large mass of brown hair. Memucan was right, he admitted almost reluctantly. She *was* beautiful.

The girl reached the edge of the canopy ledge and looked up, her gleaming hazel eyes stretched wide in terror. The girl was clad from head to foot in golden necklaces, baubles and clasps.

She bowed her head. "Your Majesty" came a small, breathy voice.

"Memucan," called Xerxes to the retreating sage. "From the look of things, I must be allowing the candidates to keep all the jewelry we put on them."

"Yes, your Majesty, although I would call it rather the jewelry they put on *themselves*."

Xerxes laughed noisily, enjoying the slight of treating the girl like she was not even present. "Yes, Memucan. I think you're right." He waved his advisor off and stood above the girl. He did not wish to be cruel to her, but the gall of piling on a fortune's worth of jewelry and then adopting the whine of a wounded lamb thoroughly irritated him. "Approach me. What is your name?"

"Olandra of Parthia, your Majesty," she gasped out.

"Well, Olandra, if you find me frightening now—"

But as Memucan reached the door, the unmistakable sounds of the poor young thing being sick once more brought him up short, and in the end Xerxes watched in disgust as Memucan ushered her out the door.

Because every candidate went to live at the permanent concubines' house rather than the candidates' harem after her first night, I did not see Olandra again. As a result it took several days for the news to filter back to us at her old home.

How long she remained with Xerxes was a matter of some dispute, but the fact that she had been unceremoniously escorted on her way after retching on the bedchamber floor was a fact. (We also heard that he had ordered all her jewelry stripped from her and returned to the display room.)

The news of this humiliating episode struck the candidates' harem like a thunderbolt. Most of the girls had intended to employ a strategy quite similar to Olandra's—to pile on the jewelry, slather on the cosmetics, lacquer their hair into an ornate sculpture and let Xerxes gape in awe at what a wondrous creation had found her way to him. He must not have been impressed, or would she not be given a second chance when she was over her illness?

Olandra's sorry experience confirmed to me that my plan was the correct one. So while the other girls gathered in huddles to reconceive their approach, I retired to my suite in order to work on the last part of my preparations, the one everyone seemed to be overlooking. The *mind*.

As little as I knew about such matters, it might require more than just abject submission to ignite Xerxes' passion, I reasoned. What about setting his mind ablaze? Everyone was aware that he had enjoyed the services of the one-hundred-strong concubines' corps for years; he must be accustomed to willing and compliant partners. Therefore, I gathered, sexual cooperation meant nothing. It would take all my youth, all my beauty *and* all my thinking processes and knowledge to give me a chance at being his queen. Toward that end I worked on my state of mind and my soul.

I not only prayed for composure before the King but asked G-d to give me, when the time came, a freedom from fear and revulsion, or even an unquenchable desire for the man.

At first the prayer had seemed misguided, even a little sacrilegious. First of all, enamoring a man who treated women as objects would be difficult at best. But it soon came to me that women like Olandra—by their attire and approach to the King—confirmed that they should be viewed only as objects. I found the avarice of it all a blatant abuse of the King's generosity. Clearly, Xerxes was a difficult man, but just as surely, the unfortunate girl had done her part to antagonize him.

My second misgiving concerned whether or not it was right to ask G-d for help in such matters. I had no idea. I carefully asked Mordecai on one morning's walk, and he repeated that I was to perform in every part of my life with all the effort and excellence I had to offer. Anything less was an affront to YHWH and to His purposes for me. He reminded me again of the Sacred Texts of Solomon, especially the part where King Solomon with a thousand wives fell in love with the simplicity of a shepherd girl, and he advised me to follow its instructions concerning the marriage bed.

So I continued with my plan. I held my image of King Xerxes from the banquet in the forefront of my mind at all times. Though the actual details of our physical contact remained hazy, as though someone had smudged the image with a moistened finger, I imagined being tenderly embraced by the King, returning his kisses.

I found that soon I began to desire the King in a wide variety of ways: to crave his presence, his words, his trust—as well as that moment of our physical union. I could now spend hours thinking about bringing a smile to his face, melting his royal reserve, causing him to laugh. At just the time when most of my competitors found themselves dreading their night with him, I came to crave all of this with a longing I never knew I possessed. I had once felt the faintest stirrings of these emotions toward Jesse. Now I consciously steered them toward the man I hoped would fulfill my destiny to serve YHWH.

One day Hegai stopped me in the hallway to give me the date of my night with the King. It was less than a week away. And as those final days passed, I began to count the hours like an impatient bride awaiting the return of a husband from war. I could feel the day waiting in front of me like a physical presence looming just beyond the horizon. The fervency of my prayers matched the fervency of my passion. Mordecai's oft-repeated words circled through my mind with growing intensity. *Who knows whether you have not come to the kingdom for such a time as this?*

## Chapter Thirty

On the afternoon of my second-to-last day in the candidates' house, I had my final hidden meeting with Jesse. I remember that although it was the middle of winter, it was one of the warmest days in months, with one of those piercing desert blue skies sprawling overhead. We sat on a pile of hay in the back of the garden. Jesse turned to me with one of the most tender expressions he had ever given me, laid a hand on my shoulder and asked how I felt about what was going to happen. After all, his ordeal was now a year behind him, but mine was just ahead. And so for the first time, I proceeded to tell him. I informed him that I had resolved to face my first night with as much competence as I possessed, that I did not understand what had brought me to this place, but that I believed G-d was going before me and had prepared me in every way for this night. And then, slowly, haltingly, I informed Jesse how well that resolve was working, how I was even looking forward—

Jesse stood with a loud groan and stomped away toward the East Wall. I had naïvely imagined that he would respond as he had before when I'd delivered good news—unqualified support and encouragement.

"Jesse! Where are you going?" I called toward his retreating back. But I received only a raised hand in reply as he broke into a run.

I jumped to my feet and ran after him. It could not end this way. I wouldn't let it. After all, should I fail to win the King's favor, I might never see Jesse again. We could conceivably roam the vast spaces of the Palace for years without ever catching a glimpse of each other.

I ran like I hadn't run since that fateful morning when I had learned of his capture and become prey myself. I found him leaning against the wall, his head pressed into the stone.

"What is the matter, Jesse? Did I say something to hurt you?" I gasped out, reaching my hand toward him. I met with the hardest part of his shoulder as my reception.

He finally turned and stared at me as if I had uttered the most foolish question in the history of humanity. "If you don't understand, then I don't want to talk about it."

"And so we leave it at this?" I had to restrain myself from shouting. "After all these years, I go to face my greatest challenge without even a good-bye? Or an explanation?"

He blinked and glanced down at his feet. "You know, Hadassah, you are so intelligent, but sometimes you can be so . . ."

"Then enlighten me," I encouraged when he couldn't finish.

He continued to speak toward his feet. "How do you think I feel, hearing you talk about feeling desire for this man? Knowing your innocence is about to be taken by the same man who stole my life, stole my chance at ever enjoying something I had dreamed of one day sharing with *you*?"

My face suddenly felt like someone had poured hot water over it. How stupid, how self-centered could I be? I had grown so consumed with my quest for knowledge and victory that I had overlooked that early bond between Jesse and me. Yes, we had since become close friends—but now I saw that emasculation had not quenched his love for me. And I know now that I felt it, too; I had simply pushed those feelings from my mind out of sheer willpower.

I softly took his hand and squeezed it hard.

"I'm sorry," I whispered. "I'm sorry I was so thoughtless."

He shook his head without ever facing me, his gaze still pointed down. "It's all right, Hadassah. You know it is. Just don't tell me any more details, all right?"

It was my turn to nod soundlessly and fight back tears.

"I'm doing this for us, Jesse, don't you know?" I said with a voice rising beyond my control. "Not only Mordecai, your family or our people. You and I are the ones behind closed walls, just one mistake away from death. I'm doing this to win, and then I can have you placed on my personal bodyguard detail. We then can be together in some way, at least."

"Yes, but you would do it as his wife."

"Oh, Jesse," I said and my eyes filled with tears. *His wife*, in Jesse's sorrowful tone echoed over and over in my mind. Finally I was able to say, "You know the King and Queen do not spend all day together. I hear she joins him for an occasional dinner. The rest of the Queen's time is spent in the company of personal staff."

He turned to me with a swiftness that frightened me. "Do you still believe in G-d?" he asked with a bitter twist of his features.

"I didn't a year ago. Not truly. But today I can tell you I couldn't live a moment without Him. I feel His presence as strongly as I feel you right here and now."

"I wish I could say that. I wish—"

"I know, Jesse. I don't understand it, either. But I'm praying He does answer you. Both of us, for that matter. I don't understand why I'm here. I only know that while I *am* in this place, He's made himself more real than I'd ever dreamed He could. And that's why I have the strength to do my best. I think He's given you that same strength to do *your* best."

Jesse suddenly smiled as though he knew that would be my

answer, then moved to my side and took the risk of openly draping his arm around my shoulder. Had anyone seen it, the obvious affection between us would have caused an uproar—maybe costing me my candidacy and him his life. Yet we walked like that for several long minutes, not speaking, savoring the bittersweet tinge of each other's company—sweethearts separated by less than a parasang of Palace grounds yet kept apart by the highest, most hopeless barriers our world could possibly erect between two human beings.

I saw Mordecai on the day before my appointment with the King. I had never seen him so adrift—his eyes unfocused in their sockets, his hair jutting in every direction, his skin the pallor of Pentateuch parchment. I knew he was only nearing middle age, but today he looked like a very old man. He stared off toward the Palace and spoke rapidly in a halting and uncertain voice.

"Hadassah? Are you—? I have done all I can. All I can for you. There is no more to be done but pray, no? Have you been praying, my dear? Have you steeped yourself in the presence of the Lord? Is the *Shekinah* with you, my little one?" He sounded more like a prophet than Poppa.

I could not speak to him for fear of collapsing in tears. I nodded fiercely, then breathed in and out several times. Finally I could respond.

"I have, Poppa. YHWH has drawn me especially close of late. I feel Him all around me. All the time."

"That is good. That is all the good I can hope for now."

"Come back for me, Poppa. I'll find you here, even from the concubines' house."

"You never know, dearest. You never know what old trick he'll conjure up to keep you right next to him."

He looked away, squinting toward the Inner Court like he was its chief inspector. All to mask his tears.

We prayed for strength and guidance, and then he clasped me again. I could tell over his shoulder, from the silent heaving of his chest and torso, that he was weeping as hard as I was. So I kissed him on the cheek, whispered the most confident good-bye I could and began to walk swiftly back to the harem.

What I did not understand, my dear young maiden, is that even while I endured these poignant leave-takings, history-making events were taking shape in the halls only cubits away—developments centered on the man I would soon meet in his bedchamber.

A great war with Greece was now imminent, the battle to end all Greco-Persian battles. Xerxes had fought an earlier war only a few years before, one in which his father was killed and the army had failed to conquer Athens. Now obsessed with sacking the Greek capital, he was in the middle of planning with his generals to march on Greece with the largest army assembled in the history of mankind.

Today, you and I both know the outcome of that campaign, for we are living through its aftermath even as I write these words. Already, the events themselves have begun to acquire that peculiar tarnish of history past—that quaint aspect of an event whose danger, whose razor-sharp edge of catastrophic risk, is eroded by the passage of time. Yet its consequences now define every day of our lives.

Back then, none of this was known. Persia was still the undisputed ruler of much of the world. Xerxes, although not claiming to be divine, was as close to G-dlike as any mortal ever born.

*Chapter Thirty-one*

$\mathcal{A}$nd then it was the eve, then the morning of that day. I remember little of the hours leading up to my departure, for my handmaidens had worked themselves into an unchecked frenzy of last-minute beauty experiments, harried arrangements and raging anxiety. I already felt like a queen, at least a queen bee surrounded by a never-ending buzz of exertion.

Oddly, I found myself slipping into a strange, trancelike contentment during those last frantic hours. I knew what I needed to do, I knew I was ready for it and I was as prepared as I knew how to be. The simple finality of those affirmations gave me a peace that thankfully settled over me while everyone else flew about on adrenaline. The handmaidens' agitation collided around me like an outer storm from which I sat insulated, even strangely calmed by the commotion. Somewhere out there, outside of myself, I could feel the passage of time. But the dwindling moments were not part of my inner world.

No, my emotions were consumed by two seemingly

contradictory truths that day. First was my desire to enter into the King's presence and please him with every part of myself. Second was an already vibrant sense of G-d's nearness. I could feel His Spirit within me, fortifying my resolve and thrilling me with a sense of purpose and destiny I had never known before. My mind could not analyze these two seemingly disparate facts, but I knew them to be.

When only a few hours remained, I spoke out in a soft voice and began to express some personal requests. First, I asked my handmaiden Vodhi to fetch her harp and play a selection of the songs from her native Syria. I requested that the other girls begin to calm down, lower their voices and move as gracefully about me as they could.

I asked for one final anointment with perfume. Four of the girls set about covering every inch of my skin with the contents of a small bottle Hegai had discreetly supplied containing the King's favorite essence. He told me no one else had used this rare oil.

Next, I had one of my handmaidens wash my hair in milk, rub it dry in woolen blankets and smooth it with oil. Another one combed it straight down with my favorite ox-bone comb. My hair was long and nearly jet black in those days, and weeks of straightening treatments had removed any of the curl that it had had upon my arrival at the harem. Tonight it hung thick, black and shiny upon my shoulders, the Persian ideal.

As the preparations wore on, I began to catch sight of glances being exchanged.

"What's the matter?" I finally asked.

"What do you mean, my lady?" asked Shakel, the handmaiden nearest me at the time.

"Everyone is acting strangely. Is it my request for quiet? Did I offend you?"

Shakel looked over at the others, then turned to me with a faint smile. "It's not that. It's just that you look so beautiful. You truly are the loveliest woman in the whole Palace. Truly. I imagine we are all asking ourselves the same question. How could Xerxes see you and not fall in love on sight?"

I could not answer the question, and I was grateful that no reply was expected of me. I knew that the girls were utterly sincere, and a feeling of gratitude began deep within my chest, spread outward and soon found its way onto my lips. My eyes filled with tears. Instead of speaking, I reached out to both sides of me and grabbed two of the girls' hands. I squeezed them tightly and gave them each a warm smile.

The youngest of them entered from the hallway and carried a mug of something steaming over to me. "Here is your traditional good-luck brew," she said, holding it out to me with a shy smile.

The tea smelled enticing, minty and sweet. I raised it for a drink, but as soon as the heat approached my lips, I realized I actually had a craving for something cool to drink. I lowered the cup and faced its giver with an apologetic look. "Thank you, Jivat. But I would rather have some spring water."

"I heard it was bad luck to turn it down," she insisted. "It seems to contain some kind of aphrodisiac."

"You heard this from *whom*?"

She shrugged. "Misgath. She seems to know a lot about the Palace's prenuptial customs."

The blood rushed from my face. *Misgath?* I glanced back at the cup. Hegai had never said anything about a traditional cup of tea.

"Who prepared this?"

The handmaiden's face fell. She no doubt had wanted me to believe she had fixed it herself. "She did, ma'am. Misgath."

Suddenly it all fell into place: how some of the girls had become violently ill just prior to their nights with the King. I sent one of my handmaidens to fetch Hathach, told him the tea's origins and asked him to find and invite Misgath in so I could express my gratitude. Apparently she had been lingering nearby, for he returned with the girl in just a few moments.

"My friend," I told her with my warmest smile, "I just wanted to thank you so much for helping me overcome my ignorance about the rituals of this day. I only wish Hegai had told me about it earlier. I almost missed out on this delicious drink."

Misgath had walked in with unusual stiffness upon entering the room, but the moment she thought I had drunk her potion, her whole body relaxed.

"Well, Star," she answered with a smug look, "Hegai doesn't know everything. I have a few sources of my own."

"Yes. I'm sure you do," I said evenly. "By the way, Misgath, I enjoyed this so much I would like to share it with *you*. Since I am done with it, I would like you to have a drink of it yourself."

"Oh, it's an aphrodisiac," she answered, suddenly appearing less relaxed. "I hardly have use for that—yet. Besides, tradition has it that only the candidate of the night can touch the drink."

"No, Misgath, I heard that it was a drink to be shared among good friends. I insist." I held out the cup.

"No." Her voice was now flat and adamant.

And that is when Jesse did something I never expected. He grabbed the cup from my hands and took a deep draught himself. His eyes remained locked on Misgath as he lowered it and wiped his mouth.

"You're going to come with me to Hegai," he said with a sudden authority to his voice. "We're going to talk about who your father really is and why you lied about it. And we're going to discuss who your secret friend is who gave you the poison I just drank. And when I become ill, your time as a candidate will be over."

The handmaidens froze in shock. Misgath's face twisted into a sneer. "Who are you to speak to me this way, Hathach? A eunuch? You'll pay for your impudence."

Jesse smiled confidently. "I am charged with serving and protecting the candidates, Misgath. And toward that end, I have all the latitude I need."

Just then he grimaced and bent over with a groan. He looked up at her. Through a forced smile and gritted teeth, he muttered,

"I don't think Hegai will lack for evidence of your treachery."

Still wincing in pain, Jesse walked over, grabbed Misgath by the arm and dragged her from the room.

As the sound of her threats and insults faded with distance, I turned to the handmaidens and breathed in deeply. Privately, I was filled with fear for Jesse's safety. Would this development somehow reveal the friendship between us? And given how quickly the other candidates had recovered from their illnesses, would his superiors believe his account of the plot? It seemed far easier to simply write off the previous incidents as crises of nerves. *Hysterical women.* I breathed a quick prayer for his safekeeping and steeled myself to the task at hand.

"Well, girls," I said, "we've had a lot of excitement added to the day, haven't we? I'm sure you'll hear more about how this turns out than I will. But I still need to get ready. Shall we?"

Strange how quickly that inner feeling of peace returned. I knew more than ever that G-d was with me.

Just as all seven handmaidens finished carefully draping the light blue sheer silk wrap around me and tying it around my waist with a flourish, I began to feel that my moment of completion had arrived. At that very moment, as if forewarned of my readiness, there came a knock on the door and Hegai looked around the edge.

"Star?"

A hush fell over all of us. The handmaidens stopped, and their hands fell to their sides.

"Come in," I answered.

Hegai entered, stopped and stared at me as I stood in the center of the room. He folded his arms over his chest and smiled faintly.

"The rumors are true," he said in a half whisper.

"What are those?" I asked.

"That the favored candidate will capture the moment."

Then he came back to himself, stiffened his back and gave the handmaidens a brisk hand gesture. On cue, they cleared out of the room like butterflies swept away by a brisk wind. I felt an immediate pang in my heart.

"Wait, girls!" I called after them. "Can we bid one another good-bye?"

Hegai reached me and touched me on the cheek with the tip of his thumb. "Do not worry, my sweet. This is how it is always done. You will see them again. As for Misgath, you and Hathach both have just rendered a great service to the Crown. Hathach is in the infirmary. He will recover fully, but he has amply proved that the girl's tea contained a strong stomach irritant. Misgath has confessed and has been taken to the garrison. You will never hear her name again, I suppose. Nor, I am sure, the name of her father, Prince Carshena."

"Hegai, if it is acceptable to you, I would like to forget about that whole thing right now. I have so much more to think about, and even allowing myself to be distracted would give her too much of a victory."

The head eunuch smiled. "As usual, you show wisdom beyond your years, Star. I could not agree more. So, my dear, let us depart."

I turned toward a deep-blue softly-woven cloak, and Hegai quickly lifted it and placed it around my shoulders. The single medallion, his early gift to me, was already in place. He nudged me forward with the pressure of his hand under my arm. I followed him out the harem's front door, and there awaited something I had never seen before: a golden litter sitting on the walk with a strapping eunuch standing beside each end of the pole. Applause rang out as I stepped forward. I looked about me and saw nearly every member of the harem stretched out in a crowd, standing with smiles of gen- uine affection and goodwill. At the front of the gathering, clustered in a group with tears in their eyes, stood my handmaidens.

Hegai came alongside me now and gestured toward me with an open hand as he faced the harem girls. "Your favored candidate!"

A loud cheer engulfed the terrace. I felt a wave of warmth wash over me. I believed I had won the hearts of most candidates there on one occasion or the other, but I had never seen it so vividly. Now all the backstabbing and grousing were forgotten, and it seemed I was truly loved. It certainly felt that way. "Thank you, G-d," I said silently as Hegai nudged my elbow toward the litter. I complied and climbed into the seat. As the eunuchs bent down and pulled upon the pole, all at once the world lurched sideways and rose. With the rising came the most unusual sensation somewhere just above my breast. It felt like the popping of some delicate thread that had once tethered me to the ground and maybe, in a deeper way, to all that had come before. The impression was almost tactile—like the head of a dandelion breaking from its stem or a thread of yarn softly giving way. It was followed by a feeling of lightness as the litter righted itself and the eunuchs began to carry me forward, at shoulder height, across the courtyard.

The trees framing the harem now stood behind us, and I soon recognized the expanse that had yawned so large when I had walked into the banquet. The last of the candidates fell away, but I heard, to my amazement, that the applause did not—the farther we proceeded, the more people walked forward, applauding, calling out to me with shouts of encouragement.

Then I heard a shout above the others and looked around for its source. And there was a sight that instantly brought a lump to my throat. It was Mordecai. A wave of loving nostalgia washed over me as his beloved face grew closer. I called his name and waved; he laughed out loud, waved back and smiled wider than he had in many, many days. I winced, realizing how far this was from the Jewish wedding he no doubt had envisioned for me. Through his grin I thought I saw tearstains lining his cheeks. I gritted my teeth, breathed in deeply and willed myself not to cry. Regardless of how deeply I loved him, now was not the moment to spoil hours' worth of cosmetic preparations. I owed it to this father who meant so much to me, who had been such an integral part of my life and even this moment, to remain in control.

He passed by, and I saw that Mordecai was indeed doing the

weeping for both of us. "I love you!" I cried out. And then he was gone, swept into the tide of humanity that seemed to part before my procession as water before the prow of a ship. It did not seem to end: the soft slapping of the carriers' sandals against the marble, the faint up and down motion of the litter upon their shoulders, the soft patter of applause, which truly did, upon this vast terrace, sound a little like the lapping of waves.

We traversed a long distance, beyond all parts of the Palace I had ever known. Finally we passed through a three-deep column of soldiers at attention whose golden breastplates glittered so brightly in the bright late-evening sun that I had to turn away.

The assault on my eyes was far from over, for overhead loomed a wall high enough that I leaned nearly out of my seat to see its top. Its surface shined even more brightly than the guards' uniforms. I squinted and then realized that its ramparts were studded with—I focused harder to make sure—*gold and silver*!

I had known the world was far larger than my experience could envision and that Persia's ruler was a mighty and wealthy man. But even that perception was beginning to pale in the face of reality. How much gold *was* there in existence? How much extravagance could one man amass—and enjoy, for that matter?

A set of high brass doors parted before us, and we entered another courtyard, totally enclosed yet nearly as vast as the one we had just left. Far away in the distance I could make out the abrupt rise of yet another wall with a similar door shining at its center. And here, too, stood people by the dozens—functionaries carrying satchels, clusters of soldiers in rows, beautiful women in robes of every color. How had I lived here a year and not known of this walled-in world and all its citizens? These also turned at the entrance of my litter and stared at me while a sudden hush fell over the place.

The pause was starting to grow awkward when Hegai, apparently sensing the odd stillness, began to shout, "Make way! Make way for the favored Queen candidate!" The people's postures soft-

ened at those words, and their stares seemed to shift from vague
alarm to curiosity. The litter began to move with purpose again,
straight toward the second wall and its door.

The groups of women must have been concubines, because I
glimpsed more than one angry glare directed my way—the same
kind of *What makes you think you are better or prettier than me?*
expressions my fellow candidates and I had been receiving all year
from the concubines across our courtyard. I sighed deeply with an
inward sense of resignation, for I obviously had not chosen this
manner of naming a queen nor inserted myself into the process. I
will tell you that I was still young and naïve enough to be amazed
at people hating me for things completely beyond my control. Life
since then has brought me to a more pragmatic understanding and
acceptance of this unreasonable phenomenon.

Like on my first visit to the Palace, the enormity of the place
was beginning to play tricks on my sense of scale, of distance, of the
relative value of things. The sun, low on the horizon, seemed to
wheel in some fiery dance around my head, and I could feel the
beginnings of a swoon assault my senses. I closed my eyes, eventually unable to care what the onlookers thought, and tried to regain
my bearings.

For a very long pause I savored the darkness, then felt the litter
pause beneath me. I opened my eyes again and found that we had
crossed the enormous courtyard and stood waiting before the next
set of giant doors. I shook my head, for this wall appeared to be
more forbidding, as richly built and as well guarded as the last! As
stunned as I had felt upon entering the banquet hall that first time
I came to the Palace, I was struck dumb by the present splendor
around me.

*Stop*—I told myself. *Stop thinking about it. Stop measuring and
assessing, and be. Simply be. Focus on the King!*

The doors opened, and yes, fate was trying to tempt my
resolve—what stretched nearly into infinity was yet another courtyard. This one was bisected by a well-worn path through a sea of

tents. Between them stood soldiers—thousands of them, by the looks of it. These men seemed to be on a higher alert than their colleagues farther out, for at my entrance they all turned as one and fixed me with suspicious stares. I could almost feel fists tighten around swords and lances in anticipation of some shouted order or negative assessment.

Hegai waved, though, and the mood looked to relax at once, starting with the soldiers nearest us. Their stares turned from suspicious to something more leering, and I looked quickly away.

Hegai appeared beside my feet and looked up at me with a smile. "Are you all right, my dear?"

I just nodded as gamely as I could.

"We're over halfway there," he continued. "I know it's a trek, but just know, you are looking exquisite. No royal approach has caused this much amazement in many days."

"I can't tell if they're watching me or ready to leap on me and tear my head off!" I replied, but I saw he had already returned to the front of the litter.

We now approached the third set of walls. I inwardly prayed it would be the last, that its opening would reveal indoor dimness rather than a repeat of waning daylight and yet another courtyard. The cordon of guards surrounding the perimeter was a dozen deep and even more rigid and alert.

Indeed, the feeling of increasing vigilance and coiled-up danger seemed to grow with every passing moment. I began to imagine what kind of man could live out his days at the epicenter of such awesome diligence and watchcare. How did he step out of bed in the morning without fearing that his tiniest gesture would set off the mobilization of regiments or the migration of thousands?

*Be quiet*, I reminded my inner self. I focused back on the peaceful glow that had permeated my final hours at the harem. *G-d, grant me peace*, I asked, and indeed I began to feel the placid quiet return.

The doors opened, and my last wish, too, was granted. I looked inside to the warm light of white marble rather than another expanse of orange and blue sky. Finally, an interior. We passed inside and my relief from the evening sun was immediate—coolness flowed over me. My eyes, while briefly blinded, soon widened blissfully at the reprieve. The sight slowly appearing before me was a hallway the height and breadth of a canyon, lined with slender pillars, indoor palms, and people by the hundreds. Men and women of every Palace variety had lined up beside our path to watch. There was a renewal of applause and cheering, but more polite this time, tinged with a definite air of obligation.

I smiled warmly, although inside I was thinking of the King. I centered my thoughts on him with all the determination of a distance runner gritting through his last few strides.

We continued along the awesome hallway for what seemed like another enormous distance—again, the span of one of those massive courtyards—then turned at a right angle and began a stretch so similar to the previous that I began to wonder if we had really turned at all. Doorway after doorway continued as far as I could see, each seeming to lead into offices—as I gazed into several, I saw rooms filled with frowning, intent generals and large tables of sand and stone, replicating battlefields and war strategies. This side of the Palace was surely in a war mode, I noted to myself. Even the hall's many couches were lined with elegantly dressed officers—no rough soldiers here—nearly all of them flirting with some courtesan woman or other. Finally I stopped trying to meet the eyes of all those lining the way, as their sheer numbers threatened to shake my concentration.

I began to wish I had merely closed my eyes at the beginning of this journey and taken a nap. But part of me knew that would not have been a very good idea.

Hegai reappeared, his eyebrows arched. "Are you ready?"

The question startled me, for a perverse voice had begun to whisper to me that we would never actually reach our destination. Yet I nodded yes and took another deep breath over my pounding heart.

*You're here*, I told myself. *You're at the end of the waiting, the preparation. You're ready to go in, into the presence of the King.*

And then a cool assurance fell upon me, as sure as the air.

We paused before another tall door, but this time we did so with a finality that told me indeed, the litter would go no farther. The conveyance began to descend to the floor, slowly, carefully. I took Hegai's outstretched hand to pull me up and—I am still unsure whether it was the sudden rush of blood or the final realization of where I stood—a shudder and a thrill rushed through my body. A strange mixture of trepidation and utter confidence took hold of me. I wanted to run away and hide, but also storm the King's room, all at the same time.

I stepped away from the litter and stood facing the great doors, guarded on either side by two Immortals. Hegai turned to me, assessed my face with several quick darts of the eyes and reached out to rearrange two or three errant strands of hair.

"Just remember," he whispered. "He'll be fortunate to choose you. He'll be the one to be congratulated if he does—not you."

As he lowered his hands I grabbed them and squeezed them tightly. "Hegai, I do not know how to thank you," I told him. "I am so grateful."

He frowned unexpectedly. "You can repay me by being a good and righteous Queen, should you win. And by being a wise advisor to His Majesty. He needs this."

Then the doors opened, as slow and ponderous as trees falling in the distance. Or at least it seemed they opened at a stately pace—perhaps my memory has slowed them out of reverence for the golden moments that followed.

In a way, the goal of this seemingly endless journey seemed at first its most disappointing. All I saw was darkness—many, many cubits of it. Then my eyes focused on a pool of light seemingly far away, and a moment later I could make out a bed canopy as tall as my old home's rooftop, surrounded by man-high torches.

What I thought was another guard appeared from behind the

door, his brow deeply furrowed. Hegai leaned in toward him. "This is Star of Susa, Master Memucan," he whispered. "My personal favorite Queen candidate. For His Majesty's company this evening."

"Is she weapons-clean?"

"I saw her dressed myself, sir. Of course, yes."

"It is on your head," incanted the other man. "As always."

Hegai nodded. "As always."

The royal Master of the Audiences, second most powerful man in the empire, glanced my way and nodded for me to proceed. He closed the door behind himself as he departed.

I was alone with Xerxes. Alone with a man I had never met yet was about to know intimately.

## Chapter Thirty-two

*N*ow, I am not sure how to describe the moments that came next, for my memory has traveled over these events so many times that the line between a wondrous memory and mere imagination or even hallucination has become blurred. I know for certain that I moved inside and took several steps forward. I know that my gaze settled upon the figure of a man standing at the edge of the ridiculously large canopy bed.

Beyond that point, the accuracy of my descriptions remains open to question.

I will tell you now, after all these years, that I have a strong memory of being drawn toward him by a longing that felt elemental, like a force of nature.

As for his physical appearance, the importance for some reason seemed almost secondary. My eyes soon captured the image of a man so handsome and captivating that I began to wonder if he was actually a mirage created by my time in the sun. Either way, I did not care. The image consisted of a man in his early thirties with bronzed cheeks and eyes glittering at me over broad, masculine cheekbones. He possessed broad shoulders, the arms of a stone-cutter and the bulging leg muscles of a distance runner.

But it was his face from which I could not glance away. He truly had the visage of a king—strong, fearless and endlessly intelligent. Eyes with such depth that I felt drawn as to a pool of clear water. They seemed to gleam more brightly as I approached, and I wondered if this was some response to my appearance or merely his usual appraisal of the candidates. I felt truly beautiful with the wrap clinging to my waist, the star medallion hanging from neck, my hair arrayed over my shoulders and behind me. (But, still, I wondered if I was beautiful *enough*. There is always room for doubt, I am afraid.)

I reached up to unclasp the Kashmiri cloak, and it fell to pool about my feet on the marble floor.

As I moved forward, I suddenly remembered the drunk who had advanced on him so recklessly at the banquet and lost his head. I risked the briefest of glances from side to side and saw none of the scabbard-carrying guards from before. We were truly alone.

I now stood at the edge of his shadow, near enough for our fingers to touch.

"Good evening," he said in a rough and weary voice. "You will forgive me, for I am very tired this evening. The rigors of the throne and all—but I have forgotten your name. Memucan told me a few minutes ago, but in my fatigue—"

"Star, your Majesty."

"Ah, yes. Star of Susa. And *that* you are. You are most beautiful." He frowned and glanced slightly downward at my neck. "Is that your only jewel, your only adornment?"

"It is, your Majesty." I felt my lips forming words as though the loftiest part of my brain had forged a direct link to my mouth and bypassed my conscious mind. "It is a near replica of a medallion I once had, my most prized possession in the world. My seventh birthday present from my father, who was killed immediately after-ward. I was named for its shape. Star."

"Well, Star, some would call you foolish indeed. Every girl who preceded you had a keen eye for the riches she would take *away* from the Palace."

"I was taught, your Majesty, that when you visit the King, rather than expect a gift, you bring the gift yourself. And this—" I reached up to my nape, detached the necklace, cradled the gem at its core and held it out toward him—"is all I have in the world."

"You are giving this to me? Why? I have everything."

"And now, sir, you have a reminder that I bring you my all. Not only my body," I said with my head bowed, "but I give you my mind, your Majesty. My heart. All of me." Words I had rehearsed but which felt as natural at this moment as if I had never phrased them before.

He seemed to frown even more darkly at that, and for the briefest of seconds I wondered if I had miscalculated badly. Then he extended his hand and took the necklace, dangling it for a moment in the light, then clasped it in his hand.

"Thank you, Star of Susa. You are a most eloquent giver of gifts. And a beautiful one. I have never received such a . . . cherished present before."

"It is only a symbol, your Majesty. The gift I most wish to give you is that of myself."

He smiled. "In due time, my dear." Then his smile faded. "And why are *you* smiling?"

"Sir?"

"Why in the name of the gods are you smiling like that? Every other girl who has preceded you appeared on the verge of bursting into tears, regurgitating or both. What is it that causes you such cheer?"

"It is *you*, your Majesty. I am so delighted to be in your presence. For a year I have bathed in your oils and perfumes until every pore of my skin emits a scent that you favor. I discovered your preferred fragrance and anointed myself with it just before coming here. I have prepared so long to come here and . . . bring you joy—

and now I find *I* am the one feeling joy at being so close to you. May I tell you: you are most appealing, even beyond your royal stature? I want to know you. And . . ." My voice trailed off, overpowered by my emotions.

I meant it, every word of it. His proximity felt like a cascade of honey down my shoulders, like an indulgence.

I, little Hadassah from the backstreets of Susa, a little Jewish girl not even allowed to leave her house for years, the most socially deprived and maladroit girl in the city, was now enjoying the undivided attention of the ruler of the world. I was being allowed to partake of one moment of a royal life, though I did not yet know it was already destined to be chronicled in the annals of history. I had succeeded in venturing beyond thousands—no, tens of thousands—of bureaucrats and officials whose only function was to keep ordinary citizens far away from this place, from the vicinity of this man. Most of his subjects would consider it the event of a lifetime to come within four or five of these royal buffers to His Majesty. And there were physical barriers, as well—all those rings of fortress walls, each one thick enough to repel an army, each one defended by legions, concentrically arrayed to keep people away.

Well, none of the ramparts or the terraces or the countless officials stood between me and the supreme ruler at this moment. I had made it past all of them. Every layer of insulation was gone, every intervening shield peeled away like the skins of an onion. It was he and I, only the air between us.

"You want to know *me*?" he asked, his voice pulling me back to reality. "Or the King?"

"All of you. The part that is King and the part that is a man. They fascinate me equally."

He smiled again—a smile of amazement, I must admit—and shook his head. Then I saw that his expression had changed. A tinge of emotion, of grief even, had stolen over his features.

"I do not know why I admit this to you, a commoner. But I am not sure I know the difference between Xerxes the man and Xerxes the King any longer."

"Perhaps I can help you find it again."

I had spoken the words before considering that I was speaking to the ruler of millions like a mother might speak to a child. Yet I was gliding on pure instinct at that moment, and considerations of tact and etiquette had now served their purpose. Having reached his innermost presence, I felt emboldened. I could sense that destiny was in full command.

And indeed, my reply seemed to find favor—no, far more than that, it seemed to touch something deep within him, for Xerxes held out a hand and touched my cheek with a wondrously tender look.

"You are a remarkable woman, Star." Then he raised my gift again in his other hand. "No one has spoken to me like this in a very long time."

"Well, how *do* your people speak to you?"

He leaned back against the bed and glanced up at the faraway ceiling to form his answer. With surprising candor, he said, "Oh, you know. Two ways, mainly. First are those who want something from me. I can see the desire, the avarice, the ambition in their eyes from a parasang away. It has nothing to do with me but what I can get them. Money, position, revenge. The others are people who for some reason have cause to fear me. Subjects, servants, prisoners—I can see the fear, even the hate in their eyes. And on those occasions the knowledge that they do not see me but my position is actually a relief. A balm."

"Is there no one close enough to your stature to whom you can speak as a true friend, who can look at you and see a person?"

"That's what a queen is for."

I looked away and did not answer, for the opportunity to serve my own ends was too obvious to be exploited.

"I see none of those pitfalls in your eyes, Star." His voice called me back to face him again. "In fact, what I see there is so rare I am not sure what to call it."

"It is attraction, your Majesty. And delight. Forgive me—I am a girl of very little experience. I did not grow up in the company of many other people. I did not ever imagine that I might be considered to spend time in your company."

"I hope you spend a great deal of it. I am enjoying our conversation."

"And I." Then my hand traveled upward. I asked him tremulously, "May I?"

He nodded yes. My hand continued upward to touch his face. His skin felt hot and impossibly smooth. Yet just beneath it lay the hardness of bone and the tautness of lean flesh. I moved my fingers ever so slightly over his face, barely grazing his thick beard, his cheek. The feeling of tenderness seemed to flow freely between my fingers and his face.

And then he did something I had never heard anyone describe him doing on a candidate's first night. He took my hand, pulled it down and leaned forward to kiss the palm.

Then his lips touched mine.

*Chapter Thirty-three*

*I* must pull away from the moment, perhaps to take a breath, perhaps to ready myself to disclose what I am thinking about revealing to you. As you may know, all sorts of assumptions have been made through the years about what I did next with the King. I have had women of highest repute turn up their noses at me. I have had rabbis denounce me in their synagogues for the laws they think I betrayed. All sorts of moralists have had their say about me even though they were not there with me and Xerxes that night nor have they lived through the experiences that led to that fateful encounter. They did not pray the prayers I raised to G-d for guidance, for rescue out of temptation, for a way to conduct myself in a manner that would please Him and exalt His name before others.

YHWH is a righteous G-d, I know, a G-d of the law. But He is also a gracious G-d who sees our hearts, our intentions, who meets us in the very difficult and nuanced situations where our lives take us. And I know beyond a shadow of doubt, as history has borne out, that He used what actually *did* occur that night for His good, for His purposes.

Why am I telling you these things? Because, my fellow candidate, I am going to tell you what I have told no one beyond Mordecai and my beloved Jesse-turned-Hathach in all the years since these events took place. It is a disclosure that might have saved me from a great deal of pain and condemnation had I made it years ago. I suppose I have been too stubborn, too ambivalent—and too offended—to offer this very tender fact up for public consumption.

But you see, as truth would have it, there was no sexual intimacy between me and the King that night.

It is not a matter of eternal importance to me, since I was fully prepared to become everything I could for him, with every womanly skill I possessed. And I also know that what we purpose in our hearts is as important as our actions. To begin with, I believed Mordecai when he told me that my being taken against my will and forced into the King's bed on pain of death relieved me of culpability. Had I given myself to him, I would have felt utterly absolved of guilt. Furthermore, as I've already said, I believe G-d had brought about this divine appointment that night for a destiny that went far beyond a King's desires.

Something far more special and profound took place between us in those precious hours. We engaged in a conversation the likes of which he said he had never enjoyed in that room before. I can say it now, too, with no fear of vanity or pride.

We fell in love.

We lay on his bed—without embarrassment or discomfort on my part, without being overtaken by lust on his part—and talked of our lives—of things Hegai had never prepared me to converse about. Only G-d himself prepared me for that night. Xerxes unburdened himself of his struggles, of years' worth of pain and grief. He talked about how it felt to come upon his father's body pierced with arrows, lying upon the field of battle like some punctured bag of corn. He described the pain of seeing his own brothers, his childhood companions, treat him like an adversary the moment his crown had settled upon his head.

I honestly began to feel his sorrow, his grief, and my eyes moistened more than once. I had never imagined being able to sympathize, let alone feel sorry for, the sovereign of my known world. Yet the honesty of his disclosures gave me a raw glimpse into his very own, very real inner pain.

I gathered up my courage and told him about the great ordeal of my childhood—what it felt like to burrow into my mother's side for protection only to find her beheaded. The disclosure created an atmosphere of empathy—he winced and held me then, and I shed several more of my belated tears at her neglected memory.

I did not reveal my Jewishness, yet I answered his many questions about the attack and where it occurred. He seemed to think hard at that moment, trying to search his memory, then shrugged and returned to our conversation. I did not tell about the twisted cross insignia, still unsure to whom the emblem belonged and having seen it now several times around the Palace.

Somehow, somewhere in the early hours of the morning, we came to acknowledge each other as fellow orphans, strangely and oddly stranded in the world by events beyond our reach. Although the means and circumstances of our respective tragedies clearly differed enormously, the more we talked the more we realized that the resulting traumas were strangely alike. He was forced as a young crown prince into the isolation and otherworldliness of Palace life, while I became a recluse and unwilling refugee at a very early age, then another kind of recluse in the Palace harem.

And strangely, as fatigue began to wear away my reserves, I ceased to see either his royalty or the danger he embodied. It may have been imprudent of me, but I began to see just a man beset by countless cares and machinations. A man afflicted with unquenchable loneliness and insecurity. A flawed man, to be sure—obsessed, for one thing, with ransacking Greece, one of the world's great civilizations, and slaughtering scores of its citizens. But for some reason, my reaction to him vanquished his defenses and caused him to reveal his innermost self to me. And that self was remarkably like other human beings I had known.

When I told him what I had seen in his eyes, he sighed and began to unburden himself even more directly. "I am weary, Star. So weary. I tire of the constant maneuvering and gamesmanship of court," he said, looking away. "I always have to keep watch behind me, careful that some hidden enemy or other does not usurp my throne. The seven Princes of the Face, to name but one group, while on the surface my closest advisers are at the same time my fiercest competitors. My grandfather was one of the Princes years ago, and he inserted himself into the throne, as everyone knows. Ever since then the other Princes have pushed and strained for the chance to do the very same thing, always trying to improve their claim to royalty, always straining to inch one level closer than the others. It is an endless matching of wits, a perpetual game of positioning and repositioning themselves. I must always be thinking of strategies to outflank my enemies, to surprise them, to pit them against one another and waste their energies on meaningless rivalries rather than on me."

He held me then, and I felt that the tighter he held me the more he was squeezing away the worries he had just listed. I tried to mentally detach myself and take stock of the incredible situation I was in—here I was in bed, having one of the most intimate and satisfying conversations of my life . . . with the King of Persia.

The King seemed in no dire need of a woman's body but rather in desperate need of a loyal soulmate. Apparently the wonder of what was taking place between us far outweighed his immediate craving to discover any sensual mystery about my womanhood, let alone relieve any pent-up tensions.

Lastly, I believe he *did* fully intend to take my virginity that night. Before he could, though, our conversation dwindled hours later, and he fell asleep in my arms, just as the torches began to gutter down to mere embers and the sun warmed the light in the room's high windows.

My fears waited until after the King's slumber to assault me. After all, the evening's most notable event, the one thing I had prepared for the most carefully, had not taken place. So with the end of our time together came an onslaught of insecurities. Had some flaw in my appearance caused him not to desire me? Had I miscued the simplicity of my presentation? Did he finally decide I was not attractive to him and that any further intimacy was futile?

I had not heard of any girl waking up a virgin after this night. Although who knows—perhaps they had simply declined to let it be known, silently bearing the ultimate rejection.

Another misgiving soon pounded its way into my consciousness. Any woman later found to be carrying His Majesty's child was guaranteed an exalted place among the concubines, for she could be carrying a future king, or at least a potential apple of his father's eye. Our platonic evening had denied me even that bit of leverage.

In fact, since only a royal deflowering ensured a girl entry into the concubines' house, I wondered—would I, still a virgin, be sent back to the candidates' harem, there to be mercilessly taunted by the other girls? The prospect filled me with dread colder than a blast of winter air.

But then, had he not profusely complimented my beauty? Had his gaze not lingered over my form in its simple silk gown?

And yet the fatigue he had spoken of clearly overtook him in the end. Xerxes had truly been a weary man.

These warnings and reassurances tumbled over one another in my mind until I became literally dizzy with anguish. Finally, exhausted both mentally and physically, I stared up into the room's dim elevations and gave up—I simply asked G-d to give me peace and direction.

Then I must have fallen asleep for some short period, for I awoke with the King moving about beside me. I immediately bolted forward with my worries fully deployed. How would he treat me now? What would the morning's unkind light reveal that had been withheld during the night's overwrought emotions?

Xerxes rolled onto one elbow and brought his face within inches of mine. And he smiled a smile that instantly left me at ease.

"I woke up wondering what you must think," he said in a throaty whisper. "I know that you came prepared to give me pleasure last night, and clearly that did not happen. But, Star, you must know this. And do not forget it. You are by far the most beautiful and desirable woman who has ever graced my bed. And believe me—that is saying much. I was a fool not to ravish you last night. But I was also enraptured by something more than your lovely form. I was completely overwhelmed by your manner with me."

I breathed in deeply out of sheer relief. "Thank you."

"And what's more, Star," he continued, "no one needs to know what did and did not take place here last night. It will be our complete secret. I will have Memucan burn our sheets and swear him to secrecy upon pain of death. Believe me, he will obey. Nor should you worry about not carrying the royal seed—"

"It was not your seed I craved," I whispered. "It was your presence. And your love."

He looked at me with the distant gaze of someone realizing that his life has just taken a major turn. "You have that, my Star. Know that you have that."

Then he kissed me again, long and hard, and bounded from his bed calling loudly for his valet.

*Esther, Queen of Persia*

KETHUVIM ESTHER 2:17

*"The King loved Esther more . . . so he set a royal diadem on her head and made her queen. . . ."*

# Chapter Thirty-four

And then everything swirled into a blur—aides poured in through the suddenly open door and a hum of activity broke out within the chamber. Two eunuchs presented themselves at my side of the bed and helped me rise. One of them must have retrieved my cloak from the floor, for he handed it to me with his eyes averted. I swept the cloak about my shoulders. I stood there, uncertain what I should do next. Did I simply walk away? I did not know my way back nor where I should go. Did I wait for someone to attend my return? I stepped off the canopy platform, was given my sandals by one of the eunuchs and looked about me. The King was already so surrounded that it would have required making a commotion to gain his attention. Perhaps this was the royal manner—a night with his rapt attention, then forgotten among all the details of running his kingdom.

Before I could grow too bewildered, however, Hegai presented himself, apologizing profusely for his delay. We walked out to the hallway from which I had entered, now choked across its width with milling throngs of people. This time, however, hardly anyone turned as we left. I was just part of the crowd drifting through the hallways adjacent to the royal bedchamber.

Hegai walked me through the crowd, over to a far wall and a small door carved out of its side. There, just outside, awaited the same litter, this time with no entourage around it or attending applause. Just as well, I thought, for I was too perplexed to endure much attention. I climbed in and the eunuchs lifted me and carried me off at a brisk saunter. Already the sun was high and hot. This time Hegai reached over and produced a broad sunshade. I accepted it with profuse thanks. He examined me with his eyes.

"Are you in good spirits, my lady? I had pictured you emerging—well, happier than this."

"I am not unhappy, Hegai. I am just confused. I thought last night went—incredibly. Magically. Yet after waking up this morning, the King jumped from his bed and launched into his affairs as though our time together had never happened."

"That is his way," Hegai called to me through his panting, for he was now running lightly to keep up with the litter. "It means nothing! He focuses intensely on one thing, then shifts completely on to another."

I wanted to seize Hegai and quiz him for hours on every subtlety of royal behavior, but Hegai had moved away; the issue was settled for him. He was, after all, a man.

I remember next to nothing of my trip to the concubines' house. Perhaps the building's resemblance to the harem I had just lived in contributed to my indistinct memory, but more likely it was just my turbulent state of mind. I do vaguely recall the litter being set down before the door. I turned to Hegai.

"What do I do now?" I asked.

He shrugged amiably. "You wait. The King has urgent business in Persepolis and will be away for several days. Do you think anything special happened between you?"

"I thought so. But now—I don't know. You're right. I'll just wait."

Waiting was, of course, far easier said than done. I spent the next few days in an unbearable state of bewilderment and torturous doubt. In fact, the interval felt longer than the twelve months that had preceded it. I retreated to my room, nearly identical to the very first one I had occupied at the candidates' house. Hegai had thoughtfully arranged for my personal items to be relocated to my new quarters. The first eight hours I spent recovering from my lack of sleep the previous night. I slumbered erratically, restless under the torment of fitful dreams in which King Xerxes berated me for being such a forward and presumptuous commoner. Both the sting and the venom of his diatribes stayed with me after I awoke, like a sour taste upon my tongue. I went through the day unable to shake the peculiar tone of his disapproval and rejection, despite knowing that it had only been a bad dream—and that Hegai had warned me against making any assumptions.

Besides fighting against feelings of dejection and confusion, I also felt adrift. I had spent the last year relentlessly focused on preparing for a single night. Now that night was over forever, and I was already living out the likeliest outcome as a new resident of the concubines' house. Odds were, I would spend the rest of my life in this monotonous luxury, waiting like all the rest for a second evening summons from the Palace.

And how would he remember my name days or weeks from now, when he hadn't even remembered it minutes after my introduction the night before? Doubts swirled relentlessly through my mind and heart. Reality seemed so cruel. I could not shake the merciless fact that unless he called for me by name, I would never see him privately again.

I had reached my goal of spending a memorable night with the King. At least it had been memorable for me—I wasn't sure about him. What now was I supposed to do?

And more important, what was *he* thinking? He had the weight of the world on his shoulders. I know now that he was planning a war of staggering proportions against the world's second greatest military power. Had I slipped from his mind the moment he had jumped off the bed platform? Where did the choice of his queen rank in his thoughts compared to world war, Palace jockeying and the affairs of state? Was I the worst sort of simpleton for thinking that little Hadassah could intrude on thoughts and plans of such magnitude?

And then the face of my beloved father flashed before my mind's eye, and I was reminded of my Heavenly Father. *Oh, YHWH, I* prayed, *show me your way and help me to trust you in all this uncertainty. . . .*

He had a wayward general, problems with the treasury, countless minutiae of the Greek invasion to think about and so much more—but Xerxes, the King of Persia, had but one thing on his mind during his land journey to Persepolis. It was the girl who had shared his bed the night before. *Star of Susa.*

Never had a woman borne herself with such straightforward confidence in his presence. He had possessed women with poise and inner reserve, but those qualities had most often accompanied coldness and emotional distance.

The warmth of Star's enthusiasm and her unabashed passion for him remained about him like a lingering scent. He could close his eyes and picture her smile so easily, those bone white teeth in a face so perfect, so appealing—and yet, was it the way she lit up around him that made her so beautiful? No, he concluded, she would have been classically lovely had she worn a frown. But she hadn't. Every inch of her seemed aglow with pleasure at simply being around him. He had felt so at ease with her. So affirmed and cherished.

She had made no pretense about her willingness, her eagerness even, to share herself with him—her mind, as well as her body contours draped in the blue silk, were seared upon his imagination like the branding of red-hot coals.

He pictured her as his queen and saw a lively, spirited woman, an engaging companion, one with whom he could discuss affairs of state along with issues of the heart. The realization struck him broadside. *He couldn't wait to start a life with her*.

But she was a commoner, and that was a problem. Everyone expected him to wed one of the candidates from a noble family, especially one with political connections. Such a choice was not only traditional but would make political sense—on the surface. But the added claim to royalty would also turn such a bride's father into an instant contender for the throne, and Xerxes could live without one more of those. Besides, the noble-born girls had so far been the worst of all the candidates—haughty and self-centered, always wanting to make sure he was sufficiently aware of their highborn state and their various allies at court. They had been less than satisfying lovers and even worse company, he concluded with a bitter wince. He would not suffer one of them in exchange for a century's worth of political stability.

Yes, it would raise countless eyebrows for him to take a peasant girl, a commoner, and make her his new queen.

He grinned. That made him want to wed her all the more.

But of course I did not know this until later. . . .

## Chapter Thirty-five

*B*y the time one moon had passed, I needed every ounce of willpower I possessed to keep from despondency. The darkness deepened when I heard the King had returned four days ago from Persepolis and still had not called for me. My hopes and expectations had been raised beyond the stars during my night with the King. Now I wandered through my days in a sort of blur, working to remain as unfocused and unthinking as possible. I hardly noticed the other concubines around me as I woodenly ate what was put before me, slept as often as I was able and implored G-d to again give me purpose and direction. My handmaidens had urged me to dress in readiness should the King call, and I let them prepare me every evening. But each day the flicker of hope burned itself out more quickly. By nightfall the girls probably recognized my humiliation at the silence from the Palace, and they tried to cheer me with promises and expectations we all knew were not more than feathers in the wind.

I had given up hope and was lying beside the courtyard pool on that fifth afternoon, covered only with a simple length of cotton, when the sound of a distant drumbeat reached my ears. It sounded martial, warlike, unlike anything I had heard in my year of Palace life. I sat up to see if any peculiar sight accompanied this noise.

I saw a dark jumble of motion on the horizon. People. Carriers of some sort. A parasol that dipped up and down, as though held by a slave over the head of someone of high rank. A caravan of some importance was approaching.

I noticed a woman standing behind me, also staring, and then two more behind her. I looked farther—within moments, a dozen concubines had silently gathered nearby, their squints turning to frowns as the drumbeats grew closer. I heard murmurs about a court official coming this way.

I thought briefly of retreating to the house and observing what happened through a window. And then it hit me—I was as likely a choice as anyone. I had forgotten! In just a few days of emotional despair, I had allowed myself to utterly overlook the fact that I was a leading contender to become the next Queen of Persia—all royal fickleness aside.

Instantly flushed with embarrassment, I quickly wrapped the cloth around me and ran inside for a long linen robe in the preferred style of the concubines. I hurried back through the hall to rejoin the others and almost ran into Carylina, the last candidate before me, as she ran giggling out the door.

Memucan, the King's Master of the Audiences, was walking Carylina's way. The assembled concubines and his own varied entourage were now a mere backdrop, arrayed behind him in myriad expressions of awe and surprise.

They were all staring her way.

My heart sank and broke at the same moment. Carylina was a fine girl, a worthy candidate, I realized. Somehow, I felt more disappointed for Mordecai and Jesse than for myself. All those certainties about G-d and His destiny, His divine interventions. We would all muddle through without it, made sadder yet wiser by our disillusion. Maybe even discover a new chastened and reasonable estimation of G-d in the process.

Then, in a sort of luminous slow-motion cadence, as though the whole scene were taking place inside a jar of honey, I saw Memucan's hand go out to Carylina's shoulder, grasp it, then, in the slowness of great moments, move her aside.

*He was walking toward me.* Or was another girl standing behind me? I glanced around and saw no other nearby.

Within three steps of me, Memucan knelt. Before I could utter a word of apology, or even surprise, he was bowing his head before me. I felt like I was turned to stone, without and within.

He looked up with an inscrutable expression on his tanned and confident face. "My lady, Star of Susa, your presence is desired within the court of His Majesty King Xerxes of Persia. Would you honor me with your hand?"

The world came to a halt. The wind ceased to blow. The clouds in the sky stopped floating past. The mouths of the women behind him remained in gaped expressions. Even my racing thoughts had come gracefully to rest like an autumn leaf gliding to the surface of the water. They delicately settled upon a single thought, which emblazoned itself across my brain and mesmerized my faculties. *He remembers my name!*

*He wants to see me. He wants me to come.* . . . And then my emotions swung between *He wants me!* and *He is angry.* . . .

A noise knocked on the door of my consciousness. It was a familiar sound—one I had heard at a happier time. A noise like water. A sign of goodwill, of celebration.

I broke back into the waking world and found that the noise was applause. It occurred to me, ever so briefly, that I might well be a queen.

My knees gave way, and I would have fallen except for Memucan's hand under my arm. I willed myself to breathe. I tried to apply the news to my brain, to make it stick like an artisan pressing gold leaf onto stone. The staggering nature of it had rendered my intellect immune to rational thought.

I tumbled into a lucid moment and found that I had grabbed Memucan's hand. "Is everything all right?" I managed to ask.

Memucan flashed the same kind of smile I had seen Rachel give Jesse when he was a little boy in our house, asking silly questions. "The only possible harm is what could befall me if I answered your question, my lady," he answered. "His Majesty will make his intention perfectly clear when we arrive. Please come with me, yet do not be troubled."

Memucan lifted my hand and led me like I was a blind person. I kept stealing glances his way, wondering one moment if what he had hinted could possibly be true.

Finally Memucan whispered to me, "Madam, please. Did I not kneel before you? I can say no more, but surely you know you have cause for joy."

*Cause for joy.*

Some part of me knew these were the best possible words I could have hoped to hear. Yet the fact they presented to me lingered somewhere just beyond my understanding, a stranger at the door. Could I fully accept their truth?

In a far grander version of my procession five days before, I walked shakily past the gathered well-wishers. The golden litter before me had room for four and was carried by half a dozen of the largest men I had ever seen, Nubians, from the blackness of their skin, with more gold on their limbs than any slave I had ever laid eyes on. Drummers and escorts dressed in Palace finery stood to one side.

*I was not ready*—in my despondency, I had failed to stay prepared for this possible outcome. Harboring great misgivings about my appearance, I climbed into the litter.

Then something unexpected happened. A thick brocade curtain was drawn around the litter's edge, and I found myself enclosed inside a sort of improvised tent, open only to the sky for light. The flap opened, and I recognized two of my handmaidens stepping eagerly inside. Their arms were filled with rich embroidered clothing.

"We've come to dress you, your Highness," said Sakyl.

I nearly fainted with relief. Within a few minutes their skillful hands had not only folded my body into the most stunning set of robes I had ever seen but adorned my face with all my favorite cosmetics. I could have kissed their feet in sheer gratitude.

Finally they both leaned back with beaming glances, smiled their approval and swiftly left. Just as quickly, the curtain was pulled back and the same crowd, still waiting, cheered my transformation. I sat down; the seat rose and began to move forward.

A group of spectators came into view, trailing stragglers back toward the royal chambers. Hundreds and hundreds of people drifted our way as though blown by some errant wind. I could see the faraway gate into the inner courtyard standing open and a faint glimpse of the gate beyond, open as well.

This time as we broke into the sunshine, I was not only shaded from its glare by a canopy but cooled by the swaying of palm branches. And now rather than the applause of a partisan crowd, I was greeted with lowered eyes and heads bowing in some sort of deference. The sight of it shocked me—I had been a concubine wondering and worrying about my future only moments before. What had I done to merit such honor?

We crossed the outer courtyard and turned for the Inner Court. As we turned, I saw through the open door another magnificent hall. Its acres of shadowed heights were cleaved in half by pillars of sunlight streaming down from windows I could hardly see. Down lower, a carpet of scarlet lay stretched onto the terrace, its edges lined with threads of gold that glittered in the sun. And on either side stood soldiers, members of the Immortals, a group of the King's personal bodyguards, in full gold-threaded regalia with their scabbards held high and their faces frozen in expressions of grim determination. The tops of their helmet plumes and the blades of their lances traced a perfect row leading inward, in toward the source of all this splendor.

We came to the end of the red carpet, and the litter, along with the whole drum-beating procession, stopped at once. The litter began to lower, and Memucan fixed me with a knowing look.

"His Majesty awaits you, your Highness."

*What had he called me?*

But there was no time for questions. The litter had reached the ground, and it was now the moment for me to step out. I felt the blood rush from my head as I took my first step, and just at the sides of my vision, I realized that I was being watched more intensely, and by a greater number of people, than I had ever been in my whole life. The crowd had knitted together into a solid mass, a human wall lining either side of my path. It was almost as if every pair of eyes was a tiny pinprick fixed somewhere upon my person. I fleetingly wished for the anonymity of Mordecai's home, its isolation and peace.

I looked ahead and peered into the shadow of the Inner Court. Some great pomp and ceremony loomed ahead, I could tell, but I could not make it out precisely. Then I passed under the portal and into the great room. And I saw.

*Chapter Thirty-six*

The grand room and its hundreds of hushed occupants seemed to swirl around a central figure. There, at the very core of my vision, stood Xerxes upon a dais much like the one I had seen at the banquet. He was watching me intently, and his smile seemed only for me. Even much of the entourage behind him was the same as the previous event—the Seven Princes, the man who had rushed out at the banquet's end, and then someone I did not recognize. An older woman scowling in my direction. The mother of the King, I instantly presumed.

I stepped up my pace along the narrowing path through hundreds of new spectators. With every successive step I took, Xerxes stepped another toward me, so that by the time I had covered half the distance to the platform, he was standing at its base with his hand held out.

He looked magnificent. A gold breastplate covered his torso and was etched with layer upon layer of fine engravings. A silk cape flowed behind him. Again—you will not be surprised—gold shone from his every extremity.

And then I was there, within just two arms' length of him. Everything else fell away—the presence of the thousands around us, the splendor of our surroundings, the grandness of the occasion. All that existed were his eyes, which bore into mine with a fire that seemed to warm every inch of my body. Despite my wish to maintain a regal expression, I could not help but shyly smile again at the sight of him.

I tried to kneel, but he took my hand and raised me up at once. He spoke in a low, intimate voice, as though all the others did not exist.

"Welcome, Star of Susa."

I could not hold back my smile. My delight seemed about to burst my heart. "My greetings to you, your Majesty King Xerxes."

Then my own joy seemed to superimpose itself onto his face, for his lips widened into a smile that seemed almost unkingly, nearly too joyous for the formal atmosphere.

He turned aside and held out his hand to the crowd. A stooped, white-bearded man stood, his back bent seemingly from the weight of an object he held in both hands. The old man—a priest of some sort, I presumed—strained to extend the object into Xerxes' grip.

I recognized what it was, as anyone would. But my mind refused to acknowledge its meaning, however unmistakable. Back and forth I vacillated between the import of this object and my mind's more fearful scenarios. Now the evidence of my own eyes was overwhelming.

Encrusted with more gems and diamonds than I had ever seen on something so compact, its circular shape was, of course, solid gold. It was actually hard to look at for a variety of reasons—first, because of all its gleam, even there in the shadows. Second, because of its breathtaking extravagance.

And third, the most momentous—the implied meaning of a *crown*.

Xerxes turned to me with the diadem held before him. He glanced down at its jeweled tips, then at me.

"Star of Susa, I choose you to be my consort, my wife, my queen."

A deafening cheer filled the room, and both of our smiles stretched even wider.

I felt a barrier give way within me—all the anxiety and pressure and grief of the last year drained away, while a flood of pure gratitude poured down from somewhere above me and filled my heart to bursting. I lowered my eyes and shut them against the tears already welling inside.

*It is over. It is over, and G-d has truly been with me, guiding my ways. He has blessed my efforts.*

"I call you Esther, 'E-star,' the beautiful Star, the Queen of Persia," Xerxes continued, "mistress of all the land that lies between the Nile and the Indus and all who reside therein. Let all who live beneath my rule hold you dear in their hearts as their beloved sovereign. Let every Persian revere you as the embodiment of all that is lovely and tender. Star, I today name you Esther. Receive your crown."

Upon hearing my new name, I once again felt that a gift had just been delivered straight from G-d. *Esther means star.* He had thought this through, remembered my name and given me a most fitting new name. The simple thoughtfulness of it, from someone like Xerxes, suddenly made me want to weep.

I knelt then and bent my head toward him. The crown was settled upon my head more heavily than I had dreamed. I thanked G-d for all the training I had received, suddenly aware that unless I wore it with unusual care and grace, it would surely fall with a mortifying thud. And then it occurred to me that the need for caution was symbolic as well as physical. The heaviest burden I would ever shoulder had just been laid upon me.

But I stood, more carefully than I ever had before, and took his hand in mine. He suddenly held both hands high above us. I caught the edge of the crown, afraid it would slip, as he stepped forward to face the crowd and shouted, "Persians, your queen!"

And with a loud rustle of fabric and shuffling of feet, the entire assembly fell into a vast communal kneel. Sound died away and left me beside him staring at a sea of varicolored backs, with only the echo of their motion to fill our ears.

Xerxes waved them up again with a magnanimous sweep of his hand, and the crowd began to stand again.

"I declare a national holiday! Let there be joy and feasting throughout the kingdom—for I, your king, declare it!" The crowd cheered.

I turned to face Xerxes. Once again, he and I were the only persons in the room. The illusion was just as quickly dispelled, for all at once he held up both of his magnificent arms and shouted, "Let the celebration begin!" Another cheer erupted, and then a wondrous series of seemingly well-planned movements swept into action around me. The crowd parted as if on cue around a column of servants carrying tables of steaming food. Another line moved quickly into their midst with great golden vats of wine. Yet a third danced in, playing lyres and harps and flutes, filling the room with melodies and songs that sent a thrill quivering through my core.

In less than a few moments of furious motion, the solemn assembly had been transformed into a lively banquet hall.

And now I was walking up the steps where once I had stood at the bottom and quaked, holding the hand of—was it true?—*my husband*. The phrase whirled through my whole being with its intensity and joy.

We reached the top of the steps, and he looked at me for a long moment, leaned over and kissed me for the second time. His lips felt strong and smooth. Again the hall rang out with thousands of *hurrah*s. He turned toward my left ear and whispered, "I am sorry for such a surprise, my dear. In order to protect your life, I had to keep my decision secret. There are some at court for whom your selection is not welcome news. But come, my dear. Let us quit this

Tommy Tenney*

place and speak no more of such things. There will be banquets and briefings aplenty for the next few days."

And so, while the celebrants ate and drank and danced, Xerxes and I and the assembled courtiers slipped away through a back entrance. The largest litter I had yet seen carried us across the courtyards and through the royal gates into the King's chambers.

And yes, even now I do not tire of telling you about the size and beauty of all that surrounded us, or the splendor of the Palace, or the grandiosity of the moment. At the risk of being overbearing, can I just tell you that everywhere I looked, my eye was assaulted with the magnitude of it all, that once again my capacity for awe was pummeled at every turn by the sheer weight of extravagance around me?

Anyway, none of it truly mattered to me. More than ever before, the world consisted of me and the King. The closer we came to his bedchamber, the smaller the world became—until it had shrunk down to little more than the space between our lips. The moment our litter nudged the landing of the Palace entrance, the King was on his feet. He turned to me and swept me up into his arms. Xerxes nearly sprinted through the short hallway into his bedchamber, calling good-humored condemnations of death along the way to any functionary who dared intrude.

I was still held closely in his arms when we entered the room. He used his back to push the giant door shut. Then, as soon as the great clang of its closing stopped echoing, he looked at me with deep longing and, yes, love. His next kiss was both intimate and powerful. I was shaken to the core of my being. Next, he laid me on the bed, and I can tell you no more.

As a candidate yourself, if you do not know the rudiments of physical love, I will not spoil your surprise—or your shock, as the case may be. Your preparations will inform you on that matter easily and thoroughly enough. But more than likely, you already know more than I did—as today's generation is so much more aware than mine.

Suffice it to say that our mutual hunger raged unchecked—at no time did I even think of demurring or becoming submissive, for my desire for him was genuine. I had fallen in love with him. I had seen past his outer facade at some hour of that previous night's unconsummated love, and now I had reached his heart. I knew the cause for my previous despondency. It wasn't about winning a contest. *I simply loved the King.*

Given the ceremony that had just ended and his bold and public declaration of love for me, the intimacy was far more than simply physical.

In fact, what followed that time of glorious passion was not more lovemaking but another long night of soul-baring conversation. To my amazement, Xerxes even sought my naïve advice on kingdom affairs during those precious moments, and he remarked on my insight when my suggestions found his favor.

It was then that I began to feel like a queen—the wife of a King.

## Chapter Thirty-seven

*I* have drawn back the curtain on this very private moment because I want to explain something about intimacy. I have heard this word used as a substitute for sexual congress, and I regret that the usage has become so common. It is an injustice to reduce such a profound and important concept down to merely a prudish euphemism.

*Intimacy*, while definitely something I felt during and after the consummation of our union, was far more than just the closeness created by the joining of our bodies.

Intimacy was the joy we felt in each other's company—joy we could have felt walking together or having a deep conversation—as well as the trust, the mutual understanding, the romantic feelings of tenderness, the visual attraction, the longing to be cherished. It was all these things and more. *That*, too, is intimacy.

You will never spark this complete array of feelings in a king or any other man unless you do much more than simply tickle his eye, teasingly drop your pretty eyelashes, or even please him in bed.

First, you must be someone who knows who she is and how she fits into the world, who needs no one but G-d to make her a whole person. Neediness can be highly seductive, but only for a very short incendiary period, and usually only with a man who is flawed in his own right. After that first blush, a healthy man will want to shrug you off as quickly as he can. What attracts him the most, and the longest, is a woman who does not need him to be complete yet chooses out of her wholeness and completeness to give herself utterly to him. This I learned from the instructions of the Chamberlain, Hegai, and, yes, from the writings of Solomon.

Secondly, you must approach him with a sincere and delicate mixture of qualities. As I have already described, I had inwardly cultivated a true passion for Xerxes before that very first night together. This ember smoldered quite well after I first met him. But that passion was not based on what I could gain from him, his position or his prestige. I had caught a glimpse of him not long before coming to the Palace and knew him to be a handsome and charismatic man. Wouldn't those qualities be winsome in even a commoner? I think so.

Xerxes could also be incredibly stubborn, subject to raging jealousies and all too quick to fear for his sovereignty. I had been told to expect these things, and I found them. But I did not view them as off-putting—merely another piece of a complex human being. It was the man himself I focused on. *Who* he was, not what he did or what he owned or what he could do for me. And as someone who wards off opportunists all day long, the King recognized that quality in me instantly.

I was interested in *him*—his thoughts, his fears, his memories, his hopes, and I expressed my interest in those matters very quickly. That curiosity, along with my inner confidence, somehow set me apart from all the others. It put him at ease. I truly loved him.

I have already alluded to the third thing. Out of this confidence, then, out of this genuine passion for him and joy in his company, there must come an attraction from you that is not abjectly submissive or needy or cloying. He must know that your desire is based on every part of him—not just his physical being—that you desire to close the final distance between you, already having bridged every other gap remaining.

I implore you, when it comes time for your own night with the King, heed these suggestions. I can tell you, no one, not even your own personal Hegai, will impart these to you as a young virgin candidate. G-d and His servants, the wise Hegai and Mordecai, graced me with the ability to discern these things.

And as sincere as I want you to be in these matters, there is a final dimension I must mention. Every other leverage I ever employed with Xerxes was grounded in this sense of real, many-dimensioned intimacy. Influence flows from intimacy—true influence based on the deepest trust flows out of the richest intimacy. The story to follow would have turned out far differently had I not first nourished true intimacy with Xerxes, along with the influence that emerged from it. I did not demand this influence as my queenly right, although I could have, and certainly many women would have relied on this leverage alone. I did not grasp it out of petulance or aspiration. I did not even ask for it as his bride. Instead, I cultivated it like a delicate flower that wilts from too much watering, just like I nurtured favor with others in the candidates' harem. (And by the way—I did not forget the other candidates. Over time I persuaded Xerxes to release them to their families, a move that brought him enormous goodwill across the Empire. They returned home rich with the jewels and robes they had chosen for their first nights.)

I did not leave the King's arms for hours. We lay like that without counting time or heeding schedules or even speaking overmuch to each other. We simply rested together, basking in a feeling of closeness that never waned from the first moment of our union. In fact, the all-encompassing intimacy continued to grow. The tenderness of his embrace meant as much as any additional overture he could have made.

After several hours—a length of time that seemed to stretch into infinity—we were both startled by the faint sound of knocking on the bedchamber door. Xerxes smiled ruefully and shook his head. "Memucan wants us for the banquets," he whispered. "We are being called for." I began to stir and comply with Memucan's impatience, but Xerxes shook his head and pulled me back. "We do not answer to him. Besides, the less they see of us, the more they'll want us. I learned that a long time ago. It's one of those secrets of being a king. And, anyway, I'd rather be here with you."

So we lay back and relished a delightful sense of occupying a cozy boat amidst the storm. For the first time in my life, I did not feel the compelling need to answer a door. I needed answer only to him—my husband.

"Are you ready to be Queen of Persia?" he asked at last.

I thought for a moment. "I have not had the time to even consider that," I answered. "But now that you ask, I am more than ready to be your wife and your confidant if I can earn that place with you."

"I think you will make an amazing Queen."

"Will the people at court despise me for being a commoner?" I asked.

He sighed deeply and pitched his head back. "Oh, I suppose some will resent you a bit. But I think you will win them over. In time."

"It will not matter, my love," I said. "As long as things are good between us. But I will work to win over your subjects. Maybe not as thoroughly as I worked to win you." At that we both chuckled. "But hard enough to be loved, I hope."

"Speaking of the people," he said as he sat up and began to dress, "I suppose it is probably time to give them a glimpse of their new queen."

And bless my handmaidens' hearts, they had lobbied Hegai long enough to be summoned for my aid at the Palace—on Xerxes' signal they poured into the room with squeals of joy and even some weeping, then swept me into an adjacent room, a dressing room of sorts. While the now-dressed King stayed and spoke with Memucan, they converged on me carrying cosmetics and a beautiful new robe for the celebrations. Ever loyal and thoughtful of my needs, they had already begun to move my things into the King's Palace. I nearly suffocated each one with hugs at the very sight of them, for it seemed their excitement over my coronation nearly matched my own.

Before I knew it I was as pampered and coiffed as the day I had finally left the candidates' house. I found Xerxes back in the bedroom, arrayed in royal splendor himself, and we left the bedchamber for the Palace hallway. The cheering began as soon as we crossed the doorsill and did not subside, it seemed, for an eternity.

Soon we approached the front door, the assembled courtiers parted in anticipation and the most awesome sight yet slowly came into view.

The courtyard before us—and beyond its walls, beyond a courtyard after that, and beyond the next walls and the vast terrace beyond—was completely covered with people. Thousands. Tens of thousands. If I have the used the term "sea of humanity" before now, I apologize, for it would have been a mere smattering compared to this endless ocean of faces.

And what's even more staggering—it seemed that every last one was fixed on us! The force of their attention struck me with an almost physical sensation, causing my knees to weaken and my heart to start racing in my chest. It took several anxious seconds to regain my composure, wave weakly and begin to sense the emotions the crowd was sending our way. It was a mixture of adulation, love and simple joy—and perhaps even a bit of envy—the sorts of emotions every wedding party conveys to the bride and groom.

Waving and gazing over the intricate variety of expressions below me, I suddenly became seized with a desire to see Mordecai, to throw myself into his arms and celebrate the victory, *our* victory, on this day. He must be out there, I assured myself. And I found out later that he was indeed. Mordecai had been on the Palace grounds all day, weaving through crowds to gain the best glimpse of me. Jesse was there, as well—in fact, he had been assigned to help move my personal belongings into the Queen's apartment in the Inner Palace. But I knew nothing of this up there at the door, waving to the crowd.

All I knew was that I was not quite finished with two decades of life, and I had just become queen of the known world.

And then, less than thirty cubits away, on the back of one of the guards facing the adoring masses, I glimpsed once again the terrifying shape of the twisted cross and realized that being Queen was not the utterly safe place I had once thought it would be.

*Chapter Thirty-eight*

You might assume the amorous king of a vast empire could indulge in a lengthy and extravagant wedding celebration, maybe even for several weeks. Yet despite his great love for me, such was not the case with Xerxes of Persia and his new bride. We had our nights together, but days were spent maddeningly in feverish preparations for war. I bit my tongue and focused on making those evenings together all that they could be. But the lack of time together during daylight hours began to frustrate me immediately.

I did take the occasion to rescind the Queen's tax, a widely resented levy that forced citizens to pay for the extravagances of the Queen's lifestyle. Memucan hailed the move as a stroke of genius, as it instantly made me the most popular Queen in Persian history. Favor seemed to follow me in those days.

However, despite my seemingly charmed life, it took a near-eternity to see Mordecai again. Once more, the handmaidens came to my rescue. Most of them had seen me slip out nearly every day of my preparatory year, and when they had asked me, I had told them the truth. After all, it was no great embarrassment that my father worked on the Palace grounds and met me in secret. So Roshana slipped away to the King's Gate, found Mordecai and delivered my instructions. Another of my girls went out to each of the four watchtowers and delivered the Queen's order, beneath my seal, that one Mordecai the scribe be accorded full access privileges into any royal space he wished to enter.

The next evening, while Xerxes attended a war meeting with his generals, I followed two of the girls through a back door in my quarters, walked through a dizzying series of back corridors and came out of the royal residence through a servants' entrance.

I barely had time to make out a figure in the shadows before he was there, embracing me. The handmaidens, already highly nervous from having led me out without protection, stiffened and nearly screamed in fright.

"This is he," I quickly called to them. "He's my father!"

They shrank back, and I continued to sway in his arms. Yes, my tears made a return appearance, as did his. He kept up a muttered monologue as we kept bending together, neither one willing to break free. "My dear, my little one," he repeated. "Can you believe it? Can you? *You are Queen!*" I felt like I was holding a ghost, for the first part of my life now seemed like some faraway dream, an ethereal reverie that had taken place in someone else's lifetime.

I was still unwilling to let him go, so I began to whisper through my sobs into his ear, "I need you, Poppa. I need you more than ever! I need your counsel, your wisdom. I need *you*! I miss you!"

Finally he pulled back, his eyes bright with a remembered question. "Have you told them, Hadassah? Have you told even the King of your—secret?"

I hurriedly waved my companions farther away and leaned into his face. "No, I haven't! But if you continue to call me Hadassah and ask about my secret in front of my servants, it will not matter!"

He winced at his thoughtlessness and frowned. "I am sorry, dear Esther. I forgot about them and your new name."

"I told Hegai only because he realized that I had invented a name. And even then, I swore him to silence. Yet I do not see why I should not reveal it now. I am married to the most powerful man in the world, if you can believe it. Surely I am now safe from those who killed our families, am I not?"

"No," he hissed in agitation, "you are not! In fact, in some ways you are more in danger than ever. You must never, ever tell."

"Have you seen the number of guard towers you just walked through?" I exclaimed. "Do you know how carefully I had to plan just to have you admitted through all of them without endangering your head? Have you seen the thousands, yes *thousands*, of guards who guard my husband's every move? And now mine?"

I believe my angst was tinged with some desire to have Mordecai appreciate the height of my ascension. I regretted my petulance immediately when I suddenly remembered that fleeting glimpse of the twisted cross on the back of that sentry guarding Xerxes and me from the coronation crowd—not a handful of steps away from me.

I quickly dismissed the idea of telling Mordecai, knowing it would only heighten his worries. And at that moment I did not want to argue with him about his perennial anxieties. I just wanted to be with him, to somehow bridge the gap between my dizzying new existence and my placid, solitary life of old.

"Look, Poppa," I continued. "Don't you want to come into the Palace? I can have you named to any post you wish. I can gain you access anywhere you want."

"I am sure you can, my dear. But someone would learn our secret. Let me just continue in my current work and keep the safe life I know."

"But don't you understand? You can live at the height of luxury. You're the father of the Queen! Can't my victory have any impact on you? Come, please! Don't deprive me of my chance to make this a good fortune for all of us!"

"My favor must be earned," he replied, "just as yours was." He touched me lightly on the top of both arms. "You can make the most of this good fortune by being a beloved Queen—by extending your influence. As for us, I have spoken with Jesse. Now that you've been chosen, he has been rewarded for helping catch Misgath by being named to Memucan's private staff. He can run errands out to the Gate and carry messages between us."

"And is that *it*? After growing up in your house, calling you my father for as long as I can remember—I never see you again? We never speak again except through messages from a courier?"

"No. No," he quickly assured me. "We can arrange meetings like this again. But they cannot be too frequent or word will get out. This night was dangerous enough."

I looked down, unwilling to face him. "All right. But I never thought it would end up this way. I thought I was fighting for both of us. I never . . ." My voice trailed off into a stifled sob.

"You *are* fighting for us, my dear. You are. But G-d has a different way than we'd anticipated. A different path, that's all. Trust Him."

"I'm trying my best, Poppa. I really am."

G-d did not take long in showing both of us that Mordecai had urged me onto the right path. Less than a month later, in his normal position as a scribe at the King's Gate, he sat praying for me, as he usually did throughout the day. Evidently the two royal guards standing above him thought he was napping, for they launched into a conversation that soon caused Mordecai to stop praying—but keep his eyes very much closed.

"You're going to have to do it," said the first, in a low, raspy voice. "Xerxes is getting ready to leave for war tomorrow, and he decided at the last moment to bring our commander with him. So I have to know. Are you ready to take him?"

"I'm ready to take him into the next life with me," said the other, a younger-sounding man. "I hate him. I hate these people and all their grand pretensions. I'm ready to help take over and to cut a few necks."

"Are you truly ready to die in the process? It may take some time for the boss to take over the Palace after you do it."

"I am ready to die, my captain. If only I have the chance to spit in that fool's eye before I give his severed head a good swift kick."

"Good. Tonight, at the stroke of seven, just after his dinner with the new Queen."

"I'll have my blade sharpened."

Although the men must have separated and left within moments, Mordecai did not know that—and he was too frightened to open his eyes for a look around. So for several long moments he sat as still as a stone, listening to the sounds around him for any signs of their continued presence. Finally he pretended to let his head fall sideways, and he parted his eyelashes ever so slightly. They had indeed gone.

In case they were watching him from the crowd, he feigned nonchalance when he stood and yawned. Nevertheless he made his way through the Gate and swiftly onto the Palace grounds.

I received word only a few moments later. A guard entered the room where I was receiving a welcome massage from one of my handmaidens and slipped another of the attendants a tiny note. She brought it to me. It read, "Mordecai of Susa wishes an audience with your Highness at your earliest convenience, in the Outer Court."

I immediately bolted upright, stunning the messenger in the process, pulled on the nearest robe at hand and made haste for the Outer Court. I knew Mordecai would never have initiated a midday meeting unless it was an emergency of the highest order.

When I found him, Mordecai's skin was the color of an overcast sky—white with a strong tinge of gray. I wanted to sit him down and feed him a good soup as badly as to hear what had brought him there. Unfortunately, Mordecai gave me no such choice. He immediately grabbed my forearms and began to pull me toward him. He spoke quickly, then caught sight of the two guards purposefully approaching him.

"Hada—your Highness, these guards must leave us," he whispered.

"Nonsense," I replied. "They are part of my personal retinue. They are trustworthy upon pain of death."

Mordecai's face tightened and he whispered, "I mean it, your Highness. Absolutely no one else can hear my message for you. No one is safe."

Mistakenly assuming that his only objection centered on the tired old ethnic secrecy issue, I began to argue. These guards did not care whether I was Jewish, Persian or a citizen of the moon. They were reliable. Besides, I was Queen of Persia, regardless of anyone's prejudice.

But Mordecai held his ground. Speaking through gritted teeth, he muttered, "When I am finished you will see the necessity for my demands, your *Highness*."

So finally, with a heavy sigh, I dismissed the guards to just inside the door. They hesitated, wishing instead to form an outdoor perimeter for my protection, but finally relented.

Mordecai was only halfway through his account when I started to feel like the ultimate fool. Without taking my eyes off of Mordecai, I called out loudly for my senior guard. "Artechim, get me Memucan."

"Your Highness?"

"Get me Memucan. *Now*. As fast as you can run."

# Chapter Thirty-nine

*A*rtechim saw the fire in my eyes and his own widened immediately as he sensed my urgency. In fact, this was the first real test of my royal authority—to give an order to someone this adamantly. He turned on his heel and was gone, the rapid slapping sound of sandals on stone fading quickly into the distance. Mordecai gave me his usual tight embrace, this time punctuated by an extra long squeeze of the arms.

"I hope this can help you gain the King's trust," he said.

"It might. But I will also tell him your name as the source," I answered.

"No. Leave me out of this."

This time I flatly refused. As much as I wanted to give Mordecai the respect he deserved, I was, after all, Queen of Persia and capable of making a few decisions for myself.

When the door opened again, he hurried off with a quick wave for a farewell, still angry at my refusal to disguise his involvement. Memucan walked over, his brow furrowed at the interruption to his day, and asked me what the problem was. I relayed the entire message to him, along with the names Bigthana and Teresh—the guards Mordecai had discreetly identified with the help of other soldiers at the Gate. He asked me only if my source was reliable; I assured him that it was of the highest order. An old family friend. He, too, turned swiftly and disappeared into the Palace.

While I stood massaging my temples and wondering if I had just proven to be an ungrateful and disrespectful daughter, I heard Memucan shout from inside the door. And a remarkable thing happened. It was as though an invisible shock wave had traveled from the depths of Memucan's larynx outward to the Palace and at the speed of lightning across the courtyards to the watchtowers. The great brass doors swung shut with a speed I never knew such massive objects could attain. Down below my vantage point, soldiers snapped into combat position, facing the Palace with their spears and swords held out before them and their knees bent. Civilians stopped walking and stiffened in their places, glancing in my direction with anxious expressions. My bodyguards rushed out from the door with panicked looks. "Your Highness, please come inside," Artechim said, out of breath, "for they're about to lock down the Palace doors. Please leave this courtyard at once!"

I rushed inside to a scene I hardly recognized. The hallway I had recently left, once thriving with milling crowds of Palace staff and functionaries, now resembled an occupied camp. All of the usual people now stood rigid against the walls, terrified of the points of weapons holding them in place by an equally motionless row of soldiers. I trod tentatively through their midst as the only person allowed to walk openly through this tense gauntlet. I thought of the last crowd I had walked through days before at my coronation. How things could change in just a few days!

I turned the corner and ran straight into a loud commotion. Screams echoed across the marble and the row of Palace staff against the walls seemed to ripple with sudden apprehension. I peered into a roiling mass of people that seemed to propel itself into the hallway from our bedchamber—I made out two soldiers being lifted at their waists by enormous members of the Immortals, Xerxes' personal contingent.

"Death to Xerxes! I curse you all!" one of them was shouting. I could not believe he was so unhinged as to proclaim his guilt like that, but then, he must have known about the swiftness of Persian justice—especially when it came to royal security. Both men, I would later learn, had been found with concealed daggers upon their persons. Upon discovery, neither man had denied their intentions but spat haughtily upon their accusers and begun this shouting against the King. Someone had already draped the death scarf upon both of the men's heads—they had mere minutes to live.

I certainly did not follow this grim procession out to its destination, but Xerxes had just the night before informed me about the gruesome method of royal execution. No swift and merciful decapitation for those who plotted against the King or otherwise angered him. No, special prisoners like these were stripped of their clothes, thrown to the ground, and impaled straight through their bodies upon the sharpened point of a very long wooden pole. As the point eventually emerged at the top of their throat—I will leave you to imagine the place at which it first entered their body—the log was raised up and dropped into a pre-dug hole, and the prisoner died a long and agonizing death as the centerpiece of an unspeakable aerial display.

Walking through the hallway, I winced as I recalled Xerxes' account and watched the knot of soldiers recede from view. The King himself soon exited his room, his face as pale as the marble underfoot.

"Esther, Esther, are you all right?" he cried. "I heard you were the source of this information. How on earth did you learn of this?"

I thought again about my decision, then silently reaffirmed it. "I will tell you in confidence. An old family friend informed me. His name is Mordecai. He is a court scribe who does his work with royal couriers at the King's Gate."

Xerxes' face grew solemn and majestic, and had I not known of the occasion I would have feared Mordecai in deep trouble. "Summon this Mordecai. I wish to speak to him."

I exulted inwardly, thinking how much he deserved the accolade that awaited him. I knew he would have a moment of panic, but his recognition as a faithful, loyal subject would be worth it.

Xerxes called for his personal scribe to come with the Chronicles of the King, and we moved into one of the private dining rooms surrounded by a phalanx of tense soldiers.

"Can we not call off the alert?" I asked.

The King shook his head. "It is not over. We do not know who these men were working for. Surely there are other traitors about, awaiting my death."

A general appeared at Xerxes' side. "We will find them, your Majesty. The gallow poles will go up all over Susa." I shuddered.

Mordecai was even paler when they brought him in than when I had seen him last. The soldiers sent to bring him had not been told whether he was a co-conspirator or a hero—only to not harm him. And since Mordecai did not know whether the plot had succeeded, none of them had any idea if he was going to his death.

Xerxes wasted no time putting him at ease. He stepped forward to greet Mordecai, grasped him by the shoulders and gave him a warm kiss on both cheeks.

"Mordecai, today you have saved my life, and for that you will have my eternal gratitude." He turned to the scribe sitting off in the shadows. "Scribe, please record in the Chronicles of the King that Mordecai gave exemplary service to the Crown this day. Xerxes will be forever in his debt."

Mordecai bowed low, the new glow on his features betraying the pride he was too humble to convey. "It is my honor to serve you, your Majesty," he said.

"I understand you have known my beloved Esther for a great many years, honorable Mordecai."

Mordecai glanced up at me with eyes frozen in shock, unable to formulate a response. Finally realizing that his pause was more pejorative than my disclosures, he spoke. "Ah, yes, your Majesty. I have known Her Majesty since childhood."

Xerxes chuckled. "Well, Mordecai, when the time allows, you and I will have to sit down and have a long conversation."

"Sir?"

"To determine how such a rare woman was raised."

Mordecai glanced rapidly from Xerxes to me, trying to assess the situation. He took a deep breath and said, "I would welcome the occasion, your Majesty."

"Upon the first opportunity available," Xerxes continued, "a banquet will be given in your honor and a generous reward will be forthcoming. Let it be known that the King's favor is upon you!"

Xerxes was not able to reward Mordecai in the customary fashion, which required two days or more to prepare, for the next day he departed for war. It was my first introduction to the truly excruciating aspects of royalty. As Queen I was obliged to wear a brave and optimistic face while constantly on the verge of weeping. We said our good-byes in the bedchamber, with a great many tears and long, wrenching hugs. Then, after an interminable dressing session in which he was fitted with a full ceremonial suit of armor, we rode through a triumphant crowd to the outer courtyard. There, we walked out to the crest of the Inner Court and looked out over the assembled troops. Once again a staggering mass of humanity lay arrayed before us, this time in perfect military rows. I stood two steps behind Xerxes as he held out a martial salute and was answered by the deafening *Hail!* in return. Then he turned back, wrapped me in a theatrical embrace, kissed me one last time and walked down to his chariot. He cracked his whip and rode off, and the Persian army followed him—taking hours to fully exit the city. I, the Queen of Persia, had to stand and wave . . . and weep inside.

## Chapter Forty

*H*e was gone for four years.

I cannot overstate to you the impact of marrying a man I had just fallen in love with only to have him depart for such a length of time. I did not fear for the country in his absence, for Memucan was placed in charge and, as he was the King's closest advisor, the transition was seamless. No, I feared for the security of the country and the viability of Xerxes' reign if things went badly in Greece. There were ominous rumors almost from the beginning; therefore, it was both a blessing and a torment that messages took so long to reach Susa from the front.

I cannot tell you how deeply I missed him. I eventually took to my bed following his departure and hardly left it for days. Once again, I am ashamed to say, my ability to fully trust G-d wavered. I could only lament the fact that the man I had come to adore would soon face the might of a great military power intent on killing him. What would happen to me if he was slain? I did not want to learn the answer.

The Palace felt empty without Xerxes. Although the halls held activity and motion, it seemed to me that everyone was merely going through the motions, acting busy while the underlying reason for their busyness was a vast distance away.

Another cause for concern was a task Xerxes had left unfinished upon his departure—the ultimate conspirator behind the captured guards was not found, let alone punished. But on the verge of his departure, Xerxes instructed Memucan to continue the investigation. He assumed that the pause for war, and his eventual triumph, would destroy any impetus for an overthrow. Time would simply sweep away the confluence of people and events necessary for a coup to succeed. But those of us remaining in Susa were left with a profoundly unsettled feeling, knowing that the plotter remained free and quite possibly in our midst. At times I could feel palpable tension in the air, and I began to honestly fear for my own safety. My only hope was that the traitor was a part of the army hierarchy and was deeply involved in the current conflict.

After somewhat recovering from the shock and sadness of his leaving, I gradually came to find that Xerxes' absence from the capital had its advantages. First of all, the heat of the public spotlight on me seemed to diminish. I was still treated as royalty, but people looked more relaxed, and their manner around me grew more natural. Secondly, I, myself, felt more free to act. I spent more time with both Mordecai and Jesse. I frequently moved around the Palace grounds.

In my short time as Queen, I had already grown accustomed to going through my day with the eyes of hundreds upon me. I had begun to adjust to the strange feeling of being watched during the most ordinary moments of my day, while quietly relishing any time I could spend alone or in the sole presence of those I trusted. I never would have imagined, while still a girl who never left home and who had spent most of her life in the company of only three people, that I would adjust so quickly to such a public existence.

And then, just as suddenly, a great deal of the scrutiny had died away. I often felt, traversing the vast hallways and glazed brick walls of the Palace, that I was just another high-level functionary with business afoot. Perhaps some of that is due to the fact that I never demanded grandiose royal treatment for myself. Vashti, from all I had heard, might have insisted on being carried in a royal litter and surrounded by a regiment every time she set foot outside her quarters. And in her defense, her royal lineage no doubt made her expectations quite different from mine, raised a commoner. All I desired was security, human respect and the proximity of my loved ones.

What I craved most in this world, of course, was the presence of my new husband. But for many, many long months, that would be denied.

As for the war news, it started out highly encouraging, with but one area of concern. It sounded as though the Xerxes I had fallen in love with, the reflective conversationalist of our first weeks together, had turned into an irrational tyrant on the battlefield. I received word of a great victory at someplace called Thermopylae, and while the outcome itself was cause for joy, I heard that when the weather did not cooperate, Xerxes had ordered the sea itself lashed with whips. Then he had ordered the summary execution of engineers whose bridge had floundered in the storm. Furthermore, Memucan had begun warning me that the scope of this war was costing enormous amounts of money and that without a quick victory, it would soon deplete the royal treasury entirely.

This made me ill at ease. From my very first entry into the Palace, it had seemed that the King's wealth was limitless—so great that it would replenish itself no matter what happened to the Empire. Now I realized that in fact these riches were finite, beset by gargantuan expenses that extravagances like palaces and foreign wars posed. Xerxes had left with nearly two hundred thousand men and 160 ships. It was at that point that I began to earnestly crave my husband's counsel. Did I have the authority to cut back somehow on the Palace staff? Should I have implemented some sort of measures to reduce costs? Or did the *appearance* of endless wealth matter more than the state of the royal finances? I decided to consult with Memucan regularly upon these matters.

Every several days, he would enter my chambers, wearing a sober and contemplative expression, to give me news from the front. For some reason he had come to consider me a confidant, someone with whom he could share his most candid observations about the Empire. From what I understood, this was a new and unusual role for a queen. I suppose his loyalty was so unassailable that he knew he could voice criticism without being labeled an enemy.

"Your husband is an impetuous man," Memucan would tell me in the quiet of my counsel chamber. "I wish he never developed this obsession with destroying Greece. I pray to the gods it is not his—and our—undoing."

In retrospect, I think Memucan had found me to be one of the few impartial and sincere people with whom he could be truly honest. My peasant lineage had labeled me to Memucan as immune from the loss of balance and perspective that afflicted so many Palace insiders. And so, as the months turned into a year and the seasons flowed seamlessly into one another, I came to rely on the Master of the Audiences as deeply as I depended on Mordecai and Jesse.

One day Memucan entered my suite at the noon hour, and his face was ashen. I could feel the pounding of impending doom throb across the Palace and across my temples.

EGALEO HILL—ISLE OF SALAMIS, GREECE—479 B.C.

Flush with the satisfaction of just having sacked Athens—setting fire to not only the city itself but its renowned Acropolis—King Xerxes of Persia strode up the mountainside to the marble throne just erected there and sat down as only the King of the world could. He grasped the throne's arms with both palms, spread his legs and smiled with the assurance of one about to watch his last foe go down in utter defeat.

Three thousand cubits below him, sprawled across a spectacular vista of shining waters and bulging island landforms, lay the two greatest navies in the world, preparing to do battle. On the island to his right the fleeing inhabitants of Athens had taken refuge. Once their naval forces had been obliterated, Xerxes would order his ships to land and his men to slaughter the Athenians wholesale.

Without even glancing aside, Xerxes took a goblet of wine from his personal aide and gulped the liquid as though it were water. He tossed the solid gold vessel into the grass, closed his eyes in bliss and smiled broadly, deeply. How sweet the next few minutes would be! At last to witness the final defeat of the hated Greeks, defiers of his rule, murderers of his father. He would soon rule not just a vast portion of the world but the entire civilized world itself.

Standing next to him, his general Mardonius pointed. Their ships were on the move. Persia had far more vessels than the Greeks, and larger ones, as well. Once they had squeezed through the narrow canal and massed in front of the island itself, the battle would be all but won.

The sails bearing his royal gryphon symbol had been unfurled, and their bold standard flapped in the wind from hundreds of ships. Actually, the biggest challenge of the day would not be defeating the Greeks but navigating so many boats through the narrow passageway separating them from Salamis. As Xerxes watched, the first wave of three boats broke from the pack and headed into the strait, which could accommodate no more than three abreast. Three more sailed in behind them, and three more after that—a juggernaut of naval might.

He was admiring the seamanship of his captains when he noticed Mardonius frowning, staring farther away.

"What is it?" he asked.

Mardonius pointed down to the Greek position. "Well, your Majesty, it appears the Greek ships have taken a head-on course and are making quite a speed in our direction."

"Is that worrisome?"

"Well, it is unexpected, sir. They're sailing right into our teeth. One would have expected them to feign and dodge to avoid killing themselves outright."

"Maybe they are trying to hasten the inevitable," Xerxes said with a chuckle. The other generals and nobles around him chuckled, also, understanding their roles.

"They are not known for taking their lives, your Majesty. As evil as the Greeks may be, so far they have conducted themselves with a measure of bravery."

"Be quiet, Mardonius," Xerxes snarled, suddenly tired of the general's endless analysis. "You're ruining my moment."

"But they certainly *have* gathered speed," said another beside him.

Xerxes squinted for a better look. It was true—a good dozen Greek ships, smaller and nimbler than his own, were sailing straight into the Persian onslaught at a velocity that seemed downright reckless. He stood without thinking as the Greeks closed the gap, racing toward . . .

The unthinkable happened: they rammed their sharp prows into his lead boats and sliced them open like overripe fruits! A moment later, the groan of severed wood reached their ears. The sound felt almost human to Xerxes, like the dying gasp of a very large man.

Or maybe the dying gasp of his own aspirations.

The sonic wound reverberated through his assembly like a thunderclap; generals and high-born civilians alike recoiled and tried to stifle their own gasps by covering their mouths.

And their sounds soon turned to moans, for the worst had only begun. The wounded Persian ships not only floundered, tossing dozens of elite fighting men into the water like swarms of tadpoles, but their useless hulks now began to block the narrow canal. The ships behind them soon began to run aground and collide into one another!

I learned later that this was among the first times the hardened rams had been used in naval battles. The rather constricted area through which the Persian ships had to sail became a noose as the suicidal attacks by the Greeks decimated Xerxes' fleet.

Xerxes stood and shook his head, trying to forestall the moment when his mind absorbed just what was taking place before him. "No. No. Mardonius, tell me this is not happening."

Mardonius did not answer. He stood scowling, with his hands on his hips. Several of the concubines brought along for the trip had wilted, physically bowled over by what was taking place.

It only grew worse. The entire Persian fleet had acquired a speed of its own entering the strait, and so the great bottleneck continued. Ship after ship plowed into the one before it—tossing men and weapons overboard like wrecks in a hurricane. Meanwhile, the Greek boats continued to speed into the melee with a disregard for their own safety, which had it been exhibited by his own captains, Xerxes would certainly have deemed heroic.

The hillsides above the water's edge now filled with Spartan swordsmen, Greece's most skilled soldiers, along with archers, and even from this height, he could see the water turn red with Persian blood. Greek soldiers were actually leaping from the deck of one ruined Persian ship to another, killing their Persian enemies at full stride. His men were being slaughtered wholesale before his very eyes.

He turned to Mardonius. "Are we going to lose?" he asked in a voice that sounded to him like death itself.

The general answered without turning from his watch. "We already have, your Majesty."

*Chapter Forty-one*

*I* will never forget the day, or the moment, when poor Memucan entered with his skin the color of cinders and his face a mask of numb disbelief. He seemed a decade older than when I had seen him last, just an hour before. I was finishing the noon meal with two of my handmaidens, and we had just been reminiscing about the seemingly long-ago candidate days. I stopped in midsentence the instant I saw him.

He sat down on a divan next to me and placed a smooth hand upon mine. "I have some bad news, your Highness. Do you wish to hear it with your companions at your side?"

I nodded silently as my food suddenly soured in my stomach.

"Now, do not fear the worst, ma'am. His Majesty is perfectly safe. You can rest assured on that score. However—" and on that word he paused and drew a tremulous breath—"our armies have suffered a terrible defeat. The Greeks have withstood us."

"But I thought we had just sacked Athens, burned the Acropolis! I thought the war was over!"

"I thought as much myself, your Highness. However, it appears that His Majesty attempted to pursue and wipe out the Athenian refugees, and our navy was ambushed in the process. They suffered a terrible defeat and are unable to resupply the army. His Majesty is en route back home to Susa as we speak, for our navy can no longer replenish the troops. I do not know more than that, dear Queen Esther."

He bowed and rose to leave, but I caught his hand and pulled him back beside me. I needed a wise and experienced presence beside me just then. I did not let him, or my handmaidens, leave me until I had fallen into bed and begun a long night of weeping and wrestling with fears that would not stop tumbling over each other in my mind.

*What is Xerxes' future as King? And by extension, mine as Queen? Is Persia in danger of being toppled or conquered by a rising power? Will the unsavory influences rising in the Palace during Xerxes' absence now feel emboldened to show themselves and challenge his throne? How much can befall a politically weakened King like this one, not to mention his new, commoner Queen?*

After hours of restless questions, I once again saw Mordecai's face and thought to pray. I wish I could tell you I left it all in G-d's hands, but at least I finally fell asleep.

Unfortunately, the defeat at Salamis was just an omen of the ill tidings to come. One of the few men to distinguish himself during Xerxes' Greek campaign was the satrap of Negev, Haman the Agagite. Time and time again his advice on how to properly round up and execute civilian populations, as well as strike terror into the Greek ranks in general, had proven absolutely essential. Furthermore, the King soon learned that his newest governor was also one of his wealthiest. Even after decades of marauding, his predatory bands had never stopped raiding caravans all over the Negev, and their haul had now grown prodigious.

As a result, while the Persian army and Xerxes' entourage made their slow and despondent way home, the truth was that Haman actually possessed nearly as much wealth as the King himself.

Neither man knew it at the time. All they knew was that Haman currently ranked as one of the fastest rising stars in the whole Empire. And Haman no doubt realized that now was the time for him to call in his favors.

News of the defeat struck Susa like a death in the communal family. An eerie stillness fell over both the Palace and the city itself. I could feel it when merely leaving my quarters; the hallways seemed to be covered by some gray blanket that swallowed all sound, all life, all enthusiasm.

Yet by the time the Persian army returned to Susa, its calamity at Salamis had been given the proper political interpretation as both a heroic survival from treacherous Greek tactics and a righteous stand against the enemy's defilement of the rules of war. Far from erasing the sour taste of defeat, the revision of history merely took the worst of the sting from Xerxes' return and at least allowed a disheartened cheer to the returning men.

All the Crown needed now to complete the scenario was a good scapegoat.

As for Haman, it took him only a day to realize he had come back to a far different Susa than he had left. His departure four years before had been a highly calculated risk—with his plot against the King only freshly foiled, his co-conspirators still displayed on the logs of their gallows, and he not knowing how much information they had divulged before their executions. Leaving for war alongside the King, he had gambled that his role at the heart of the coup attempt was still unknown. And he had won. This, of course, we did not know at the time.

Furthermore, the capital of old had been a jubilant launching point for what promised to be a historic and triumphant military campaign. Now the King was diminished and cowed, and the entire picture had altered.

One thing Haman knew for sure. Xerxes' impulsive behavior on the battlefield had cost Persia the war, and the Amalekite must have felt more certain than ever of his chances for an overthrow. To put it mildly, he told his lieutenants in his sumptuous tent, Xerxes was a fool. A man like that did not deserve to stay king, let alone possess the acumen to stay in power. It would be a stroll through the poppy fields to pick off this weakened king. Maybe he'd even to take this Queen for himself. . . .

In fact, Haman had already set the stage for his next move. His own private army had galloped into Susa at the rear of Persia's downbeat ranks. Mordecai discreetly joined me, and we had watched the ragtag procession from the top of the King's Gate. All of a sudden, a band of horsemen arrived, completely unlike the soldiers who had preceded them. Their faces were taut and determined, their mounts of a different breed and a different gait than all the others. They didn't appear weakened or disheartened, as the regular royal troops had. They cheered and waved their swords about them as though they had won and were receiving their triumphant entry.

And then we both saw their backs—the symbol of the broken cross.

A foul wind blew through me as if I were made of straw. I reeled back, took a deep breath, and burrowed my fingernails into Mordecai's arm. He did not notice the pain, for he was reacting as spectacularly as I, standing as though made of stone. I was immediately in tears; yet because I was standing atop a reviewing post and knew others were watching me, I tried my best to rein in my emotions.

But I could not help it. Every terror that had ever beset my childhood had just returned tenfold.

The faithful Memucan, on whom had fallen the onerous task of reporting every piece of bad news since Xerxes' coronation, now bore the awful burden of telling a defeated King that he was also depleted of his wealth. The conversation did not go well. I was not in the room when Memucan delivered his dark report, but I was nearby, and I heard Xerxes' shouts clearly. How could the King's most trusted advisor allow this to happen? How could he have failed to stanch the flow, without even warning the innocent monarch of what was happening?

I could not make out Memucan's response, but I can imagine his rightful riposte—that he was not the cause, nor Susa the site, of the financial hemorrhage. Indeed, it was Xerxes' foolhardy military jaunt and the extravagance of his own demands that had caused the losses. But the defeated King, the spoiler of Persian invincibility, wanted to hear no such thing.

Memucan was ejected from Xerxes' presence with shouts and thrown shoes, plates and even a piece of silverware or two. Knowing the King, I am surprised the poor man left with his life, although Xerxes' angst was only momentarily directed at the loyal Memucan.

As for my reunion with the King? I am sorry to say that it took several days to happen, for Xerxes was preoccupied and angry in those first few days, far too distracted to entertain my joy at his return. Beyond that, I am also sorry to say, I had heard rumors that he had brought along a contingent of his favorite concubines on the trip. (Not exactly my favorite aspect of royal life.) I waved at him from a high balcony, and he waved back with a smile, but that was all.

And once again, I allowed the worst of my fears to overcome me. Today, I am certain that he actually waited to see me because he wanted nothing to intrude on the joy of our being together again. He was indeed assailed by a hundred pressing issues upon his return, and he hardly slept for his first three days back. But I once again began to question both his love for me and my continued viability as Queen.

Finally, on the night of the third day, he called for me. And the moment I entered the bedchamber and he turned around to meet my eye, it was as though no time had elapsed at all since our last night together. His face brightened and a broad though slightly weary smile creased his features; he held out his arms and braced himself, for I was running toward him from the first moment our eyes met. I leaped into his arms and thankfully the momentum forced us backward and onto the bed, not collapsing in an undignified heap on the floor.

Now, I know it may seem silly or incredibly naïve of me to be so in love with a man who had just deserted me for four years and who had generally behaved like a capricious maniac the whole time he was gone. But you must realize this: sometimes what might seem capricious to you and me is wisdom for a king. I was forced to realize early on that Xerxes knew more than I did about kingdoms, authority and the seemingly irrational requirements of staying in power. So I worked very hard not to question his decisions—but to love him.

And you must know—it was as if G-d had given me a mad love for the man. An irrational one, perhaps, but undeniable nevertheless.

He muttered, "I can't believe how much I missed you," and I believed him, for better or worse. And we spent the next two hours delightedly retracing the intimate territory that his absence had denied us for so many nights.

# Chapter Forty-two

*I*t started with a knock on the door.

Xerxes bolted upright at the sound, his face flooded with a mixture of rage and apprehension. "Ignore it," he whispered to me with a dismissive gesture toward the sound.

But the knocking continued; in fact, it grew louder with every passing second. I recoiled inside, for I did not want this glorious reunion tainted by the memory of seeing someone beheaded—which appeared to be this ignorant interloper's upcoming fate. No one interrupted times between the royal couple; not even the Master of the Audiences, who could approach Xerxes when no one else could.

I saw Xerxes glance around for some sort of weapon or projectile to use. His eye settled on the sword lying to one side of the bed, where he had undressed. He walked over and brandished the weapon, then turned for the door.

"What?" he shouted with venom toward the unfortunate one on the other side of the door.

The door opened slowly. I winced, preparing for the worst. Then I hazarded a glance, and my eyes widened once, then again.

Jesse stood in the doorway, his face the whiteness of marble. He advanced more tentatively than any male I had ever seen in my life. He did not so much as look my way; he kept his eyes aimed straight at his feet in a terrified sign of submission.

"Your Majesty, I beg your forgiveness for this most importune intrusion. And I implore you to listen to my news before you decide on taking my life. It is my wish only to bring you grave tidings that your Majesty should know at the very soonest opportunity."

The sword lowered. Xerxes glared at him expectantly.

"What is it now, eunuch?"

"Your Majesty, it is my deepest sorrow to inform you that Master of the Audiences Memucan has been murdered."

I did not see Xerxes' initial reaction, for my own eyes shut themselves in shock and sorrow. At the same time, understanding settled over me—as Memucan's chief aide, Hathach was the logical choice to deliver this news.

Within a split second, a loud clatter filled the room. Xerxes had dropped his sword, and he stood motionless, incapable of further movement. He fell to his knees, and I rushed to his side. Xerxes neither embraced my coming nor shrugged me off; he was too overwhelmed to react at all. The next thing to emerge from his mouth sounded like singing, so melodic was his lament.

"*Nooooooo . . .*"

And that is when I caught him, about to pitch over sideways. He swayed in my arms for a moment, then finally regained his composure.

"Have the murderers been captured? Do we have any idea who did it?"

Jesse shook his head. I then thought I saw him glance toward me from the corners of his eyes. "No, your Majesty," he answered. "No one has any idea."

Xerxes swore under his breath and buried his face in my neck.

What we learned later was this: while we all were sleeping, several men slipped through the building's darkest shadows and into Memucan's quarters. In much the same manner as Vashti had been killed, the loyal advisor was stabbed repeatedly in the chest; then he rose in his bed only to have his screams stifled by strong hands and a tightly pulled strip of fabric. None of the other occupants of the house heard a thing.

Eventually, I knew that these men had ridden into Susa that very week with the returning troops, and I knew who their leader was. I also knew their murderous legacy stretching back decades, for the source of my knowledge was a twisted cross appearing on an errant cloak accidentally dropped during the grisly assignment. It was many weeks before I learned of this item, but I immediately knew how this terrible thing had occurred and who had ordered it.

Haman the Agagite did not even wait for Memucan to be buried before presenting himself to the King. He had, after all, just spent four years at the monarch's side and distinguished himself in Xerxes' military service. Haman was plausibly as close to a friend as Xerxes could ever have. He had worked hard to position himself as first among the Princes of the Faces.

But Haman's next step had nothing to do with soldiering. Since Memucan had been the man who managed Xerxes' schedule, and because approaching the King uninvited meant risking instant execution, Haman sent an initial letter instead. In the missive he offered his services as the new Master of the Audiences. He was now wealthy beyond measure, and he wanted to "give back" to the Empire.

Xerxes did have a few misgivings about Haman, since his chief specialty seemed to be robbing and pillaging innocent people, but he accepted his offer nevertheless. Haman had been the only Persian to distinguish himself on the battlefield. His ruthless tactics had served Xerxes well, and the King now felt that he owed the Agagite. So, bypassing a host of Palace functionaries who had jockeyed over the post for decades, as well as the fact that usually this position was held by a eunuch, he quickly named Haman the Agagite his new Master of the Audiences.

As I may have mentioned before, this made Haman essentially the second most powerful man in the Empire. The Master of the Audiences controlled the Immortals, the thousand-man bodyguard force that camped perpetually in the outer courtyards. He also had complete sway over the King's schedule, able to lock out with complete impunity anyone whom he found unworthy of Xerxes' time. He alone could interrupt and enter the King's presence at any point—except for private meals with the Queen and the King's evening trysts. That was infinitely more than could be done by average citizens, who would surely pay with their lives for an impromptu approach to the sovereign.

And all the promotion had cost Haman was direct supervision of his band of thugs. That task he duly relegated to his ten sons, each of whom was already more bloodthirsty than he had ever been.

Perhaps this next is so striking because Memucan had occupied his post for so long and with such grace and ease, but you never saw a man as thoroughly transformed by a new appointment as Haman. He seemed to grow a cubit from the moment Xerxes laid the medal of the appointment over his neck. In fact, when he rose from the brief commissioning ceremony, which was attended by all high-ranking Palace bureaucrats, he turned his face to the assembled crowd with an expression that can only be described as gloating. In any event, a discernible aura seemed to emanate from the man, and his posture changed demonstrably.

It was not until Xerxes publicly announced the new title that Mordecai and I fully realized what had just taken place. The King loudly intoned, "People of Persia and servants of the Crown, I give you this day my new Master of the Audiences, Haman the Agagite of the Negev. It is my will that each of you obey and treat him in every way exactly as you would regard your King."

Upon hearing those words I felt my heart pound and my breath quicken. I swiftly turned toward the audience, where Mordecai occupied a prominent seat. Our eyes locked with an implacable expression of dread.

My first instinct was to run straight to Xerxes and tell him what a murderer he had just appointed. But the tiny voice of prudence warned me to consult first with Mordecai, and as usual my poppa convinced me to keep still for the time being. He wisely reasoned that unraveling the whole story to Xerxes would reveal my Jewishness and would throw me into a pitched battle with a Palace official whose power, at least as decreed, could be said to rival my own. Remember Memucan's ability to have Vashti deposed, Mordecai somberly reminded me.

And then it struck me. The true field of war was not Greece, a thousand miles away. It was right here, in my own residence. I could not have stood in a more exposed and perilous spot if I had stood upon the prow of that doomed lead ship bound for Salamis.

For the next few days I went about my business, secretly consumed with a lingering sense of dread and alarm. I met Mordecai for another covert meeting outside the walls of our private quarters. He seemed both as troubled and as irresolute as I. "I have spent the last three nights in the Palace library poring over the archives. Esther, I finally found the proof. An old volume of the Chronicles of the King records a tidy sum of money paid to one Haman of the Negev for services rendered in the 'pacification' of Babylon. The time period is right. We already know his emblem is that of the twisted cross. He most certainly is the man responsible for the murder of our families."

But then, seeing the helpless rage mixed with fear upon my face, he quickly added, "I am sure he knows nothing of our identity, so we are in no immediate danger. Please do not do anything rash. We may find a way to bring him to account for his crimes, but it will take time and a great deal of careful planning."

"I could have him executed at once," I fumed recklessly.

"I doubt it, my dear. Any other citizen, perhaps. But do not forget—he is the newly appointed second-in-command of the Empire. You might have a difficult time. No, I implore you, let me devise a way to reveal him for who he is. Do not worry that I will let the issue drop. You know how driven I've been to seek justice for what happened to us. Just be patient. Please?"

I exhaled. "All right, Mordecai. But I don't know if I can treat him normally."

"I know. I know."

Mordecai's understanding made his wise counsel acceptable to me. After a quick hug, we went our separate ways.

It was Mordecai who had the most difficulty treating Haman normally. I learned of this only much later, but the next day Mordecai was sitting in his usual seat near the King's Gate when Haman entered the Palace grounds. Evidently he had taken seriously Xerxes' order that everyone treat him as they would the King himself, for he had several of his largest men precede him with swords in their hands, yelling, "Everyone bow before His Excellency, the King's Master of the Audiences, Haman the Agagite! Everyone stand and bow!"

At once, the hundreds of onlookers bowed forward at the waist, just as they would before the King himself. That is, they all bowed except for Mordecai. He sat as still as his posture would allow and gritted his teeth against the dust whipped up by Haman's horses.

The thug closest to him walked over and brandished his blade high in the air. "Did you hear me right?" he shouted. "Bow at once for the King's Master of the Audiences! Have you not heard? There is a new master in the kingdom!"

Mordecai did not even deign to look the man in the eye for several long seconds, so intense was his disgust. I know because he later told me that his mind raced with thoughts of death with honor—*Kill me, you swine, for I long to go the way of my mother and*

*father and sisters, not to mention Esther's beloved family, and I welcome
the chance to turn every one of these onlookers into a witness to your bru-
tality. Come on—raise your blade, you coward.*

Instead, the man swore repeatedly, then turned and rode on—
clearly not authorized for killing that day.

Then Haman himself rode by in a chariot inlaid with rare and
precious gems. His eyes never left Mordecai's figure during his ride
through the portal.

As quickly as he'd come, he was gone. After several long
moments, the grit settled, and the hundreds of bowed torsos slowly
straightened. Every eye was darkly fixed upon Mordecai, the one
who had not budged.

A fellow scribe groaned from the back strain and turned to his
stubborn colleague. "What is the matter with you, Mordecai? Why
did you disobey the King's direct order and refuse to pay homage?"

"It is none of your business."

"Come on, Mordecai. You and I have known each other since
you came to the Palace. You've always been a reasonable, accom-
modating man. You've bowed to the King and his high officials in
the past. Why not bow to the new Master of the Audiences?"

When Mordecai finally spoke, he settled a heavily lidded gaze
upon his questioner. "I bow to no man but the G-d of Heaven and
my King, Xerxes," he said slow and level.

"What is happening here?" asked a deep voice from over the
companion's shoulder. It was a royal guard who had stepped off his
post to investigate the problem. "Why did you defy the King's command?"

Mordecai said nothing and looked straight ahead like a man
scanning the horizon for some approaching danger. A razor-sharp
blade found its way beneath his chin, deeply indenting his neck but
not quite puncturing it.

"Answer me, you luckless soul. I already have the grounds to
haul you in."

Mordecai's back grew straighter, his gaze even more resolute.

"Sir," interrupted the bystander, "the man refuses to bow to the King's emissary on religious grounds."

"What is your name, my man?"

"My name is Mordecai."

"And what religion do you practice?"

Mordecai paused and made the decision that I always knew he would make when the occasion warranted. "I worship the one true G-d," he replied. "YHWH. The Creator of heaven and earth. The G-d of Abraham, Isaac, and Jacob."

*Chapter Forty-three*

pparently the soldier in question was familiar with the influence and autonomy that Jews enjoyed in Susa, for he nodded, shrugged and returned to his post, harassing Mordecai no
longer. He did not even stir the next day when Mordecai repeated
his defiance, or the day after, or the day after that when my poppa's
back remained unbent and it seemed the passing Haman would
burst a blood vessel from apoplexy.

On the fourth day, the scribe who had overheard Mordecai's
startling admission was mysteriously called in for a day's work with
the King's Master of the Audiences. Once alone with the man,
Haman wasted no time in inquiring why his neighbor was showing
such disrespect. He asked the question almost mournfully, as
though he felt nothing more than a vague disquiet at this strange
scribe's behavior.

At first, the scribe resisted. After all, he was not eager to bring
about his old colleague's demise. They had become good friends
over the years. But sensing his prey's reluctance, Haman resorted to

threats. "Perhaps we did not see correctly. Perhaps it was you, sitting so close to this man, who refused to show me the proper respect."

The colleague sighed, then began to speak. He restated his conversation with Mordecai and told Haman the surprising disclosure that his old friend was actually a Jew, though Mordecai attempted to keep this a secret.

Haman smiled and inhaled, deep and long. He leaned back on his couch and sighed.

Finally, one of the Susa Jews—in person.

*Perfect.*

He knew better than to mar his first week in his new position with the indiscriminate killing of a Palace scribe, so he merely reached out and clenched his fist in the air. There would be time enough—soon.

Mordecai's friend left the encounter shaken to the core of his being.

On the terrace of his palatial villa, Haman nodded to one of his men for the plot to begin. His henchman had ushered in a soothsayer, who pulled two handfuls of small clay cubes from a bag, separated them on the tabletop with deft stabbing motions and dropped the respective piles into two thin-necked urns. He looked at Haman and nodded. The casting of the *pur,* the lots, was set to begin.

He shook the first urn, tossed a half-dozen cubes down upon the wood and looked up at Haman. He had his first result.

"The pur show the month of Adar."

He picked up the second urn and repeated the process.

"The thirteenth day."

Haman was at first a little disappointed that it would be several months away; then he decided it would give time for his plan to reach every province and time to prepare every detail.

Finally Haman smiled. "Just so! The thirteenth of Adar is the beginning of the Persians' feast of the goddess Anahita. There'll be drinking and revelry . . . topped off with a little slaughter and plunder, courtesy of the King."

It must have taken enormous effort for Haman to appear hurt, incensed and concerned before Xerxes later that afternoon. Inwardly, he no doubt felt buoyed by a sense of relentless destiny, of staggering opportunity. Finally his time had come. Not just as a man, as an official of the Empire, but in a role that stretched back centuries—as a son of Amalek, a descendant of Agag.

Finally he had both the influence and the pretext with which to exterminate the Jews. He could have wept with humble gratitude, wishing his father could have been there to see him—and more importantly, there to see the stacks of Hebrew corpses that would soon line ditches and alleyways the world over. He breathed deeply to hold in his emotions, remembering all the generations of Amalekites who had lived and died in exile because of the Israelites and their hateful G-d. He would soon avenge them. When Xerxes remembered the meeting later, he concluded that Haman would have been nearly overwhelmed with the potential for revenge.

But Haman obviously swallowed all these feelings in favor of a mask of simmering rage and victimhood as he approached Xerxes' side that day. Never one to ignore a courtier's emotions, the King looked up from a parchment he was reading and asked, "What is the matter, my new Master of the Audiences?"

"Sir, I am naught but your servant; you know it no less than I."

"Oh, not so sour, Haman. It is but a jest. Now tell me what troubles you before I grow angry."

"Your Majesty, I have just encountered one of the gravest threats to your reign and to this Empire that you will ever imagine."

All the mirth drained instantly from Xerxes' face. A threat to his reign was always something to be heeded. His gaze now bore into Haman's face with an almost visible force.

Haman took a deep breath, as though he were too deliberate a man to launch into such a painful subject without enormous reluctance. "I am speaking of the Jewish people. I've become aware that during your absence, they have been fomenting a massive coordinated conspiracy against your Majesty's rule. In the last few hours alone, your Majesty, evidence has come to light that Hebrew killers were responsible for the murder of Memucan. I have sworn witnesses in my custody right now—two experienced Palace guards who detained three men leaving the area of Memucan's quarters quite late on the night in question. Both men independently swear that the trespassers were clearly Jewish in ethnic origin."

"Did they arrest the intruders?"

"Sadly they did not, your Majesty, and for that oversight they will be punished. But please remember, sir, that they had no idea what had just taken place inside Memucan's quarters. Besides—the Jews had Palace passes, maybe forged or even stolen—which allowed them access, even if the hour seemed suspicious."

"This is most distressing," Xerxes whispered.

"Most regretfully, your Majesty, that is far from all. Jewish insolence against your authority has become an open practice, even within the Palace itself. Today I passed a Palace scribe, a Jew who tells everyone who will listen that he bows only before his god. He was resisting obeisance to me at the time, but he could have just as easily been speaking of your Majesty or any authority outside of his cult. He openly flaunts his refusal to stand at my passage, despite your Majesty's clear instructions."

"Is this man in custody?"

"No, sir. I did not want to tip off the conspirators that we are aware of them. But think of it, your Majesty. Open rebellion, starting within the walls of your very own palace!"

"What a betrayal," Xerxes said, shaking his head. "I've known and worked with Jews all my life. My own grandfather allowed many of them to return to Israel and rebuild their temple!"

"Exactly! And how do they repay the Crown's generosity? With plots and treachery! You see, sir, it is nearly impossible to know just what these people believe without firsthand knowledge. And as a former inhabitant of this area of Mesopotamia, I am intimately aware of their twisted beliefs. They recognize no authority but their own bloodthirsty god. They will work insidiously to undermine any leadership aside from their bizarre priests. They are a rotten plague in the kingdom, relentlessly eating away at its strength, eroding everything you love and that loves you."

"I have simply never heard this before," Xerxes insisted.

"As I said, your Majesty, they specialize in covering their shrewd designs. It is one of their greatest strengths—their ability to completely mask their evil."

"Haman, all my life I have known them as a weakened people. They were brought to Babylon as slaves. They have little organized leadership. They barely have control of their own capital city. Jerusalem, I believe it is called. They don't immediately strike one as a potent threat."

"Yet wherever they're allowed to breed and settle, they grow stronger. And whenever they reach sufficient numbers, they always seize the reins of power. No treachery is too low, too revolting."

"How did you become such an expert?" the King asked.

Haman paused, and his eyes seemed to fill with tears. "Your Majesty, could I tell you the story of how they exterminated all but a handful of my people?"

Startled, the King said, "Of course. Tell me all of it."

"Well, my ancestors, the Amalekites, tried to make peace with the Jews for centuries. When they first emerged from Egypt, their own women and children starving and emaciated, we offered them food and shelter. They repaid us by stealing our crops and burning three of our villages. Then they settled in our prime farming areas and simply began to take our lands by force. Still, we sought to coexist in harmony. But once their population grew large enough, they chose a king and began to make war against us in earnest. They systematically slaughtered men, women, children, even our livestock, by the thousands. They killed all but a tiny remnant of helpless Amalekites, my own people, my heritage, deliberately trying to wipe us from the face of the earth. And they robed it all in religious excuses. It's a matter of historical record, your Majesty. I encourage you to have your scholars research it themselves in the royal library."

The King shook his head, consumed by dark thoughts. At long last, he looked up. "So what do you propose I do? Eradicate them? They are not only numerous in Susa but all across the Empire. They are well-respected merchants and—"

"I know, sir. That is part of their plan. To fit into the Persian population and disperse evenly across your districts, waiting for the signal to strike. But they are so relentless, so unceasing in their vile efforts, that the only way to save your kingdom is to make an example of them. Kill them all."

"All? You must be joking. Our citizens would never understand."

"Leave even a remnant, and it will redouble its struggle to destroy you." Haman allowed a thoughtful pause to settle over the exchange. Then he pounced. "And, my King, I have something else to make your decision easier." He took another of his ponderous breaths. "As it is no secret that my people have an ancient stake in seeing these vermin wiped from this earth, I will pay into the treasury ten thousand talents of silver upon the issuance of a royal edict authorizing their liquidation."

"That is a most generous offer, my friend," Xerxes replied thoughtfully. "And yet, such a rash action. I just returned from a disappointing war. I have hardly the goodwill or the pretext to deploy my troops across the realm to kill a civilian population."

"You are king, sir. You do not need a pretext, especially where national security is in the balance. The Hebrew threat is its own justification. And yet—do not send your troops. There is a simmering jealousy toward Jews among your loyal citizens. Simply give them the authorization to kill all the Jews in their midst and take their possessions for themselves. Many Jews are quite prosperous, you know. And remember that my contribution alone will restore health to the royal treasury."

Haman smiled his best compliant grin at those words, for he was already planning in secret for his henchmen to plunder the wealthiest Jews upon the chosen day—amply reimbursing him for the outlay of blood money he had just offered the King.

Xerxes fell into a long, meditative pause. Having been in his post only a short time, Haman was not supposed to know about the treasury's plight. Yet the King overlooked the unauthorized knowledge as just another fact of Palace life and considered the plan with a slow nodding of his head. The last thing he needed now was a rebellion at home after such a costly and embarrassing defeat abroad. *Yes*, he thought with a clench of his jaw, he must appear strong now. Or others would arise to exploit his weakness—others who were already watching for the least sign of encouragement.

"That is a most helpful idea, my friend," he said at last. "You have clearly given this a great deal of thought. This Jewish scribe, by the way—he must have truly stirred your ire."

"Clearly he did, sir. Every person at the King's Gate, hundreds of your Majesty's most faithful subjects, bowed to me in respect. Not respect for me, mind you, but by extension for the Crown and for your Majesty. This man's rigid back made him stand out like a torch at midnight. Every eye turned from the King's chief servant—me—and was drawn to this seditious display. It was a powerful gesture of rebellion against you and your stated authority, your Majesty. And it may have been a public sign of what has been brewing in private."

Xerxes' face went grim and tense. "That will not do, Haman. You are right. I saw your quick eye on the battlefield, my friend. You saw enemies coming before others did. I value that talent most highly." The King reached one hand over the other and yanked off his jeweled royal ring. He held it out to Haman. "Here. Use my signet ring to make this into law. The Jews are yours to do your bidding. But remember, my friend"—and at this, Xerxes grabbed

Haman's wrist and fixed him with a piercing gaze—"once that signet ring stamps the wax, it is done. The law decrees that it cannot
be changed. So do it right the first time."

My husband recounted to me this whole conversation in vivid
detail when later he discovered how he had been manipulated. I
don't mind telling you he was both extremely angry and mortified
to have been deceived by someone he trusted. But I am getting
ahead of my story.


As occurred whenever an urgent proclamation was to be dispersed across the kingdom, the Master of the Audiences summoned
every Palace scribe into his presence for dictation. Mordecai, as an
experienced member, usually was situated in the very front row. But
seeing who was in charge of the meeting, he chose a seat farther
back.

Without greeting or preliminaries of any sort, Haman began to
elaborate on their assignment.

"On the thirteenth day of the month of Adar, all citizens of Persia are exhorted by His Majesty King Xerxes to destroy, to kill, to
annihilate every person of Jewish blood, whether man, woman or
child. On top of that, the populace is fully authorized to plunder
these dead traitors' possessions. Signed into royal law on this day."

Now, you must understand—Mordecai was already most agi-
tated at being in such close proximity to the man who had murdered his family. He was using every ounce of self-restraint and
natural common sense to keep his mouth shut. But when he heard
these words, his lungs nearly emptied of air. The vessels of his brain
seemed to void themselves of blood. He fought to keep himself
upright. While his head swam, he managed to still its motion by
thinking of his family and allowed the rage to keep him conscious.

He focused his gaze on Haman.

"Does this edict actually come from the King? Does it bear his
royal signet?" asked a brave scribe.

*Maybe, just maybe, this evil man is acting without approval,* thought Mordecai.

"No," Haman said flippantly. And for just a moment, Mordecai's heart again soared with sudden hope.

Then Haman held up his hand with a faint smile, allowing the King's ring to glitter in the light. He slammed the jewel and its seal down upon the questioner's parchment, indenting the royal seal across the document.

"*Now* it does." He stared straight at Mordecai for a long moment.

That next dawn, the King's Gate shook with a sound like an onrushing tornado, rousing me from my sleep. A moment later, the cause of the awesome sound materialized: it was the thundering hooves of 127 of the Empire's fleetest mounts, each one bearing a royal courier and storming through the portal in a cyclone of dust and noise. I watched from a small Palace balcony, awakened by the noise but as yet unaware that each rider carried, in a leather pouch upon his back, sealed with the King's signet, a copy of the edict authorizing the extermination of my people. As I learned later, much too late, each horse and messenger would scatter to each of Persia's 127 provinces in twenty-three nations, delivering their tidings of death to each of the provincial governors in person.

Haman had wasted no time.

I also did not know that Mordecai, who had personally prepared twelve copies in the last twenty-four hours, himself stood at the King's Gate during that evil moment and watched the dark shape of the convoy recede from sight while he swayed from sheer grief in the retreating daylight. He reached up to his brow, wiped it clean of a sweat that bore no relation to the weather and fought to keep his balance.

Mordecai had been so proud of being a royal scribe. All over Susa, Jews accorded him great respect, despite his lack of involvement in their community, because of his work and the status it afforded him.

Now he wanted to vomit, thinking of what he had just helped to expedite. And even worse, he could not let himself even consider the thought that his refusal to bow to Haman had been the spark that launched this evil attack on his people.

*Chapter Forty-four*

At first, I thought little of not seeing or hearing from Mordecai over the span of several days. After all, the King had just returned after four years' absence, which had caused my own schedule to accelerate dramatically. Court was back in full swing, my social calendar had gone from dormant to hectic, and my free time was largely spent in useless yet time-consuming court appearances about the Palace.

In fact, the demands on my time escalated even more sharply because of a most disquieting turn of events.

You see, matters between Xerxes and me did not permanently return to the ecstasy of our first few nights together so many years before. What sank my spirits as surely as anything was the lack of a summons to his side—or his bed. Slowly, it grew clear to me that the magic spell of our time together had been shattered by the rigors and traumas of war. The initial period of bliss and harmony appeared to be over.

My nights spent alone during his absence were nothing compared to the lonely nights after his return, which gradually increased in number until more than a month had passed. I began to catch the tail end of gloating looks and snippets of gossip from ladies of the court, and I wondered who *was* gracing the King's bed. As usual, my faithless mind raced far on ahead of the facts.

Certainly, I was not the only one being neglected by the King. His deflated retreat from Greece, combined with the disastrous news of the treasury, the murder of Memucan and the subsequent report of a grave threat within the Palace walls—all had combined to render Xerxes listless and despondent for the very first time in his reign. I began to hear of canceled engagements, of days when Xerxes never left his chambers. I longed to reach his side and do my best to restore his morale, but even the most basic mealtime summons never arrived. And so, as my popularity still soared with the people following the Queen's tax repeal, I began to make appearances in his stead, dismissing the urgent inquiries about his health with a quick laugh and a confident shake of my head. . . . *Oh no, fear not, Vice-Chancellor. His Majesty is merely in a war council, conferring with his generals on the impending counterattack. . . .*

To make all of this even worse, I remained tormented by the fact that Haman, the now-proved murderer of my family, was my husband's top advisor—a man who now spent much of his day just a short distance from me, constantly trying to become as trusted and close to me as Memucan had once been. His ingratiating efforts, of course, only made me want to publicly scream out my accusations. But I bit my tongue and gave him my best winning smile. Truth be told, it was only after witnessing how the King's reclusiveness bolstered Haman's status as the Empire's most powerful figure that I started attending court functions alone. Someone had to blunt the Agagite's sudden rise to power, and at the moment I seemed to be the only person in a position to do it.

Yet once again, the overwhelming fears of my childhood started to make repeat appearances. I began having nightmares of that horrible night, only now Xerxes and the Palace court stood watching the carnage, laughing and pointing out its most spectacular highlights. Perhaps worse, that gray cloud started to haunt my waking hours again, coloring my daylight with its haunting and shadowy gloom. I grew fearful and jumpy. Sudden gestures and people turning corners too quickly caused me to scream, ready for a blade across my neck. As a result I became irritable and critical.

Worse still, I had begun to hear Palace rumors of impending civil unrest. The whole city wallowed in confusion. Indeed, the world seemed to be unraveling at every seam! How far I had come from the wide-eyed girl who once imagined life among these golden walls as a blissful idyll of joy and leisure. All the prestige and privilege had now faded utterly from my mind—replaced only by gnawing fear and grinding stress.

As a result of all these distractions, I was completely caught off guard when one of my handmaidens quietly tapped me on the shoulder and whispered, "Your eunuch friend, Hathach, is waiting outside. He has an urgent message he will deliver only to you."

For some reason, I instantly knew it was about Mordecai. I had not heard from him in several days and I sorely needed a dose of his calming wisdom. A plunge of fear stabbed through me—had he suffered an illness? Had his delvings into Haman's complicity caused him to be hurt—or worse?

I immediately stood and made my way to the door where I knew Jesse awaited, an anxious look on his still-handsome face.

"Hadassah—I mean, Esther—" he smiled gamely at his inability to use my royal name—"there's a problem, but I don't know what it is. I have been ensconced in the archives on an assignment from the King, but when I finished this morning, I heard some most disturbing news. I know it's serious, because Mordecai paraded through this city in full Jewish regalia, crying loudly in Hebrew. It's as if he now wants the whole world to know what he kept under wraps for so many years. And even worse, he has now clothed himself with sackcloth and ashes and spends all day at the King's Gate moaning loudly."

"Did he say why he is so upset?"

"No. He barely acknowledged my presence, he was so distraught. He will not move any more than he will speak. All I know is he is wearing full Jewish mourning garb. He must have told everyone he was a Jew, because all the symbols are now there for everyone to see."

"He is certainly in mourning—there is no other meaning for sackcloth and ashes. But mourning *what*? Are there any tragic deaths he could be upset about?"

Jesse shook his head. "He keeps mumbling something like 'only she can save me now.' You must go to him, Esther."

"I can't. I must not. But, please, go to him for me. Take him a change of clothes and tell him that he must stop this dangerous display and be more discreet. If he wants to continue keeping the truth about our relationship a secret, I simply cannot come to him. He must stop what he's doing and tell *you* what is the matter."

Jesse nodded somberly and hurried from the room through the hidden exit. Although he was now Haman's chief assistant, he spent some of his time working on my behalf—errands that were naturally kept hidden from his new superior. In that role he had learned all the Queen's hidden exits and corridors.

I was just finishing a solitary supper when the same handmaiden rushed in and summoned me with frantic hand motions. I hurried out to our usual meeting spot and found Jesse sitting against the Palace wall with his face in his hands. Without a moment's care for appearances, I rushed over, knelt and pulled his hands back. The face before me bore little resemblance to the one that had left me such a short time before. Jesse's face was streaked with dust and tear tracks, and his features were so twisted in anguish that he did not look like himself.

"What is the matter, Jesse? Tell me, what were his tidings?"

He shook his head, initially unable to even form the words. I felt my heart plummet and shook his wrists wildly.

"What? What?"

"*Your husband* has just issued an Empire-wide edict stating that on the thirteenth of Adar all Jews are to be killed—men, women and children."

I recoiled as though a physical blow had struck me across the face. I began to pant, for the invisible shock had knocked the air out of me and I literally could not breathe. I fell back and sank into the dust—hardly a regal pose. Yet I could not gather the composure to regain my feet.

I wanted to race through the usual preliminaries—whether he was joking, whether there could be some mistake, whether this interpretation was all the result of some simple misunderstanding. But I knew that neither Mordecai nor Jesse, both of whom I trusted above all others, would have told me this without absolute certainty. My mind reeled instead from one futile reassurance to another, none of them satisfactory. The inescapable verdict was like some child's leather pouch I could not allow to fall to earth, that I had to keep swatting about in my brain and keep airborne as though my life depended on it.

I tried to twist the news into some pretext for blaming Mordecai—that perhaps if I had been open about my Jewishness the King would not have issued such a decree. But then again, it occurred to me, I might have never become Queen if it had been known in the first place.

There was no way to absorb this, no way to process its full import. Not only could I not think it through, but I felt I was fighting to survive my very next breath.

The handmaiden who had escorted me hastily called for soldiers from the Palace. Half a dozen men poured out from the door and rushed to my side. Their captain knelt and leaned into my face.

"Are you ill, my Queen?" he asked. "Should I call a physician?"

I shook my head no—that was the most I was able to convey.

Jesse crawled over into the middle of this panicked group, reached out and, again disregarding appearances, gathered me into his arms.

"Her Highness has just received some very grave news about a beloved relative," he rasped out to the captain. "She is in the throes of severe grief and only wishes for some cover from the prying eyes of others. Will you form a circle around us and give the Queen a few moments to recover?"

The captain's eyes darted suspiciously from Jesse—who was, after all, a mere eunuch virtually ordering around a captain of the army—to me. I managed to nod and confirm the truth of Jesse's words; the man shrugged and turned around to the rest of his men. Within seconds a cordon of soldiers' backs shielded the pathetic scene from the eyes of any courtiers who might have wandered around this corner of the inner courtyard. Whether the measure actually protected us or simply attracted more attention, I would never know.

For the next few long moments I swayed silently in Jesse's arms, overcome by a dizzying, even nauseating sensation of freefall. He told me that the entire Jewish community was in mourning. "Mordecai gave me a copy of the edict. He had to transcribe it himself," Jesse whispered to me. "His thought is that perhaps you might go in to the King, implore his favor and plead for the sparing of our people."

I shook my head, for this had been one of the first ideas my desperate mind had rejected.

"It won't work, Jesse. Don't you remember your training? Have you forgotten how unforgiving Palace protocol is? You know as well as I that any man or woman who approaches the King without being summoned is immediately decapitated—unless the King lowers his scepter to spare their life! And do you know how long it's been since the protocol of the scepter has seen it lowered in invitation? Years! Besides, Xerxes has not summoned me into his presence for over a month now. Remember what happened to Vashti—that even a queen is not above losing her life over a matter of protocol. And Haman would be delighted to eliminate any rival for the King's attention. I just cannot do this. Please, Jesse. I am all right now. Go and tell Mordecai what I have told you."

One of the handmaidens, thank G-d for her, brought me a veil. I rushed through the hallways to my private quarters. Once inside, I retired to my bed with a tall goblet of sedative-laced wine prepared by the Palace physician. Hours later, I was awakened from my slumber by Jesse shaking me by the shoulder. He had barged past the guards, reminding them he was Hathach, aide to Memucan. I stirred upright and stared at him in amazement, for in normal times the impudence of such an intrusion would have likely caused his own immediate execution. Yet my guards, knowing him well, had apparently allowed him free access.

"What did he say?" I asked, coming immediately awake.

"He did not receive your reply well," he said as he crouched before me at the side of my bed. "He acknowledged that you may well risk execution in any attempt to reach the King, but he also wished me to point out that the King's Palace is no escape from the force of this edict. He said to remind *you* of Vashti and her fate. He said you will most likely die with all the other Jews when the truth is known and the order is carried out."

I reluctantly had to nod my agreement with Mordecai's dark appraisal. As much as I hated to admit it, he made sense.

"Mordecai made me vow to quote him accurately. He said, 'Furthermore, if you remain silent now, G-d will surely raise a deliverer from some other source. But you and your father's house would perish forever in the process.' He said, 'Who knows, Hadassah, but what you attained the Palace for such a time as this?'"

And then Jesse put into my hands a copy of the written edict. I held it like it was on fire as I read the pronouncement of death and destruction *on all Jews.*

## Chapter Forty-five

*M*y dear young maiden, I know I have described several periods of great despair and anguish in my life. I hope they seemed understandable to you and that I have not appeared as someone flighty and unbalanced, for I certainly do not see myself as that kind of person. And indeed, these *were* unusually tumultuous times, such as I have not endured since.

But let me assure you: no matter how intense and difficult any previous period of grief may have seemed, none compared to this one. To have survived my childhood, to have overcome Misgath's plot, gained the King's love and favor and become Queen of Persia, only to face a brutal execution by my family's murderers along with every one of my countrymen—it seemed a cruel, sadistic fate. I felt I was spinning uncontrollably into some black, hopeless pit. An abyss where either end was equally horrific—to continue falling or to strike bottom.

I took to my room and paced about, calling on G-d and challenging Him to tell me why He would allow such a horror to take place. Completely forgetting all the times He had rescued me before, I once again allowed myself to doubt His power and His care for me. After all, what could be done? Even if he wanted to, Xerxes himself could not reverse a royal order stamped with his signet ring. The law of the Medes and Persians, acknowledging how notoriously fickle its sovereigns could be, made it utterly impossible to change the law after that stamping had taken place. The situation seemed impossible—I could think of no way out. Our lives were as good as over. Even if Haman were somehow dispensed with, the law would still be enacted.

I found myself considering whether it would be more dignified to take my own life. Yet the moment I seriously entertained the notion, it seemed like an obscene and impossible thing to do. I owed it to everyone—Mordecai, Jesse, even the Jews of Persia, to embrace my fate—and theirs—with courage.

And when that thought occurred to me, I sat down on my bed and realized the way before me. No matter how hopeless, I would go in to Xerxes. Regardless of the outcome. It was a risk I could take, and I would take it.

As soon as I made the decision, my grief and rage seemed to ease somewhat. In its place came an inexplicable sense of repose. While I did not deny or ignore the fate that hung over me and my people, the knowledge of what I would do gave me direction, a sense of purpose.

To preserve the feeling and prepare me for what was to come, I retreated to my private chambers and summoned my handmaidens for a three-day period of fasting. I hoped the time would resemble those halcyon days spent together just before my very first night with Xerxes. By now these wonderful women knew my needs and moods seemingly long before I even recognized them, so they were not dismayed at my request for a quiet and subdued atmosphere.

I sent Jesse to find Mordecai and tell him this: "Please go home, assemble all the Jews in Susa and ask them to fast and pray for me for three days. My handmaidens and I will do the same. Then I will go in to the King unbidden, even though it is against the law. And if I perish, I perish."

The handmaidens and I spent the most peaceful and serene three days I have ever lived through, before or since. They seemed to delight in serving me, in giving me comfort and ease through the fasting period. And my state of mind grew so tranquil that after the first few hours of their ministrations, I did not even feel the hunger.

Yet from the first morning I found myself spending more time talking with G-d than anyone else. During those three days I prayed by the hour, simply pleading and imploring and, yes, cajoling Him to show me why He would visit such a fate upon His people—why He would allow their systematic deaths in this way. And the more I spoke with Him, the more I was certain He was answering, quietly exhorting me to have faith and remain intent on Him.

Finally I had an answer to the lament that had always afflicted me during times of trouble: *Why? Why take me so far only to let this happen?* This time I knew precisely why I had been allowed to go this far.

And the strange thing is, I did not have an inner assurance of success—that the King would lower his scepter, spare my life, then heed my pleas and somehow right this terrible wrong against my people. Of that happening, I had no certainty whatsoever. It had been a very long time—maybe decades—since the scepter had been lowered for a supplicant. Who was I to flaunt the laws of the Medes and the Persians? I did not even know for certain if he would notice me—especially with Haman's constant distraction. I did, however, in spite of all that the Persian tradition and law was telling me, have a very real conviction that I was in the right place, doing exactly the right thing. And for some strange reason, despite the threat of death, that was enough.

And so once again I underwent an abbreviated version of my long-ago preparation for the King. I bathed in myrrh. I had scented oils rubbed into my skin. I knelt over the incense burners to infuse my hair and skin with fragrant smoke. I asked the handmaidens to adorn my face and hair with the finest cosmetics, remembering exactly the combinations of colors and aromas that the King had responded to most strongly in the past. I summoned the Palace cooks to my side and ordered them to prepare a sumptuous banquet for that evening, for a small group—only three people. I clothed myself in my royal robes to remind him of our covenant, choosing again the King's favorite style and colors, and then, escorted only by Jesse and two Immortals whom he trusted, I opened the door to my chambers and began the long journey to the Inner Court. *Uninvited* hammered into my mind with each step.

A passing throng of Palace functionaries turned with surprised looks at my approach and parted before me. I had been gone from public sight for a noticeable period. And undoubtedly, many rumors about my state of mind must have arisen following my collapse the day I had received Mordecai's news. Lastly, I am sure that my appearance without the King—especially given that he was already holding court that day without me—along with my dress and demeanor and the unusual composition of my party, was quite unprecedented. The Queen usually wore royal robes to accompany the King to court, and then only with the traditional contingent of soldiers, aides and eunuchs.

I ignored the stares, neither smiling nor frowning, allowing the flinty resolve that I felt to show upon my face. Inwardly, I was speaking to G-d almost constantly, asking Him for favor and begging Him for the lives of the Jewish people. My own survival did not seem so important that day for some reason, but in another odd twist, the population I had once largely ignored now struck me as infinitely valuable. They were depending on me. I could feel their communal anxiety, their thoughts, even their prayers surrounding me like a shroud. I had heard the entire city was in an uproar—what would the court scene be like?

I suppose I have exhausted your patience with all my descriptions of how I felt at each stage of this story. I have done so because

I wanted you to know that I was little more than a frightened young girl trying to do her best, not some exalted figure of history whose fate was predetermined and whose composure was perfect at all times. Yet I must once more indulge in an account of my feelings, for today was both unexpected and strange. Instead of foreboding or anxiety or any of the expected emotions, I felt like I had passed into some high place of serenity with a peaceful resignation, almost as if I were drifting above a mass of storm clouds—floating calmly among the thin wisps of vapor that crown the uttermost heights of the heavens.

The feeling grew with every step closer to Xerxes and my fate. I truly believed that if I died, so be it. G-d could somehow use even that to save His people. It was beyond me now. If her husband does not grant her quarter, what is a queen's life worth anyway? And if the decree went forward, who was I to grasp at my own survival? Everything that mattered most to me would have already been swept away. I had only one course of action before me, and that singleness of purpose was itself a great relief. I had done my best, ridden the buffeting winds of fate as carefully as I could, and now I stepped willingly into a date with destiny. The horizon of that day stood dark with thunderclouds holding no portent of whether they would linger or benignly pass over.

I mean that last description only symbolically, of course. There were very few stormy days in Susa. And as I stepped from the doors of the Palace, the sun assaulted me mercilessly. I winced and Jesse turned to me with an apologetic look, realizing that no one had any sort of shade to offer me. I simply shook my head and waved away his concern.

Thankfully he did have the small litter waiting for me, so I did not have to walk the great distance through the terraces to the Inner Court. A part of me silently bade good-bye to the place as I proceeded through it, for the prospect of this being my last day was growing more distinct with every passing second. I could picture the moment of upcoming death with as much reality as any other outcome. *Maybe a quick demise.* I pictured Xerxes' fist tightening upon the scepter as he glanced away and refused to lower it, the brief hiss of air across the edge of the approaching blade, the initial slice of metal into my neck.

And then, the hereafter. A reunion with my family. With my mother, who had suffered the same form of death.

I shook my head and willed these thoughts away from me. Continuing to pray was far more important than these morbid contemplations. Despite faithless meanderings, another part of my being could feel G-d drawing closer than ever to me.

And then is when it struck me. Despite all my thoughts and meditations—and now in hindsight it seems hopelessly ignorant of me—I had failed to remember the initial source of my insights about how to approach the King.

*Jacob. The Holy of Holies. The Shekinah. The incredible joy of approaching G-d like a small child running into the arms of a returning father.*

I am ashamed to say it, but it was not until then that I remembered it all again. That the King of Kings *was* my father, that he missed me and longed for my presence as dearly as my own father had—and as urgently as I had come to crave the presence of Xerxes. And just as I had come to anticipate those times of fellowship with Mordecai and Jesse—simply basking in the warm glow of their nearness—G-d looked forward to my being with Him.

# Chapter Forty-six

So that day, with the eyes of hundreds still upon me, the motion of the litter lulling me into a meditative state, with the heat of the hour and above all the gravest risk I had ever faced—I closed my eyes and began to trust in the simple presence of the Almighty. And He took the occasion to flood my senses with an overpowering awareness of himself. I actually pictured myself as a toddler climbing into His vast and all-loving arms. Although I never lost sight of His other attributes—His righteousness and power, even His jealous anger—the side of Him that then poured into my awareness was the tender and loving YHWH of my earliest childhood.

I found myself praising Him in simple terms. "Dear G-d," I prayed, "thank you for your mighty and righteous deeds, for who you are. Thank you for meeting me here, for bringing your presence to my aid. You are so holy, so faithful. . . ."

And I began to recognize, pouring from my spirit, some of the same words that had left my lips when I had met Xerxes for the first time. Somehow my delight and praise seemed to have found its truest recipient. I had come full circle, a journey that brought me back—to YHWH.

And G-d's presence was indeed the most amazing distraction; in fact, it soon began to make the momentous occasion of the day almost pale in significance. And still I did not gain a sense of certainty that my quest would prove successful and my life spared. Instead, it continued to become clear that *this*—this intimacy with Him, this joy at His presence—was itself the true substance of life. That it actually dwarfed my life in importance, not to mention some fleeting moment of fleshly pain upon death.

So strongly grew this inward peace that when the litter settled upon the threshold of the Inner Court and I stepped upon solid ground again, I was almost entirely consumed with my spiritual life rather than the gravity of the moment. And I was glad for it, of course—for the distraction was at the very least a welcome respite from what lay ahead.

The doors of the court were crowded with supplicants and bureaucrats. I suppose most of them knew that the Queen was not scheduled to enter the King's presence that day—as I had not entered it for quite some time. So shock and consternation grew suddenly very plain on the hundreds of faces around me. I kept my gaze fixed ahead and simply walked, just concentrating on placing one foot in front of the other. Even though the red carpet was clear of loiterers—kept so by the threatening stares and weapons of the Immortal guards—an even larger swath began to part open before me. The hall in which I had been crowned suddenly opened wide in all its majesty, culminating in the marble platform of the throne itself.

As I came closer, the surprise grew audible; it sounded like a long, shared gasp emanating from the assembled crowd. I also caught more of the knowing looks between ladies of the court, perhaps inwardly celebrating the fact that I might be soon to share Vashti's fate. If she could be deposed for not coming when bidden, I could certainly be disposed of for entering unbidden! Oh, I knew how rare it was for the scepter to be lowered and intruders spared. I did not care. I was destined to take the next step and the one after that.

"Dear Father," I prayed, "I embrace your plan, your destiny for this moment. I want no other outcome but the one you have ordained. Please do not let me take one step outside your will."

Time seemed to stretch into infinity the nearer I approached. Those final strides seemed to last a lifetime. I know that my ears shut themselves down somehow—all sound died away except for the beating of my heart. I continued walking and kept my eyes away from the King's, even though he was now but a few dozen cubits away. I was not yet ready for that moment of truth. I kept my head slightly lowered. Another sight from which I averted my gaze was the pair of Cushite soldiers flanking the throne, their gleaming swords held at the ready behind their backs. Yet I could sense them nervously shifting to their ready position—unsure of their next move, afraid to take action yet fearful of doing nothing.

But then I was there; my feet struck the first step of the platform as I woodenly forged ahead. I stopped. And then it was time: I looked up into the eyes of my husband, who at that moment was anything but my spouse but instead my King, my earthly sovereign and perhaps soon to be my judge and jury.

His lips were pursed and his eyes questioning; he was genuinely surprised at my entrance. He cocked his head and peered at me, like someone trying to query the other without using words. As though he was asking, *What is it? Can't you let me know your errand somehow, before I have to speak?*

Another endless moment passed. I felt I could have left my body, gone home to the Palace and lived several years in the pause that stretched between us. I heard, behind me, a great hush fall over the entire hall as if they, too, had entered into this moment of suspended time.

I saw the King's fingers flex and unflex around the scepter, appearing to decide on their own whether to grant me my life.

"Please, Lord," I whispered, "give me wisdom. Give me *your* direction on what to do next."

And then the strangest thing yet happened—I felt the corners of my lips begin to tug upward. My cheeks start to flex. My spirit begin to lift. It made no sense, yet the muscles of my face began to act in one accord, disobeying my every command. I smiled.

Xerxes frowned.

"Why do you smile, my Queen? Most people at an intrusive moment like this would look like they'd soon faint with fear—as well they should. What causes you to smile so oddly at this moment?"

My smile broadened, because even though his expression remained grim and surprised, I knew he was remembering the moment we had first met and the similar words he had spoken then.

"Because, your Majesty," I answered in a soft voice, "even at this moment of highest danger, of which I am well aware, your presence fills me with joy. I am overwhelmed when I come close to the one I love."

The shared memory flashed between us. His head nodded slowly with a suppressed chuckle—I could tell he was gladdened that we had both kept that distant moment hidden in our hearts.

And then that which I had not dared to hope for: King Xerxes lowered the scepter. The gasp that now arose from the spectators was neither soft nor wavering. In fact, the clamor of shared surprise—and I hope relief—nearly caused me to swing around in alarm.

There remained one more part of this ritual to perform. I had to accept his grace, his mercy. I leaned forward and touched the tip of the scepter and felt a wave of gratitude—toward him, but most of all toward G-d—wash over my senses.

I removed my fingers from the scepter's jewels and leaned back again. But Xerxes took the occasion to lean closer to me. "What troubles you, my beautiful Queen? And what is your request? I will surely give it to you, my love, even if it is half the kingdom."

"You will be glad to know, my lord, that I do not come for nearly that much."

"Yet I hope it is an errand of great importance."

"The highest, your Majesty."

And I took a breath. I glanced from side to side and realized immediately that I had made the right decision about how to proceed next. This was not the right place, not the optimal setting for me to state my plight. There were too many prying eyes in here, too many distractions and competitors for his attention. I needed to speak on my territory, on the ground of my greatest strength. So, realizing the absurdity of what I was about to say, I closed my eyes for a split second, opened them again and said, "I offer only one simple request." I took a deep breath. "But not at the moment. If it pleases the King, may the King and Haman the Master of the Audiences come today to a private banquet that I have prepared for you."

Xerxes visibly stiffened at my strange reversal, yet he kept his eyes glued on my every move. Finally his stare broke and he turned to an aide beside him with a smile. "Quickly, find Haman and bring him here so we can do as Esther desires!" Then a quizzical look spread slowly across his face.

Before he could question me further, I hastily asked to be dismissed so that I might prepare for the evening. I left the room using every ounce of Palace protocol I could remember—curtsying perfectly, glancing with a smile at every court official, walking at just the proper gait—and thanked G-d when I passed the threshold and left the throne room behind. I don't mind telling you my legs could barely hold me upright as I found my way back to the litter, which returned me to my quarters. I was enormously relieved, as you might guess, but I also knew it was not over yet.

My private Palace cooks did not disappoint. They prepared a lavish meal of spit-grilled pheasant, kebabs of beef and peahen, roasted potatoes, grilled asparagus tips and desserts from around the world. And, of course, wine—this night the finest Chaldean blends flowed freely into our cups. I had chosen one of my favorite spaces in the Palace: a high balcony overlooking the sprawling grounds of the citadel and the city beyond it. Far ahead, beyond an intricate latticework of streets and rooftops, the sun sank onto a thick horizon of sand and cloud and inflamed the western sky into a riot of reds, oranges and turquoise.

For the first part of the meal I sat and listened, striving to appear calm, trying to eat, attempting to slow the pounding of my heart as Haman, the source of all my worst nightmares, sat within one cubit of me. Close enough to smell sour wine upon his breath. To count his pulse in the vein of his neck and the pores bridging the tip of his nose. I watched the moist wrinkles of his lips as they opened and closed and twisted a hundred ways. All the while, the man never stopped talking.

It's strange, I thought to myself. He *looks* like a human being. A loathsome specimen, to be sure, but a cunning re-creation of humanity nevertheless. I closed my eyes and pictured something closer to the truth: a long, stooped creature with a scimitar rising from one fist, its reptilian maw barely visible beneath the overhanging cowl of a loose black robe.

To regain control of my imagination, I willfully pictured another truth that caused me to wince outwardly, although neither man noticed. *My mother's death*. I forced myself to remember the beloved mouth that had kissed me goodnight lifelessly kissing dust in some corner of the floor.

I looked across the table at her executioner, and I resolved that his evil edict must be thwarted, even if it cost me my life.

## Mordecai, son of Jair

KETHUVIM ESTHER 3:2, 4

*". . . but Mordecai would not kneel or bow low. . . .*
*They spoke to him day after day,*
*and he would not listen. . . ."*

## Chapter Forty-seven

*I* turned my gaze upon Xerxes—nothing else, *no one else at all*. I had already taught myself to delight in his presence. Now that discipline had met its greatest test.

The murderer prattled on with Xerxes and virtually ignored me, as though I were beneath his newfound prestige—despite my being the source of his invitation. He drove the conversation upon every subject in which his status had given him exclusive knowledge—as though Xerxes needed reminding of how intimate they had now become.

Growing ever more intoxicated on the wine and his precedent-setting status as sole dinner guest of the King and Queen, Haman grew louder and more repulsive with every passing moment. Xerxes was far more alert, though. Knowing that something important was afoot with me, that I would never have risked death to invite Haman without some dire provocation, he kept his gaze half fixed on his obnoxious guest and half on me. I could see his thoughts reeling, his quizzical stare trying to grasp the meaning of this odd trio and failing to understand.

At last, when Haman had finally lapsed into a sort of waking stupor in his seat, the King turned to me and repeated privately what he had proclaimed so publicly in the throne room. "So, what is your petition, my Queen? It will indeed be granted to you, even if it is half the kingdom."

I took a deep breath. "My petition and my request is . . ." And I knew in an instant. The time was not right; Haman had made himself the focus of this meal, ruining the planned moment in the process. So I continued—". . . if I have found favor with the King, and if it pleases you to grant my petition and grant what you request, would you and Haman come to a second banquet that I will prepare for you? Tomorrow I will do as you ask and tell you what I seek."

He nodded slowly, boring into me with his eyes. I realized then that if my sudden reticence had produced an unintended benefit, it surely was to pique the King's interest. My delays had intrigued him even more than he was already. As so often happens between men and women, he sensed that something major was in the works yet lacked the acumen to discern just what it was. And I, remembering the immense nature of my request, had grasped intuitively that he was not yet ready to hear it, that this night was not the one on which my purpose should be revealed.

It was still early evening when the King and Haman left my banquet to return to their various duties. Haman had spurned the relatively spartan yet prestigiously situated quarters that Memucan had occupied, instead taking over a recently built villa not far from the King's Gate. On his way out of the Palace grounds, he spied a lone figure in the shadows.

It was Mordecai, still clad in sackcloth and ashes, sitting numbly in the portico after many days and nights of fasting and prayer. (In fact, had I known how badly he had neglected his health and pushed himself to extremes during these times, I would have forcibly summoned him to the Palace and personally fed him meats and wine.)

I am not even sure Mordecai saw Haman pass, so deep was his combination of fatigue, despondency and fervent prayer. Of course, even had he been in the heartiest of health and good spirits, Mordecai still would not have risen to bow for Haman.

So when the man passed, still basking in the glow of his ascendancy, of his favor with the King and Queen, of his overall high station in life, Haman's entire mood crashed to earth when he saw the lone Jew oblivious to his glory. He glanced aside from his litter, gritted his teeth and swore loudly. Mordecai did not even stir at the sound. Not only did he fail to honor Haman, but he did not even seem to notice his presence.

The Amalekite spat angrily and waved his carriers onward. To exact his revenge within sight of the Gate guards without the King's authorization would have invited disaster. This could wait— although not for long. He would indulge his rage and his upcoming revenge once he arrived home. And he did just that a few minutes later, storming into his living quarters and loudly ordering everyone into his presence: his wife, his ten sons and a few trusted lieutenants who had stayed around to celebrate his ascendancy and hear the reports of this most unusual meal with the royals.

"What a night!" he exclaimed, waving his arms wildly as he spoke. "This was probably the pinnacle of my existence—the summit of any man's aspirations! Picture this: me, Xerxes and the Queen dining alone on this Palace veranda with the whole citadel and capital city spread out below us. Discussing affairs of state—me regaling the King with all this nonsense from the top of my head about how he can replenish his treasury and vanquish the Greeks and generally become the most exalted ruler in human history. Blah-blah-blah. And the Queen just sitting there, soaking up my every word. I tell you, the woman dotes on the very ground I walk on. Oh! And she invited me back for another banquet tomorrow night! Certainly you can detect a pattern here, my entrance to an even greater position with the King *and* Queen, also! Can you believe my good fortune?"

He paused, and his head seemed to sway, whether from drunkenness or an inability to further describe the grandeur of it all. "And it occurred to me"—and at that he turned to the warriors beside him—"that maybe this is the best position I could possibly have. Even better than the throne itself. I mean, think about it. First, there are risks in making another overthrow attempt. Second, there's the fact that I am not descended from their precious Persian nobility, so even if I seize power, I might never be accepted. Third, this King is foolish, weakened, financially dependent on me and enamored of every golden word that drips from my mouth. I mean, when I proposed exterminating the Jews, he acquiesced so quickly I was astounded. I made the most rudimentary defense for my position, and he accepted it immediately. He gave me his signet ring—the second most powerful symbol of authority in the Empire after the scepter itself. On my word he sentenced tens of thousands of people to death. Fourth, I already occupy the second highest position in the land, higher than the generals, higher than the seven Princes of the Face, higher than any Palace official—I even control the King's schedule. Many believe my post is as powerful in reality as that of the King! Wouldn't you agree that this is the best position I could occupy? It's ideal!"

His oldest friend and captain raised a toast to Haman the Magnificent. Haman drank deeply, then looked into his glass with a reflective, even sentimental look. "I am truly humbled to see how far this life has taken me. To work a heartbeat away from the throne of the world's strongest kingdom, to be rich beyond measure, to have ten strapping sons already beginning to lead my troops in my absence, carrying on my tradition—I am truly blessed by the gods."

"Wife," he said abruptly, turning to Zeresh, "did you hear they have even invited me back for another feast tomorrow night? It seems I am to become a regular dinner guest with the royal couple!"

But then, in a transformation so lightning quick his listeners jerked back in shock, he scowled and began to snarl.

"Oh, but then the indignity that stole all the joy of it! It makes it seem like nothing! That worthless piece of—"

"What is it, Haman?" interrupted Zeresh. "Tell us!"

"Mordecai! That moldy little worm! He was at the Gate as I passed. Did not even stir, let alone rise to pay me the homage I am due—and that Xerxes ordered for me. Ah! Isn't it amazing how quickly one insult can ruin even the highest satisfaction? All the heights of the evening, the contentments of a lifetime, then seeing that creature sit there in his stench steals away all my happiness! All my triumph!"

Zeresh laid a hand upon his arm. "Well, then, do not let him rob your joy. Take the initiative. Maybe now is the time to put all that immense influence to good use."

"What are you suggesting?"

She chuckled, then went silent for a moment. "Have a gallows pole built fifty cubits high tonight, here in the yard, and in the morning ask the King's permission to execute Mordecai upon it. Then go to your private royal banquet tomorrow night in peace and vindication."

A broad smile crossed Haman's face. He leaned forward and gave his wife an unusual embrace. "She really has good ideas, don't you think?" he said to his lieutenants.

Goblets of wine raised up across the room. Haman nearly wept with joy. Mordecai, the bane of his existence, now had mere hours to live.

Within minutes Haman was shouting at workmen to hasten the process of preparing the longest private gallows pole ever seen in Susa. His plan was already in place—he would only bring it out in public view minutes before the execution, stunning both the condemned man and the whole city in the process. No one would ever disrespect him again. He tried to imagine the sight of Mordecai impaled atop the shaft, but the thought was too blissful for him to even contemplate.

But this eventful night was not yet spent of its surprises. Deep in the innermost chambers of the Palace complex, King Xerxes was suf-

**314**

*Tommy Tenney*

fering through a sleepless night. He knew from my demeanor that
something significant was brewing. *What was it?* No matter how
relentlessly he tried to clear his mind, it would not stop tumbling forth
with a cavalcade of anxious and even irrational thoughts. He was simply not at peace; his mind could not digest the myriad events and
threats to his power churning like bile through the pit of his stomach.
He briefly thought of calling for me, but he quickly put the idea aside.
He was not at his best—body and soul—and far too restless.

Now, you *could* say that intestinal indigestion kept the King
awake. In fact, he had indulged heartily at my banquet. He had not
been eating much of late, or so I had heard, but that night he had
stuffed himself on the feast I had prepared. I suppose it was impossible for him to resist my urgings to eat.

Or perhaps the cause was his bewilderment over my strange
behavior and my even more mysterious request. Or even the many
cares that afflicted him in those days—finances, Palace intrigues, his
stubborn obsession with exterminating the Greeks.

But I say it was the Spirit of the Most High sent down to trouble his slumber and cast his attention in a direction of G-d's own
choosing. The only insomnia cure Xerxes could think of at that
moment was to have someone read to him from the most lifeless
and stultifying document in the Palace's world-renowned library—
the Chronicles of the King, the court records, if you please.

He had a vintage volume brought to him, a huge, bulky tome
with a cover that resembled a richly jeweled tapestry more than the
front of a book. It took the labors of both his eunuch and another
aide pulling a specially-built wooden stand to even open it.

"Do not try to apply your talents at making this interesting,"
Xerxes warned Harbona. "I did not call you here to be informed. I
summoned you here in order to fall asleep at last. Start at the beginning. By the way, how far back does this volume go? Does it extend
back more than four years?"

Harbona nodded yes.

"Good, because I need to be able to say that I've 'read' the records of what transpired during my absence at war. Proceed."

And so the eunuch launched into a mind-numbing list of ancient administrative budget meetings, of endless appropriations and favors given and received. Events that had taken place just before Xerxes' departure for the ill-fated war with Greece. The King's eyelids were predictably starting to weigh heavier and heavier when the reader began an entry that caused them to jerk open again.

". . . that Mordecai of Susa has on this day rendered an exemplary service to the Crown by thwarting an attempt on the life of the King and of his kingdom. Xerxes will be forever in his debt."

Suddenly recalling those memory-jolting words, the King sat upright in his bed with an alarmed expression. "Read that again."

Harbona did just that.

"I remember that! Is there any record of us having done anything to reward this man?"

He peered down and scanned several lines before looking up again. "No, your Majesty. There is none. It is noted that Bigthana and Teresh were executed, but nothing of a reward."

"You know, I left for war shortly after that. I would not be surprised if we failed to do anything to recognize Mordecai."

On the surface, it might have seemed insignificant, his failure to show the usual extravagant gratitude to a man of little consequence. After all, the lowly scribe had probably gained a great deal of notoriety from the incident. Some might say that was reward enough. But something about the oversight bothered him. How many other matters had fallen through the cracks during his absence?

To not honor loyalty could weaken the Empire! After several hours of tossing and pondering, Xerxes resolved to do something, something beyond the norm. While he felt strangely calmed by the decision, it was not enough to grant him sleep. The King continued to lie awake, tortured by anxious thoughts, while Harbona droned on.

*Chapter Forty-eight*

*I*n the morning after his sleepless night, the King found that Haman was waiting outside his chambers well before his right-hand man's usual hour of arrival. He had no idea, of course, that his Master of the Audiences had arisen early for his own reason—supervising the erecting of the tallest impalement pole Susa's horizon had ever seen. The task had required half a dozen men to accomplish.

Haman considered the early start crucial to carrying out the plans of the day. He could now gain a head start on Mordecai's execution and move on with his life hours before anticipated. After being summoned to the King's bedside he stood before the monarch, swaying slightly with a good-natured air of anticipation and compliance.

"How may I serve you this morning, your Majesty? And by the way, I am so glad to see you a bit early, for I had a pressing request to make of the King."

"Really. Would you like to go first?"

Haman made a mock frown. "No, sire. Your assignment comes first, obviously."

"Well, Haman, I have a thorny question which afflicted me sorely and kept me from sleep last night," he answered. "And it occurred to me that you might help solve it."

"I, too, was up planning something. But, after you, your Majesty."

"Well, I wonder how you suggest that I honor and reward a man who has rendered exemplary service to the Crown and who has gone too long unrewarded."

Haman reared back, his eyebrows shot up playfully and a wry smile toyed with his lips. "A man? And who might that man be, if I may ask?"

The sleepy royal insomniac did not smile, although Haman certainly must have tried to imagine that he could discern the faintest hints of a grin somewhere in his expression. It had to be him the King wanted to reward.

"Let us keep him nameless for now," the King replied.

Haman crossed his arms confidently and looked upward to feign the search for a difficult answer. "Well, your Majesty, if this man has truly rendered valuable service to the Crown and the Empire, I would say . . ." He rolled his gaze all about the room. And he began to describe his own personal dream, full of his seditious desires for the throne.

"First, take a royal robe, one that your Majesty himself has worn in public, and place it upon this man's shoulders before a large audience of courtiers. Then have a high-level dignitary, a well-known trusted servant of your Majesty—maybe Carshena—place this man upon your most imposing warhorse arrayed in full royal regalia including the royal crest, and have this dignitary lead him through the main streets of Susa for hours, proclaiming at the top of his voice that 'here is a man whom the King wishes to honor for great and meritorious service.'"

Xerxes considered the suggestion with a slow nod. "That would certainly make a lavish show of gratitude. And that is what I need."

"Do you?" said Haman, obviously already savoring the sound of his own name as the recipient of this treatment.

"Yes. Indeed, you have served me well, Haman."

For Haman, this statement must have sealed his hopes. He was indeed the man to whom the King was referring. "It is my honor, your Majesty," he said with a modest bow.

"So what I want you to do is arrange for all these things—the robe, the horse, the royal proclamation—and make certain it is done exactly as you suggested! The man I wish to honor is a royal scribe here in Susa. His name is Mordecai. But I choose you, Haman, to be my high dignitary and lead Mordecai on a parade of tribute through the streets of Susa."

Of all the things I regret in this life, one of those I lament most is not having been in the King's chamber at that moment to see Haman's face. However, having quizzed the King for hours and hours on the subject, I can paint the ensuing reaction with utter confidence and accuracy.

Haman first became completely still. The color drained from his face so swiftly and dramatically that Xerxes blinked several times to make sure some trick of the light was not deceiving him. Haman's eyes first narrowed inquisitively, then furrowed with incredulity, then finally widened with pure shock. The King did not give him the least encouragement with a smile or a wink, for of course he was not being facetious; Xerxes was naturally innocent of any subterfuge. He had no idea of the private feud Haman had been pursuing, nor of Mordecai's Jewish heritage.

Haman looked around him as if someone had scribbled a solution for exiting this conversation gracefully somewhere upon the Palace walls. Finally he fixed the King with as much irritation as he would dare exhibit.

"Your Majesty, surely you jest—"

"And why would I jest on such a matter of import?"

Haman squinted to see if he could discern any deception in the monarch. But Xerxes' gaze was level and honest. Yet Haman would not, could not, allow himself to even consider what might be the truth: that the King had possessed no foreknowledge of Haman's intentions, that all this had been nothing more than some sort of diabolical coincidence.

When, of course, it was a "coincidence" of completely different origins. I know it was entirely divine.

"I said, your Majesty, that your assignment for me is—well, perhaps a jest in a highly ironic sort of way—but given the totality of the issue, well, perhaps not the best chosen . . ."

"What in the name of our god Ahura are you talking about, Haman? I simply asked your advice on a troubling question, and given your most astute reply, I gave you a straightforward assignment. What is ironic or comical in any of this?"

Haman took a step backward, obviously just beginning to absorb the terrifying truth. Xerxes was serious, and he was completely unaware of Mordecai's ethnic origins. Haman would not get his hanging today—nowhere close to it.

"Nothing, sir" came his eventual reply.

"Good. Then obey my order at once. And don't go pawning off this task on some subordinate. I want this recognition to come from the King's Master of the Audiences himself. I will meet you at my royal viewing balcony in one hour. And there had better be a crowd below, Haman. Then I will see you at sunset, dressed for tonight's banquet."

"Let it be done, your Majesty."

Shortly thereafter, an Amalekite guard appeared before Mordecai. I am sad to say that my poppa had lapsed into an even more stupefied state of disorientation, hunger, dehydration and fatigue. His cross-legged form there in the King's Gate appeared to have sagged with time and stillness, like some great statue that the centuries and the elements had mercilessly sculpted and eroded.

The guard, no doubt aghast at both the identity and the disheveled state of the person they would soon have to exalt, bent down and poked Mordecai with an emphatic finger jab. Mordecai's head only pitched forward a few more degrees.

The guard called sneeringly to this castoff from society.

There came no reaction.

"Are you, sir, Mordecai? Of Susa?"

The grizzled head rose a bit, and his eyes now bore into the guard's own.

"Sir, His Majesty King Xerxes wishes to see you. At once. On a matter of the utmost national urgency."

Mordecai's eyes locked onto a sight across the man's shoulder guard—a sight that turned the blood in his veins to ice. *A twisted cross.*

"Yes," came Mordecai's voice, low and gruff. "Most likely my death."

"Hardly," responded the guard under his breath.

But Mordecai did not hear the whispered rejoinder; he was in the throes of trying to stand. He grabbed both of the man's hands and pulled himself up, his knees shaking from side to side.

"No matter, I am ready," Mordecai said. "It is before the date, but I understand. I am not surprised." In near delirium he began, "Dear YHWH, I come to you. . . ."

Mordecai already believed himself on the way to heaven when he opened his eyes and, through a swirling mist of various bodily agonies, glimpsed the King and Haman standing before him. The sight confused him, for he had expected to see them upon the moment of his demise, not after the passing of his soul.

*Maybe I have not yet died,* he corrected himself then. *Perhaps the moment is at hand.*

And then the figure he had taken for Xerxes bent over and brought a goblet of wine to his lips. That certainly made no sense. The liquid burned a welcome path down his throat and ignited a fire in his stomach that at least brought the sights before him into a clearer focus. He would have preferred food first, but who was he to complain, standing as he did on the brink of eternity?

It was honey wine, his throat soon told him. Soon strength and alertness began to seep back into his limbs. The man who resembled Xerxes then fed him some goat cheese and a little bread.

"Am I dreaming?" he asked.

"No," said the King, or some royal impostor. "But you are in dire need of a bath and a meal. Why are you attired such?"

"I am in mourning, Your Highness. This is the ritual garment of sackcloth and ashes."

"Oh. I am very sorry. I hope today's events help in some way to soothe your loss. Can you stand, my dear Mordecai?"

And my poppa found that indeed, he could—with the Xerxes person supporting him about the shoulders.

Mordecai looked out, and the scene below him almost caused him to lose consciousness—a crowd like the grains of sand on a beach stood waiting before him. "Let us give them what they wait for, shall we?" asked the King. He leaned forward and removed from a box at his seat a long velvet robe. A royal robe. He raised the shimmering garment high in the air, and without a second's delay the crowd below roared its approval. Xerxes raised it even higher, turned slowly on his heel and said, "My fellow Persians! Please witness with me the placing of this royal robe upon one Mordecai of Susa, for whom vigilance and loyalty will prove this day to be fortuitous qualities indeed. For let it be known that four years ago, Mordecai undertook great danger to warn me of an impending plot against the royal person. And thanks to his prompt warning, my own life was spared. The perpetrators were duly punished, and now the loyalty is being belatedly rewarded. Let all within this kingdom know that Xerxes rewards those who serve him! Reward delayed is not reward denied. Let this be a sign to all of you! Let the King's gratitude be known, and let honor and respect fall like rain upon the shoulders of this most beloved of servants. Hail!"

"Hail!" came the shouted reply, a rampart of jubilant sound rolling across the Palace grounds to the astounded ears of the Jew Mordecai.

# Chapter Forty-nine

*A*nd so it came about that on a certain day many years ago, a ragged Jew was given the ultimate tribute by a grudging Amalekite, their respective races mutual enemies from time immemorial.

For several hours the streets of Susa bore tribute to one of YHWH's most delicious ironies, that the very man who had plotted Mordecai's death the night before now led him on the back of the King's mightiest steed, arrayed as no one had ever seen the lowly scribe—his erstwhile executioner shouting praises and honor to this great friend of the King, this heroic Mordecai of Susa. The streets' fringes grew thick with spectators, especially those of Susa's Jewish quarter—where Mordecai had specially asked to be taken—and where many frowned in utter bewilderment. They had heard of Haman and the decree he had spawned. Their knowledge of it had made their recent days a living hell. Most of them even knew of the conflict that had given rise to this impending doom. And so the sight of these two men even occupying the same proximity was more than they could comprehend. Some of them shouted confused queries at Mordecai, which the dazed man failed to hear or answer.

As for friends and acquaintances of Haman, most later commented that they had never seen the Palace luminary so glaze-eyed, so mechanical in his steps, so aimless in his direction. The usually keen-eyed Master of the Audiences seemed to have been struck by a heavy wooden beam. Those members of his family and his band of killers who watched the event came away utterly disoriented, unsure of what might arise next. Should they flee for their lives? Preemptively attack the Palace? Rush out and stop the ridiculous charade before them? None of them could marshal the proper clarity to choose a path of action.

In fact, Haman's own daughter provided the day's crowning moment. Seeing the impromptu parade approach from her rooftop parapet, and knowing that her father was preparing to execute Mordecai with the King's permission, she decided to do her part. As she had been cleaning out her bedchambers at the time and happened to be holding a full chamber pot with the intention of hoisting the contents out the window, she devised her own form of degradation. She waited and, at the final moment, emptied her container of human waste upon the downcast man pulling the horse—whom she assumed to be Mordecai. Only when the befouled figure glanced up her way just in time to see the rain of slop reach his face and for her to recognize his features did she realize her terrible mistake. The surrounding spectators erupted in shocked yet raucous laughter. It is said she never recovered.

As the hours wore on, Haman's steps grew slow with fatigue and his voice hoarse from shouting Mordecai's praises, and he began to edge back toward the King's Gate. As for Mordecai, he had now fully regained both his energy and his morale, and he sat as straight as a spear atop the royal stallion. He still did not think too hard about how he had arrived there or what had taken place to bring about such monumental irony. He certainly had no way to discern whether this meant the end of the murderous decree hanging over his people's heads. He had barely grasped that this was reward for a deed he had long thought overlooked.

He was, literally and figuratively, simply there for the ride. But it turned out to be the ride of a lifetime. The prayers silently moving his lips were no less full of gratitude to G-d and further requests that He protect His people.

I did not even hear of Mordecai's baffling afternoon until after it was finished, as I stood busily watching over the final preparations of the banquet and Jesse barged in, panting and laughing at the same time. Jesse told me the story of the parade, of Haman's demeanor both then and at home later when Jesse and Harbona had arrived to escort Haman to the Palace—seeing the man standing forlorn among his family, everyone looking like they had just seen a ghost. Haman's wife stood berating the man in a loud voice, exclaiming that if Mordecai was of Jewish descent, he could not stand against him, that his fate was sealed! And somewhere in a back corner a daughter was cowering, afraid to meet her befouled father.

When Jesse had softly spoken up to say that it was Haman's time to leave for the Palace banquet, he and his family had turned to the eunuch with openly incredulous looks.

"Are you mad? I need at least an hour to clean up, to prepare!"

Jesse had shaken his head, managing to banish the amusement he felt from his expression. "Master, her Highness insists on starting precisely at sunset. If I do not have you there right on time, not only may I lose my head, but you will certainly be shut out of the dinner. Her orders were most explicit."

"But I smell like . . ." Haman waved his arms and glanced about him with a wild stare rather than elaborate on the nature of his stench. "Give me ten minutes!"

"I am sorry, sir. We are already late leaving, and I fear we may still not arrive on time to walk over with the King. If you do not come with me now, I will have to decline her Highness's invitation on your behalf."

"Go!" Haman's wife shouted in exasperation as she pulled a fresh robe around her husband. "Just go! Do you want to compound the day's misery? Go and be with them, make excuses, douse yourself with perfume on the way—just *go*!"

I laughed so exuberantly upon hearing the tale that I dropped something loud, a large silver mirror I believe, upon the marble tile.

With every peal of laughter I could feel my inner strength to face the evening's challenges grow.

And the evening's challenges did arrive, both of them, within minutes of the appointed time. Jesse's insistence had borne fruit.

This night the banquet took place in my private quarters—my most familiar and comfortable environment—lavishly decorated for the occasion. Veil after veil of wispy curtains were suspended from ceilings, anchored to walls, and shimmered softly in the evening breeze that swept in from opened doorways. The arrangement gave the rooms an evanescent appeal and separated the main spaces in a most ethereal yet effective manner. In a corner, largely out of sight, one of my handmaidens sat fluidly playing the harp.

And finally, the air inside was redolent with every form of delicacy most favored by the King. Roasted lamb, slow-baked venison, vegetables steamed in the meat's own vapors. Vast quantities of wine, of course. Bowls of curdled cream laced with honey and studded with every sort of berry and fruit.

I hope my own appearance was in keeping with my quarters' beauty and taste, for I had certainly endeavored toward that end. As men's preference in women and female attire seldom changes much over time, I will not repeat for you the now familiar adornments and anointings in which I had indulged. Suffice it to say that I had worked hard to make myself the evening's ultimate enticement—for the King, that is.

The two men swept in. At this banquet it was Haman, appearing strangely disheveled and smelling rather farmlike, who proved the quieter of the two. But all the better. I blossomed that night into a vivacious hostess, reminding Xerxes all the while that I could hold my own at conversation. I even courteously tried to engage Haman in talk of his family and other innocuous subjects. But his reponses were brief. I also recall that, for some reason, the food that night bore the most exquisite taste of any dishes I have ever eaten, before or since.

Haman confined himself to attacking the wine riatins on each side of the table early and often, which of course did not disappoint me in the least. For most of the evening he sat on the other side of the table and gazed blearily into thin air. Neither Haman's aroma nor my appearance compelled the King to favor our guest's side of the table. And so it did not take long for Xerxes to venture closer to me, then launch into the salient question at hand.

"Finally, my dear Esther, what is your request? For it will still be granted, to be sure—even if it is half the kingdom."

And now the moment had come—no more delays possible, no more strategic retreats from the urgency of my plight. Now was the time to risk my favor, to achieve my ultimate purpose. This was the instant of my greatest influence and the reward of intimacy. I took a deep breath, looked him straight in the eye and softly launched into my plea.

"If I have found favor in your sight, your Majesty, and if it pleases the King, my petition is to be given my *life*, and my request is the life of my people. One man has schemed a monstrous plot against my whole people. We have been betrayed, I and my people both, to be destroyed. Killed. Annihilated. If we were only going to be sold as slaves, I would have kept silent, for it would not be worth troubling the King. But I believe my life and that of countless innocent men, women and children is worth begging your mercy."

I did not look at Haman as I said this. I remained totally focused on the King—refusing to empower my enemy with so much as an inclusive glance. Yet I could see that the Agagite had emerged from his despondent state and sat listening with as much concentration as he could muster.

The King, for his part, became instantly enraged. His complexion flushed, his eyes narrowed in anger. His fingers gripped the stem of his wine goblet so tightly that they turned white. His voice came out as the perfect combination of a hiss and a low growl.

"Who is he, and where is he? Who would dare to do such a thing?"

In one of the most exquisite, destiny-defining moments of my life, I turned to Haman. I watched his eyes begin to widen in fear. I pulled my arm up above the tabletop and pointed, right in his face.

"The very same man who murdered my family. This wicked, evil Haman is my foe, my enemy, your Majesty! *For I am a Jew.*"

At once, Haman's breathing went from a contented purr to a frantic pant. He jerked upward in his seat and put on a groveling expression for probably the first time in his adult life. He almost fell backward, so great was his terror.

"Oh no, your Majesty. There's been a mistake. A terrible misunderstanding. . . ."

Yet something in Haman's face, in the manner of his speech, virtually radiated guilt. Xerxes stood so abruptly that the table jerked backward with a clatter. He threw down his napkin, turned on his heel and marched out the door into the gardens. Rage seemed to have rendered him speechless.

"Oh, your Highness, I had no idea!" Haman yelled, nearly weeping as he knelt abruptly and, to my astonishment, clutched my leg. "I mean, yes, your race and mine have been at odds for centuries, but that is a cultural matter—if I had known you were of Jewish blood, I would have never considered the edict! I would have found another way! It was nothing personal, it was just a terrible old Jew who sits at the Palace gates who refused to—"

"That 'old Jew' is my *father,*" I interrupted, feeling a bit dizzy from the extraordinary irony of my declaration.

At that news he sank down onto the floor, and the seal of his impending death imprinted itself upon his face. Yet he turned to me again while a final hope of survival flickered upon his countenance.

"Please, your Highness. You are a person of mercy. You have

received mercy yourself, on occasion. Please grant me pity."

"The same pity you would have granted to the children and babies of Jewish mothers?" I asked. "No, I fear the only reason you mention pity is because you have been caught and exposed. If you want any quarter, you must ask the King."

"No, your Highness!" he cried, barely coherent now. He grabbed my wrists and nearly pulled me to the ground. "Only your kind heart can save me now!"

Something about Haman's desperation suddenly made me fearful of being alone in the room with him. I quickly turned from him and retreated to a couch in the corner to await Xerxes' return. As I did, Haman fell headlong upon the floor and, actually clutching a corner of my dress, tore a piece of the fabric. I turned, gave him my most fierce scowl and took my seat. Haman, in the full throes of death-panic, was not to be deterred. He followed me and cried out in a voice unlike I had ever heard from the throat of a man, "Please! Oh please, your Highness!"

And in the very next moment, two things happened that sealed Haman's fate—first, the evil one fell in his desperation upon my couch, nearly covering me with his body, and second, my dear Xerxes returned from summoning the bodyguards he had stationed a discreet distance away in the garden.

I saw only the onrushing form of Haman descending upon me, then heard a voice of animallike rage erupt from across the room. "*What?!* Will he even assault my wife while I am in the house?"

Xerxes, the source of the outburst, turned to Harbona—one of the attending eunuchs whom he had apparently summoned during his absence—and motioned toward Haman. The aide pulled a black scarf from his tunic, walked over to where Haman knelt in frantic tears and draped it over his face. *The scarf of death.*

Then Harbona turned to Haman. "Your Majesty, were you aware that the tallest execution pole Susa has ever seen now stands in Haman's yard? Word is he built the gallows pole in order to kill Mordecai upon it. Mordecai—the same man you sought earlier to honor for heroism and service to the King."

"And my father," I added. "The one who raised me."

Xerxes shot me a look of greater amazement than I have ever seen on the face of any human being. Then he whirled upon his heels and fixed Haman with a gaze so icy cold that it gave me shivers just being in the same room. It lasted only an instant. He walked over, reached out to grab Haman's right hand and yanked the signet ring from his finger. Then he turned away, and anyone watching would have known the King would never set his gaze on the man again.

"Impale him on his own gallows. At daybreak."

And on that order soldiers scurried in, picked Haman up and carried him from the room—a once haughty man now whimpering softly like a half-starved newborn.

# Chapter Fifty

*T*he dawn was just a warm glow upon the horizon and the awakening city still largely unaware of the night's events when Haman was dragged into his yard to stare into the eyes of his own aide—the eunuch he had tormented for these past several weeks.

My Jesse of Susa, known to the Palace as Hathach the Good Man.

Haman at this moment was incapable of coherent speech. He had now reached a point of human consciousness capable of evoking pity in even his most enraged victim—sunk to the state of a whimpering, incontinent, jabbering fool. The condemned creature put up little resistance as his clothes were torn from his body and his nudity exposed before not only the whole execution party but his assembled family—who stood nearby, forced to watch. Glaringly, the once secret twisted cross tattoo on his back now announced him to the world as the scheming murderer that he was.

I will spare you the terrible details of his death by impalement, but you do not need a reminder of the unfortunate souls he had sent to their death in similar fashion.

The pole's absurd height, intended to display Mordecai's fate before the whole city, now helped Susa bear witness to the punishment of its most devious traitor.

In other quarters, Haman's remaining foot soldiers began ripping the twisted cross emblems from their uniforms and trying to smear the tattoos on their skin with dyes. Some even scraped their forearms with knives to remove the evidence—for they knew their day of reckoning had arrived.

Mordecai and I did not watch the execution. We spent the morning on a Palace balcony as far away from the sight as possible. As we talked together, Mordecai hugged me tightly and said, "You did it, my Hadassah. You were faithful to the position where G-d placed you. You were brought to the Palace for this purpose. To save our people."

I held him as close as I could and nearly collapsed from sheer relief.

Later that day, King Xerxes called a grand audience in the Inner Court. There, in front of a packed crowd, he held up the signet ring that he had removed from Haman's finger and unexpectedly slipped it onto Mordecai's. I could hardly believe my eyes. My poppa, faithful Palace scribe of so many years, had now risen to the post of Master of the Audiences. He looked again like the Mordecai of old, hardly a young man yet standing straight once more with the old gleam in his eye and the bearing of a Palace veteran.

Xerxes held out his hand toward him and said quietly, "Years of delayed reward proved you to be truly loyal." Turning to the crowd the King shouted, "People of Persia and servants of the Crown, I give you this day my new Master of the Audiences, Mordecai, son of Jair, a child of Israel and citizen of Persia! It is my will that each of you obey and treat him in every way exactly as you would regard your King!"

A deafening cheer went up from the spectators, many of whom

had dealt with Mordecai for years. I thought I saw a decade of cares fall away from Poppa's countenance in the moments that followed.

Then came my turn. I took both of Mordecai's hands in mine—hardly a conventional gesture for the Queen, but it seemed everyone was now aware of our relationship—and said, "Master, as the Queen's gift in your newly installed post, and at the King's request, I give you all the goods and riches from the household of Haman the Agagite, enemy of the Empire and plotter against its citizens."

At those words Mordecai, whom I had not forewarned of this gift, blanched and seemed to sway a little. I had just given him a fortune equal to that of any nonroyal in the Empire. I stepped closer and we exchanged a tight, lingering embrace.

Making this gesture touched my emotions in a way I had not anticipated. Finally I had been able to do something for him as Queen that he was not able to shrug off or dissuade me from doing like a father scolding his little girl. Between the appointment as Master of the Audiences and the granting of Haman's wealth, Mordecai's life had just been transformed forever. And I, his daughter, had played a strong hand in both. He had taken me in when I was young—I had brought him in when he was old.

And then I turned away from Poppa and steeled myself for an entirely different gesture. I walked over to the King, who was still guarded by his soldiers and their ready swords, and abruptly fell upon my face. Despite my joy of only a second before, I broke into loud sobs. Tears began to flow down my face.

"Please, your Majesty," I pleaded, "please thwart the evil scheme that Haman left embedded as law! Please stop this plot against the Jews!"

From the stunned look overtaking his features, Xerxes was as clearly shocked by the swift turn in my emotions as anyone in the room. He lowered the scepter and my breathing settled a bit. I stood and approached him.

"I know that even your Majesty cannot change a law of the kingdom sealed by his signet ring," I said. "But if it pleases the

King, and if I have found favor with you, and if it seems proper and I am pleasing in your sight, then let it be ordered to revoke Haman's order calling for the destruction of the Jews throughout Persia. For how can I endure to watch this awful fate come to my own people? How can I endure the destruction of my own flesh and blood?"

Xerxes reached out his hand and grasped my arm, his eyes glittering with a powerful intent. "Now listen. I have already approved giving Haman's goods to Mordecai because of his plot against the Jews. I am not about to let his treachery prevail now. So, you write a letter to the Jewish people, anything you see fit, and you may seal it with my signet ring, and it will be binding law."

So I retired to a back room with Mordecai and a hastily called assembly of royal scribes—the same kind of conference Mordecai would have attended as a mere functionary only days before. And as one of their own, he dictated to the staff with a mastery of language and protocol that they had never before seen from a Master of the Audiences. Speaking in the name of King Xerxes, he announced— and the scribes translated into every alphabet and language of the Empire's 127 provinces—a most audacious proclamation. He declared that on the same day that had been designated for their extermination, the Jewish people would have the right to assemble and defend themselves as a group. They could destroy, kill and annihilate anyone who rose up against them, including women and children. They would even be allowed to plunder their enemies' spoils—and know that they enjoyed the King's blessing as they did so.

The sound of Mordecai's voice slowly echoed into silence in the stone room as his former colleagues scribbled furiously to render his words into the proper form. Then, after a long pause, they approached him one by one while he emphatically stamped the King's signet ring onto each copy of the new edict. Immediately following the procedure, each one filed out of the room and walked to an outer door where a small army of royal couriers awaited, each one mounted upon an offspring of the King's own stallions. Immediately, each cavalier grasped his designated copy of the decree and rode out of sight.

When the last of the scribes had left us, I grasped the King's robe from a nearby handmaiden and laid it again across Mordecai's shoulders. And then, to my eternal gratitude, Poppa was able to share with me one of the great sensations of my life—to step out upon a terrace, look out across a sea of faces and know that the roar engulfing the platform was composed of cheers directed at no one else but him—at least until the King and I followed behind.

The city so recently shrouded in confusion was now engulfed in celebration.

Oh, I wish you—I wish anyone—could have seen him on that day. My dear Mordecai, who once had to be reminded not to wear the same clothes for a week straight—now stood resplendent in a suit of fine linen and purple Kashmiri wool, a golden crown upon his head, a royal robe of blue and white draped across his shoulders. He was splendid, I must admit. I have never been so proud, and I despair of ever feeling such pride again. I wept with joy to look across and see him brace himself against the wave of love as if it were a stiff desert wind.

He deserved it, of course, as much as any occupant of the Palace had ever deserved a wild ovation. His loving obstinacy had helped bring about every good thing of that day. He was as great a hero as any soldier of Xerxes' army. And the crowd was filled with Susa's Jews, I later learned, for whom Mordecai had just attained the status of liberator.

He leaned to me and whispered, "Esther, always remember that favor can restore in a day what was stolen over a lifetime." I felt his hand squeeze something into mine—a strangely familiar shape in a velvet cloth. I unwrapped it and gasped as I held up the old star necklace given to me by my parents.

Mordecai continued, "I guess now that everybody knows who you are and what you are, you should wear this again."

He raised it in trembling fingers and slowly lowered it around my neck. I embraced him with all the strength in my arms. Of all the spectators watching that moment, only he and I knew everything that gesture meant to us.

Across the Empire, the Jews began to call Mordecai the Exilarch—leader of those in exile. And it appears the title will continue on even now that Mordecai is in his old age. Wherever one of his couriers rode in with Mordecai's edict held high in the wind, there was feasting and rejoicing such as Jews had not enjoyed in decades. The name of Mordecai was celebrated in word and song.

And, in the quarters of the wicked, mightily feared.

After the death of Haman until the counter-edict took effect on the thirteenth day of Adar, Haman's sons continued their father's ethnic hatred against the Jews. But as the months passed and the strength of the King's favor became more apparent, they went into hiding. Of course, the real liberation occurred when Haman's supposed day of Jewish extermination finally dawned. Mordecai's subsequent proclamation had produced its desired effect, for anyone with an ounce of political savvy had come to realize that the weight of imperial support now rested on the Jewish side. As a result, none of the government officials, from satraps to local governors, lifted a finger against my people. The only ones who did attack us would best be described as roving thugs, a few remnants of the Riders of the Twisted Cross hoping to strike at opportunistic targets like undefended homes or houses of worship. I am sorry to have to report that Elias, Mordecais' father's friend, was killed during the street fighting.

But the hoodlums met a Jewish people heartened by the King's support and steeled by the knowledge that Persia's second-in-command—a man reputedly more influential than any non-royal in recent history—was in fact one of their own. The Jews had planned long and hard for this day and organized themselves into local militias who defended the weak and helpless with a fervor that left the streets littered with corpses and their opponents running away in panic.

I myself spent that day upon the Palace ramparts flanked by Jesse, who was now Xerxes' head eunuch, and a contingent of heavily armed bodyguards. Even my limited view gave me a heartening appraisal of the day's eventual outcome. I saw well-coordinated bands of Jewish men pursue erstwhile attackers down the streets with flying arrows and knives and even flaming clay pots of oil. I gasped as I watched one reckless youth strike an old Hebrew woman only to be beaten to death by a passing band of Jews. It was not pretty, but every time I grew revolted, I reminded myself of the bloodshed that would have taken place had Haman's edict been carried out. What I saw was nothing compared to what might have befallen my people!

I was in the King's bedchamber that night preparing to retire—for indeed, the turn of events had given our marriage another of its periodic revivals—when Mordecai knocked and entered with the day's tally. I must admit that I startled at the sight of my father entering my marriage bedroom, until I remembered that of all his subjects, the Master of the Audiences had the greatest access to the King's presence.

I realized at once that Mordecai was even more startled than I. He stood motionless, his gaze transfixed upon the jeweled star lying against Xerxes' breastbone.

"Your Majesty," he finally said, haltingly, "that is a most—unusual—and beautiful medallion upon your person."

"It should be! It was given to me by the Queen herself."

Mordecai's eyes shifted to the familiar medallion around my neck, and his amazement seemed to grow dramatically. I realized instantly that Mordecai had not known of the second one given to me by Hegai. I quickly explained, and he was dumbstruck by the resemblance between the two.

"So, my most excellent Mordecai," Xerxes called out in a hearty voice, shattering the silence, "how have your people fared on this day?"

"Well, of course, being the first eve," Mordecai answered with a moment's pause, "I can speak only for Susa and the nearest outlying cities. But in my limited vision, it appears the counter-edict was an enormous success."

I breathed out with a sigh so loud that both men paused and turned in my direction.

"In Susa alone," Mordecai continued, "we killed and destroyed five hundred would-be murderers and plunderers."

Xerxes blew out his breath with an amazed look. "Five hundred men! If you did all that in Susa alone, who knows what your countrymen have done across the kingdom! I hope I have subjects left!"

"You do, sir," Mordecai assured with a smile. "And with your leave I took the initiative of ordering that all spoils of the conflict go to your Majesty's treasury to restore what our valiant war on Greece had, ah . . . withdrawn."

"Excellent," Xerxes exclaimed. "You are a most astute advisor, indeed."

"Were all the Agagites killed?" I asked Mordecai.

"Pardon?" he asked, not quite understanding my question.

I fixed him with a knowing, intense look. "Were all the Agagites killed?" I repeated, each word distinct.

And Mordecai smiled again—recognizing the grasp of Jewish history I was now exhibiting. He smiled at my memory of all those bedtime stories he had forced me to endure. "No, my Queen," he replied. "There remain Haman's own sons and a group of his gang who escaped retribution."

"So Samuel's ancient order to Saul remains unfulfilled."

"I'm afraid that is the case."

Upon those words I turned to Xerxes and, perhaps without completely needing to, I fell prostrate before him.

Xerxes laughed. "Now what is your petition, my Queen? It will be granted you, make no mistake. You have probably just helped rid the Empire of several thousand undesirables, including the traitor Haman. So name your request."

I rose into a kneeling position. "If it pleases the King," I answered, "let tomorrow also be granted to the Jews of Susa, to follow the edict one more time."

I had stretched my royal influence to its limit, yet the King, bless him, agreed despite not quite understanding the ancient blood feud that had provoked my request.

It was simple—I knew that any remnants of Haman's followers would probably be hiding among the population of Susa. And I wanted to finish what King Saul, five hundred years before, had failed to do. Exterminate the final ranks of Israel's oldest and most evil foe. Correct a centuries-old mistake.

And indeed, across Susa, Jews sought out the men who had worn the twisted cross, gathered around them and slaughtered them. Their foul garments, along with the evil insignia they had tried to hide, were promptly burned.

By the next day they had ferreted out Haman's ten sons. When the last one had been captured, Mordecai ordered them to also be impaled on gallows as their father had been. He sent out a pronouncement to all 127 provinces of Persia that the circle was complete and a five-hundred-year-old omission reversed. The bodies displayed on the gallows were the evidence. An ancient enmity upon the Jewish people was purged. Not to mention an entire race saved.

And a little girl's grief avenged.

## Chapter Fifty-one

*I*t has now been many years since these historic events took place. If you are indeed, as I suspect, a Jewish girl, then you heard songs sung in your nursery rhymes recounting the Feast of Purim, the holiday established to celebrate our deliverance from the evil I have recounted here.

Today, I am no longer a woman spoken of for her youth and beauty. Constant tending with myrrh massages once delayed, even softened, the onset of wrinkles. At least for a time. No, I am a source of legend perhaps, yet no one will still call me the fairest maiden in the kingdom.

But that is far from the only bittersweet gift the years have wrought. As you probably know quite well, Xerxes was murdered in his bed only four years after all this took place. I made certain my dear husband was buried with the medallion I gave him on our first fateful night. I still miss him terribly, especially those glorious evenings we shared at the beginning of our marriage. The breathtaking Palace at Susa burned to the ground six years later, which is why I took such pains to describe its splendors to you. I wish you could have seen it, my dear, when it was the virtual center of the world and seemed to contain half its people.

Indeed, you could no longer say that being King of Persia is to be King of the World. Persia is a far weaker empire than it once was, and its military might is now a patchwork reflection of what I remember. I hear that our current King would rather hire foreign mercenaries to do our fighting than drag our citizens into one more disastrous campaign.

So, my dear girl, you enter into Palace life at a time probably as perilous and unsettled as my own. Mordecai's admonition may well apply to you—". . . *who knows but that G-d placed you here for such a time as this?*"

As you face the "competition," remember the protocols of the King's presence, my dear. Heed the Chamberlain as though your life depended on it, because it may. The man has the ear of the King himself, so his advice outweighs that of a thousand others. Bear gifts; do not ask for them. Keep your motives sincere and pure. Remember that this is not about you—your beauty, your charm, your allure. It is about *him*. Focus on the King. Delight in his presence, and you'll already have all the attractiveness you need. Cultivate true intimacy, not just sensuality, and influence will come with it. The King's favor is worth more than all the titles and pomposities a person could ever hoard—as Haman's fate will readily attest.

I hope this too-lengthy account of my story proved to you that these maxims are no mere platitudes. Learning and understanding the protocols of the King's presence could save your life—even the lives of our whole race. At the very least, they could earn you a lifetime's worth of favor with the King.

As for me, I can truthfully say that the years have been kind—and mercifully, I can add, free of the excitement that seemed to lurk around every corner during those earlier days. The people remember me warmly, and indeed their adulation has helped keep me safe and protected these many years.

After Xerxes' tragic death, I took up residence in the candidates' harem, in the same favored suite that holds so many fond memories for me. And I find that I have a soft place in my heart for the harem girls, once discarded and now stranded among the careening monoliths of history. I find I hold a great deal in common with them.

I rejoice to know that Mordecai became one of the most beloved and revered figures Persia has known—the Exilarch, and perhaps the ablest Master of the Audiences any king ever took to his side. As such, he no longer was able to slip anonymously in and out of the Palace grounds to converse with me. And the strange thing is, as I am now the *ex*-Queen, Poppa became the one with greater access around the Palace. It was I who became compelled to sneak in to see *him*. And of course, even today in his extreme old age, he still acts like my father. Which I know he is—I suppose I mean that he acts like the father of a ten-year-old. I love him for it. Sometimes I wish I could bring myself back in time as the Hadassah of old, then climb up into his lap for another of those endless stories he once told me about the history of Israel.

And Jesse, our Hathach the Good Man? He rose to the rank of King's chief eunuch, with the primary responsibility of managing the royal harems. That's right, my dear. The very Chamberlain who greeted you on your first day and who this very moment oversees your own year of preparation. So when I tell you to listen to the Chamberlain, it is important. He happens to be my very oldest and very best friend.

To this day, he and I meet in the Palace orchards as we did so long ago. We reminisce with laughter and not a few tears about the extraordinary events of our youth. We share each other's burdens, hopes, fears and deepest yearnings. We even shed a few tears for the irrepressible Rachel, whom I brought to live with me in the palace and who lived long enough to see Mordecai save the Jews of Susa.

I suppose if it were not for the terrible loss inflicted upon Jesse, as well as my very public legacy, we might have married. I cherish his company and rely on his advice, and I could not last a day without our conversations. Besides, I'm sure you'll agree that he grew into a very handsome man.

In fact, it was on one of our clandestine walks through the gardens that we spotted you, in some of the very places I once retreated to, clearly praying to G-d. We shared a look charged with decades of history, and I resolved there and then to give this account to you, one that I have been researching and writing for many years.

Of course, there is another character in this drama, the One who, despite our limited view of circumstances, watched and cared for His people through every twist and turn. He is the One who oversaw its whole outcome—and with whom I still revel in a rich and amazing relationship. He is YHWH, the G-d of my fathers. I cannot pretend that I feel Him every day as strongly as I did during some of those times of agonizing crisis. Yet I do feel His Spirit with me, I speak to Him constantly, and sometimes at the oddest of moments—watching a sunset over the Palace mount, holding a small child, walking with Mordecai or Jesse—I feel His presence as vividly as ever.

During such occasions I am given to laughing out loud, shouting out a word or two in His praise, raising my hands to the heavens and even weeping uncontrollably. I wish more than anything that I could see Him with my earthly eyes at those times—so I could run to Him like that tiny child seeing his returning father and jump blissfully into His arms. Instead, I content myself with a few feeble old lady's leaps or two. And then I bask inwardly in the embrace of His presence, exulting in His love and praising Him for all that He is—to me, to my people and now to you.

They say I am turning into an old woman and that old women are given to this kind of eccentric behavior.

*Hah.* I only hope they—and you—will someday share my lunacy.

For now, this side of paradise, the best substitute I can think of is to return as fast as I can to the bosom of my people—the land of Israel. And that is my dream. I am hoping to soon join a countryman named Ezra on a caravan and return across the deserts to live my last days in the land of my fathers. I do not know if you will have spent your night with the King by the time I depart. I suppose it is of little consequence to your chances, either way. But I will pray that you experience the love that I knew with my Xerxes.

And I will pray that, as it did for me, your one night with the King changes everything.

> Signed,
> Hadassah,
> Esther, Star of Persia

### Hadassah ben Yuda

THE *JERUSALEM STAR* FRONT PAGE

"... *Prime Minister to meet with Minister of Defense*
*regarding current conflict* ..."

# Chapter Fifty-two

JERUSALEM—PRESENT DAY

*H*adassah turned the final page slowly and, with a palpable feeling of regret, closed the cover. The young bride turned to her father. It was the final afternoon, her wedding only hours away. She had promised him she would finish reading the book before the moment came, despite all the preparations at hand. With a long sigh, she laid her head upon his bony shoulder and grasped his arm in both her hands.

"So, Poppa, do you think she made it?"

"Who?"

"Esther. Do you think she made it back to Israel?"

He smiled and narrowed his eyes ever so slightly to gaze out over the valley of Kidron and the Temple Mount. "Well, my love, experts will tell you there is no historical or archaeological record of Queen Esther ever leaving Persia, let alone arriving here. And I sort of like it that way."

"So do I."

"But between you and me, I'm sure she made it. In fact, I'm

certain of it. Whether she stayed there for the remainder of her days, only G-d knows."

Then he turned in his chair, winced slightly with the aches and pains of an old man and extracted a velvet box from his suit pocket.

"Here, my dear. Your old aunt wanted you to have this."

She knelt before him and reached out delicately to open the box. Inside was an obviously ancient and weathered, yet still exquisite, piece of jewelry—a golden medallion engraved with the Star of David.

She frowned and glanced up at her father. "What aunt?"

"Oh, you know. Queen Esther. And she gave it to the young candidate to whom she wrote—"

"Oh, Poppa," she gasped, reeling with the knowledge of what she cradled in her hand.

"I am going to find out the name inscribed second to Queen Esther's on the memoir," she finally said to her father when she had her emotions under control. "She is my ancestor, and I feel like she's here for my wedding."

Her father laid his hand on her head and recited the ancient Hebrew blessing that was many times older than the medallion.

The moment had come. The bride stepped down the aisle of the synagogue just as the sun set upon Purim's second and final day and the finest view in Jerusalem just beyond. Its final ray sparkled on the spectacular Star of David around her neck. She arrived at the canopy and her groom at last, and he reached forward to pull back her veil. When he saw her face, he frowned at once.

"What's the matter?" he whispered.

"What do you mean?"

"Why are you smiling like that? Is everything all right? Do I look—?"

"You look wonderful," she said, smiling even more.

"Most brides I've seen looked like they were about to pass out right about now. You're—"

She laughed infectiously and reached out to hold him lightly about the neck.

"I'm smiling because I'm so overjoyed to be in your presence. You are the most desirable and intoxicating man alive—did you know that?"

Just then, long before the ceremony's end called for it, the groom bent down and engulfed his bride in a deep, impulsive kiss that did not break until impromptu applause from the guests reached its crescendo. It was such a clearly spontaneous and genuine display of passion that no one had the heart to object. The abashed groom finally pulled away, and laughter rose above the scene.

His young bride heard the sound of mirth drift up over the nearby rooftops, out over the Kidron Valley, toward the ancient wall that encircled the Old City of Jerusalem. Here was the ancestral home of the Jewish people—beloved children of the Most High G-d who always, even when He is silent, watches over His own. She could not help but smile.

ATOP THE MOUNT OF OLIVES—LATER THAT NIGHT

Nestled in each other's arms, the wedding couple glanced out their French doors toward the lights of old Jerusalem spilling down into the moonlit Kidron Valley.

"This is a new perfume you wore today," he said, nuzzling her neck.

Hadassah laughed. "Yes, dear. It is."

"Why would you wear something new like that? Don't get me wrong—it's a wonderful fragrance, but it isn't like you to change something at the last minute."

"It's an old family recipe."

"And what is the name of this recipe?"

She laughed. "Essence of myrrh."

"What? Where did you—your family—come up with such a thing?"

"An old aunt. Aunt Esther."

"All right, I give up. But that's not the only last-minute change you made. I've never seen that necklace you wore today, either. That's a stunning piece of jewelry. Even though it's a replica, it must have cost a mint."

She smiled demurely. "It's not a replica."

"No way. I know my Jewish icons, and if that were real, it would be thousands of years old."

"It is."

He bolted upright. "You're joking? You've got to be kidding."

"No, I'm not. It's an ancient family heirloom. It truly is real. I was shocked myself—you should feel how heavy it is."

"Hadassah, for that to be real, the historical period would have to date from the time of the Exile."

She looked at him for a while, then nodded slowly.

He paused with a scowl, pondered for a moment, then turned to her again. "Where is it now? If it's really that old, you can't leave something like that lying around!"

"My father has taken it back to the House of Scrolls." Finally she laughed deeply, heartily, and took his hand tenderly in hers.

"Why didn't you tell me these things before?" he asked, searching her face.

"I only learned of them this week. You and I have been so busy, I haven't had the chance."

"Well, it isn't too late to start."

She laughed. "Jacob, there's a story I need to tell you."

It was a long story—a *very* long story, and before she was ten minutes into it, his head had settled against her chest, and he had begun to snore lightly. She shook her head with a rueful smile.

There would be no honeymoon for this Hadassah, either. Jacob could not spare the time. Nor could the nation. For even the first day of marriage would be a busy day in the life of Jacob ben Yuda—Prime Minister of the nation of Israel.

TOMMY TENNEY, along with his wife Jeannie, has been a world traveler for more than 30 years. An avid reader and relentless researcher, Tenney is a highly acclaimed inspirational speaker and bestselling nonfiction author with combined sales of over three million copies. He has here turned his hand to fiction and the captivating story of Esther.

Tenney says, "In attempting to understand and more fully appreciate my wife, the queen of my life, I discovered Esther's fascinating story. Totally powerless, she fully prepared herself to finally maneuver a powerful king toward a destiny larger than either of them."

The Tenneys and their family make their home in Louisiana.

For more information, you may access:
*Hadassah-onenightwiththeking.com*
or
*TommyTenney.com*